D1544436

Just After Midnight

Center Point
Large Print

Also by Catherine Ryan Hyde and available from
Center Point Large Print:

The Language of Hoofbeats
Allie and Bea
The Wake Up

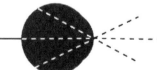

**This Large Print Book carries the
Seal of Approval of N.A.V.H.**

Just After Midnight

Catherine Ryan Hyde

CENTER POINT LARGE PRINT
THORNDIKE, MAINE

The text of this Large Print edition is unabridged.
In other aspects, this book may vary
from the original edition.
Printed in the United States of America
on permanent paper.
Set in 16-point Times New Roman type.

ISBN: 978-1-64358-194-1

Library of Congress Cataloging-in-Publication Data

Names: Hyde, Catherine Ryan, author.
Title: Just after midnight / Catherine Ryan Hyde.
Description: Large Print edition. | Thorndike, Maine : Center Point Large Print, 2019. | "Originally published in the United States by Amazon Publishing, 2018"—Title page verso.
Identifiers: LCCN 2019007373 | ISBN 9781643581941 (hardcover : alk. paper)
Subjects: LCSH: Female friendship—Fiction. | Large type books. | Domestic fiction.
Classification: LCC PS3558.Y358 J87 2019 | DDC 813/.54—dc23
LC record available at https://lccn.loc.gov/2019007373

Just After Midnight

MID-JULY, RIGHT IN THE MIDDLE
OF THE THING

Chapter One

I'm Worried About Sarah

Faith stood in line to buy two chicken soft tacos from the food truck that serviced that weekend's dressage show.

Bag in hand, she cut across what might have been green lawn if this hadn't been the Central California Valley. If it hadn't been more or less one hundred degrees all summer, including now. Instead her boots crunched over a sea of wood chips on the way to Barn C. She had to take a "long cut" to avoid a watering truck that was spraying down the path to keep the dust to a minimum.

Halfway there, a few yards past the warm-up arena, Faith heard a clop of steel-shod hooves and looked over—and very much up—to see John Wintermeyer ride up behind her on his dark bay Dutch warmblood gelding.

"Just finish your ride?" she asked, craning her neck to see his face. She had to shield her eyes against the midday sun, which seemed to hang directly over John's head.

"Yup." Then he seemed happy enough to let it go at that.

They set off walking together side by side, if

such a thing can be said when one person's side is nearly six feet higher than the other. They kept pace more easily than Faith might have imagined.

He was a bizarrely tall man, John. About six feet five, she guessed. Maybe even six feet six. As a result, he made his massive dressage horses look like ponies. At the top of his withers, this gelding was taller than Faith. When the huge beast was saddled, she could not peer over the horse's back, not even on tiptoes. But the bottom of John's boots, where they sat in their metal stirrups, hung more than a foot below the bottom of the huge horse's barrel. John's legs looked toothpick-thin in their clean white English breeches. Faith thought she could wrap both hands around the widest part of John's thigh and have her fingertips touch on both sides. Though, for obvious reasons, she had never tried.

"How did it go?" she asked, more or less to have something to say.

"Could've been better." His voice sounded small. Or just too far above her. Or both.

"Actual errors? Or you just didn't like the way he was going?"

"Somewhere in between. The canter pirouettes were only so-so. His haunches came around too much. That's my fault as much as his. But I was pretty disappointed with the tempis."

It was a dressage word Faith didn't think she

10

had heard before, and could not have written out correctly. But it sounded like John said "tempeeze."

"I don't know what that is," Faith said.

They walked by another mounted horse, a young-looking, slim gray who froze, backed up two steps, then reared while its rider hung on and tried to spur it forward. At one time Faith would have cleared the area fast at such a disturbance. These days she just kept walking.

"Tempi changes," he said. "You know."

"I swear, John, I'm learning as fast as I can. Some days I feel like my head is going to explode, and I still don't know five percent of what you and Sarah know."

For a moment they just walked, Faith listening to the reassuring clop of his horse's hooves. She noticed John had kicked out of the stirrups and was letting his long legs hang freely. He might easily have bumped the back of the massive warmblood's knee with the toe of his high black boot.

They passed Barn A, and Faith was glad to see that they were almost back. It was such a long walk from everything on these showgrounds to everything else. And in this heat.

"It's when you do a flying lead change every x number of strides," he said. "These were two tempis. With a lead change every two canter strides. You saw me doing one tempis the first day I met you, and you said it looked like the horse was skipping. Remember?"

"Right," Faith said. "Right. Got it. I remember that now. So did he not change leads every two strides?"

"Oh, it wasn't all *that* bad," John said, but he sounded discouraged and tired. "He was just uneven and not a hundred percent straight. Once he was actually late. I don't know. Him or me. Probably both. He's just not his best self today, and neither am I. We're both tired." They passed Barn B in silence. "I'm worried about her," he said, his voice stronger. "I'm not sure if that's an okay thing to say or not."

Faith stopped. John and his horse stopped. She tried to look up at him, but there was too much direct sun in her eyes.

"Who? Sarah? Or the mare?"

"Both, I guess. But I meant the girl."

"You can *say* it. I'm not sure what I'm supposed to do about it. More than usual, you mean?"

John unclipped the chin strap of his black helmet and pulled it off, holding it between his thighs on the pommel of his saddle. He scratched behind one ear through his closely cropped hair as the gelding shifted underneath him, the horse scratching his bridled face on the inside of one muscular front leg.

"Maybe more than usual. Hard to say. I haven't known her that long. She's just been striking me as . . . I mean, granted, she's a teenager, but . . . the word that keeps coming to mind is *volcanic*. Like there's some pressure building up in there. I understand all about her and the horse, and I'm not saying I blame her. I'd be upset too if I were her age and my father'd done a thing like that to me. But, I don't know. Now I'm feeling like there must be even more. But . . . you know what? *So* none of my business. How about you forget I even brought it up?"

They walked together again, then turned down the long aisle at Barn C. Faith could feel the warmth of the tacos through the white paper bag. She could feel her stomach rumble with hunger pangs. She had waited too long to brave the long walk in the heat for dinner.

"Well," she said, and then paused. And doubted whether she should go on. But then, suddenly and without a great deal of thought on the matter, she spit out the information. "There's the fact that her mother died a couple of months ago. I don't know if she told you about that or not."

John and his horse stopped. Faith stopped. She looked up at the pair, no longer handicapped by sun in her eyes. Blessed shade fell in the aisles between the barn rows. They both stared at her. Man and horse. Or, at least, it seemed that way to Faith.

"I thought *you* were her mother," John said.

"Me? No. I'm not anybody's mother."

"Just somebody who's known her all her life?"

"Not even that."

"Known her a long time?"

"Less than two months," Faith said, feeling as though she might have missed her conversational off-ramp.

"You do have her with permission, though, right? I mean, you didn't steal her?"

He laughed. Or tried to, anyway. It fell flat.

"Her grandmother knows she's with me. I have her as sort of a . . . favor. To her grandmother."

It was a factual statement, but one carefully constructed to avoid the truth—that Sarah was, to some degree, stolen. At least, by technical standards of legal custody.

They stood silent for a moment. Then John swung down off his horse in one smooth motion, bending his knees slightly as he dropped into the dirt. He took the reins over his gelding's head, and they walked again.

"So her mom died and her dad sold the mare out from under her in more or less the same week?"

"That's about the size of it."

"That explains a lot. Poor kid."

They reached the section of stalls marked by the canopy labeled "John Wintermeyer Dressage." He led his horse into an open stall and began to unbuckle the girth.

"I still worry about her, though," he said.

"I know," Faith said. "You should. So do I."

• • •

She found Sarah in Midnight's stall, which was hardly a surprise.

The jet-black mare had been beautifully groomed while Faith was out in search of food. Her tail had been conditioned and combed, her mane braided into neat plaits and then folded into knobs that looked like little flower buds every few inches along the horse's neck. The mare held so still as to appear hypnotized.

Sarah had the horse's saddle on, and was standing in the ankle-deep shavings, holding the leather strap of one stirrup in her hand and staring at it strangely close-up.

Faith waited, but the girl's concentration never seemed to waver.

"I brought tacos," Faith said.

Apparently Sarah was not startled by Faith's voice or presence. She did not so much as look around.

"I'm not hungry," the girl said.

"Shouldn't you have some energy to burn while you do this?"

"It's so hot. I'm afraid I'd throw up."

Faith assumed the girl's potential nausea was more a result of nerves than heat. She didn't say so. She didn't say anything.

"Thank you anyway for bringing me something," Sarah said, still staring at the leather strap. "It was nice of you. Can you eat them both?"

"I could try. I feel like I could be hungry enough for both of us."

But for a long, overheated moment Faith just leaned in the open stall door and stared at Sarah's back. Faith could clearly see the horse's deep, liquid eye. It was watching her, that eye. Taking her in, but with no apparent opinion, pro or con. As though Faith were of no genuine consequence in the mare's world at all.

"I missed this," Sarah said suddenly. Her voice held that deep, intense tone she fell into when something was so important she could barely process it.

Faith laughed, but it came out as more of a forced bark. "I know you don't mean that strap," she said.

"I sort of do. And it's called a leather."

"That's a weird thing for it to be called."

"Why is it weird?"

"Because every part of that horse's tack is leather. So why single out that one pair of straps?"

"It's called a stirrup leather," the girl said. "Because it just is. And because that's as opposed to the stirrup iron. And I missed it."

"More than the noseband of the bridle, say?"

"No. I missed all the tack the same amount."

"I thought it was the horse you missed," Faith said.

"Well. Yeah. Of course. The horse, yeah. But I

knew I missed the horse. I had no idea how much I missed *this*."

Then she dropped the leather suddenly and turned to face Faith. Looked into her eyes for maybe the first time that day. Hell, maybe for the first time since they'd fled the beach together.

"Faith. What if it works this time? What if I ride her and make her look really good, and it works, and somebody buys her? Then what?"

"I . . . absolutely don't know. I'm sorry, Sarah, but I really don't know about any of this. I wish I had answers to everything that's weighing on you right now, but I don't. But, really . . . when you think about it . . . is it that much worse if somebody new owns her instead of John?"

"Yes!" the girl shouted. Loudly enough that Midnight spooked slightly—just one big jolt that didn't move the mare's feet much. "Yes, it's much worse. They could take her out of state. They could not let me hang around. John lets me hang around."

"I don't know what to say, kiddo. Sooner or later we were going to have to go home anyway."

"I gotta go change," Sarah said.

She pushed past Faith almost violently on her way out of the stall.

Faith slid onto a bleacher seat beside the arena where the Sales Horse Presentation Class was already taking place. She pulled off her outer shirt and sat in just her sweat-soaked T-shirt, even though it offered no protection from the sun. She swept her long hair off the nape of her neck.

A rather unusual-looking horse was being shown. He had a roan coat, and was heavily built. Faith heard the announcer say that the gelding was a cross between an Oldenburg and a quarter horse.

"That explains so much," one of two women sitting in front of her said to the other.

Faith glanced over at Sarah and Midnight, warming up at a canter in an arena a couple of hundred feet away. Faith could see the way the girl's riding jacket was safety-pinned on the inside to draw it in at the waist. She hoped no one else would be looking so closely.

Meanwhile Faith heard the announcer tell the crowd that the Oldenburg/quarter horse gelding was a perfect gentleman whether trailering, clipping, tying, or riding on the trail or at the beach.

Her attention was pulled away from the girl when the announcer stated a price for the gelding. Faith thought she heard the announcer say eight thousand dollars, which sounded absurdly low. She assumed it was the mixed breeding, combined with the fact that quarter horses are rarely used for dressage. Still, she couldn't imagine why someone would even haul a horse to a show if they were only asking eight thousand dollars for him.

The two women on the bleacher seat in front of her hooted under their breath. Both of them.

"Oh, who is she *kidding?*" one of them asked the other, her voice a deep hiss in her friend's ear.

They looked wealthy and thin and fiftyish and haughty. The kind of women no one should be surprised to encounter at a dressage show.

"No one is going to pay her eighty thousand dollars for that gelding."

That's when Faith realized she had misheard the announcer.

"Notice she has the announcer say he got a nine on his canter pirouette?" the woman continued. "One score. Of one movement. Give us the overall scores from his last six tests or I'll assume it's a fluke."

The quarter horse cross and his rider left the arena.

Sarah and Midnight rode in.

"Next we have a real beauty of a Hanoverian mare," the announcer said. "This is Falkner's Midnight Sun."

After that opening line, Faith completely lost track of the announcer and fell into the conversation of the two women. She couldn't help it. It was closer. More compelling. Besides, she had already read everything the announcer was saying in the sale catalogue.

"Oh, it's that rude girl," one said. "Why does John let that rude, difficult girl ride her?"

"Why?" her friend asked, as though it should be obvious. *"Why?* Have you ever seen how that mare works for John? Or doesn't work, I guess I should say."

"No, but John's a good rider."

"Not on this mare, he's not. Why do you think he's selling her? She's completely unwilling under him. He can't even keep her on the bit. Half the time she's above the bit and on the bottom neck, her back all hollow. It's just total resistance and it looks dreadful. He can't even get her scores up into the sixties. Who's going to pay seventy-five thousand dollars for that? Look how the mare goes for that girl. She comes alive under that girl."

"She does look like a different horse. What's she got, though, that John hasn't got?"

"The mare's trust, I suppose. She's the former owner. I don't know what difference he thinks it's going to make, though, because nobody's going to spend that kind of money without riding her first. He's going to lose his shirt on that mare."

Meanwhile, against this backdrop of conversation, Sarah rode the mare in an extended trot, with that lovely forward movement Faith had once thought she was supposed to call *overstep.* Turned out that was a term used only for the walk. But it seemed as though it should apply.

Then they transitioned smoothly into a working canter. Sarah executed several twenty-meter and then ten-meter circles, sometimes in the counter canter—which Faith now knew meant leading with the outside leg—other times with flying lead changes on every change of bend. Faith knew the girl was showing off how the mare would refrain from anticipating and wait for her rider's aids.

If her rider was Sarah, that is.

And still the women were gossiping.

"She's such a difficult girl, though," one said. "Remember when *we* were young enough to know everything?"

And they both laughed.

"Were you there when she went off about the 'mare-ish' thing?"

"No. What mare-ish thing?"

Sarah and Midnight performed a beautiful movement (which Faith had learned to call a *passage,* with a French-sounding pronunciation) down the far long-side rail, the mare's hooves lifting breathtakingly high and pausing in the air on each trotting stride. It was a thing of beauty.

The ongoing soundtrack was not.

"The only other mare in the sale catalogue . . . Jesse Rich's Westphalian . . . the catalogue description made this simple statement that she's not 'mare-ish' at all. That she's always mistaken for a gelding because of that. And that little girl, she just went *off* about it. Told everyone who would listen that being a mare was not a flaw, and anybody who thought their mare was too mare-ish just wasn't riding and handling her right. That you *use* traits like that, you don't fault your horse for them. Bent everybody's ear until no one would stand still and listen to it another minute."

Sarah and the mare transitioned into an extended canter—a thundering, thrilling thing that would probably be called a gallop in some other sport. They looked as though they were riding into battle together. Bravely.

"Life is so simple," the other woman said, "when you're . . . like . . . twelve."

They both laughed again.

"Actually," Faith said, "she's fourteen."

The women spun around to look, then quickly averted their eyes when they saw who had spoken. They didn't know Faith, and she didn't know them. But they knew that Faith and Sarah went together.

Their faces twisted into two different versions of humiliated, forced grimaces, and they eased off their bench and slithered away.

Faith sat back and breathed deeply. The announcer, whose words she could now focus on, was noting that it went without saying that the mare was suitable for a junior rider, since the rider currently showing her was only fourteen years old and had brought the mare up to fourth level with only a modest amount of professional training.

Then he intimated that this made her suitable for a beginner, which Faith knew was nowhere near the truth. She wasn't even suitable for John.

Sarah and Midnight moved diagonally across the arena in a long, crisp free walk, bent the corner snugly, halted at the letter marker A in a perfectly square halt. A brief pause fell. Then the mare began to piaffe, lifting her hooves high without ever moving forward. High-stepping in place, her neck beautifully rounded. The light smattering of spectators broke into intermittent applause.

Sarah rode the mare out of the arena, and the strained tension was over.

Unless someone decided to buy her, in which case it was only beginning.

"Don't sleep in the car," Sarah said. "You have to try it here in the stall with me. It's so much more comfortable than the car could possibly be."

She had hot-walked the sweaty mare, hosed her off, and put her away in her stall with a light fly sheet on. Then Sarah had come back to find Faith, who was sitting in the barn aisle on a rectangular bag of stall shavings, eating the second taco.

"I don't know about that," Faith said when her mouth was not too full.

"Wait till you see how much straw I put down. You think it's hard. But it's not."

"It's not just that. It's that horses have been in that stall. And you know what horses do in their stalls. It just seems unsanitary."

"No, it's not like that at all," Sarah said. "It's a concrete stall floor, but this one has brand-new rubber mats on it that never had a horse standing on them. And then the straw I put down myself from a fresh bale, and then I put a clean horse blanket over the straw. It's sanitary. I swear."

Faith could hear something mildly desperate in the girl's voice. It was important to Sarah that Faith agree, but Faith wasn't sure why. Maybe the girl was feeling depressed or scared and wanted the company.

"That doesn't sound so bad. But, actually, I was considering driving into town and treating myself to a night at an inexpensive motel."

Faith regretted saying so immediately. The girl was nearly begging.

I should have been more gracious, she thought. *Just gone along.*

"Do that tomorrow night. Tonight just give this a try. Please?"

Faith shoved the last bite of taco into her mouth and followed Sarah to the stall in question. Still chewing, she spread her arms wide and fell facedown onto the deep bed of straw. She turned her head to speak.

"Better than I imagined," she said with her mouth still full.

• • •

It was not long after midnight. The stall was not completely dark. A soft glow stole in from LED lights that had been placed at intervals along the barn aisles to allow the horses to see a bit of their surroundings. It made them less panicky in their unfamiliar venue. More secure.

A light breeze blew in over the stall door, but it was not cool. Faith felt as though it had never been cool. That it might never be cool again.

The horse across the aisle, belonging to no one they knew, was doing his neurotic dance, head over the half door, swinging his shoulders back and forth. Making a rhythmic thumping sound against the wood and steel of the door.

Faith sat up and looked at the odd horse. He looked back but did not stop swaying.

"You're not asleep," Sarah said.

"No. And apparently neither are you."

"But it's not because it's not comfortable in here, right?"

"No, it's not that. It's fine. It's just too hot to sleep. The car would have been worse, though." A hotel would have been heaven, but she didn't say so. "So was there any response?" Faith asked. And immediately wished she hadn't.

"I have no idea what that means," Sarah said.

"Never mind. Forget I even asked."

"No. Really. Tell me. What did you mean?"

"I meant did anyone approach John and want to buy her?"

"I have no idea," Sarah said. Her voice had gone dull and cold. "He tells me nothing. Why should he? She's his mare. She's not mine. I guess nothing that happens with her is any of my business."

They fell silent again, and lay still for two or three minutes listening to the thump, thump, thump of the neurotic horse across the aisle.

"I need to tell you something," Sarah said.

The whole middle of Faith froze. Because she knew in that moment that Sarah had needed to tell her something since the first morning they'd met. Needed to tell someone, anyway. And it was a big something. Faith could feel how big it was. She wanted to question how and why she had stepped into the role of being the one to hear it, but it was too late for that now.

"Shouldn't you tell your grandmother?" she asked, thinking she could hear the crystalline ice of fear in her own voice.

"I wanted to. Don't you think I wanted to? But she would've . . . I don't know. I think she would just lose it. She's just hanging on, you know? Just barely. Like those people in the old movies who go off a cliff, and then you see them and they're just holding on to this one tiny little weed. And the dirt is starting to fall out around it, and it's pulling out and getting longer, and you can see the roots. I don't want to be the one to do that to her. You know? She's trying to hold on."

"Yeah," Faith said. "I think I know."

"It's about the night my mom died."

"Is this something we maybe should be telling to the . . . you know. I hate to even say the word." But then, after a choking pause, she did. "Police?"

"I don't know. Maybe. Yeah. But first I have to at least say it to someone I know well enough to say it to. Right?"

"Yeah," Faith said. "That sounds reasonable. Okay. I'm listening, then. Go ahead and say what you need to say."

Chapter Two

Respect

"It didn't happen the way my dad said it did," Sarah began. "Not at all."

They sat on the makeshift straw bed in the empty stall, nearly shoulder to shoulder. Watching the neurotic horse rock and sway. He watched them in return. Faith briefly wondered if they looked troubled to him as well.

She waited for the girl to continue. She did not care to push. But no more words seemed forthcoming.

"Well, honey," Faith said at last, "I'm at a handicap here, because I don't know what he said happened."

"You don't know how my mom died?"

"No."

"I thought my grandmother would have told you."

"She didn't. And I didn't want to pry."

"Oh. Okay. Well. They had a fight. Everybody agrees on that part. It was a little after midnight, and they were having this big screaming fight in their bedroom. And then my dad told the police he went downstairs and had a drink and turned on the TV. And then he heard the gunshot. And then he ran back upstairs. And she . . . had . . . you know."

A silence fell, save for the stall-door thumping of their four-legged across-the-aisle neighbor. Faith's stomach broke into a cold sea of tingling, as if someone were trying to electrocute her on a low setting. Because she was beginning to get a sense of where this was headed.

"Okay," Faith said. "Okay. That helps. Now I know what everybody *thinks* happened. Now go ahead and tell me what really happened."

"I was in my room." Her voice had fallen to a soft whisper. She leaned in closer, so Faith would hear. "It was just after midnight. The fighting woke me up. And then I heard the gun go off. And then I ran out into the hall. And I saw my dad. He was just coming out of their bedroom. And he looked at me. And the look on his face . . . it was like . . . I don't know. I don't know how to say it."

"Did he have the gun when you saw him?"

"No."

"Was there any time between when you heard the fighting and when the gun went off?"

"No. It sounded like she was right in the middle of a sentence."

"So what you're saying is . . ."

"I don't know," Sarah said, and pulled her head away again. "I don't know what I'm saying. Well. Maybe I do. I guess maybe I do. But I don't know."

29

"You know I have to tell your grandmother this."

"I hate to do it to her."

Faith looked at the neurotic horse in the dim light, and he looked back. Just in that split second his movements stilled.

"This is big, Sarah. This is a huge thing. She's trying to dig up anything she can use to get legal custody of you. She needs this. And even beyond that . . . I think you know it's one of those things we can't keep to ourselves. It's too important. I think if you didn't know that, we wouldn't be having this talk."

"Right. Yeah. I know. But just . . . not *today,* okay? Let me just get through today, and worrying if someone is buying Midnight. Let me just have one day to get used to the fact that I even told *you.* Before you tell my grandmother and she tells everybody in the whole world. Okay?"

"I guess one more day wouldn't hurt," Faith said.

And with that, the horse resumed his swaying.

They sat in silence for a time. A few minutes at least.

Faith lay back down on the clean horse blanket on the soft bed of straw. A few minutes later Sarah stretched out as well. As though they would sleep. It seemed like a pathetic charade to Faith, to pretend they could sleep after a revelation like that one.

A stretch of very awake time went by. It might have been fifteen minutes, or it might have been an hour. Either way, it was painfully clear that no one was sleeping.

Faith heard footsteps, and for a moment it alarmed her. Caused her heart to race wildly. As it so often did. But she lay still and listened, and soon realized it was probably just the person who did the stall checks on the horses at night.

"I do know," Sarah said when the footsteps had faded away again.

"What? What do you know?"

"The look on his face. When he saw me see him. I do know what it was. He was . . . ashamed. Like . . . really, really ashamed."

Faith waited patiently, in case the girl wanted to say more.

But the rest of the night crawled by, with no sleep for Faith, and no more words spoken.

"Wake up, sleepyhead," an unexpected voice said.

Faith opened her eyes to see John leaning over the stall door. She realized she had been drifting, almost ready to drop off at last. But now it was light, and John was here. And her chance was over.

Did he always come and wake Sarah up this early? Faith had no idea.

She looked down at the girl, who appeared to have slept straight through the in-person wake-up call.

Faith looked at John, and he looked back.

"I hate to do this to her," he said. "But I might have a buyer. I can't just take the horse out while she's sleeping. It might be the last they ever see of each other and then she'll never forgive me."

The news settled like a heavy and spoiled breakfast into Faith's stomach, which was always rocky anyway as a reaction to missed sleep.

She looked down at the sleeping girl and almost couldn't bring herself to do it. But John was right. Sarah would never forgive them if she missed her chance to say goodbye.

"Hey," she said, and rocked the girl's shoulder.

Sarah sat bolt upright and rubbed her eyes.

"What?"

Faith pointed to John, his elongated torso leaning over the stall door. Sarah's face fell. As if she already knew what John had come to say.

"Hate to do this to you, kid," he said. "But a potential buyer wants to ride her. Kind of cold, I know, asking you to get her ready for a buyer. And if you don't want to do it, that's okay. I'll do it myself."

A long silence.

Faith could feel them pitched into a new day, following another wild swing of events in an unexpected direction. As if the revelations of the night had never happened.

"I'll get her ready," Sarah said.

Faith followed the girl as she hand-walked the fully tacked-up mare. They seemed to be headed for the warm-up arena at the farthest corner of the property. John was there waiting, talking to a much older woman—old enough that Faith did not assume she was the buyer.

It was still early, not much after six, and the sun was barely up, but on a long slant. It did not punish Faith. Its light simply fell on her, reminding her that this day was entirely new. That it could contain anything. That she did not control it. Birds twittered contentedly in the trees as they passed. What did they know of all this trouble?

Then Faith saw a man standing in the distance, and just for a jolt of a split second she thought it was Robert. Her brain made him into Robert. She stopped dead, and stared, and the man turned back into himself—into no one she knew. She walked on, heart pounding, reminding herself that no one would think to look for her or Sarah here. Not Robert. Not Sarah's father. There was no logical reason for anyone to think they would be here, and that made them safe.

John saw them and trotted to meet Sarah and the horse.

"Where's the buyer?" Sarah asked him.

"Right there. Where else? I was just talking to her."

"That old lady? Don't you think that's a mistake? If she falls off, isn't she about ten times more likely to get hurt? That's as bad as putting a kid on her, John. You know? I just don't think this is the right horse for her."

John took hold of the sleeve of Sarah's T-shirt and marched her along beside him, the horse following the reins, which were still in Sarah's hands. Together they all three walked up to the older woman and stopped there, giving Faith a moment to catch up.

They seemed to be almost the only ones awake, except for some light, scattered movement in the section where horse trailers, most equipped with living quarters, sat parked.

"Sarah," John said in his best formal voice, "this is Estelle LaMaster. You may have heard of her. She represented Canada in the Summer Olympics in Montreal in '76. Took the bronze in individual dressage."

"Oh," Sarah said, looking at the older woman with a new expression. "Well, then . . . I guess maybe you can handle this mare after all."

Estelle laughed. It was a light, infectious sound. Against odds, she was utterly unoffended.

She was a sprightly-looking, thin woman of perhaps seventysomething, face tanned and weathered by sun, her long white hair pulled back in a ponytail along her neck. She wore riding breeches with short brown paddock boots, and a T-shirt with very short sleeves. Her arms looked surprisingly slim and toned.

"Estelle," John said, "this is Sarah. She was the mare's owner until just a few weeks ago. Sarah is going to want to give you endless advice on how to ride the mare. Endless. I sincerely hope you won't be put off by the sheer volume of it. Just take it as a sign that she cares."

"Oh, nonsense," Estelle said, a lightness in her voice that made Faith want to move closer—a sureness about the world that drew her in. "Why would I be offended? She knows the mare. I don't. There's value in that. Besides," she added, turning her face down to the girl's, "I saw you ride her in the Sales Horse Presentation Class. You did a lovely job. I can't remember when I've seen a rider so in sync with her horse. And such a young rider, too. You've come much farther than most junior riders your age. What are you, about thirteen?"

"Fourteen," Sarah said. "Almost fifteen."

Her voice had grown small, and Faith knew why. It was because she wanted to dislike Estelle, but she couldn't. There was just no way to make such a thing work.

Estelle raised her clear, light blue eyes to Faith, who stood a few steps behind. "You must be very proud of this lovely girl," she said.

"I am," Faith replied. She did not bother to correct the impression that Sarah was her daughter. In the moment, it didn't matter much.

"Now let's have a look at this fine animal," Estelle said, and extended her hand respectfully toward Midnight, palm up. When she opened her hand, a grain-and-molasses horse treat sat exposed in the middle of her palm. "I hope you don't mind," she said more or less in the direction of John. "I know not everybody approves of hand-feeding. But first impressions are important, and when a new person thrusts herself at a horse, you really can't fault the animal for wanting to know, 'What's in it for me?' Now tell me, young lady. How does this lovely mare care to be ridden?"

Faith watched the girl's shoulders drop slightly as the bulk of her tension drained away. Meanwhile Midnight, still chewing slowly around her bit, continued to nose around in Estelle's empty palm, which seemed like an encouraging sign.

"She's very sensitive," Sarah said. "*Very* sensitive. So the worst thing you can do is override her." She glanced back over her shoulder and shot John an accusing glance. He rolled his eyes. "Especially the leg aids. Just whisper to her with your aids. Don't yell or she'll get upset. And you don't want to be on her back when she gets upset, believe me. But if you give very soft, light aids and trust her to hear you, she'll be brilliant.

She likes to feel your legs on her the whole time. It makes her feel more secure. As far as the reins go, she likes a nice, steady contact. But she better not feel like you're walling her in or she'll panic."

John moved closer, took the reins from Sarah, and handed them to Estelle. Then he took hold of Sarah with a hand on each of her shoulders and steered her away.

"I believe it's time to trust Estelle to know how to ride a horse," he said.

"John Wintermeyer!" the older woman said in a voice that could freeze the blood of any grown man. "You unhand that poor girl this very instant! She's being helpful. Stop micromanaging. I know you need to get out from under this horse, we all do. And don't think I don't know that she's fussy and needs to be ridden just so. Some of the best horses I've ever ridden were exactly that way, so stop trying to hide it, because it's already known, and it's not as bad a thing as you make it out to be. Now I need a helmet. Run and get me one I can borrow, John, will you please? At my age it doesn't pay to get up on a horse without that very inexpensive form of insurance. And bring me back a mounting block if you have one you can carry all this way. If not, a leg up will do. But I'd rather have the block."

John pulled in a deep breath, sighed it out, then trotted away.

Estelle, who still held the mare's reins, turned to Faith and Sarah, her blue eyes dancing. "Anything to get rid of him, right?"

Sarah laughed out a snort of sound. She liked Estelle. Faith could tell. It was hard to imagine how anyone wouldn't. But it had clearly taken the girl by surprise, and she didn't seem settled into the feeling yet. It felt as though she hadn't quite let go of her need to dislike any potential buyer.

"Oh, he means well, poor John," Estelle continued. "His head is just so busy. And he's always worrying. I wish he could relax and enjoy life for his own sake, but I suppose he's doing the best he can." She turned her attention to Midnight, stroking smoothly and softly between the horse's eyes with the flat of one hand. "Now, my lovely girl, I know you don't know me. I'm a total stranger to you, and why should you put up with much of anything from me? But I promise I'll take your feelings into account, and no harm will ever come to you when I'm around. Will you take me at my word on that?"

Faith looked around to see John sprinting toward them again, shortcutting across the empty arenas by jumping over the very low railings. He was dangling an enormous three-step mounting block from one hand. In the other hand he held two helmets, their chin straps flapping.

Midnight saw the movement, too, and spooked one long step sideways.

"Oh, think nothing of it, lovely girl," Estelle cooed to her. "It's just that silly man, and you won't have to put up with him much longer." Then, turning her attention back to Sarah, she asked, "Now then, what else would you have me know about your beautiful girl?"

"Nothing," Sarah said. "Not another thing. I'm sure you'll do fine."

Before she finished the thought John arrived, panting heavily. He looked at Sarah curiously, as though she were a total stranger. But he wisely did not argue with her assessment.

There was a plain wooden bench at the side of the warm-up arena, and Faith and Sarah walked to it together. Faith already felt the need to sit down after her rough night. She couldn't imagine Sarah felt much better, especially considering the way the day had begun.

"I have to say," Faith told the girl as they sat together to watch, "that's the least I've ever heard you say to a potential rider of that horse."

"She doesn't need all that. All the mistakes I try to tell people not to make, she's not going to make them anyway. She's gentle, and she respects the horse. So Midnight will like her, and they'll do okay."

"John respects horses. Doesn't he?"

Sarah sighed theatrically. "John is impatient. That's the last thing you want to be with Midnight—impatient."

Meanwhile Estelle was already on the horse's back. She rode by them in a gentle free walk.

"We'll just start slowly," the older woman said in Sarah's direction. "Not ask for too much too soon. She just needs a little patience, don't you think?"

Sarah said nothing. Just sat with her mouth open. Faith had no idea whether they had been overheard, or if that had only been a coincidence.

On her next ride by, Estelle said, "I think my granddaughter is not as patient as I am. But I still believe I can teach her to be."

Sarah leapt to her feet. If anyone else had moved that fast in Midnight's presence, the mare would have launched across the arena before anyone could so much as blink. But the horse just kept walking.

John came over, quickly, and firmly encouraged Sarah to sit back down on the bench.

"She's buying her for a *kid?*" Sarah hissed in an almost comically loud stage whisper. "This is not the horse for a kid, and you know it. You're going to get somebody killed, John Wintermeyer!"

Faith wondered briefly if the girl had adopted that first-and-last-name chastisement style from Estelle.

"Will you keep your voice down?" John hissed back. "Her granddaughter is twenty-two years old and shows in Intermediare 1."

"Oh," Sarah said.

It was the second time that morning that the girl seemed disappointed she could not assume an attitude of furious disapproval.

"The horse is not Intermediare," Sarah said, her voice full of hurt. "She's barely Prix St. Georges. You pushed her to Prix St. Georges too fast."

"So you keep telling me," John said. "But she'll get there. Estelle thinks she can be Grand Prix."

"The granddaughter or the horse?"

"Both."

A silent moment.

"Well. Of course she can be Grand Prix," Sarah said, sounding a bit huffy. "That goes without saying."

"Then what's the problem?"

Another uncomfortable pause.

Then Sarah said, too loudly, "I can't watch this."

She leapt up from the bench and stomped back to the barn.

Faith arrived back at Barn C after a very long walk to a restroom. In the shade of the barn aisle, she was surprised to see John down on his knees in the dirt in front of Sarah. Literally on his knees in casual black breeches. Begging.

He was still every bit as tall as the girl, even in that kneeling position.

As Faith walked closer, the wide-awake show scene buzzed around her. Dogs sat tied outside stalls. People rode by on bicycles and tiny motor scooters. A man hosed off the mats of a stall across the aisle and several places down. A horse whinnied desperately—and somewhere, far away, another horse answered.

Faith walked up behind John and caught the tail end of his begging.

"I know you think I'm flush," he said to the girl. "Some years I am. This year I'm close to the line. I can't afford to eat what I paid for that mare. It'll bury me. Please. I'll pay you to do it."

"I don't want your money," Sarah said.

She glanced past him to Faith. He didn't seem to notice.

"Take the money," Faith said. "We need it. This is all coming out of my pocket."

John spun around and pushed up to his feet at more or less the same time.

"My grandmother gave us money," Sarah said.

The girl was in one of those moods again. Faith could hear it in her voice. See it in the set of her jaw. This time Faith was having none of it. She hadn't slept. She was hot. The balance on her credit cards wouldn't last forever. She wanted to go home, but she wasn't sure she knew anymore where home might be.

"Yes, well, we spent it," she said, matching the girl's vehemence.

"How did we spend it?"

"It's not as hard as you make it sound, kiddo.

We ate half of it and put the other half in my gas tank. Now I'm stressing out my credit cards keeping us out here. So if the man wants to pay you money for something, take the money."

"I'll leave you two to work this out," John said, his face deadly serious. "Sarah, when you make your decision, you come let me know."

He strode away on those amazingly long legs.

"What does he want you to do?"

"The lady thinks she wants to buy her, but first she wants to see her ride a test. John doesn't want to ride it for obvious reasons. The scores he's been getting on her are not exactly a selling point."

"He wants you to ride her."

"He wanted me to ride her in the Prix St. Georges, but I can't do that. I've been schooling fourth level every day. We're barely back to where we left off. I could ride her in the fourth level junior class, but I don't know if I should. Why should I? If I'm good, I just lose her all over again."

Then she walked off to sit in the lawn furniture under John's canopy. And Faith was too tired and discouraged to argue.

She just let the girl go off to figure it out on her own.

Faith looked up to see Sarah ride up on her mare and halt. It was a few hours later. Faith had been hiding out in the tack stall to beat the heat. Half reading her book, half pausing to fan herself with it.

Sarah peered into the open stall and down at Faith, as if convinced Faith knew exactly what to do and was only being difficult by not volunteering to do it.

The mare wore a number on her bridle: 227. Her mane had been carefully braided. Sarah was dressed in her finest borrowed riding clothes.

"So, are you coming to watch me ride, or what?"

"I didn't even know you'd decided to ride," Faith said, setting down her book.

"Well, that's a bit of a duh, don't you think? I mean, look at us."

"Right," Faith said. "Now that I look at you, it does look that way. Don't you need to warm up?"

"Already did. I ride in, like, three minutes."

"Do you need me to read the test for you?"

"No. I thought I might. But I studied it out of the book while I was waiting. I know it. I'll be okay."

Faith pushed herself up from her lawn chair and stepped out into the aisle. She fell in beside the girl and the horse, and they walked together.

"This is a good thing you're doing for John," she said as they approached the arena.

"I'm not doing it for John. I'm doing it for

Midnight. If she has to get sold, I want it to be to Estelle. Even though I don't know her granddaughter. Still, I think she'll be okay at Estelle's. And if I let this chance go by, who knows what kind of person might want to buy her next?"

They stopped about a hundred feet from the arena and stood side by side, watching a compact chestnut with a heavy woman rider complete their third-level test.

"I'm thinking about calling your grandmother," Faith said.

"Now?"

"Yeah, now."

"Why now?"

"I was thinking maybe we could do a FaceTime thing. So she could see your ride. Does she know how to do that?"

"Yeah. She does. So . . . okay. That would be good. But don't tell her . . . you know. Anything important. Not right before I ride. That would ruin everything."

Faith slipped her phone out of her pocket and made a regular voice call to Constance, who was slow to pick up. Five rings. By the time she did, the heavy rider and her chestnut horse had ridden out of the arena.

"Faith," Constance's voice said. "Is everything all right?"

"We're fine. Sarah is about to ride Midnight

in fourth level. Test two. Kind of a long story. I thought you might want to wish her luck."

She handed the phone up to the girl, whose face softened. In fact, she looked like she might be about to break down in tears.

"Hi, Grandma," Faith heard her say.

Then, "Thanks, Grandma."

And, "Okay. Me, too."

Finally, "I have to go now. I have to be ready when the judge rings the bell."

She handed the phone back down to Faith and cantered the mare into the outer arena.

Faith put the phone to her ear again.

"I was thinking . . . can you call me back as a FaceTime call? Then I can hold up the phone, and maybe you can see her ride. It'll look pretty far away, but . . ."

"Better than nothing," Constance said. "I like the idea."

"Oh," Constance said on a long breath. "She's doing so well. Those half passes!"

"Yes, it's a beautiful ride."

Sarah and Midnight were just finishing their ride with a change of rein—a diagonal pass across the arena to change direction—in extended trot, then a shorter "collected" trot followed by a turn down centerline and a halt and salute at X, the very center point of the arena. Faith was standing outside the arena but close to the rail at E—the equivalent of the fifty-yard line on a football field—holding up the phone so Constance could see.

"And it would have been so easy not to," Faith added.

"I'm sorry. What?"

"Never mind," Faith said. "Not important."

Horse and rider halted squarely. Sarah took both reins in one gloved hand. She saluted to the judge by dropping her free hand and her head, then let the reins go long. The girl fell over the mare's neck, petting and praising her. A smattering of applause rose up in the sparse crowd as the horse stretched her neck out and down and moved to exit the arena in a long, relaxed walk.

Faith turned the phone around.

"Let me talk to her one more time, please," Constance said, and she had tears in her eyes. "So I can see her."

"Sure. Of course."

In that moment, looking at the older woman's face, it struck Faith—hard—that she should not be keeping a secret from Constance. Especially not a big one, like the one she'd been told shortly after midnight, at the beginning of this painfully long day.

Faith walked with the phone to the break in the railing, the spot where Sarah would ride out of the arena.

They met there.

"I was good," Sarah said.

"You were."

"I didn't have to be."

"No," Faith said. "But you were." For a moment, Faith almost forgot she held Constance in her left hand. "Oh," she said when she remembered. "Your grandmother wants to talk to you one more time."

She handed up the phone, and the girl rode away holding it. And talking. She seemed to want a bit of privacy, away from the near-constant presence of Faith. Faith allowed that, because she understood it.

A minute later Faith looked up to see the girl ride back, holding the phone out for Faith to take. The screen was blank, or rather, back to the home screen. The call was over.

Faith reached up to accept the phone, double-checked that the call had been ended, then slid it into her pocket again.

"I just want to say this now, Sarah. Two things. One, that's the last time we talk to her without telling her everything. Two, as far as anyone else is concerned, you told me tonight. Not last night. I don't want to be on the hook to explain how I could sit on a thing like that. Even for one day."

Sarah nodded. She understood.

She swung off Midnight's back and dropped into the dirt. She took the reins over the mare's head and stood, holding them, looking into Faith's eyes.

She opened her mouth to speak.

The reins disappeared from her hands.

The girl looked down at her gloved but empty hands, as if she could not imagine where the reins had gone.

They both looked up to watch John lead the mare away.

"I know what you're thinking," John called over his shoulder. "But it's better this way. The long goodbyes will kill you. Trust me. Just clean like this is best."

Faith and Sarah stood transfixed, watching them go.

Once, just as John and Midnight disappeared behind a row of trailers, the mare turned her head to look back. Presumably for Sarah.

The girl looked away.

EARLY JUNE, WHEN IT ALL BEGAN
Six Weeks Earlier

Chapter Three

There's Something You Should Know About Sarah

Faith woke suddenly in the pitch-dark. She sat up in bed in a panic, with no idea where she was. Or why.

It was more than just a momentary need to reorient herself to her new surroundings. Somehow a dream had not let her go. *Would* not let her go. And in this dream state it was essential to grasp everything she could not currently grasp no matter how desperately she tried.

A couple of elongated seconds later she heard a wave roll in and crash on the sand. The panic fell away. She gasped oxygen as if it had been unavailable for days.

The beach house. She was at the beach house that belonged to her father and stepmother. She had driven up just the afternoon before.

Her heart calmed. Her mind tried, against her will, to turn back in time to what had chased her out of her home and all the way to the beach. She firmly turned it away again.

Faith rose and walked to the window.

She had fallen asleep in her clothes after dinner and three glasses of wine—the last two of which were unlike her. The master bedroom was upstairs in this two-level vacation home, and Faith stood at the window, drew back the gauzy white curtain, and looked down over the beach, her eyes adjusting to the dimness.

A yellowish full moon was setting at the horizon, its outline dulled by a foggy mist. And there was someone sitting on the sand directly in front of the house.

Just for a split second her heart jumped, thinking Robert had found her here. She'd half expected him to. Every time she'd left the beach house to fetch another suitcase from her car, she had nervously glanced around, scanning the yard for him. It would not have surprised her to see him. It was not like Robert to let anything go. Especially her.

Faith breathed deeply again and let such thoughts fall away. The person on the beach could not possibly be Robert. It was a female person, by the look of things, and it was unlikely that she was even a full-grown adult.

She was sitting in what looked like a lotus position in the sand, just a few feet down from Faith's porch. Her hands rested on her knees, palms up. As if she were meditating. As Faith's eyes continued to adjust to the dark, she was able to see that the girl was wearing a sleeveless tank top in the chilly fog.

Faith turned to go back to bed. But she paused.

And stood. And could not let it go. Could not ignore it. The girl looked, from behind, to be no more than twelve years old. What was she doing in front of the beach house in the middle of the night?

Faith drew on her sheepskin boots and trotted downstairs, pulling her light jacket off the hook on her way out the door.

The girl heard her as she padded down off the porch—Faith could tell. Before her boots touched sand and could no longer make a sound, Faith saw her tilt her head slightly, as if turning an ear to listen. But the girl never looked around.

Faith sat in the cold sand a few respectful feet from the girl's bare left shoulder.

"I'm sorry I interrupted your meditation," she said.

"It's okay," the girl said. Her voice was filmy and insignificant. Still, it told Faith she was not twelve. More of a teenager, though likely a young one. "I'm not meditating."

"You look like you are."

"I was trying. But I can't do it. I don't know how my grandmother does it."

"Do you live around here? Or are you staying here for a vacation?"

The girl flipped her head to indicate one of three or four houses farther up the beach. Faith wasn't sure which one. Then again, it didn't really matter.

"So what are you doing out on the beach in the middle of the night?"

The girl looked at Faith for the first time. Right into her face. As if looking for something. As if gauging the intention behind what she obviously found to be an odd question.

Faith was struck with the unwelcome sensation of her life changing in that moment, transformed by this meeting. By that glance. But she hated it when such glimpses of the future reared their heads. She fought them hard, every time, and continued to regard herself as someone who knew nothing beyond what was right in front of her face to be seen, touched, or smelled.

"It's not the middle of the night," the girl said. Tentatively, as if testing the limits of Faith's silliness.

"It's not?"

"No. It's almost five in the morning."

"Oh."

They sat a moment in silence. Listened to the waves come in. Or Faith did, anyway; she could not say what the girl was listening to. In her peripheral vision, Faith saw a faint orangey glow to the east, which was not directly behind her on this partly south-facing beach. It was early June, when the days were long, and civil twilight was about to break.

"My grandmother gets up at four a.m. and meditates for hours," the girl said, startling Faith slightly. She didn't seem like the chatty type, that girl. Faith had expected the silence to last. "I came down here so I wouldn't disturb her. She doesn't know I'm up."

"Couldn't you meditate *with* her?"

"That never works. I can't meditate. I told you. I just can't do it. My brain is too busy. It runs everywhere and I can't stop it. So I always end up sniffing and scratching and shifting around trying to get comfortable. She never *says* I'm bothering her, but I always know I am. I came down here because I thought there was nobody staying in this house."

"Aren't you cold, though?"

"Freezing."

"Can't you just go in and get a jacket?"

"I don't want to disturb her while she's meditating. I told you."

The girl stole a glance at Faith. Or, at least, it looked as though the glance was something she wanted to steal. She did not appear to want to be seen openly taking it. But Faith met her gaze head-on, and the girl quickly looked away again.

Faith pushed herself up, her hands sinking into the loose sand, and moved back toward the house. She looked back to see the girl glance over her shoulder, watching Faith go. Uncomfortably, from the look of it. As if she had not been ready to let their conversation end.

It was an odd sensation, because Faith felt

strangely sure that this young girl avoided conversations with grown-ups. It was something she knew by feel. But the girl was leaning toward Faith in a way that was deeply contrary to her own nature. And Faith had no idea why.

Letting herself in through the door she had left unlocked, she grabbed the alpaca throw off the back of the living room couch.

She carried it out to the beach and draped it over the girl's bare shoulders. Then she sat again.

"Thanks," the girl said. Before Faith could open her mouth to say she was welcome, the girl added, "That wasn't true, what I said to you before."

"What? Which part of what you said wasn't true?"

"When I said I thought there was nobody staying here. I saw you come in yesterday. I watched you bringing in all your stuff. I don't usually do that. I usually only say stuff that's true. But I was embarrassed."

"Oh," Faith said. And was unsure what else to say.

"I should go," the girl said, fairly leaping to her feet.

The alpaca throw landed lightly on Faith as she raised her arms to receive it.

She watched the girl trot about fifteen houses down the beach, then noted which house was hers as the child ran back into the safety of her grandmother's home.

• • •

Faith tried her best to get back to sleep for another few hours.

Sleep never came.

In time she sat up in bed, blinking into the light from the window. She reached for her phone. Woke it up. It informed her that it was almost eight o'clock in the morning.

She had turned off the ringer. She instinctively moved her thumb to turn it back on. Then she thought better of it. She pressed her thumb onto the keypad to unlock it.

There were two missed calls. Both from Robert.

There were three texts. All three from Robert.

There were seven new emails. One was from Robert.

Faith touched the phone icon and pressed the green call button twice, knowing it would call Ava. Ava was the last person Faith had called. Ava was almost always the last person Faith had called.

Ava picked up on the second ring.

"You okay up there?" her friend asked in place of "hello."

"Yeah. Fine. So far."

"What's the weather doing at the beach?"

"Foggy. Cool."

"Lucky you. It's going to be ninety-seven here today."

"Yeah. Lucky me. I feel so very lucky these

days. So, look . . . I was wondering if you knew how to block a contact on an iPhone."

"Robert?"

"Who else?"

"I do, actually. I do know how to block a contact on an iPhone. I also know you can ask Siri, 'Siri, how do you block a contact on an iPhone?' And I know you know it, too."

"I didn't want to talk to Siri. I wanted to talk to you."

"Got it," Ava said. "And, also . . . that was not a complaint."

It was the following day, or possibly the one after, when Faith saw the girl's grandmother for the first time. Faith was just beginning a morning walk along the beach, passing the houses to the north of her own. She instinctively turned her head to look more closely at the dark red one-story bungalow the girl had run to after their meeting. Faith thought maybe she would see her.

Instead she saw a woman who she knew must be the grandmother, though she did not look much the grandmotherly type. She looked to be about fifty, with big, dark hair, curly and wild, wearing a long, soft-looking skirt that seemed to have been created from a woven South American fabric. She was moving from one outdoor plant to another—mostly hanging spider plants and creeping Charlies—and watering them from a red metal watering can.

Faith paused a moment too long, and it caught the older woman's eye.

"Good morning," the woman said, her gaze drilling right into Faith even at some distance. She had a strength, an intensity about her that Faith found almost unsettling.

"Good morning," Faith said in return. Her voice sounded lighter and more unconcerned than she felt—an imitation of a person more relaxed than she had been for as long as she could remember.

Faith walked on, but didn't get far. Five steps, maybe. Then she stopped. Almost walked north again, but didn't.

She turned back and strode to the woman's porch, leaving no spaces into which her hesitations could wedge themselves.

"You must be the grandmother of that girl I was talking to the other day."

The intensity of the woman's eyes, her gaze, returned. Faith had no choice but to hold it all up for a few seconds.

It wasn't easy.

"Sarah?" the woman asked. Almost more curious than the conversation seemed to warrant.

"I'm not sure. She didn't tell me her name. But she looked to be thirteen or fourteen years old. She was sitting in a lotus position in front of my beach house like she was meditating. But when I asked her, she said she can't meditate. She said she tries, but she just can't do it. She told me her grandmother gets up at four in the morning and meditates for hours."

Faith watched the woman's eyes narrow slightly, as if she were under some kind of strain. As if she were doing math in her head.

"That would be my Sarah, all right. But . . . it's not like her to say that much to a stranger. She barely says that much to me. I would have been surprised if you told me she'd said 'hello.' "

"You know," Faith said, "I got that feeling, too. That she wasn't much of a talker. That she was making an exception for me, and I had no idea why. She seemed a little uneasy about it."

"I can't imagine why, either."

A silence fell, punctuated only by the waves breaking onto the sand. Then the sound of human voices, people laughing and talking, turned Faith's head. She saw a couple at the far end of the beach throw a ball into the surf for their yellow Labrador retriever. Watched the dog bound into the water after it, jumping up and washing back as a wave crashed into its chest.

"Oh," she heard the older woman say. And it was a monumental "oh." It contained something of importance. Faith just had no idea what it might be. Yet. "I do know why. I see it now."

Faith looked back into the woman's face. This time the older woman looked away.

"What? What do you see?"

"You look a little like Sarah's mother. My daughter. Heather. When you were looking at me head-on and talking to me, I didn't see it. But when you turned your head partway away . . . your hair is a lot like hers. And something about your movements. It just hit me. I'm not saying anyone would mistake you for her, but it definitely catches you. Kind of took my breath away for a second there."

"Is Sarah separated from her mom in some way?"

A long pause. It had been the wrong question. Faith could feel that now. If only her words had come equipped with a handle or a tail, she would have grabbed hold of it and pulled them back again.

"Constance," the woman said, still without meeting her eyes.

It took Faith a moment to realize it was a name. An introduction. For a split second it struck her as a one-word inspirational suggestion.

"Faith," Faith said in return, and then laughed. "We sound like a bunch of advice on how to live comfortably in the world, don't we?"

Constance smiled, but did not laugh. Faith thought maybe she saw the woman try. But it was too far from where she currently lived.

"Would you like to come in and have a cup of tea, Faith?"

"I really didn't mean to intrude."

"No, you're not. Not at all. I left behind every friend I have to come here to the beach with Sarah. It would be nice to have a conversation with a grown-up again."

"Where *is* Sarah?" Faith asked her host, who was puttering in the kitchen.

Faith sat at the table in a nook of dining room in Constance and Sarah's one-story bungalow. Across from her, in the living room overlooking the beach, Faith saw a meditation cushion in front of what appeared to be a Buddhist altar. It was hard for her to take her eyes off it.

"She's out walking. She walks for hours. I'd feel better about it if she would eat a little more. You know. To support all that exercise. But there's only just so much you can tell a girl that age. Do you have children?"

"I don't."

Faith looked away from the altar—looked up—as Constance came to the table with an Asian-looking cast-iron teapot. She set it down on a bamboo mat in the center of the table, then placed a handleless cup in front of Faith, and another at the place across the table, where Constance then sat.

"We'll just let that steep a few minutes," she said.

After a few awkward moments, during which

they both stared out the window at the surf, Constance asked, "Didn't want them?"

"I'm sorry. Didn't want what?"

"My fault. I was picking up a thread of conversation that had been set down too long. We were talking about children."

"Oh. Right. That. I did think I wanted them at one point. But that was a long time ago now. I lost one after three months of pregnancy. But then things weren't good between my husband and me, and I guess I instinctively knew better than to bring a child into that environment."

"I'm sorry if it seemed like too personal a question."

"I suppose it was my choice to give a personal answer. I could have just said yes or no. But I didn't."

They fell silent again, the soft roar of the waves reminding Faith that sound still existed. That no one had pressed a mute button on the entire world.

Meanwhile Constance was gearing up to speak. Faith could feel the gathering of it.

"Sarah's mother died two weeks ago," Constance said. "Two weeks almost to the day. She was my only daughter. My only child. So it's been just devastating for me, too. I'm trying my best to be everything Sarah needs—to have everything she needs to get through this. But I don't even have everything *I* need. I used to meditate twenty minutes morning and night. But she's right. It's turned into hours. I know she feels left out. But if I don't hold myself together, then what will she have?"

Constance allowed a pause, followed by a deep breath. It seemed to stall her momentum. To settle her.

"I'm so sorry."

Faith poured herself a cup of the green tea to have something to do with her hands. She wanted to ask *how*. *How* had Sarah's mother died? But that might have been more than Constance cared to share.

Instead she asked, "Was it sudden?"

"Very. Very sudden. Nobody saw it coming."

A sound made them both jump. It was a whoosh of air as the door opened, and the amplification of the noise of the surf. Faith and Constance both looked up to see Sarah standing in the living room. The door continued to yawn open as the girl stared at them.

Faith took the girl in with the help of daylight, since none had been available on their first meeting.

Sarah was painfully skinny. No wonder her grandmother worried about how much she ate. Her light-brown hair fell thin and straight to her shoulders, half covering one eye. Hiding her the way young teenagers love to be hidden. She looked like a girl who could be notably pretty if only she wasn't trying so hard not to be noticed in any way.

"Oh," the girl said. "*You're* here."

"Your grandmother invited me in for a cup of tea."

"I can see *that*," Sarah said, a note of derision in her voice. She swung the door closed behind her and it latched into place with a whump. She came closer to the table and flipped her chin to indicate the obvious trappings of tea. "What were you two talking about?"

Constance looked flummoxed, so Faith took the lead.

"I was just telling your grandmother about that nice talk we had the other morning."

"It wasn't that nice," the girl said. "I don't mean . . . I mean, it wasn't your fault that it wasn't nice or anything like that. It just wasn't that much of a talk. All I said was that my grandmother meditates a lot, and I can't do it at all."

A silence fell, and all three of them seemed to sink into it and get lost. At least, that was how it felt to Faith.

Then the older woman gathered herself to speak.

"After Sarah's mother died—" she began.

Faith had no idea where Constance was going with that thought. And she would never learn. Because Constance would never arrive there.

Sarah's mouth fell open. She glanced quickly at Faith to see if this was new information to her.

"You *told* her that?" the girl bellowed. Faith had never imagined that so much vehemence, so much volume, could be hiding in that narrow frame. "Why would you *tell* her that?"

Then the girl was in motion.

She stamped into a bedroom and slammed the door. Hard. The glass shade of a lighting sconce rattled on the wall, and a soft pastel painting of the ocean ended up askew.

Faith heard Constance pull in a long breath and slowly let it out again.

"I played that all wrong," the older woman said. "I used to have good instincts. I trusted them, and not for no reason. Now it seems like whatever I land on is just exactly wrong."

"I'm thinking of going in and talking to her. Is that even a remotely good idea?"

"Don't ask me. My instincts are always wrong."

Faith rose from the table, surprised that her heart was hammering. She could hear it and feel it in her ears.

How can I be afraid of a skinny teenage girl? she thought as she walked to the closed bedroom door. Then she decided it wasn't the girl that was scary, but the loss. What Constance and Sarah's loss said about the world. How it withdrew Faith's ability to pretend that the world could not—would not—strike with no notice, offering up a loss that could take a person's breath away. *Of course it can,* she thought, *and you know it better than just about anybody. We only pretend it can't, a minute or two at a time, to help us get up and out of the house in the morning.*

She rapped on the door. The sharp sound caused a jump in her own belly, the way a sound would startle her if she were half-asleep.

"Go away, Grandma," the girl called through the door.

"It's me," Faith said.

"Oh."

Then . . . nothing. For an uncomfortable length of time.

"May I come in?"

"Why?"

"I just want to tell you something."

"What?"

"I'd rather not yell it through the door." Another long, awkward silence. "Well," Faith began again. "Can I come in, then?"

"Whatever."

Faith swung the door wide and stepped into the girl's room.

It took her several seconds to even notice Sarah lying facedown on the unmade single bed. At first her attention was totally captured by the photos on the walls. There were three or four dozen of them. All blown up to eight by ten or larger. None framed. They were, instead, laminated and mounted to the wall with pushpins, nearly floor to ceiling in most places.

They were all photos of the same two subjects. A girl and a horse. The same girl. The same horse.

The horse was tall, fine boned, leggy, and jet black. It wore a classic English saddle. Formal English tack. It trotted with an extension that enthralled Faith, reaching out with those long legs to cover ground in a way Faith thought she had never quite seen before. And it cantered in a similar style, hind legs gathered underneath its haunches, front legs reaching.

In most of the pictures the horse had a number on its bridle. For a show, she assumed. She stepped closer to see: 289, 122, 419. Its mane was beautifully braided, the plaits gathered and folded into little knobs that looked like dark, tightly closed rosebuds seated every few inches along the crest of the horse's neck.

The girl on its back appeared just as classically formal, in bright white breeches, tall black leather boots. A black riding jacket. White stock tie with a jeweled pin. Black brimmed helmet apparently made to look something like an old-fashioned English hard hat.

In one photo, girl and horse stood before a row of neat stalls with half doors. Beside them a canopy read, "Dressage Journeys, Moorpark, California."

Faith looked to the girl on the bed who, she now realized, was watching her take in the photos.

"Is that you in these pictures?"

"Who else would it be?"

"It's hard to tell with the brim of that helmet. It casts shadows on your face. So . . . is that your horse?"

"Was," Sarah said. And did not elaborate.

Faith opened her mouth to ask another question. Sarah cut her off.

"You said you wanted to tell me something."

"Right."

"So tell me the something."

"Okay." Faith felt herself gather a larger-than-average lungful of oxygen in preparation for the task. "I wanted to tell you that my mom died when I was only twelve."

Faith stole a glance at the girl. She was staring out the window, despite the fact that there was nothing to see out there but the house next door. But she was listening. Hard. Faith could tell.

"How did she die?"

"Plane crash. Small private plane."

"Oh," Sarah said, still staring out the window. "Your father wasn't with her?"

"Actually, he was. But he survived."

"Oh. At least there was nobody to blame."

"Well, that's not entirely true. The pilot had been drinking."

"At least you had someone to hate."

"It wasn't quite that easy."

"Why not? I sure would have hated him."

"The pilot was my father."

Sarah looked at her then. Quickly and sharply. As though she couldn't stop herself. Before Faith could meet her eyes in return, the girl looked away again.

"So . . . ," Sarah said. Then she stalled. As if there were no more words in the universe. At least, none that she could reach.

Faith could feel the girl gird herself to say more. It took a minute or two. She waited patiently, her eyes straying back to the photos.

"What did you do?" Sarah asked at last. Her voice had grown small again.

Faith laughed, but not the way a person laughs at anything genuinely amusing.

"I don't know. What *could* I do? The sun still came up every morning. Which, I have to tell you, seemed like quite the personal insult for the first few months. I put one foot in front of the other because I didn't have any other choice. I was alive, whether I liked it or not. I lived because I had to."

A long silence. Faith turned her eyes back to the amazing performing horse. The four-legged dancer with a girl on its back.

Nobody seemed willing to wade any deeper into the conversation.

"Well," Faith said. "I'll leave you alone now."

"Thank you." Then, just as Faith was slipping out the door, Sarah added, "Thank you for telling me."

"I don't know that it was all that helpful. It's not like I could tell you how to get through a thing like that."

"But you know how I feel," the girl said.

There was a catch in her voice on the word "feel." Faith purposely did not look back to see if she was crying.

"Yes. I know how you feel."

Faith closed the door softly behind her. With all of the reverence the situation demanded.

Chapter Four

Women's Self-Defense

"I should get us each another beer," Ava said.

They sat on the front porch of the beach house, watching the surfers. It was late on a Saturday afternoon. The sun had fallen to a long slant over the water. Ava had driven up much later than promised, as was her habit.

"I can't believe you've even finished your first one already," Faith said. "I mean, you've been here for about a minute."

"I'm thirsty. It was a long drive. Four hours plus, with traffic."

"Fine. So grab another. Maybe just bring me a can of that sparkling water. It's on the bottom shelf of the fridge door."

Ava got up and walked into the house.

Just as she did, Faith noticed the girl. Sarah. She had stepped out of her dark red bungalow in shorts and a sleeveless tank top, and was headed straight for the water. The girl glanced south. She seemed to identify Faith sitting on her porch. She raised one tentative hand in a wave.

Faith waved back.

"So are you actually, literally going to file for divorce?"

Ava's voice startled her. An aluminum can of cherry-flavored sparkling water appeared near her left shoulder. Faith took hold of it, appreciating the sweaty coldness of it. Popped the top.

When she looked north again, the girl was just jumping up over a wave. Then she sank beneath the surface and seemed to disappear.

"Who were you waving at?" Ava asked, sitting on one of the wicker porch chairs again with her beer.

Faith said nothing for a moment, intent on watching the waves. Sarah couldn't simply be gone. And what if she was? There was no lifeguard on this beach. And Faith was not a strong swimmer.

"Hello? Earth to Faith?"

"Wait a minute," Faith said.

On the second syllable of the word "minute," she saw the girl's head break the water. Saw her begin to swim south with sure strokes. Faith breathed again, deeply and audibly.

"I was waving to this girl from a few houses up," she said.

"And I notice you're using that to duck my original question."

"No. I'm not. I'm not ducking it at all. I just got distracted for a minute. I already filed for divorce."

A reverent silence as Ava absorbed the gravity of that statement.

"You didn't tell me that," Ava said after several seconds and a long slug of beer.

"Sorry. I was busy fleeing."

"What was his reaction?"

"No idea. I got out before he could have one. Before he was served."

"Are you sure you're okay here? Doesn't he know your father has a beach house?"

"He doesn't know where. It's always been rented out. He has no idea my dad unrented it for me. Dad and Marilyn know better than to tell him where it is. Or where I am. I have them trained."

Faith scanned the surf again and caught another glimpse of the girl, her head a mere dot beyond the breaking waves. Still making a beeline south, parallel to the shore. In Faith's direction. Faith wondered whether she would turn and swim back the way she had come or swim ashore in front of Faith's house.

"Is actual violence a possibility here?"

"Oh, I doubt that," Faith said. "He never hit me before."

"You never left him before," Ava said, then set about draining her beer in more or less one long swallow.

"True. But I really think the worst that could happen—if he even found me, that is—would be maybe . . . I can picture him doing something like grabbing me by the arm and trying to put me back in the car and take me home. So just to be on the safe side I got pepper spray. And I'm taking a women's self-defense class in Morro Bay. But that's more for the inside of me. My own confidence. I really think he would make my life unbearable in mostly nonphysical ways."

" 'Mostly,' " Ava repeated. Then, "I hope you're right. I'm getting another beer."

"Whoa. Slow down, girl."

"Bad advice. Or, anyway, unwanted advice. It's the weekend, and I'm free. And this is what I want to do with it."

She disappeared into the house again.

Faith looked toward the water to see Sarah walking out of the surf. A wave broke against the back of the girl's legs and pushed her forward as she shook water out of her hair. Sarah looked up. Saw Faith watching her. Waved again.

The dripping girl walked up to the porch and leaned on the rail from the outside.

"I wanted to ask you something," she said.

"Go ahead."

But then, for a long minute, the girl didn't. She looked down at the sand as if ashamed of the whole world, and especially her place in it.

"Do you hate him?" she asked at last. Quiet. Small.

Faith felt her head rock back slightly.

She had never said a word about her estranged husband to the girl, or to Sarah's grandmother.

That she would ask about him was downright spooky.

"How do you . . . I mean, how did you even . . . who even told you about him?"

"You did."

"I never—"

"When you were in my room. You told me about your father. Don't you remember?"

"Oh," Faith said. And all the alarm and confusion drained out of her. She pulled a deep breath, released it, and felt it all go. "My father. Right. No. I don't hate him."

"But it was his fault."

"But he didn't mean for it to happen that way. He didn't want that."

The girl fidgeted with her dripping hair, as if trying to pull it over her face. But there wasn't enough of it when wet. She seemed to be regretting her own exposure.

"But it was his fault."

"I think maybe if he'd gone on drinking I might have hated him. But he never drank after that. Not so much as a sip of champagne at a wedding. Not even his own, when he got married again. So that let me know how sorry he was, and I think that helped. He wasn't an alcoholic or anything. He just drank the way a lot of people drink. They'd been to this party on Martha's Vineyard. My dad had something like three drinks. Maybe four, I don't know. He said he was thinking they'd stay longer than they did. But then my mom wasn't feeling good, and she wanted to go back. And it was a plane. You know. A plane is not a car. He couldn't just hand her the keys and say, 'Here. You fly.' I guess he thought he was okay. Or okay *enough,* anyway. It was one of those bad judgment calls that I guess can happen to anybody."

"But you were mad at him, right?"

"Oh, I was furious. For the first couple of years." Faith paused, and let the truth of those years catch up to her. For the first time in a very long time. "You know . . . now that I think about it . . . I guess I did hate him at first. Hated him and loved him both. You can hate someone and love him at the same time."

"I know," Sarah said. Her voice sounded grounded. Sure. Strangely adult.

Ava appeared on the porch again with her beer, and Sarah backed up several steps.

"I have to go," the girl said.

"No, you don't have to. You can come sit with us."

"No," Sarah said. "I can't. I have to go."

And with that she turned and sprinted along the sand toward home.

"What was that all about?" Ava asked, getting comfortable in the wicker chair again.

"Just a girl who's going through a hard time. Lost her mom. She wants to hang around me and talk to me because I told her my mom died when I was young."

No reply.

Faith watched in silence as Sarah ran up the steps to the bungalow and disappeared inside.

Then she turned to look at her friend, who was taking her in with an odd expression, her eyebrows crooked and high.

"I'd known you for a year and a half before you told me that."

"I know. But she's right in the middle of it, and she needs some help. I'm trying to do some good here."

"Okay," Ava said. "Okay. I guess I see your point about that."

Ava left for Southern California the following afternoon, and it was more of a relief than Faith would have cared to admit. Her best friend could be draining.

More importantly, Faith had been wrestling a curiosity that clung to her like an itch—in the very middle of her back, where she couldn't quite reach it. She'd been wanting to find a way to scratch it ever since that girl had come ashore in front of the house to ask her freighted question.

Faith gathered up the muffins Ava had brought despite knowing Faith was trying to stay away from sweets. She arranged them on a clean kitchen towel in a basket that her stepmother might not have wanted her to give away.

Then she folded the towel over the top of them and walked them down the beach to the dark red bungalow, where she rapped on the door.

Constance answered quickly, and Faith was relieved to see the look in the older woman's eyes in that moment. That telltale moment when a person opens the door and sees who's come calling. Faith had learned to read her welcome—or lack of same—in a person's expression. Fortunately, Constance was not unhappy to see her.

"Did I take you away from your meditation?"

"No. Not at all. I was reading. Come in."

Faith stepped into the living room and held the basket in the older woman's direction.

"I'm not sure how you feel about baked goods," she said. "I'm trying to avoid anything with sugar. It's hard on my mood. Makes me hyper. And then, when I'm done being hyper, I get a mood crash. These were given to me, and I didn't want them to go to waste."

"I like muffins," Constance said. "And it might be just what I need to get Sarah to eat something."

Faith sensed that the second part of that sentence was more true than the first. But Constance accepted the basket graciously.

"Is Sarah here?" Faith asked, moving in the direction of the girl's room. Staring at the horse photos through the open door.

"No, she's not. She's out on one of her 'forever walks' again."

Faith felt the older woman move up beside her and stop near her right elbow. Together they stood and stared into Sarah's room.

"She's a beautiful horse," Constance said, "isn't she? They were beautiful together."

"I'll say. It's hard to take your eyes off them."

"I wouldn't ask her about the horse, though, if I were you. It's a very, very sore subject. I swear she'd almost rather talk about what happened to her mother."

"Did the horse die?"

"Oh, no. Nothing like that. She's nine years old and healthy, wherever she is. Right after Sarah and I came up here to the beach I called the barn in Moorpark where she was boarded. I was going to make an arrangement for a professional hauler to move her up here. I'd found her a barn only about twenty minutes away. But we ran into some very bad news instead. They informed me that the mare was no longer there. That she'd been sold."

"Wait. They can do that? Didn't she belong to Sarah?"

"No, *they* didn't do it. And, unfortunately, when you're fourteen nothing really belongs to you. Her father sold the horse. It was devastating for the poor girl. Absolutely devastating. Hardest thing I ever had to do in my life, to tell her."

"Any idea why he would do a thing like that?"

"Just an educated guess. She's a valuable horse. I'm guessing he needed the money. Could have been hurt and anger over the fact that Sarah didn't want to stay with him. But he's a gambler. Sometimes gamblers need money, and they'll do anything. If that's true, it's ironic, because the horse came into the family on a good gambling streak. But I guess we may never really know. It's not like you can trust what he says."

They stood in silence for a moment, Faith changing her mind every few seconds as to whether she should ask her question. Then, without feeling she had come to any firm decision, she heard the words come out of her mouth.

"Does Sarah blame her father for her mother's death?" She immediately regretted asking. The words felt like weapons in the air, some hovering danger waiting to cut anyone who touched them, drawing blood. "I'm sorry. I guess I shouldn't have asked that. It's just that she came to my house yesterday and was asking some odd questions that made it sound like she did."

In the brief pause that followed, Faith could hear the older woman's exaggerated breathing.

"I don't know," Constance said after a time. Her voice sounded solid and calm. Weirdly, artificially so. "I don't know if Sarah blames her father for what happened. I know *I* do."

"I think I'm really wishing I'd never brought it up," Faith said. "I didn't mean to pry. It's just that I feel like she's reaching out to me for some kind of help. And I don't know what to do to help her."

"No," Constance said. "Neither do I."

A much longer silence followed.

Then the older woman said, "Stay for lunch if you'd like. I was just about to make something."

"Oh. Thank you. But I can't. I have a women's self-defense class in Morro Bay. I have to be there in about twenty minutes."

"Self-defense?"

"I guess it sounds silly."

"No. Not really. It sounds scary. Like you think you have a reason to need it."

"Oh, no. It's not that bad. I doubt I'll ever use it. But I'm going through a divorce. And my husband . . . well, he's never been all that physically violent, but he can be so horrible emotionally. And verbally. I guess it just . . . kind of leaves a person wondering if he could cross a line with no notice. But it's not even that so much. I mean, that's not the biggest part. It's that a couple of people have told me it's good for the inside of a person. Good healing, when you've been through a lot. Makes you feel like you can take care of yourself, and that changes the way you carry yourself through the world."

An entirely new voice entered the conversation.

"*I* want to take a self-defense class," it said.

Both women spun to see Sarah standing in the living room behind them.

"Fine," Constance said. "I think it's a fine idea. I'll look into signing you up for one."

"But she's going *now,*" Sarah said, a distinct whine in her voice. She brushed her hair off her face with one impatient movement. "Why can't I go *now?*"

"She can come to mine," Faith said. "I really wouldn't mind at all."

"So what do you think will happen when you see him?" Sarah asked on the drive. It was a question that sprang from behind the thin waterfall of her hair.

"My husband?"

"Right."

Faith had been wondering how much of her conversation with Constance the girl had overheard. Now she could stop wondering.

She had taken the exit at Morro Bay Boulevard, encountered a traffic circle, and then realized she had no idea where she was or where she needed to be.

"Get that flyer out of the glove compartment, please," she said to the girl. "And I don't know that I *will* see him."

"Don't you have to be in court when that whole thing gets worked out?"

"Maybe you do if you want things from the property settlement. I don't want anything. He can have it all. I just want to get away and start over."

Faith pulled over to the curb to examine the flyer close up. Get the address again. Maybe enter it into her navigation system.

Before she could, she noticed a car half a block behind her. She had seen the same car behind her on the highway. Now that car was pulled over as well. She peered at the driver in her rearview mirror, her heart hammering, but it was not Robert. It was a man more refined looking and slight. She was only letting her imagination get the best of her. She breathed deeply and looked at the little hand-drawn map in the corner of the flyer.

"Oh," she said. "It's exactly behind us. I have to find a place to turn around."

"You shouldn't let him have everything," Sarah said.

"I don't care about any of it," she said, making a possibly illegal U-turn. "I just want him to let me go."

"My grandmother says when women do that it's because they don't think they're worth it. They don't have enough self-esteem to demand half of everything they both worked for together."

"That's interesting," Faith said.

"Interesting how?"

"Interesting because I didn't realize your grand-mother was the judgmental type."

"She was only judging herself. She said that about herself. A few years after she divorced my grandfather."

"Oh. Okay. Well, my self-esteem is fine, thank you very much. I just don't want the mess of it all."

"My grandmother says—" But then the girl glanced over at Faith before continuing. Sized up the look on her face. "Never mind. I guess it doesn't matter what my grandmother says."

The community center shared a parking lot with a supermarket, a dollar store, a payday loan establishment, and a mailing center. As Faith locked up the car, she glanced around to be sure she and Sarah were about to head to the right building.

She saw a slight, refined man step out of his car and spin away immediately, just as she turned to look in his direction. She could only barely see the car—a big SUV was blocking it—but it looked like the same silver color as that car she kept seeing behind her.

"What?" Sarah asked, startling her.

"Nothing."

"What are you looking at?"

"Nothing. Seriously. It's nothing."

Because by that time she was able to see that the man had only turned away to look at the screen of his phone without the glare of full sun. And by then she had decided he might not be the same person anyway. And she had begun to feel quite silly. Ashamed, in fact.

"I just thought I saw something," she added. "But now I think I was wrong."

The floor of the community center's main room was covered with thick gymnasium mats. A man wandered back and forth in an eerie amount of padding, including a massive padded helmet that made him look alien and completely obscured his face. Faith thought she could guess why, but it gave her the creeps.

A petite and classically attractive blonde woman handed them each papers to sign. Release forms, Faith assumed.

But Faith was already off on a bad footing, because women like this always made her feel horsey, clumsy, and unattractive. It had been that way since she was a child. Telling herself she "should" outgrow it had done nothing to ease the situation so far.

"You have to sign your daughter's release," the offensively attractive woman said. "You know. As her legal guardian."

"I'm not her legal guardian," Faith said without thinking.

Then she kicked herself. She could have just signed the form. If no one got hurt, what harm would be done? Even if someone did, Sarah was here with her grandmother's permission.

But it was too late. She had said it.

"Uh-oh," the blonde woman said. "That'll be a problem."

"We could take the paper back to Cayucos," Sarah said, "and get my grandmother to sign it."

"But then we'd miss the first half hour of the class," Faith said.

"Oh." The girl was disappointed and not hiding it.

"Besides," the blonde woman said, "we like to have a legal guardian actually present during the class."

In the silence that followed, Faith looked through the big plate-glass windows to the parking lot, which she scanned. In case someone out there appeared to be following her. But there was nothing and no one as far as she could tell.

"I'll just sit in the corner and watch," Sarah said. But she sounded crushed.

"No," Faith said. "Never mind. I'm not doing that to you. I'll just take you home. I'll just take us both home."

They handed their forms back to the petite woman who clearly had everything in life that Faith did not.

It was a relief. One that Faith might even have admitted if someone had called her out on it. The scene of the class was new, which made it feel vaguely threatening. It was poised to imitate violence, which made it scarier. And Faith tended to pick up too much energy from others in big rooms like that one, leaving her feeling jarred and alarmed.

She steered Sarah toward the door.

"I hate that I made you miss your class," the girl said as they stepped back out into the sun.

Faith shielded her eyes and scanned around again, but it was just a parking lot in a small town, containing nothing and no one bent on threatening her.

"Don't worry about it," she said. "I was starting to have mixed feelings about the whole thing anyway."

"Oh," Faith said just as she pulled into the driveway of the beach house. "I was going to go to the supermarket while I was in Morro Bay."

"Cayucos has a market," Sarah said.

The girl was staring down at her own hands, as if deeply ashamed. Had been since leaving the community center.

"Yeah. Whatever. That's fine. The local one will do."

They just sat a minute, the engine running. The car not even in the parking gear. The girl seemed not to realize that she needed to jump out now.

"Oh," Sarah said suddenly. "I just got it. You need to go again."

She tried to apologize again to Faith as she was climbing out of the car, but Faith was having none of it.

"Don't," Faith said. "Seriously. Just stop worrying about it. Things have a tendency to work out the way they're supposed to."

Faith was just walking into the market when she saw him again. This time there was no doubt in her mind.

He had just parked his silver car in a much closer space than the one Faith had found. He stepped out briskly, slammed his car door, and fell in line behind her to walk through the automatic double doors of the market.

Faith stopped in her tracks, her heart pounding. The slightly built man stopped, partly in surprise, partly because she was now blocking the entrance. He looked to be in his early forties, and he wore a panama hat and dark sunglasses, making it hard for her to assess him in any useful way. But he did seem to be shooting her a questioning look.

Are we going? It was that sort of look.

Meanwhile they were close enough to the automatic door that it had opened with a whoosh and was now standing open as she confronted him.

"Don't think I don't know what's going on here," Faith said, her voice trembly. In a strange and sudden thought, she wished she had just taken a women's self-defense class.

"Well, that makes one of us," the man said. "Because I have no idea what's going on."

His voice was light and calm. He seemed amused. Like someone who was always sure of himself. Faith had never understood self-assured people.

"I know he paid you to have me followed."

"Who do you think paid me to have you followed?" he asked. Then, a bit wryly, he added, "Though I guess it doesn't matter, because I can tell you right now nobody paid me to have you followed."

She stood her ground. Narrowed her eyes at him. "If you're a private investigator, and somebody asks you straight out if you're a private investigator, are you legally required to tell them?"

The automatic door lurched toward closed, then stopped and sprang open again.

"I have no idea," he said. "Not being a private investigator, I have no idea what rules they have to follow."

That was the moment when Faith's doubt broke through. Until then, she had been strangely sure. Now she allowed for the humiliating possibility that she was yelling at a total stranger for no reason at all.

"Why have I seen you everywhere I go today?

I mean, not everywhere. But, like . . . three times. In one day."

"Because . . . ," he said, drawing the word out long, ". . . it's a very small town?"

"Oh," Faith said. And the doubt flipped and pinned her.

"You're not from a small town," he said, "are you? You're from the big city."

She opened her mouth to answer, then realized that the fact of his being a random stranger could be a good thing in this moment. She could abandon her horrendous mistake and never have to see him again.

"My apologies," she said. "I misread the situation."

She stepped sideways out of the entrance. He tipped his hat and walked inside. The door closed with a whoosh.

Faith slipped her phone out of her pocket, took a deep breath, and did something she had not done since leaving home.

She unblocked and then texted Robert.

He would be at home, she knew, with his phone by his side. Working at his desk, most likely, on a laptop computer, which would also show his messages.

Are you having me followed? she typed.

She pressed send.

Then she added: Tell me the truth please or don't answer at all.

She waited in the warm sun. Wondering if it had been crazy to open that communication. Wondering what kind of flash flood would come spilling out in her direction.

The little *boop* sound of a reply made her look down at the screen again.

I am not having you followed, it said.

Promise that's the truth?

Send.

Then a longer wait. She could see the image of a thought bubble, indicating that Robert was typing. And typing. And typing.

Boop.

Look. Faith. I'm not stupid. I know why you left. You think I'm too controlling. So I'm being as non-controlling as I can. I want you back. So I'm showing you I won't drag you back.

Faith just stood a moment, breathing. Feeling the ocean breeze on her face. She realized she couldn't say nothing. Or at least, she didn't feel right offering no reply at all. Especially to a statement so uncharacteristically reasonable.

She typed, Thank you.

Then she stepped into the market, her phone still in her hand.

The little *boop* sound made her look down again.

Now that we're talking again let's talk.

She slid the phone into her pocket.

She found the slight man in the produce section, picking out avocados. He looked up, his expression a cross between amused and braced. His sunglasses were off now, so she found herself looking right into his eyes. They were almost colorless—gray probably described them best— and light and clear. Faith's first impression was to think they might be intimidating or beautiful, depending on how you looked at them.

"Come to accuse me of something else?" he asked.

"No. To apologize for the first thing I accused you of. I'm sorry. I'm very embarrassed about it, but I know I owe you an apology. I'm going through a tough divorce. I thought my husband was having me followed. That's why I thought you were a private investigator. But I just found out you're not."

"Ah," he said, standing still with an avocado in each hand. "I'm way ahead of you, see. Because I knew all along I'm not. I'm actually in IT."

"You know," Faith said, feeling herself relax and uncoil, "I always hear that acronym. IT. And I'm never quite sure what it means. I mean,

I know generally. I know what it means you do. You work on computer systems."

"That I do," he said, placing the avocados in a plastic produce bag, then in his cart.

"But I don't know what the *I* and the *T* stand for."

"Information technology."

"See, now I could have sworn the *I* stood for internet."

"Common mistake," he said. "But my work has almost nothing to do with the internet. It involves intranets. Internal networks for businesses and big corporations. But you don't want to hear about all that. It's boring."

Faith felt herself blush slightly. She wasn't sure why. Something about his tone. A turn it had taken.

"I just wanted to say I was sorry."

"I'm sorry, too," he said. "I'm sorry your divorce isn't more amicable. I'm sorry you have to go around in this beautiful beach paradise worrying that anybody might mean you harm."

"Thanks," she said.

She turned away. From her pocket, she thought she heard the faint tone of another reply. She took a few steps.

Somehow the man with the gray eyes was not content to let her go. And she wasn't sure why. But he reached out again to extend the conversation.

"So . . . was I right? You're from the big city?"

Faith stopped walking. Stood staring at row after row of strangely green bananas, wondering if she should tell him . . . well, anything.

"I'm from Southern California," she said.

"As am I!" he crowed. As though they had won some sort of prize together. "Now, as one SoCal person to another, I just have to ask you. How does one go about choosing a melon? Like maybe a nice cantaloupe? They're such a mystery to me. All closed up and secret. How do you even know if they're ripe? By the time you get it home and cut into it, that's a little late to find out the truth. Don't you think?"

They moved together to the cantaloupes, Faith purposely avoiding his eyes. She found them intimidating now, those eyes. Either that or she found them beautiful, and found that truth intimidating.

"You just have to press gently on the stem end," she said. "Are you looking for one that's ready right now?"

"Oh yes. Right now. I'm very impatient when it comes to fresh fruit. I don't like a melon to keep me waiting."

She pressed the stem end of three or four, then picked up one she liked and handed it in his direction.

"Maybe this one."

He took it from her, his hand brushing hers.

She couldn't get a sense of whether he'd done it on purpose or not. It made her face flame humiliatingly red. She knew by the tingly feel of the blood in her cheeks.

"Thank you," he said. "Why do all women seem to know that? And why do men almost never know?"

"I don't know," she said, anxious to get away now. "But I have to go."

She hurried down the produce aisle to the market's front door.

"Maybe I'll bump into you again," he called after her, "this being a very small town and all."

She hurried out of the market without answering, and definitely without glancing back.

When Faith arrived home, she saw Sarah sitting on the beach near her house. Just sitting. Staring at the waves.

At the sound of Faith's car door slamming, the girl turned and saw that Faith was back. She pushed up out of the sand, brushing off her shorts. Then she waved and walked closer.

"I thought you were going to the market," the girl said.

"I did. I did go to the market."

"So . . . where are all your groceries?"

"Oh," Faith said. And felt embarrassed for what seemed like the hundredth time that day.

For a long moment she said nothing, which embarrassed her further.

"It's kind of a long story."

She stepped into the house, realizing as she did that she had very little food in the fridge.

Then she remembered the message in her pocket.

She slid the phone out into her hand. Unlocked it with her thumb.

Okay, it said. In your own time.

She powered off the phone without replying. Just before she shut it down, she blocked his number again.

Chapter Five

The Terror of Paper Notes

Faith stepped out through the beachside sliding glass door with her mug of coffee and stood on the patio, breathing. The early-morning air was crisp. Cool and salty, with a good breeze already up.

She watched the waves roll in for a minute or two, sipping at the hot coffee. Blowing into it to send steam up to her face. It filled her with a sense of lightness, as though she could truly breathe in and out for the first time in as long as she could remember. Fill her lungs to an unfamiliar degree. As though everything would really be okay. Or maybe it already was.

She turned back to the house, and the feeling dropped away.

There was a note taped to the glass of the door.

It hit her like a bucket of ice water. Froze her everywhere at once. Her head spun, and she instinctively reached for the back of a patio chair to steady herself.

Robert found me here. That was her immediate thought.

But it wasn't like him to quietly leave a note and slip away. She had been upstairs sleeping.

Her car, parked in the driveway, was evidence of that. Why would he not have pounded on the door? Wakened her up and insisted on talking? Or even insisted on leaving together?

As if in a dream—a heavy, unpleasant one— she crossed the patio and pulled down the note. It had been folded in half before taping. She tore the paper in the process of opening it. The handwriting was entirely unfamiliar—a neat, careful block printing she had never seen before.

A big chunk of fear exited her body on a long, audible outrush of breath.

"Hey," the note began. "Didn't want to freak you out. Turns out my beach rental is right next door to yours. Coincidence. But I know you're not a big believer in coincidence, so I thought I'd better warn you. No stalking intended."

And he had signed it "The guy you yelled at in the market."

Then, "PS: The melon is terrific."

Faith let her hand, holding the note, fall to her side. She looked up at the house next door. She knew it had to be the one to the south of her. She had seen the neighbors on the north side as recently as the evening before.

Nothing moved inside that house, at least, not as far as Faith could tell. All the curtains were drawn. It seemed no one was awake.

Faith moved back inside with her coffee. She wanted to shake the last of the upset, but it didn't shake. It was there, and she could do nothing with it.

She moved to the coffeemaker almost without thinking. Poured a warm-up she didn't need.

Then her eyes landed on the note on her kitchen floor. It was sealed into a small light-blue envelope, and had apparently been slid under the door. Her blood froze again, and this time Faith felt intensely aware of how much she hated the feeling. How weary she was from the fear. The realization did nothing to relieve the sensation.

No way Robert leaves a note in a neat little blue envelope, she thought as she crossed the linoleum floor and bent down to pick it up. But if it was from the guy next door, that was also not a good sign. *Surely he could see that one warning was enough. If not more than enough.*

She ripped open the envelope, her hands shaking.

"Faith," it said in a barely legible scrawl. "I know I ruined that class for you. I'm sorry. I ruin everything. If you want me to leave you alone, I will. —Sarah."

Faith opened the kitchen door on the off chance the girl was still there.

Nothing. No one.

She stepped out into the cool morning again with her coffee. Walked around the house to the beach and looked north. There she saw the girl sitting on the sand in front of her grandmother's bungalow. Waiting.

Faith knew exactly what she was waiting for.

She walked along the beach to where the girl sat, veering closer to the waterline because the wet sand made for easier walking.

The girl looked up when she saw Faith approach her. Then she cut her eyes away, dropping her head so that her long hair fell over her face.

"I don't need you to leave me alone," Faith said, settling carefully in the cool sand with her coffee.

"You should." A barely audible reply from behind the hair.

"Why?"

"Because I ruined that class for you. You didn't get to take self-defense, and it's all my fault. I was just being selfish saying I wanted to go with you. And I messed it all up."

"You didn't mess anything up. It wasn't a fault sort of thing. It was just a problem that popped up that nobody saw coming. It's not a big deal."

A silence. Faith glanced over to see the girl stealing a peek at her from behind her hair.

"You sure?"

"Positive. I'm not even sure it was a good idea to take self-defense. I don't even think I need it. I'm wondering now if I was being stupid to even think I would. Need it, I mean. My husband might not ever try to hurt me. I was being paranoid."

"I don't think you're being paranoid," the girl said. "I think you need it."

For a minute or more, Faith listened to the sound of the breaking waves and a seagull screaming in an almost human-sounding voice as it wheeled through the air above the water's edge. There was nothing else to hear.

"Seems like an odd thing to say," Faith added after a time. "You don't know him."

"I know *you*. A little bit, anyway. And I know you're scared. And if you're scared, you're not scared for no reason."

"I wouldn't go that far. People are scared for no reason all the time."

"No they're not," Sarah said.

Faith had never heard the girl sound so sure about anything. In fact, she struggled to remember when she had ever heard *anyone* sound so sure about anything. She opened her mouth to argue, but Sarah plowed on.

"Sometimes people are scared of a thing that won't hurt them. But they're not scared for no reason. They're just not scared for the reason they think they are. Like when I was a kid. I liked to watch scary movies, so then I could be scared and tell myself it was about the werewolf or the vampire. But I was already scared. I was just looking for something to feel it about."

"That's a pretty mature observation," Faith said, and took a long gulp of her coffee. *And*

104

strangely accurate in ways I don't want to admit, she thought but did not add.

"I don't see why. It's right there for anyone to see. Tell me right now. Don't think about it. Just answer. Are you right to be afraid of him?"

"Maybe," Faith said.

"So, yes."

"No. Maybe is not yes. It's maybe."

"But if something will maybe hurt you, then you're right to be afraid of it. Like if you're scared to drive your car on the freeway. My mom used to be scared of that. She would drive on streets, and it took hours to get anywhere. But she knew *probably* nothing would happen on the freeway. But something might. So that's enough reason to be scared. Get it?"

"Yeah," Faith said. "I get it."

"So you should go to that class again, and this time I'll stay out of it."

"No. I'll go to that class again and take you with me, but this time we'll bring your grandmother."

"Really?"

"Really."

Faith reached out to place a comforting hand on the girl's shoulder. But it was a mistake. Sarah flinched away.

"Why are you being nice to me?" the girl asked, her words cloaked in armor.

"Why shouldn't I be nice to you?"

"Why should you?"

"Because . . . it's better when people are nice to each other?"

"Is it because your mom died, too?"

"Maybe. Partly. But it's just natural to want to help somebody if they need help."

"Not for me," Sarah said, her voice small.

"Okay," Faith said, feeling suddenly done with the conversation. "When I find out when the next class is, I'll let you know."

She used her left hand, the one not holding the coffee mug, to push herself up and out of the sand.

Faith had moved three steps toward her own house when the girl called after her.

"Thank you."

Faith stopped. Turned back. The girl looked away.

"It's not a problem," Faith said.

Then she turned back toward home to hide what she was feeling. In case it showed on her face. In many ways it *was* a problem. Not taking her to the next class exactly, but . . . she had befriended a girl with no shortage of problems. And now that she had taken on the girl, it seemed she had taken on the problems as well. They now felt uncomfortably like her own.

Added to the problems she had brought to the beach with her, it all felt like too much for Faith to hold and carry. Then again, it felt better than setting it down and turning her attention back to her own life, since she more or less did not have one at the moment. She had left the old one behind, and building a new one from scratch felt too overwhelming to contemplate.

It was after dinner, with the sun on a long slant—maybe forty-five minutes from touching the ocean's horizon—when Faith decided to go for a swim. It was her first swim since arriving at the beach.

Normally she was not a fan of ocean swimming. When she had been a child, strong waves had grabbed her and held her under one time too many while she gasped for breath, fearing her life was suddenly over. Still, she changed into her one-piece suit and grabbed a towel all the same. Because something needed washing away. That young girl's shame, maybe, and her sureness that Faith would want nothing to do with her. Or the cool gray eyes of that man, and knowing he was right next door, waiting to turn them on her again. Or maybe the jolts of fear that lay just beneath the surface of her midsection, needing nothing more than the sight of a folded piece of paper taped to her glass patio door as an invitation to jump up into her throat and choke her.

All of the above, she thought on her way out the door. She wrapped herself in the big towel to make herself feel more secure.

The man was home, and out sitting on his patio.

She could barely see him, because he wore that hat and dark glasses. In fact, until she was nearly at the water's edge she saw nothing but his legs, bare in Bermuda shorts. He was hiding behind a huge, colorful patio umbrella, tilted to protect him from something on the north end. Faith's house? It seemed strange until she realized that the beach faced southwest, and the umbrella was turned more or less toward the sun.

When she was able to see the whole of him, she gave a slight, awkward wave. He waved back.

Then she just stood, the cold water rushing in around her ankles, not wanting to drop the towel. It seemed like a strange thing to do with that man watching her. Then again, she had clearly come down here to swim. So wouldn't it be far stranger not to?

Faith pulled a deep breath and yanked off the towel, tossing it as far inland as she could, in the hope that it would land in a spot where the waves could not take it up and wash it away. Then she ran into the surf. A wave hit her smack in the belly, but she jumped up just in time, and was able to float over it and not be pushed back much. Shocked by the cold, she began to swim hard, diving under the next wave. Then she was out beyond the breakers, and unsure of her next move.

For a moment she held more or less still, treading water and berating herself. Surely other people lived their lives in a place of more sureness. Life could not be this complex for everybody, with every possible human interaction seeming to lurk like a trip wire or a deep hole into which Faith was certain to fall. She watched the man on his patio, but found it impossible to tell whether he was watching back.

A moment later she waded ashore again. She grabbed her big towel and wrapped up in it. Then she walked to her new neighbor's patio, shaking water out of her hair.

"I can tell you got my note," he said when she was a few yards away.

"How can you tell that?"

"Because you're not accusing me of anything."

Faith stopped short and stood in the sand a moment, feeling her face warm and probably redden. She didn't want to move closer, because she didn't want him to see the evidence of her embarrassment.

"I'm never going to live that down," she said. "Am I?"

"I'm sorry." His half smile dropped away. "I was trying to be funny, but in this case I guess I missed. I promise I won't bring it up again."

Faith moved no closer for a time. She made no move at all save for rubbing her hair with a corner of the towel, hoping it didn't leave her too exposed.

"Show me you forgive me," he added. "Come sit a minute."

Somewhat reluctantly, she did. She pulled a webbed lawn chair a few inches farther away from him and sat, crossing her legs at the knees. She tried to cover more of her legs with the towel, but mostly failed.

She looked at his face to see if he was staring at her legs, but his glasses were so dark she was unable to tell. His own legs were hairy and strong looking. Wide, muscled calves. His feet were bare.

"Short swim," he said.

"I don't really like swimming in the ocean."

"It's not mandatory, you know."

So it's always this way with him, she thought. Always some pointed or otherwise sharp remark. Some observation to upend her balance, keep her continually slightly on the defensive. And yet it wasn't an unpleasant sensation. For better or for worse, she was used to such exchanges. They felt familiar. Almost comforting. But she chose not to let him take her around in an off-balance circle, so she did not reply.

Instead she asked, "Why come to the beach at all if you don't want the sun to find you in any way?"

"Oh, this," he said, touching his sunglasses and then the brim of his hat. "I'm sensitive to the sun."

"This might not be your ultimate vacation destination, then."

"Where do you suggest I go? Do you know a place with no sun?"

"Maybe north of the Arctic Circle in the winter."

He laughed. It came out as something like a wheeze.

"I come to the ocean because I love the ocean," he said. "Always have. Even as a kid. When I was a kid, and I mean like a *kid* kid, not a teenager . . . I wanted to run away from home. I grew up in Orange County. In Bellflower. And I had some money in my piggy bank. I smashed piggy with a hammer and got on a bus and rode all the way to Long Beach. I'm not even sure how I knew the right buses to get there. I think I just stuck my head into every bus that came along and asked the driver which way they were going. I knew if I just kept riding west I'd get to some beach, and I really didn't care which one. And then when I got there, I just sat on the sand all day. I had no plan. I hadn't packed anything. I didn't have enough money left over for a phone call. When the sun went down it got cold. I walked until I saw a policeman, and he called my parents. My father came to pick me up, and wow, was he ever mad." He stopped talking briefly. Tipped his head, as if listening to something. Some audible mystery, but one that only he could hear. "I wonder where that came from. I haven't thought of that in years."

"Why did you run away from home?" she asked, and then immediately wished she hadn't. "If it's not too personal a question," she added to modify the request for information, because it was too late to grab it back.

"Something my father did, but I don't recall what exactly. It was always something with him."

"I'm sorry I asked," she said, and thought seriously of a hasty exit.

"If you don't mind my saying so, I think you spend too much of your life being sorry."

It struck her as a strange observation, based on how little they knew of each other. But then she decided it had been an easy one, an observation that anyone could make at almost any moment after meeting her. The shame of that realization stole her wind and welded her to the webbed chair.

For what could have been several minutes, they watched the sun inch down toward the horizon. It was so close to setting that it didn't hurt to look right at it for a moment. Or, at least, it didn't hurt Faith. This man—whose name she still did not know—was more sensitive.

As if using a listening device trained to her thoughts, he said, "Greg," and held out his right hand for her to shake.

She shook it. It felt warm, and utterly uncalloused. Like a man who had never done a day's hard labor in his life. Then she remembered he worked in IT. It also felt uncomfortably intimate. A genuine touch between two people, something Faith was in no way prepared to feel.

"Faith," she said, quickly letting go of the hand.

Then they watched the sun setting for another minute or two.

"In my own defense," she said, "the hat and sunglasses do add to the impression that you're a stalker sort of a person."

"And that's another thing," he said. "Why defend yourself? You seem to feel the need to defend yourself. You were using the level of caution you thought was appropriate at that moment. Why apologize?"

"Because I was wrong? Because it was a mistake?"

"People make mistakes all the time. That's more or less the definition of a person: we're a bunch of walking, talking mistake holders. When I make a mistake, if I was doing my best, I let myself off the hook."

"I'm not sure how that goes."

"I can tell," he said.

And with that, Faith fell silent for another extended time, poking at the sensation of being consistently knocked off balance by the sheer directness of him.

She watched in silence as the top edge of the sun touched the water—and for the first time in her life saw the green flash. It was more muted than she might have imagined, and over very quickly. It left her feeling that it almost could have been her imagination.

"Did you see that?" she asked Greg.

"Did I see what?"

"The green flash."

"Oh. No. I've heard of it. But I didn't see it just now."

"My mother used to tell me that when someone saw it, they usually felt like it changed their lives somehow. But I don't know if that's just a legend."

"Do you feel different?"

"Not really," she said, poking around for anything she might be feeling. "I wonder if I imagined it," she added out loud, wishing she had only said it in her head. "Since you didn't see it."

"It was probably my sunglasses," he said.

"You can take them off now."

"Excuse me?"

"The sun is down. Even *you* don't need a hat, a beach umbrella, and sunglasses when the sun is down."

"Better yet," he said, removing nothing, "we could move this conversation into the living room. I have a nice bottle of wine in there, breathing."

Faith leapt to her feet, almost before she realized she was about to do so. She stood in front of him, covering as much of herself as she could with the towel, wanting to speak but feeling the next words out of her mouth would be sputtery and embarrassing.

She risked it.

"I don't think that's a good idea," she said, sounding sputtery and embarrassed. Perhaps even more so than she had imagined. "I'm right in the middle of an ugly divorce. Well, I shouldn't say 'ugly' like I know it for a fact, because I really haven't even heard his reaction to my filing for divorce. I left before I could hear how he planned to handle it. But I've known him for nine years, so it's a pretty good guess that it'll be ugly. It's only been a few days, and I just . . ."

Then she stalled, and realized she had no end for that sentence. She had no idea what she "just" was.

He pulled off his sunglasses. She wrapped the towel more tightly around herself, awkwardly aware of her bare legs. But he looked directly into her eyes, catching her with the clarity and intensity of his own.

"I think you read too much into the invitation," he said. "I was just being neighborly."

"Oh," she said. "I'm sorry." Then she squeezed her eyes shut with shame. "Damn," she added. "There I go again."

"Sometime while we're both here," he said, smoothly talking through her discomfort, "I hope you'll come over for a bite to eat. I've been fishing off the rocks up around San Simeon

Point, and having a lot of luck. Coming home with rockfish and once even a big cabezon. I fire up the grill in the afternoon, and they're delicious because they're so fresh. I promise you it's an invitation suitable for a woman only a few days into an ugly divorce. But only if and when you're ready. I won't bring it up again."

For a moment she just froze there, caught in those amazing eyes. It felt almost as though she couldn't go until he broke off the connection, freeing her. She squeezed her eyes shut to extricate herself. As she did, her mind filled with an image of a fish snared on his hook and line.

"Thank you," she said. "I might take you up on that."

She hurried back toward her own house and its safety. But a step or two later he stopped her with a small, unusually sharp collection of words.

"Tell me about the girl," he said.

She turned back to face him, feeling her eyes narrow.

"Ah," he said before she could speak. "That supermarket look again."

"How did you even . . . ?" But then she couldn't figure out a good finish to the question.

"I saw you sitting on the beach talking to a girl this morning. I just wondered who she was to you."

"Just a neighbor."

"Is she staying in that house she was sitting right in front of?"

But something in the back of Faith's brain did not want to give the whereabouts of a young girl to a man she barely knew.

So she only said, "She's staying near here."

"Right," Greg said. "I get it. I just moved back into possible stalker territory by asking. And I didn't mean to. I just saw you having what looked like a heart-to-heart with someone, and it was someone much younger, and it just made me curious as to what brought the two of you together."

"She's going through a rough time," Faith said, relaxing some. "Having some problems I can relate to. I'm just trying to be a decent person and help her in any way I can."

"Well," he said, sliding his sunglasses back on, for reasons Faith could not imagine. Force of habit, maybe. "That's definitely a point toward your being a good person, which I already pretty much figured you were. Sorry if I made you uncomfortable by asking."

She smiled slightly to show she no longer minded. Then she turned for home.

Halfway there it struck her. Why was he wearing shorts and bare feet if he couldn't tolerate any sun exposure?

For a minute or so, well into her own kitchen, it felt like an inconsistency. Her brain worried at it like a dog obsessed with a bone or toy. At first it felt almost as though she had caught him in some sort of lie. Then she decided it was only his eyes that were so sensitive, and the hat brim and umbrella were all part of his eye protection.

She put the question away again, but it left her wondering when she had become a person who found it so hard to trust.

About an hour after going to bed, in a complete and utter absence of the ability to sleep, Faith reached for her phone and texted her friend Ava.

So, this is weird, she typed.

Then she hit send.

She lay awake and waited. Mostly because she wanted to be sure her friend was even still up before triggering another notification tone on Ava's phone. But also she wasn't sure she wanted to go on and tell the story. She was torn as to whether she was ready to rat herself out to anybody. Even herself.

She listened to the surf through the open bedroom window for five minutes or more, until she almost felt she could sleep.

The tone of an incoming text startled her wide awake again.

She picked up her phone and read Ava's reply.

How long do I have to wait to find out what's weird?

Maybe it isn't weird, Faith typed back.

Okay. How long do I have to wait to find out what isn't weird?

Faith sighed deeply. Part of her wanted to ditch the whole idea and just try to sleep. But she was in it too deeply now.

Would you think it was weird if I told you I met a man?

Depends on the definition of met. You mean met in the biblical sense?

Faith laughed out loud, which felt good. Then she typed again.

There is no met in the biblical sense. That's "knew."

You got my drift.

Nothing happened. I just met him.

Something must have happened on some level or you wouldn't be keeping me awake with it.

Faith sighed again. And, for a moment, typed nothing. Was something happening? She was of two minds regarding the answer.

I just met him. That's all. End of story.
It's just that . . . Just the fact that I met a
guy who made me think I remember what
it feels like to meet a guy . . . Oh hell.
This isn't coming out right at all. I'm just
wondering, isn't it too soon?

A pause. No sound from the phone. Nothing appeared on the screen but the thought bubble of Ava typing.

Then the reply popped onto her screen.

I was starting to type this long reply, but
then I remembered that you totally know
the answer to that.

So I shouldn't see him again?

I have no idea what you should do, kiddo.

For several long moments there was nothing in Faith's world but the sound of breaking waves. Neither one of them seemed to be typing. Faith wasn't even sure whose turn it was supposed to be. After a time she stopped looking at the phone to see if Ava was typing.

The sound of a new message startled her.

Look. Faith. You're asking the wrong
person. I don't tend to stay in any

relationships ever, and you tend to stay in ones you shouldn't. This is the blind leading the blind.

Faith closed her eyes. When she opened them, she could see the thought bubble of Ava typing again. She stared at the screen for a long time, but apparently her friend just kept typing.

The longer Ava typed, the more it made Faith uneasy. In time she got up, wandered to the window, and drew the curtain back. The moon was up, slightly illuminating the water, causing it to sparkle in places. She looked at the house next door and wondered if Greg was asleep. If he was unnerved by their meeting as well.

Probably not, she decided. He wasn't the unnerved type. That was Faith's wheelhouse.

She heard a new message come in. For a moment she did not cross the room to read it.

Then, after a time, she did.

You told Robert it's over. So you can do what you want. It's not cheating. But of course it's too soon. We both know it's too soon. Stop ten random people in the street, they'll all tell you it's too soon. But you met him. So what'll happen now is you'll try to go slow. Because it's too soon. But your heart will go fast. And then you'll tell me you won't let it. But hearts don't do what you let them do. They do whatever the hell they want. So just be careful. Okay?

Okay, she typed back. I get it. I'm going to sleep.

Not surprisingly, she never did.

Chapter Six

Anger and Padding

They sat cross-legged in a small circle on the mats of the community room floor, Sarah oddly close to Faith's hip. Faith assumed the girl was afraid, though she knew it was unlikely Sarah would ever admit to such a thing.

The male instructor had set down his padded handheld shield and joined them in the circle to talk. Faith found this unnerving, since his job was to play the role of the violent attacker.

The young woman instructor, the one who had refused to teach Sarah without a signed release from her guardian, made a point of catching Constance's eye where the older woman sat on a metal chair in the corner of the room.

"You can join us in the circle," she said.

"But I'm not part of the class," Constance replied.

It struck Faith that she was not the only adult here who felt uneasy. Even playacted violence for the purpose of teaching women to counter violence had a frightening edge to it.

"But you're here to support Sarah," the instructor said. "So you won't be part of the actual lesson, but you can be part of the circle."

Constance seemed reluctant. Maybe even afraid. But she crossed the room and sat on the other side of Sarah, taking and squeezing the girl's hand. The other women in the class—four of them—shifted over to give her more room.

"So, this is a smaller class," the instructor began. "Which in some ways is good. You get a little more personal attention, each of you. We start by introducing ourselves and talking about why we chose to learn self-defense. And I just want to say before you begin . . . if you're seeing a therapist, we like to talk to the therapist. Have him or her 'sign off,' as it were, on the idea of your doing this. And if you're in a relationship that's physically abusive, that can be a problem. If you're in a violent situation, you need to move out of it first. We'd like you to leave the dangerous situation before we teach this. We're not trying to arm you to do more damage in a fight you knew was coming. Our goal is that you never actually have to use what we're about to teach you. Does that make sense to everyone?"

The women looked around the circle at each other, briefly locking gazes and then cutting their glances away. They all nodded, some a bit hesitantly.

"Would you like to start, Anne?"

A mousy, frightened-looking woman of about thirty jumped at the mention of her name. She had huge hair, curly and dark, maybe three times the size of her head. Her baggy clothes covered so much of her, and so loosely, that it was hard to tell if she was overweight, but Faith suspected she was. Not that it mattered. Except to the extent that they were all on guard, but not always in ways that showed on the outside. It was hard not to scan for the signs.

"Okay," Anne said, her voice suiting her by sounding like that of a small mouse, "I guess you know my name is Anne. When I was a kid I was abused, and I'm sorry but I'd rather not say how. But I'm grown up now, but I don't feel grown up; I feel like I'm afraid of everyone, and I'm just so tired of it. I'm just tired of feeling scared all the time."

In Faith's peripheral vision, she saw Sarah nodding slightly.

"And are you seeing some kind of therapist?" the instructor asked.

"I am. But she thinks this is a good idea. She's actually the one who suggested it."

"All right," the instructor said. "That should be fine. Just please leave us her name and phone number before you go. We'd love to talk to her."

Anne nodded, her eyes trained down to the mats. The instructor raised her eyes to Constance, who seemed alarmed. Faith saw Constance's eyes go wide.

"Who, me?" Constance asked.

"You're part of the circle."

"I'm just here to support my granddaughter. Sarah," she added, draping an arm around the girl's shoulders.

"And your name is . . . ?"

"Constance."

"Okay. Thank you, Constance. Welcome."

The instructor's eyes fell on Sarah, who shook her head vehemently.

"I don't want to go," the girl said. "Somebody else go."

"I'll go," Faith said, wanting to rescue the girl. "I just left my marriage a handful of days ago. It wasn't an abusive relationship in a physical sense. Well . . . borderline. Emotionally, I think it probably was. He was definitely verbally abusive. Very controlling. He never hit me or injured me in any other way, but when I said that to my best friend—and she knows him pretty well—she just said, 'You never left him before.' And I think there's some truth to that. Part of me thinks I'm being silly, that if he never hit me before, he won't now. I don't even think he knows where I am, but of course I'm always worried he'll figure it out. Anyway, my brain keeps saying it won't be a problem. But this place in my gut is still really scared. So a friend of mine, a new friend, got me thinking about the fact that maybe I should trust my fear. Even if there's no guarantee he would hurt me, maybe just the slight chance he might is enough to act on. So maybe my fear is justified, and I should just stop arguing with it. I hope that makes sense."

"It does," the instructor said. "Thank you, Faith. And welcome."

A little bit of Faith's instinctive dislike of the woman fell away.

The instructor turned her eyes to the older woman seated on Faith's left. But just then Sarah spoke up.

"I'll go," the girl said, "because I just want to get it over with. But I don't want to say that much. I just want to say that stuff happens, and it just happens so fast, and I have no idea what we're supposed to even do about it. And it's like that lady." Sarah tossed her chin in the direction of Anne. "I forget her name. But you just get sick of walking around scared all the time. You get tired, you know? But that's all I want to say. Is it enough?"

The instructor nodded, a soft look on her face. Another chunk of Faith's dislike of the young woman broke away. It made Faith wonder what any of it had been doing inside her in the first place.

"That's just fine, Sarah," she said. "Thank you. We're glad you're here."

Faith stood with her back against the wall, ready to watch Sarah take her turn. And, at the same time, very much not ready. Her belly still burned and buzzed, trembly from the leftover fear of her own moment with the male instructor. The way he grabbed her hair from behind. Of course he had been careful not to pull. Not to hurt her. This was playacting, after all. Still, her hands shook at the memory of it.

She watched the girl walk across the mats, and, as the instructor came up behind her, Faith felt her own back come off the wall. The instructor reached out, lightning quick, taking hold of Sarah's hair, and every muscle in Faith's body flinched. It was a jerky attempt at moving forward, into action. But she stopped herself. Because this wasn't real danger, and Faith's brain knew that. But her body, her gut, her cells wanted to save that little girl. Wanted to defend her.

Faith watched as Sarah kicked backward, stomping on the arch of the man's foot, as she had been taught. Then the girl swung around and struck toward the man's nose with the heel of her hand, her arm held stiff for power. Of course, the instructor raised his shield to protect his face. Then Sarah swung her knee up and forward, toward his groin area, and he lowered the shield.

"Excellent, Sarah," he said, loud enough for the whole class to hear it. "Very well done."

But the girl didn't do what she was supposed to do. She didn't go back and stand against the wall. She charged the instructor, slamming her shoulder into his shield and knocking him over backward onto the mats. She fell on him, fists swinging, and he wrapped his arms around his head for protection.

This time Faith did allow herself to fly into motion.

In her peripheral vision she saw the female instructor rush in to mediate. But Faith was closer. And faster.

As Faith crossed the mats, barely feeling her feet touching the ground, Sarah stood up straight and aimed a fierce-looking kick at the instructor's midsection. He had dropped his shield, and was still using his arms to cover his head, leaving his belly unprotected. Fortunately, Faith reached the girl in time.

She grabbed Sarah around the waist, pinning her arms to her sides, and spun her away from the downed man.

For a strangely long moment they just stood, frozen in that position. Both bent forward at the waist, Faith holding the girl tightly, her arms still pinned. Sarah didn't try to break away. Her body felt tight, but she didn't resist. Faith could feel the girl's heart pounding through her narrow back, and the panting of her breath.

The moment seemed to stretch out.

"I think you had a chunk of anger come up there," Faith whispered into the girl's ear. But it was unsurprising. The girl had plenty of reasons.

Sarah let out a sound that Faith initially took to

be a grunt. A couple of seconds later, hearing the sound on replay in her own ears, Faith realized the girl had said, "Duh."

She loosened her grip and they straightened up.

The female instructor was standing right in front of them. Faith still had her arms around the girl's waist, but in less of a restraining way now. More of a supporting way.

"Do I have to get out now?" Sarah asked the female instructor in a small, chastened voice.

"No," the woman said. "It's very common for anger to come up while we're doing this work. We're not here to judge you. We just want to show you how to use it more appropriately."

"Your hands are shaking," Sarah said.

They were driving home to the beach together, Sarah in the front passenger seat, Constance in the back.

Faith looked over to see the girl staring at the spot where Faith's hands gripped the steering wheel.

"Yeah," she said. "That thing with the hair . . ." Then she chose not to finish the thought.

"It was only playacting."

"It brought something up for me."

"Oh."

For a mile or two, no more words were spoken. Sarah didn't ask any questions, and Faith didn't volunteer any information. Then Faith decided suddenly that the mess of her emotions might feel better on the outside.

She glanced at Constance in the rearview mirror, but the older woman seemed to be in a world of her own.

"A bunch of years ago," Faith began, then paused. She pushed harder at it, needing it out. "I hadn't been married long. A few months. My husband was furious at me for something. Doesn't matter what. It was nothing. But he came at me really suddenly. I thought he was going to hit me. But instead he grabbed me by the back of my hair. Right where it met my neck in the back. He didn't pull it. He just held me by it. And this tiny thing he was mad about, he was telling me about it right into my ear. Not yelling. He sounded weirdly calm. It scared the hell out of me."

She glanced again in the mirror. This time she could see that Constance was listening.

"I thought it was going to be the tip of the iceberg. That I'd find out more and more that I'd married a violent man. I kept waiting for more. But he never did anything quite that scary again. Well . . . he did. Different things. But it didn't escalate. And I never told anybody, because I wasn't really sure what to say. I couldn't really say he'd been violent with me. Because it wasn't really. Violent. He didn't hurt me. But it came back up today and it scared me even more, and now I think about it, and it feels violent." She met Constance's eyes in the rearview mirror. "Do you think that's violent?" she asked.

"I think it's menacing," Constance said. "It's too close to the line of violence for my tastes."

Faith focused her attention beyond the windshield again and realized they were almost home. She had been driving in some kind of stupor resembling autopilot.

A few seconds before Faith pulled up in front of their bungalow, Sarah said, "You should come to dinner at our house."

Faith stopped in their driveway and turned her attention to the girl. "Don't you want to ask your grandmother about that?"

"I already did."

"She already did," Constance said, opening the back door of the car and stepping out. "You're welcome anytime."

"Any day you want," Sarah said.

"Okay. We'll pick a day."

They sat quietly a moment, watching the older woman unlock the door of the bungalow with her key. Faith was absentmindedly fingering the heavy card stock of the certificate she had been given for completing the class, which was sitting loosely on her lap.

"Tonight," Sarah said.

"Can't be tonight. I already have plans."

"*Plans?* With *who?*"

Faith opened her mouth to tell the girl she was being impolite. But she never got the chance to say so.

"I'm sorry," Sarah said. "That came out sounding rude. I just meant . . . I didn't think you knew anybody else here besides my grandma and me."

"I didn't. Until a few days ago. But then I met another of our neighbors."

No reply for a beat or two. Faith glanced over to see the girl looking at her with raised eyebrows and wide eyes.

"A *man* neighbor?"

Faith felt her face redden. "It's a man, yes. But it's not what you're thinking."

"How do you know what I'm thinking?"

"It's not a date."

"Are you sure?"

"Actually . . . not positive. No."

A long, stinging pause.

Then the girl said, quietly, nearly under her breath, "Good for *you*."

They paused there a moment, Faith thinking the girl would jump out of her car. Sarah didn't.

"I saw what you did," the girl said after an awkward pause.

"What did I do?"

"When that guy grabbed me by the hair. You almost came charging in."

"Oh. That. Yeah."

"You were going to defend me."

"I guess I was."

"Why?"

That sat in the air for a moment, feeling utterly unanswerable.

"I don't even know where to begin with a question like that," Faith said. "I seem to be of the opinion that it's natural for people to want to help each other. And I guess you're not."

"He grabbed *those other women* by the hair, too. And you didn't start to rush in and help them."

"I know you."

"Not even that well."

Faith sighed deeply. Reached further down into herself for a better answer.

"Sometimes I think we feel the most for the people who remind us of ourselves. It's not the absolute best part of human nature. But it seems to be who we are."

They sat in silence for one more moment. But this one felt still and comfortable. Not awkward at all. As though they had finally hit the vein of understanding they had been digging to find.

"Okay," Sarah said. "Have a nice *date*."

She stepped out of the car and moved toward her grandmother's rented home. A second or two later, before Faith could even put the car in gear, a knock on the passenger window made her jump. She powered the window down, her heart hammering.

"Sorry," Sarah said, leaning in. "I was just thinking . . . the people from that class . . . you should have told them that story."

"What story?"

"About the hair. Your husband. And the hair. I mean . . . that's the kind of stuff the circle would've been for. Don't you think?"

"Yeah," Faith said, feeling how much she'd wanted to keep the hair story to herself. "I think that might've been a circle story. Except I really didn't want to tell it there."

He was on the south side of his rented house, in a tiny strip of yard between his kitchen window and the neighbor's fence. That's where he had placed the barbecue grill.

Faith assessed the grill for a moment to see if there was anything stationary about it. A gas line, for example. But it was a charcoal grill, with wheels on one side. It just happened to be placed in this alley of sorts between houses.

An overhang of roof threw him into shade, but still he wore his ever-present hat and sunglasses.

Faith moved closer to watch him work. He had a fish basket for grilling. It held the fish on both sides in crosshatched wire, so it could be flipped over without flaking apart and falling into the coals. In a similar basket, marinated asparagus grilled. And right down in the coals themselves

Faith could see what she guessed were baking potatoes wrapped in foil.

He saw—or felt—Faith looking over his shoulder. He looked back and smiled. The smile put her at ease. It was a strange sensation, because she hadn't known how uneasy she had been feeling.

"I have a confession to make," he said.

And, just like that, there it was again. In her belly. Wedged under her ribs. That cold, tingly, explosive fear. It must have been with her all the time, she realized, or it couldn't show up so fast, and with so little provocation. No wonder she was tired.

She waited for him to tell her that he really had been hired to follow her. Waited for a seeming hour, one that she knew in her head was probably only three or four seconds long.

"Go ahead," she said when she couldn't stand it any longer. She thought she could hear her voice tremble. She hoped he couldn't.

"I came home empty-handed this morning."

She had no idea what he was trying to communicate. And yet she just stood there, not asking. Feeling foolish. Maybe she didn't ask because she was processing the fear. Letting it go. Whatever it meant for him to come home empty-handed, it did not seem to mean this man had been hired by her angry ex.

"From fishing," he said.

"Oh. From fishing."

"I told you I was doing great out there."

"Anybody can have an off day."

"Yeah. Well, I did. The only thing I caught was a gigantic red rock crab. He grabbed onto my bait and wouldn't let go. Usually they let go when you lift them out of the water. They get it then, that they made a mistake, and they drop back in to save themselves. But this guy was really tenacious. Or really stupid. I was actually able to grab him by his back legs. You have to hold them that way, or they'll pinch you so hard, you'll stay inland for the rest of your days. I almost brought him home. But they're so damn hard to clean. So much trouble for so little reward. I ended up tossing him back."

Faith breathed deeply, and moved a step closer to his shoulder.

"So what's this?" she asked, indicating the grilling fish with a flip of her chin. "Something from the supermarket?"

"Oh, no. It's not that bad. I promised you fresh. No, I went down to that little fish market on the Embarcadero in Morro Bay, where they sell you the fish right off the boat when it comes back in."

"Oh. Should be good, then."

"Ah. I don't know. Tastes better if you catch it yourself. Did save me cleaning it, though."

"That's something."

"It's yellowtail," he said. "So you would have caught me anyway."

"Excuse me? There's no part of those last two sentences I understood."

"It's yellowtail tuna."

"So?"

"It's a deepwater fish. No way I would have caught a tuna off the rocks."

"Oh. See? Now . . . I would not have known that."

"You never know what you can get away with and what you can't."

And that stopped the conversation somehow. Those words seemed to have a gravity that brought light chatter to a halt.

"This is good," she said, after nibbling her first tiny bite.

He raised his wineglass and held it out toward her, and she clinked the rim of her glass lightly against his.

"Not the rockfish I had in my head—the one I planned to best in epic battle. But I do like a good yellowtail."

They sat at a small round table in a tiny dining room. It did feel a little bit daring to be inside the house with him. Faith couldn't help focusing on that. And he'd fallen into a brisk small talk that made her feel he was breezing over the top of something. But for several minutes, until her balance was better established, she chose not to go digging.

"You actually cook," she said.

He laughed. A light-sounding thing, slightly forced. "Well, there's this." He indicated the food with a sweeping hand.

"No, I mean really cook. Not just grill things like guys tend to do."

"Not sure how you gathered that from what's right in front of you. Since it's all grilled."

"Little clues," she said. "The chopped chives for the baked potatoes. Real chives, not green onion tops. The way you put onion slices and sprigs of dill on the fish while it was cooking. The lemon wedges. The way you marinated the asparagus and topped it with shreds of lemon zest. I don't know. Maybe I'm making too much of little things. I could be wrong. But my husband never cooked. If you asked him to grill fish, he'd put it on the grill till it was done and then slap it on a plate. I'd probably have to get up and go back into the kitchen for the salt and pepper."

She was watching him as she spoke, her eyes resting on those clear gray ones—safe in observing them because his gaze was turned down to his plate. But when she stopped speaking he looked up, locking his gaze with hers.

"Then he was a boor, madam, and did *not* deserve you."

Faith turned her eyes away.

"What brought you here?" she asked, suddenly hitting the edge of her patience with small talk.

"I told you."

"No. I don't mean why the ocean. Yeah, you told me that. I meant why aren't you in Southern California doing IT things?"

He seemed suddenly fascinated by the cloth napkin in his lap. For several seconds, he didn't take his eyes off it.

"Just needed to get away," he said after a time.

A silence fell, and it was awkward. Deeply awkward. It made Faith feel she wanted to go home. But she had barely begun eating. So she shoveled food into her mouth in big bites, moving as fast as she could toward the end of the meal and some sort of exit.

It might have been a mistake to come here, she thought.

And then, the inevitable back and forth in her head.

You're making something of nothing. No, you're ignoring a thing that's right in front of your face to be seen. No, you're treating him like he's Robert, and he's not. But something doesn't feel right. No, that's just you. You always feel that way. You just can't seem to trust anybody anymore.

He spoke, startling her.

"The last couple or three weeks have just been the absolute worst ever. I mean the worst. I'll just never understand how everything horrible pours down at once like that. You're just going along thinking everything's okay. And then stuff happens that you never meant to have happen, and you can't even understand it. But I'm not ready to talk about it any further than that. It's too fresh. I just have to say I don't understand life at all sometimes."

A long pause.

Faith wanted to know what all had happened. Because she wanted to know if it had happened *to* him, or *as a result* of him. She didn't ask, because it was too personal. She didn't know him well enough. Also because it wouldn't help. People will look right into the face of something they caused and tell you all day long how it wasn't their fault. How they were only an innocent victim. No, you had to know all the circumstances and decide for yourself.

Meanwhile he was still staring at his napkin.

"Is that just me?" he asked when the silence grew too heavy.

"Which? The not understanding why life is the way it is?"

"Yes, that."

"That is definitely not just you," she said.

"I should probably be getting back," Faith said.

She knew it would land awkwardly, and it did.

The problem was that they had only just barely finished eating. It was a ridiculous time to leave. Like drawing a bold line under her fear and indecision, or pointing to it with a blackboard

141

pointer. The only thing she could have done to save face would have been to stay longer.

She was not willing to stay longer.

She braved a look at his face. He looked crestfallen. She quickly looked away again.

"I was going to serve ice cream with fresh melon," he said. "But okay."

"I'm sorry. I'm just really tired. I took a class in women's self-defense today, and it took a lot out of me."

"Are you telling me that so I'll know you can defend yourself?"

He rose from the table and began collecting the dishes.

"No. I'm telling you that so you'll know why I'm tired. And then hopefully you won't take it personally."

By the end of the last sentence he had wandered off into the kitchen with two handfuls of dishes. She waited for him to come back out. For a strange length of time, he didn't. She listened carefully for the sound of dishes being rinsed or stacked. Or loaded into a dishwasher. She heard no sound.

She stared out the front windows for a moment, watching the surf. The sun had just gone down behind a dense bank of fog at the horizon.

When she looked up again, he was leaning in the kitchen doorway, watching her intensely. With those eyes.

"But it *is* personal," he said. "Not your fault,

but it is. I made you uncomfortable, talking about how miserable my life has been lately. It was too much information too soon, and I'm sorry."

Faith rose from the table and moved toward the door as she spoke.

"It wasn't too much information at all. It was hardly any information. You didn't say a word about what happened that was so bad."

She stood at the front door, he at the doorway to the kitchen. He was looking out the front windows now. As if he'd never seen surf before.

She was fishing and she knew it. But she had put it out there. All she could do now was wait to see what he would do with her bait.

"Not entirely different from your situation," he said after a time. "I had a marriage. Now I don't."

Something in Faith's gut relaxed slightly.

"That can happen to anybody," she said. "Trust me. I know."

"You wanted to know if it was my fault, what happened."

"No," she said, even though she knew the real answer was yes. "Everybody makes mistakes in relationships."

"Maybe so," he said, still staring at the surf. "So I guess all that's left is just to tally up if they were little ones or huge ones."

"Thank you for dinner," she said. "Everything was delicious."

She turned the knob on the door. Swung it open.

Before she could step out, he spoke again to stop her. It seemed an odd time to strike up a new thread of conversation. But that's what he did.

"So, how's that friend of yours?"

She turned back to him, the door still open. She could feel the sea air rushing by her. Cool and damp. She could hear the sound of waves breaking.

"What friend?"

"That young girl you were telling me about."

That fear spot under her ribs woke up again. It tingled.

"I didn't exactly tell you about her. You asked. And now you're asking again." *Which seems a little strange,* she thought. But she didn't say that part out loud. "You've never even met her. Why would you ask how she is?"

"Because you told me she was having a hard time. Remember?"

"Oh. Right. I did, didn't I?"

"Is she okay?"

"I'd say she's doing as well as can be expected."

Faith turned into the open doorway again to exit the place.

"Can I see you again? Or did I make a total mess of it?"

"You didn't do anything," she said, stepping out onto the porch as she spoke. "I'm just tired. And . . . not as trusting as I used to be."

She pulled the door closed behind her and hurried home.

Chapter Seven

Those Eyes

When Faith woke in the morning, she lay still in bed for what seemed like a long time. Several minutes at least. Then she reached for her phone and turned it on.

No texts, no messages. Of course, it helped that Robert was blocked.

She opened the message app and typed a text for Ava.

I'm not so sure about this guy, it said.

She pressed send.

For about another two minutes she lay still, listening to birds in the trees and the ever-present breaking surf.

Then she heard the light *boop* of a reply.

Keep talking, it read.

There's either something off about him or it's me.

Not sure why you assume those two are mutually exclusive.

Ha ha, Ava. He's just getting out of a marriage. But I think he was hinting that he'd made a really colossal mistake. Probably cheated. Which I don't think people should even describe as a mistake. I mean, it's not like anyone does it accidentally.

You're making assumptions, Ava typed back.

Well, that's what people do when you won't tell them. But it's not just that. Sometimes I feel really drawn to him and then all of a sudden he scares me. And I don't know if he's scary and I shouldn't be drawn to him or if he's fine and the fear is all in me and I'm bringing it to this new situation and it doesn't belong here at all.

She waited. For several minutes, she waited. But Ava did not even appear to be typing a reply. You're not saying anything, Faith typed.

I wasn't sure if you were done.

I was.

Okay. Not sure what to say. If you can't sort it out, neither can I from a distance. Must be quite a tricky landscape.

Faith sat up in bed. Rubbed her face. Tried to breathe more deeply.

I know you have to get ready for work, she typed.

Pretty soon here.

He keeps asking about Sarah.

Sarah who?

That neighbor girl you met.

Oh. Does he know her?

No.

Then why would he ask about her?

That's my point.

You're worried he's a pedo?

It's crossed my mind.

Well, stay on the safe side and don't be part of bringing those two together.

Check, Faith typed. Now go to work.
A little smiley face emoticon popped up on the screen.
Then all was back to silence, and Faith felt distinctly aware of being alone.

• • •

Faith was rattling around her kitchen, strangely distracted by her own mind, when he knocked on the door. She knew it was him because she'd caught a glimpse of him crossing her porch. And, as always, her immediate reaction was frozen, sickening fear.

She opened the door, and he smiled in a way that disarmed her. He stood grasping a small brown paper bag, which he held out in her direction.

"I realize I was not invited," he said. "You might not like people who pop in uninvited. In which case I'll go. But in my favor . . ." He shook the bag lightly. "I have bagels. From a real bakery. Fresh. Slightly warm from the oven."

Faith froze in the doorway a moment, saying nothing. Not sure what she'd have wanted to say if words had felt possible.

"Also cream cheese and smoked salmon," he added. "But that's not the main thing. The main thing is, I need to apologize for last night."

Faith took a deep breath and found her voice. Dug down deep for it.

"I don't know that you owe me any apologies," she said. "But anyway, come on in."

They sat at Faith's kitchen table together, drinking coffee. Faith was nibbling on a bagel with cream cheese and smoked salmon. He seemed to have forgotten they were there. And for several minutes, he had not alluded to any apology.

Then, suddenly, he did.

"So I get why you might think it was a little strange, me asking about that girl. I can only imagine what you must be thinking about me. But I'll put my hand on a stack of a thousand Bibles and swear I do not have a thing for little girls. And not because I'm a big liar. Because it's true. Here's the thing. This is the truth, right here. I was a sad kid. So when I see a sad kid, my heart goes out to them. I spot them a mile away. And then I guess I relate to them too much, because I can't stop thinking about whether they're okay."

Faith worked to finish chewing before she could answer.

"That makes sense," she said. "And I'm really sorry I wasn't more trusting. I was married for nine years, and I'm only just now realizing how far I've drifted away from being the person I was when I got married. You just fall into a new life, a new way of doing things, and it feels normal. And you don't see how much you're changing. And now I'm stepping back and looking at myself and realizing I don't trust anybody anymore. It's kind of a rude awakening."

He sat back in his chair. And, to her surprise, he smiled. A natural, comfortable-looking smile.

"There," he said. "See? We're being honest with each other and getting along just fine."

"Yes. I suppose we are."

She took another bite of bagel and chewed slowly, looking out the window and realizing his assessment had made her feel slightly awkward again.

"So we should go to a movie," he said.

"I'd like that."

"So you'll ask her?"

Faith stopped chewing abruptly. When she spoke, her mouth was still full.

"Ask her?"

"Yeah."

"I thought you meant you and me."

"I meant all three of us. But . . ."

Faith's head filled with the words Ava had typed to her. Her friend's only real advice for the morning. *Stay on the safe side and don't be part of bringing those two together.*

"Uh-oh," he continued. "I'm looking at your face right now and realizing that I most definitely should *not* have meant that. Okay. So I don't mean that. You don't know me well enough yet, and I get that. You'll get to know me better. We'll go slow."

He rose from the table. Moved around to her side of it, close to her. Faith wasn't sure whether or not she should be alarmed. But she was, because that was her new default setting.

He pecked her lightly and briefly on the cheek.

Then he let himself out.

. . .

It was five minutes later when she heard the knock on the door, unless it was ten. And it wasn't so much a knock as a pounding. The way the police pound on a door, or the way a person who is deeply alarmed and needs help might do.

Faith caught the alarm like a virus, and her heart hammered as she crossed the living room and opened the door.

Constance stood on her porch, her face tight and dark. The fear flared up under Faith's ribs again, because she assumed that something had happened to Sarah.

"Well?" Constance asked. Her voice came out so hard that it fell on Faith's ears as utterly unfamiliar.

"Well what?"

"You're honestly trying to tell me you don't know why I'm here?"

"I totally don't," Faith said, her heart pounding harder. It was making her a little dizzy, that rush of blood.

"What was he doing here?"

"Bringing me bagels?"

"Is that a joke?"

"No! I'm . . . I'm missing something. I don't understand why you're upset."

Constance's eyes came up to Faith's face, and searched around for an uncomfortable moment.

"You don't understand why I'd be upset that Sarah's father was at your house?"

"That wasn't Sarah's father! That was Greg, from next door."

"You think Sarah doesn't know her own father when she sees him? She saw him just now, walking out of your house. She's very upset, and I don't blame her. She never wants to see you or talk to you again."

Faith reached out for the doorjamb to steady herself. The whole world seemed off-kilter, as if she were swimming through it, searching for the surface.

"Mistaken identity," Faith said. "I'm sure of it. He always wears a hat and sunglasses, because he's very sun sensitive. So she must have just glanced at him from a distance and gotten the wrong impression."

"Would you know your father if you saw him, even if he had on a hat and sunglasses?"

For a moment, Faith didn't answer. She felt stunned by Constance's unwillingness to accept that this was all a misunderstanding, and she had no idea where to go, verbally, to make things right again.

She heard Constance let out a big, deep sigh.

"Okay," the older woman said, "I at least get that you had no idea he was Sarah's father, and I'm awfully glad to know it. And Sarah will be glad. She felt like you'd betrayed her. But it's not a betrayal if you didn't know."

"That's not her father," Faith said. "I know it's not. This is a misunderstanding. Come over there with me, and I'll introduce you to him, and then you'll see that Sarah got a wrong idea."

Constance shook her head hard. She laughed a bitter bark of a laugh. "I'm not going anywhere near that man. You come over to my house, and I'll show you a picture of Sarah's father, and then you'll see what's what."

"Okay," Faith said. "Fair enough."

She stepped out onto the patio and pulled the door closed behind her. Together they walked down the steps to the beach. Then along the sand in silence.

"What's Sarah's father's name?" Faith asked when the silence grew overwhelming.

"Harlan Deaver."

"Well, see? Can't be him. This guy is named Greg."

"You know that? Or he told you that? Did you see his driver's license?"

"No, of course not. You don't ask a guy to show ID before you have dinner with him."

"Right," Constance said, her voice still cool. "It wouldn't be the first lie he ever told."

They fell into silence again, and as they walked, Faith's mind filled with the mystery of why he kept asking about her young friend. Just for a moment, almost against her will, she tried on the idea that Constance was right. But it was such a disturbing, impossible thought that she pushed it away again.

They stepped together up onto the front porch of the dark red bungalow. Then through the door.

"Sarah?" Constance called. "Sarah, Faith is here, honey. But it's okay. She didn't know. He lied to her like he lies to everybody. So it's not her fault. Come on out and show her a picture of your dad, because she still doesn't believe that was him."

Silence. Faith stood beside the older woman in the living room, waiting. Waiting while nothing happened. The world in that moment felt deeply unreal to her, like a gauzy dream. Faded at the edges and not distinct enough to be anyone's actual reality.

"Sarah!" Constance shouted, startling Faith and making her jump. "It's not her fault, honey. He fooled her. Now come show her a picture."

Another strange, dreamy pause.

Then Sarah's bedroom door opened, and the girl slipped out. Her face was streaked wet from crying, her eyes puffy and red. She held her gaze trained down to the floorboards as she moved in Faith's direction, holding out her phone.

Faith just stared at the offered phone for a few tense moments. It felt as though the girl were trying to hand her a tarantula or a snake. No part of Faith wanted to move into this next moment of her life.

Then, as if independent of the rest of Faith, her hand reached out to take the phone.

On its screen was a photo of Sarah at a birthday party. In front of her was a cake with its candles still burning brightly. On either side of the girl were, Faith could only assume, her parents. Under any other circumstances, Faith would have been fascinated by a photo of the girl's late mother. But she barely saw that part of the photo. She could not take her gaze away from the addictive, scary, compelling gray of those eyes.

Those painfully familiar eyes.

She felt around in her gut for the fear, but there was nothing there as far as she could tell. The inside of her was solid and inert, as if it had been filled in with damp, packed earth. Or concrete.

She moved backward to a chair and sat, still staring at those eyes.

"Oh my God," she said. And then, for lack of access to other thoughts, she repeated those three words. "Oh my God."

They sat in Faith's car on the spit of land known as Coleman Park, all three of them, Morro Rock looming behind them in the rearview mirror. In front of them lay the narrow mouth of the estuary that led out to the breakwater, dotted with detached kelp and nearly a dozen floating, lounging sea otters. Boats came and went in the one deep channel in the center of the water, but sufficiently far from the otters, who paid them no mind.

They had come here together because their only thought, the only thing all three of them had immediately agreed upon, was the need to get away from that beach and that man.

In a long silence, Faith watched the otters floating on their backs, their faces calm and puppylike in their cuteness. It seemed a nearly impossible juxtaposition with the lives of the three women in Faith's car. For a brief moment she longed to be an otter.

She pushed the odd sensation away, and spoke. "I still don't understand why he would even do that."

"Seems clear to me," Constance said from the back seat. "He's trying to get Sarah back."

"But he knew what house she was staying in. So what did he need me for?"

"He wanted a chance to grab her up when I wasn't around," Constance said. "He knows better than to mess with me. I'll fight him, and he knows it. So he was trying to separate her off from me."

For a strange moment, Faith reflected on coyotes. Her brain filled with an image of them. A few years earlier, she'd had a small older dog, since deceased. She'd been walking in the hills with him, the dog off leash, and two coyotes had tried to separate him off from her. One tracked

156

them from behind while the other hid behind a bush in front of them on the trail. If Faith had passed that bush without noticing the situation, they'd have flanked her poor little dog, and he would have been gone. She would have had no choice but to watch in horror as they carried her beloved little Harry away.

She shivered slightly at the thought and pushed it as far from her mind as possible. It didn't go as far as Faith had hoped.

"He knows I would run from him on the beach," Sarah said. "He was trying to get me someplace I couldn't run."

"But you have custody of her," Faith said. "Right? So even if he did take her, you could just call the police and get her right back."

An odd silence fell. Just a beat or two, but it meant something. Faith could tell.

"First of all," Constance said, "if he grabbed her up and ran, who's to say the police could even find them again? And also . . ."

Constance paused, and Sarah jumped in.

"She doesn't have custody of me," the girl said. Flat and simple, as though it depressed her to have to say it.

Faith met the older woman's eyes briefly in the rearview mirror. Constance quickly looked away.

"You don't have custody? You have her illegally? Did you just take her?"

Faith regretted her confrontational tone, but not

enough to repair it. There was too much going on. It was all too confusing.

"I didn't just take her," Constance said. "He asked me to take her. There was so much going on, and he couldn't really look after her properly. And she didn't want to be with him. She wanted to be with me. So I took her with his blessing. But then after a few days he started calling, and he wanted her back, but she didn't want to go back with him. So we came to the beach instead. I'm working on getting custody based on the fact that Sarah's choice is to be with me. But I need more time."

Silence fell again, and Faith watched one of the otters rubbing its face with both furry little paws. Such a jarring meeting of two worlds.

"Here's what I don't get," Faith said after a time. "If he still has custody, and he knew where she was, why didn't he just call the police and have her picked up and returned to him?"

"A very good question," Constance said. "And I'm wondering if I can even use it to help with the custody fight. It seems like cognizance of some kind of guilt."

Another charged silence.

Then Sarah said, "He's worried what I would say to the police."

Constance sat forward in the back seat and tried to put a hand on the girl's shoulder. Sarah pulled away sharply.

So it's not just me having trouble with her trust, Faith thought.

"See, you say things like that," Constance said, "and I want to know what they mean. What is he afraid you would say?"

"Nothing," the girl said, sounding like a typical whiny, irritated teenager. "Just tell them that, okay? It's just what you need to tell them."

For a few minutes they fell silent again. A fishing boat, two sailboats, and a sightseeing vessel full of tourists slid out to sea. A young man in a wet suit glided by, standing on a paddleboard.

"I guess we just need to talk about our next move," Faith said. "We can't go back to the beach. And that's a problem."

"Sarah and I will take off," Constance said. "You can go back."

"I don't want to go back there, either. Next time he sees me he'll know right away that I know. I don't have what you might call the world's best poker face. And then he'll see that you and Sarah are gone. I have no idea what he would do."

"True," Constance said. "You never know with him."

"Faith and I should take off," Sarah said.

For a moment those words just hung there in the air of Faith's car, a thing out of place.

"That's . . . ," Constance began. "Why would you even say that, Sarah?"

"Because you need to work on the custody

thing," Sarah said to her grandmother. "Which means you need to go back home to Thousand Oaks. And I don't dare go there, because he'll know right where to find me there. This way you can go home and go to the court and the police and whatever and tell them I don't want to be with him, but in the meantime I'll be where nobody can find me, because nobody will know I'm with Faith."

But that might not be true, Faith thought. *At this point he might know enough to guess it.*

She wondered if he had bothered to write down or memorize her car's license plate number. She made a snap decision to trade her car in at the first possible opportunity. For a different one, at least. She could not afford newer.

"Honey," Constance began, "I still think that's—"

"I think it's a good idea," Faith said.

"You do?" The girl and her grandmother both said it more or less in unison.

"Yeah. I do. I can't go back to the beach now. And I can't go home. I have to go somewhere entirely new, and I haven't even figured out where yet. Sarah should come with me. She'll be safer. We'll keep in good touch. And Constance, you should go home and work this out. Legally work it out. Now let's find a safe place to leave Sarah for a few minutes. Maybe the library. And then Constance and I will go back to the beach, and I'll pack a few of my things, and Constance will pack a few of Sarah's things, and then I'll pick Sarah up at the library, and we're gone."

A long, awkward silence fell.

Then Constance said, "I'm really in this deep now, aren't I?"

Sarah was only staring out the window, so Faith answered.

"Not sure what you mean."

"First I take her without having custody. Run off with her. Now I'm supposed to turn her over to someone I barely know? I mean, no offense. I know you're okay. I just know it. I'm just picturing having to explain this thing we're about to do. To the police. Or a judge. Or . . . I don't know. Anybody."

Another long silence. Faith thought the emotional strain it contained was almost audible.

"I can't make that decision for you," Faith said. As gently as possible. "Nobody can decide this except you."

"She's better off with you than with him," Constance said. Her voice had grown stronger. More settled. "I know it, no matter what anybody thinks. Just take her and go before he finds her. And before I have time to doubt myself again."

Chapter Eight

Day Sheets

As Faith drove herself and the girl out of the library parking lot, she felt something in her gut give way. It was such an unformed plan, which made it terrifying. She literally didn't know which way to turn the steering wheel of the car.

"I have no idea where to go," she told the girl, hearing the whiff of desperation in her own voice.

"Let's go to Paso Robles."

"Why Paso Robles?" Faith asked. But she had already turned in the direction of the highway north, because it was as good a plan as any.

"I don't know," Sarah said. "Why not?"

The girl was doing something on her phone as she spoke. Texting, most likely. Her focus seemed strangely intense.

"I'm just wondering how that town jumped into your head."

"It's less than an hour away. And he won't think to look for us there."

"That's true, but it's also true of all the other towns less than an hour away. In every direction."

"We're on the coast. There are no towns to the west of here."

"You're talking around an honest answer. I can hear it."

The girl opened her mouth to speak. Just then the phone in her hands rang.

"I gotta take this," she said. "Sorry."

For the next several minutes Faith drove toward Paso Robles—for reasons she didn't understand—and listened to the girl's end of a conversation. She couldn't have avoided hearing it if she'd tried. Though, truthfully, a great deal of it made no sense. Big sections seemed almost to be spoken in another language, despite being filled with English words.

"Dean, yeah. Hey. I thought you would just text me back."

Then a pause as the girl listened to whatever Dean had to say.

"Yeah. I'm okay. I was with my grandmother.

"Yeah. We knew. We called and tried to get her back, but she was already gone.

"I know. I hate him. I'd like to kill him for it."

A longer than average silence.

"Look, Dean . . . I mean, thanks. But . . . I can't even get into that now. I can't even think about it. I just can't even . . . Well, that's it, I guess. I just can't even.

"So do you have the day sheets?

"No, not for today. For tomorrow. This is Friday.

"No it's not. It's Friday."

Faith knew it was Saturday.

The girl covered the phone with her hand. "Is this Friday or Saturday?"

"Saturday," Faith said.

"Damn it! Okay, for today. Is she there?

"Okay, good. I figured she would be. I missed her rides, though, right?

"Oh, one thirty-two? What time is it now?"

Faith looked at the clock on her dashboard. It was 12:47.

"We could maybe just barely make it. Are you there? It is hot?

"Damn. That *is* hot. If I miss it, does she go again tomorrow?

"Okay, good.

"Who's she with? Who has her now?

"Oh. Yeah. Him.

"Well, no. I never met him. I've just heard of him. He's from Los Alamos, isn't he?

"*Prix St. Georges?* Why is he showing her in Prix St. Georges? He's had her, like, three or four weeks! There's no way. He's pushing her too fast.

"Okay, what?

"No, really. What's the other thing?"

Then a long, long silence. Faith glanced over and watched Sarah's face collapse. It was hard to imagine more bad news falling into the girl's life. But clearly more had just fallen.

"Okay, thanks, Dean.

"No. No, really. I would have found out anyway, when I got there.

"Okay. I'll stop by and say hi if I can find you.

"Okay, thanks. Bye."

The girl touched a button to end the call, then
dropped the phone onto the seat and stared out
the window for a long time, saying nothing.

"So," Faith said after a time, "if we can just
barely make it in time for some event, then I
sense there's a pretty specific reason for being
there."

"Yeah," Sarah said. But then she didn't go on
to state the reason.

"And I'd like to know it."

The girl pulled in a huge, audible breath. Then
she let it out as a noisy sigh.

"My horse is there," she said. "I figured she
would be. Because it's a big show this weekend.
It's at the Paso Robles Horse Park. So I asked my
friend Dean from my old barn to look at his day
sheets."

"And I don't know what a day sheet is."

"It's the list of everybody's ride times."

"Oh."

"I thought if you knew that's why I wanted to
go to Paso Robles, you wouldn't take me."

"Why would you think that?"

"Oh, I figured you'd go all grown-up on me
and tell me she's not mine anymore, and it'll only
make me more upset to see her, and I should just

let it go. But I just have to see her, Faith. I have to. I didn't even get to say goodbye. I only just now found out who bought her. I have to see how he rides her, and if they can work okay together. Otherwise I'll never stop worrying about her. I can't even sleep the way it is now. I'm up all night worrying about her. Just please take me to the horse park so I can see that she's okay."

"Fine," Faith said.

"Really? You'll take me?"

"In case you hadn't noticed, kiddo, we're a full plan short of a plan here. We need to be somewhere, and I have no idea where that should be. So if there's something that'll make you happy at the Paso Robles Horse Park, then I'm glad to have some direction for now."

"Wow. I had no idea you'd be so nice about it."

"I can be nice."

"I know that. I didn't mean it like that."

They rode in silence for a mile or two, the girl glancing at something on the dashboard now and then, but Faith wasn't sure what.

"Um. Not to be a complainer," Sarah said at last, "but if you really want to be nice to me, she has a ride starting at one thirty-two. So could you maybe drive just a little bit faster?"

Faith sighed. Then she checked the rearview mirror for any possible sheriff or highway patrol cars. Seeing none, she pushed the throttle a bit harder.

"What was the bad news?" Faith asked a minute or so later.

"Oh. He's just rushing her into too high a level. She's not Prix St. Georges. You're supposed to show one level lower than you school, and he's doing practically the opposite."

"I didn't understand a word of what you just said. But I meant the part after that. At the end of the call."

The girl's face fell again. For a strange length of time, she didn't answer. Then, when the silence grew too onerous, she spoke up.

"She's also in the Sales Horse Presentation Class tonight. Right after the last class. Probably six o'clock or so."

"I don't know what that is, so maybe tell me why it's bad news?"

"It means he's selling her."

"Oh."

"It's a thing where they show the horses that are for sale. You know. Show them off to buyers. So even if she's okay with him, she's about to go to somebody else."

Faith wanted to offer a reply, but could find none. So they drove in silence for quite some time.

They only spoke one more time on the drive, and the girl initiated it. Much to Faith's surprise.

"I'm sorry I didn't trust you," Sarah said.

"When didn't you trust me?"

"When I sent my grandmother over to tell you I never wanted to see you or talk to you again. I never thought about how maybe you didn't know who he was. But now I wonder why I didn't think of that. I just right away thought you were a big betrayer. And I feel bad about that now."

"It's hard to know who you can and can't trust," Faith said. "If anybody gets that, it's me."

They pulled through the big, wide-open gates of the horse park. The property was sprawling and huge. Dusty-looking brown hills and waves of heat. Faith could see an area with parked horse trailers, and a few parked cars. She could see tops of what looked like barn rows. But she wasn't sure which way to go.

"Do you know this place?" she asked the girl. "Have you been here before?"

"You turn here and go down the hill. No, not here. Here. Like, there."

Faith turned the car down the hill, and then the show lay spread out below her, and she was able to get her bearings.

She saw three formal-looking white-railed arenas with horses currently performing. Their riders shone in the hot sun with their tall formal black boots and gleaming white breeches. The horses sported braided manes and perfectly combed blunt-cut tails. Just outside the low rails of the arenas sat a series of carefully placed freestanding white markers with large black letters, but Faith had no idea what they signified. In other arena-like fenced areas, horses and riders seemed to be warming up, seven or eight at a time, narrowly avoiding each other on canter circles.

There was a short line of porta-potties with a handwashing station out front, and several rows of vendors selling boots, saddles, riding apparel, horse blankets, cold drinks. A strong wind buffeted the white tents and canopies that kept vendors and onlookers in the shade.

"Stop here!" Sarah shrieked.

Before Faith could even brake to a full stop, the girl was out of the car and running down a grassy hill, cutting straight across to one of the arenas. In it, a strangely tall and thin man rode Sarah's horse. Faith recognized the mare from the photos on the girl's bedroom wall. But the horse was far more beautiful in person, and in motion.

Faith stepped on the gas and drove the rest of the way down the hill. She quickly parked her car and jumped out just in time to witness what happened next.

As Faith was jogging toward the arena, Sarah's horse spotted her. And stopped dead. She had been crossing the arena diagonally in a flashy, extended trot. So the sudden loss of forward momentum nearly threw her rider down against her neck. But he was able to recover, and remain mostly upright.

He put his spurred heels to the horse's sides to make her go again. She did not go. Instead she raised her head as high as the short reins would allow, fighting against them, and let out an ear-piercing whinny.

Her rider grew more insistent, popping her flank with the whip. Nothing as serious as beating the horse, but making it clear he wanted no more misbehavior.

The horse responded with more misbehavior.

First she backed up several steps and rose up on her hind legs in a half-hearted attempt at rearing. Then she came down hard, stomping with both front legs at the same time, like a child throwing a tantrum.

Her rider spurred her again, and it proved his undoing.

The horse wound up and exploded into furious bucking. Her rider sat the first two bucks, but the third sent him flying out of the saddle and over the horse's neck. He did a full somersault in the air. While he flew, Faith heard the sparse crowd collectively draw an audible gasp. Then he landed hard on one hip in the groomed dirt of the arena.

The horse took off running and jumped the rail that formed the boundary of the dressage arena. It looked to be no more than a foot tall, maybe eighteen inches, but she vaulted high into the air, stirrups flapping against her sides, reins off-kilter, and cleared it with a good two feet to spare.

She galloped hard to Sarah, and Faith jogged as hard as she could in the oppressive heat, and they both reached the girl at approximately the same moment.

The horse halted suddenly, throwing dirt, and Sarah took hold of the mare's reins and stroked her long, shiny black face. The horse blew panting breaths through widely flared nostrils, and leaned forward to blow directly into Sarah's face. Sarah pursed her lips and blew back. The mare's sides heaved and shone with sweat. Her neck looked foamy where the reins had brushed it.

"I'm thinking this is your horse," Faith said. "Not sure how I knew."

To her surprise, the girl laughed. Faith was fairly sure she had never heard Sarah laugh before. And now, when the horse had just unseated her new owner and ruined his ride—as he limped in their direction with an ugly smear of dirt on his white breeches—well, it struck Faith as an odd time for mirth.

"That's funny," Sarah said. "You're funny sometimes."

She sounded almost giddy. Apparently seeing and touching her horse had revolutionized her mood—changed it entirely for the better. The rocky circumstances of their reunion seemed not to register with the girl at all.

But they would in a minute. Because the fallen rider had almost arrived.

"I have no idea what got into her," the man called to Sarah, sounding strangely jovial under the circumstances, "but thanks for catching her for me."

"I didn't exactly catch her," Sarah said. "She just came right to me."

He had reached them by that point. He stopped, and turned his eyes onto his new mare. This time his expression was more what Faith would have expected—perturbed and resentful. The mare did not bother to look back. She was staring into the eyes of the girl, and the girl was staring into the eyes of the mare. Nothing else seemed to exist for them in that moment.

"You okay?" Sarah asked him, not taking her eyes off the horse.

"I'll live. Landed on my hip, but probably just bruised it. More my ego I'm worried about."

"Yeah," Sarah said. "That was not pretty. Sorry."

"Wish I knew what got into her. Why would she run right up to you and stop?"

"Because she's mine," Sarah said.

In that moment, the bubble burst. The girl looked away from the horse. Sarah's world and its unwelcome reality returned. The giddiness was lost. Vanished, just like that.

"Well, she *was* mine," Sarah added. Sullen now.

She handed the reins to the man. To say she did so hesitantly and resentfully would have absurdly understated the case.

"I see," he said, taking them from her. "So you're Harlan Deaver's little girl."

"Yeah."

"I saw you riding her. That's why I bought her. Because of the way I watched her working for you."

"Where?"

"Just on a video."

"Oh."

A silence fell, and nobody seemed to know what to say next. While Faith waited, she watched the man's expression change. He was no longer jovial and self-deprecating. Nor did he seem to hold any of the admiration for the girl he'd expressed just a moment earlier.

He was growing angry.

"Oh, I get it now," he said. "*You're* what got into her."

"I guess. Yeah. I said I was sorry."

"Well, I take back the 'Thanks for catching her.' Now we're into 'Thanks a lot' territory. The sarcastic kind. Your timing stinks. You had to come in while I was right in the middle of riding a test? That's another entry fee I'll never get back again. Not to mention my reputation. I'm trying to sell this mare, and who do you think will want to buy her now, after they watched her buck off an experienced rider right in the middle of the Prix St. Georges?"

"Speaking of being in the middle of it . . . ," Faith interjected. Hesitantly, but still she spoke up. "Don't you want to get back on and go finish your . . . thing? Ride?"

He turned his angry eyes on Faith and stared into her face as if trying to take some kind of measure of her.

"Is that a joke?"

"No. I just meant—"

"He's disqualified," Sarah said. "Because he came off." Then, to the man, "She's not a horse person. She didn't know."

"Yes, I'm disqualified," the man repeated. "And more than a little bit humiliated."

He turned to walk away, pulling the horse along behind him by the reins.

"I'm sorry," Sarah said, and fell in beside him, walking toward the barn. Faith followed. "I don't know how many times I can say I'm sorry. I didn't know she would do that. How could anybody know she would do that? If I could make it up to you, I would."

The man stopped abruptly, and Faith almost ran into his back. The horse reached the end of the slack in her reins, and stopped.

174

"She's hot," he said to the girl. "Make it up to me by walking her till she's cool enough to put away. We're at Barn C. I have to go change my breeches."

He stomped off, still with a slight limp, leaving Faith and the girl in the baking, sizzling heat, alone with each other. And a sweaty horse.

Faith sat alone in a folding camp chair in the shade, under a canopy that read "John Wintermeyer Dressage." It had been set up with its back against the barn row where John was stabling his horses for the weekend.

Sarah had not come back from hot-walking the mare, though Faith had a hard time imagining the horse had not cooled down by then. The girl had been gone for nearly an hour.

Faith took out her phone and checked the reception.

Then she texted Ava.

So, you're not going to believe this.

A short pause.
Then Ava typed back, Take a run at it anyway.

That guy? The one I thought I was maybe almost sort of about to date? That was Sarah's father.

Tell me again who Sarah is?

That girl. My neighbor.

Right. Right. Coincidence? I don't get it.
How did you not know?

Because he made sure I didn't. He lied to
me. He was trying to grab her back.

For a minute or two, no reply. An older woman
walked by with a tall gray horse, all tacked up
and being led by the reins, and smiled at Faith.
Faith smiled back. Then a little scruffy dog came
out of nowhere and went after the gray, barking
and nipping at its heels, and almost got himself
kicked. But the owner, a young man in a sweat-
stained blue T-shirt, came running and scooped
him up just in time.

"Don't bring him to a show if he can't handle
himself around the horses," the woman said.

"Sorry," the boy said. Then, "Sorry," again.
And he slunk away.

Faith heard the tone of an incoming message.

That really makes everything so clear.

You think so? It confuses the hell out of me,
Faith typed back.

I mean like the way he kept asking about
her.

Oh. Yeah. It does shed light on that.

Sucks.

I know. Right?

Then there was the thought bubble of Ava's typing, but it just went on and on. Faith leaned back in her chair and closed her eyes. For a moment she just sat there, feeling herself perspire.

The girl came around again, sweaty and dirty and tired looking, and plopped into a chair beside Faith.

"You were right," she said. She sounded dangerously down.

"About what?"

"You said I shouldn't come here, because it would just kill me to let her go again. That I'd see her, and it would make things even worse, and then how would I ever say goodbye, and you were totally right."

"I didn't say that. You said you thought I was about to, but I didn't."

"Oh. That's right."

Faith's phone announced that the long, long message had finally arrived. Her screen had locked, so she woke it up again with her thumb and read.

Here's the thing. It also sheds light on some other issues. About you. This is not an insult. I just notice that you were going back and forth a lot on whether you should trust this guy. And you go back and forth on whether you have anything to fear from Robert. And I just think it's weird, because you're better at knowing things than anybody else I've ever met. You pick right up on what people are thinking and feeling. So I'm figuring you know, but then your brain tells you maybe you don't. So what if you just tell your brain to shut up and go with the part of you that knows? Does that make sense?

Faith typed back, Unfortunately, yes. It does.

"Who are you texting?" Sarah asked.

"My friend Ava. You met her once."

"What about?"

Faith thought a moment before answering. Took time to decide if she should. It was a personal question, but also an innocent one.

"I wanted to talk to somebody about what happened with your dad. Because I'm still upset about it."

Sarah clapped one hand over her mouth, then moved it just long enough to say, "Oh my God."

"Oh my God what?"

The girl dropped the hand into her lap. "I just realized. He was the guy you thought you were dating. I mean, I knew that. But it just now hit me how awful that must've felt. I was only thinking how it was for me. I just now realized what a weird thing that must've been for you."

Faith opened her mouth to answer. Before she could, they both looked up to see the slim giant John Wintermeyer standing over them. His face looked neutral. Neither angry nor particularly at peace.

"She's back in her stall," Sarah said. "I washed her down and then walked her till she was mostly dry. And I picked her hooves. And cleaned your tack and put it back in the tack stall. I don't know if I put it in the right places, but you'll find it. I left the braids in because I figured you'd want her braided for the sale class thing. The braids may need some repair by then, but I can do that if you want."

John looked down into the girl's face as if unfamiliar with her language.

"Still making it up to me for that disaster in the Prix St. Georges? Or you just like to spend time around her?"

"Yeah," Sarah said. "Pretty much both."

"Well, whatever. I have nothing against free labor. What fool would?" He paused. Wrinkled his forehead as if doing mental math. Then he squatted down, moving closer to her level without getting dirt on his clean white breeches. He had clearly changed them. "I can't believe I'm about to ask you this, but here goes." For a long moment, nothing. "Argh," he said, drawing out the syllable. "How can this be happening to me? I'm a professional rider and trainer. I do this for a living. But maybe later . . . when I go to warm her up for the sale class . . . maybe you can . . . you know . . . sort of . . ."

"Jeez, John," Sarah said, as if she hadn't only known him for a matter of minutes. "Spit it out already."

"Show me what I'm doing wrong with her." He shook his head as if disapproving of himself. "What is *happening* to me? It's like a nightmare. I'm asking riding advice from a thirteen-year-old girl."

"I'm fourteen."

"Your dad said you were thirteen."

"He doesn't pay good attention, and he doesn't keep track. I'm not sure you're doing anything so wrong with her. It was just a weird situation. She wanted to come to me."

"It's not only that. I wish it were only that. Yes, that was by far the most dramatic and painful example, but we're not getting along at all. Our scores are terrible. Everything is a battle."

"It's only been a couple or three weeks, John. It takes time to sync up with a horse. You should know that. You're a professional. You do this for a living."

"I'll ignore the sarcasm for now and just say it's getting worse. And the worse it gets, the harder it'll be to sell her. I can barely show her for sale now in a way that'll draw a buyer. If we sink down any further than this, I'll lose my shirt on her."

"Did you buy her to sell?"

"No. Maybe eventually, but I bought her to ride. But it's not working out, to put it mildly. Laughably mildly."

"Okay, fine," Sarah said, followed by a sigh. "I'll come by and see if I can give you a few pointers."

"Great," John said. "My humiliation is complete."

He pushed to his feet and wandered off, mumbling to himself and shaking his head.

Chapter Nine

Kids, Don't Try This at Home

Sarah cupped her hands around her mouth and shouted into the warm-up arena in the general direction of John and the mare.

"You're overriding her. That's the problem."

Faith watched from a place in the shade, a few feet away. But the girl leaned on the railing of the warm-up arena, not seeming to care that she was baking in the full sun. It was after five thirty in the afternoon, but still in the high nineties.

John rode over to the rail and the girl. Faith moved out into the sun to hear their exchange.

"Would you please keep your voice down?" John hissed under his breath. "I have a reputation, you know. And it's suffered enough today."

"If I keep my voice down, how are you supposed to hear me? You want me to run along beside you while you ride?"

"I'll come back to the rail now and then to hear your thoughts. Your *quietly* expressed thoughts."

"Fine. Just gives you more time to get in trouble with her. It's your life."

John only sat the mare for a moment. He didn't speak or ride away.

"Overriding her in what way?" he asked after a time.

"In every way. With the rein, with your leg. Even your seat is too loud. If you whisper the aids to this mare, you're still being a little too loud. She's incredibly sensitive. Try just *thinking* the aid. Think about putting your leg on her. Your leg'll do something because you thought about it, but barely. Then you might have a chance with her."

"I've ridden sensitive horses before," John said, ignoring the mare's impatient shifting underneath him.

"I don't think you've ever ridden a horse *this* sensitive."

"Okay. Let me take another go at it."

John rode away from the rail and trotted the horse into the center of the warm-up arena. There he attempted a canter transition. But the mare balked on the depart, gathering her haunches underneath her weight and then kicking out violently behind, throwing John forward in the saddle. He tried again and achieved an awkward canter with the horse's head too high.

He rode back to the rail at a trot and halted in front of Faith and the girl.

"I might as well scratch her in the sales class if this is the way it's going to be. Word gets around, you know. Dressage is a very small town."

"Duh," Sarah said, shielding her eyes from the late sun to stare up at her mare.

John sighed. He lowered his head in a defeated-looking gesture. Then he swung a leg over the saddle, leaning his weight on the pommel for a moment as he kicked out of the second stirrup. He dropped lightly into the dirt.

"Here's a thought," he said to Sarah, "and it's only because I'm desperate. Show me how you ride her as well as you do. Maybe that will work better than telling me."

For a long moment, the girl just looked down at herself, then up at the horse.

"I don't have my boots," she said.

She was wearing jeans, a red T-shirt. Athletic shoes.

"Should be okay for just a few minutes. You can wear my helmet."

"Which will be, like, twenty sizes too big."

John took off his helmet. His short hair shone with sweat. From inside the leg of his boot he produced a rag, which he folded into a long strip, like a sweatband. He arranged it inside the helmet, then plopped both onto the girl's head.

"Still kind of big," she said.

It was a complaint, but underneath it Faith heard excitement. The girl understood now that she was about to get back on her horse. For the first time in weeks. Long after she had grudgingly accepted that she never would again.

Faith thought about what Ava had said. *You're better at knowing things than anybody else I've ever met. You pick right up on what people are thinking and feeling.*

It was true, and Faith had always known it. She just hadn't talked about it, or even paid it a great deal of conscious attention.

Meanwhile John was adjusting the chin strap of the girl's helmet. Tightening it by several inches.

"I think that'll be okay," Sarah said. "So long as I don't come off, anyway. Then again, if I don't come off, which I won't, who needs a helmet?"

She walked around to the horse's left side, and John gave her a leg up. She fairly flew into the saddle. As if she weighed nothing at all.

"I don't have gloves," she said to John. "And my hands'll be sweaty. But here goes."

Girl and mare moved off at a brisk walk. The horse's neck was beautifully rounded. Her hooves reached out to cover ground.

They transitioned into a trot with no urging that Faith was able to see. It was not the posting trot that Faith would have expected. Sarah seemed to be welded to the saddle, and no amount of motion on the part of the horse seemed to cause her rider to bounce. Sarah's seat was still. Her legs were still. Her hands remained still and low in front of the saddle, the double reins held short.

The mare lifted her legs, her whole body, in a manner that looked almost like dancing. The amount of air underneath the horse nearly took Faith's breath away.

She heard John whistle softly under his breath.

She watched for a minute or two before she realized that a small crowd had formed. A dozen or more people were now standing in the hot sun, voluntarily, watching Sarah ride the mare.

One of them, an older woman with a weathered face, elbowed John in the ribs. "So *that's* why you bought that mare," she said. "We all wondered."

"Right," he said. Sounding despondent. "Now if I could just get her to go like that for *me*."

While they spoke, Sarah halted the forward motion of the horse. But the mare's feet did not stop moving. Instead she seemed to trot in place, a strangely high-stepping movement, hooves reaching straight up into the air in rhythm.

Faith heard a few of the people around her suck in their breath and/or murmur approvingly.

"Nice *piaffe!*" one said. "Look at that *lift!*"

Then Sarah had the mare in forward motion again, but with that same incredible lift of the horse's legs, and a pause at the top of each upstroke. As if she were reaching for the sky on every step.

"Is there a name for that?" Faith asked John, leaning in his direction.

"That's a passage," he said. But he gave it a French-sounding pronunciation, with the emphasis on the second syllable. "Much as I hate to admit it, it's a damn good one. I'd give it an 8.5 if I were judging."

Sarah let the reins go slack and walked the mare back to the rail in a long, stretched, relaxed walk. The smattering of people who had gathered wandered off again, one man clapping his hands slowly for emphasis.

"See?" the girl said to John. "Not so hard if you know her."

"Okay," John said. "Okay. I'm getting an idea. It's kind of crazy but it might be enough to pull my buns out of the fire here, and at this point I'll try anything. We'll borrow you some boots and clothes. Or I'll even buy you something if I have to. And *you* ride her in the sales class."

"Fine by me," Sarah said, but it was more than fine. The girl was clearly elated. "But we better hurry. The thing starts in just a few minutes."

Sarah rode the mare up to the rail of the warm-up arena and looked down at Faith.

"Take Midnight's boots off for me," she said. Then, when Faith only stood there for several seconds, saying and doing nothing, Sarah added, "Please."

The girl was wearing a hastily assembled riding outfit. The tall leather boots were a little too short at her knee, but Faith would not have noticed that. Only John and Sarah noticed, and Faith only knew because they had said so. Her white breeches were far too big, and the girl had been forced to gather the excess and pull it up

187

where her black riding jacket would hopefully hide it, securing it with a belt. Fortunately the jacket was big enough to swallow all that. Faith had safety-pinned it from the inside, to draw it in at the waist. Sarah's borrowed helmet and the gloves John had bought her were the only part of her apparel that fit as intended.

"Where's John?" Faith asked, not knowing what it meant to take a horse's boots off, and not wanting to know.

"I don't know. But he's not here. And I'm about to go in. And she can't go in with her boots on. Well . . . it's not really a regulation CDS or FEI or anything class, I suppose, so I guess technically there aren't rules like that. But it would look terrible. So, please."

Faith took a step back and assessed the situation.

The mare was wearing something white wrapped around each of her lower legs. Faith wouldn't have called them boots, because they did not cover the horse's hooves. They seemed to be some kind of white vinyl on the outside, with a sheepskin lining that Faith could see at the top and bottom edge.

She did not want to move that close to the horse's legs. She had already seen what the mare could do when she decided she was unhappy.

"I don't know how to—" she began.

"It's Velcro. You know how to work Velcro, right?"

The girl was being snappish, but Faith knew she was nervous about the ride ahead, so she let it go by.

"You sure she won't mind me—"

"She's had people take off her boots before. Please, Faith. I don't have much time."

Moving slowly, careful to telegraph to the mare what was about to happen, Faith reached down and pulled off the Velcro straps on one front boot. The mare seemed unconcerned. Faith lifted the boot away. She took off the other front boot, then straightened up and looked around for John to save her.

He was nowhere to be seen.

"She won't kick you," Sarah said, seeming to read Faith's thoughts.

Faith sighed and went to work on the rear boots.

When she was done, she stood in front of the girl and the mare, hugging the boots to her belly. They were still warm and slightly damp from the heat of the horse's skin.

She looked up at Sarah, who looked back. The girl was clearly a tangle of emotion. Anybody would have seen it.

"Faith," she said, just barely over a whisper. "Why am I doing this?"

"Because you love to ride your horse?"

"But I'm helping him sell her. Why am I helping him sell her?"

Faith pulled a slow breath before answering, and dug deep for the right words.

"Because John's not happy with her, and she's not happy with John. And you want her to be happy. I know, I know, you want her to be *with you* more than anything in the world. But she can't be. So you want her to be someplace where she fits with her rider and they get along well. Because when you really love someone, you want them to be happy. Even if it can't be with you."

For a moment, the girl just sat her mare, head slightly tilted. As if still listening. As if the words were playing on a slight delay in her head. Then she nodded.

"Right," she said. "Wish me luck."

But she rode away before Faith could.

Faith called it after the girl. "Good luck!" But she wasn't sure if Sarah ever heard.

Faith trotted across the hard dirt, following Sarah and her horse to the edge of the arena, where she sat on a warm metal bleacher bench.

A thought came into her head. If the horse was for sale again, maybe Faith could buy her for the girl. She probably didn't have nearly enough money. Still, until she knew how much money was at issue here, the idea was unlikely to leave her alone.

A girl a year or two younger than Sarah—in full riding gear with her helmet over one knee—sat a few yards off Faith's right, a parent on either side. The girl had what looked to be a program for the Sales Horse Presentation Class. Faith could see it turned to a page with a color photo of John riding the mare.

She was just about to lean over and ask to see it when it struck Faith that the announcer was giving much the same information that she guessed was written in the booklet. He had been talking all along, but she had been too preoccupied with her own thoughts to listen.

Not a sentence after she gave him her attention—and just as Sarah and the mare thundered by the rail in a breathtaking extended canter—the announcer killed her idea.

"This beautiful and very talented mare is practically a steal at seventy-five thousand dollars," he said.

And with that sentence, the dream died.

She sat a moment, thinking nothing. Not really listening to the announcer. Not really watching the ride.

"You know that mare, right?" an unfamiliar voice said.

Faith looked over, bounced out of a stupor, to see the girl in riding clothes sit next to her on the bench. Sarah was still riding, but Faith hadn't been able to bring herself to look. They were too beautiful together. Too *meant to be*. And the fact that they wouldn't be was too sad for Faith. It was more than she could hold up in the moment.

She glanced over at the girl. She looked to be twelve or thirteen, with braided long hair and a shy, hopeful expression.

"A little bit," she said. "I know the girl who's riding her much better."

For a strange moment, Faith couldn't imagine how this girl knew she was connected to the horse and rider in the arena. Then she realized she was still holding the horse's white boots clutched to her belly.

"She'd be okay with me, wouldn't she? My dad said no because he heard the horse caused some trouble for that man today. But she's great for this girl, and I'm almost as old as her. So she'd be a good horse for me, right?"

"I . . . ," Faith began. Then she allowed herself to stall. She knew the answer was probably no. But, more to the point, it was not a call she was qualified to make. "I really couldn't say. I don't know much about horses. You'd have to ask her owner about that."

Faith looked up to see Sarah ride the mare out of the arena. She had missed the bulk of the ride, utterly preoccupied with other thoughts.

"Okay, thanks," the girl said. "We'll go find her owner and tell her I want to try her out."

Faith stood, still clutching the mare's vinyl boots, and walked to meet Sarah just outside the arena. She felt a sense of dread on every step.

As if walking to the principal's office. Or the gallows.

When they met up, Faith looked up at the girl, who looked down into her face.

"Now we just hope nobody buys her," Sarah said.

"Yes. We can hope," Faith said.

Because she couldn't bring herself to tell the girl it might be time to say goodbye again. Already.

"No, don't put her away," John said, catching up to the three of them—Faith, Sarah on the ground now, and the horse. He grabbed the mare's reins and turned her back toward the arenas. "We're bringing her up again."

"Why?" Sarah asked. "Aren't we done?"

Faith could hear the beginning of the panic in the girl's voice.

"We have a nibble," he said.

He pulled the reins out of Sarah's gloved hand. All Faith and the girl could do was follow along.

In the distance, Faith could see the girl she'd met during Sarah's ride. She was standing with a parent on either side, halfway between the porta-potties and the end of Barn A.

John led the mare right up to them, and the girl reached out a gloved hand to touch the mare's face. The horse's head jerked up, evading that touch.

John looked around for the first time, checking to see that Sarah was still with him.

"Sarah, this is Mercedes," he said. "And her mom and dad, Dan and Mary Anne. Do me a favor and give her a few pointers to get her off on the right foot with Midnight."

Faith glanced over at Sarah. The girl stood like a statue in the slant of late afternoon sun, her face white.

John tapped his foot in the dirt a few times, impatient for Sarah to awaken. Then he turned his attention back to Mercedes.

"Come on," he said. "I'll give you a leg up."

It woke Sarah—shocked her into motion—to see the girl swing up onto the back of her mare. She stepped in quickly and grabbed the horse's reins just behind the double bit.

"Okay," she said, her voice sounding a little shaky. "She's very, very sensitive. So don't stick your spurs into her sides, and don't do anything sudden. Don't kick her if you want her to go. Just use a tiny bit more leg pressure. You should have your legs on her all the time. Otherwise she won't feel you there, and she'll get panicky. So to move out or transition up, just a whisper more pressure."

Sarah let go of the reins. Hesitantly. Mercedes sat the mare like a statue, nothing appearing to move. She looked more than a little bit afraid.

It took a moment for Faith to realize Mercedes was concentrating on making the mare walk forward. Trying to perfect an aid so subtle that it was invisible to her onlookers.

"It didn't work," she said to Sarah.

"Okay, well. That's unusual. But I guess a tiny bit more of a press with your legs until you get what you wanted."

Still no aid that Faith could discern. Still no forward movement on the part of the horse.

"Do it again," Sarah said, and took hold of the mare's reins.

As the girl pressed with her legs, just hard enough for Faith to see, Sarah used the reins to move the mare forward. Then she let go. Like a father running beside his child's bike, then stepping back and letting her fly solo.

The mare took a few more steps and stopped. Mercedes applied her legs to get Midnight moving again. But it was too much. The mare bolted forward, nearly unseating the girl. Then she spun back to the safety of Sarah, throwing Mercedes off balance. By the time the mare and young rider arrived back at the group of adults, Mercedes was desperately holding on to the horse's neck to stay in the saddle.

John ran to them and took the horse's reins.

Dan, the father, arrived just a step behind. "See, I didn't think so, honey," he said. "Now jump down."

But the girl only froze there, still clutching the horse's neck.

Mercedes's father grabbed her around the waist and pulled her off the horse, gently setting her expensively booted feet in the dirt between his. He looked up at John and shook his head.

John led the horse away with a visible sigh.

For a moment, they all just watched the mare go. Then Dan left his daughter and walked up to Sarah, stopping just inches from the girl, his face close to hers.

"You know that horse," he said, "better than that John guy does, and I'm sensing you're not the one who needs the money. So you tell me. Please. Is that horse suitable for a rider like my daughter?"

Sarah remained absolutely silent. But the barely perceptible shake of her head said everything that needed saying.

Dan nodded, as if he'd known as much all along. Which Faith figured he probably had. "Thank you," he said. "I appreciate the honesty."

Then he gathered up his family and walked away.

They stood at the front desk of a Paso Robles hotel together, Faith digging through her wallet for the credit card that was furthest from being maxed out.

After hearing the price for two rooms, Faith had booked one room with two beds.

"This is going to get too expensive," she said.

"I don't know how we're going to swing this if we need a motel room every night."

"I can sleep in the car," Sarah said. Her mood had clearly crashed. Exhaustion and depression had gotten the best of her. Her lips barely moved as she spoke.

"That's not really the answer. We can't both sleep in the car. It's not big enough for that. Besides, if I have a hotel room, you're welcome in it. But I can't afford one every night."

"My grandmother gave me a little money," she said.

"How little?"

"Well, it was Saturday. Which I didn't know at the time, but now I get it that she couldn't go to the bank. She had, like, seventy dollars in cash in the house, and then she gave me a check for six hundred that I can take to the bank on Monday."

"That's helpful for food and gas," Faith said. "But for hotels it won't last us a week."

"Can I worry about that in the morning?" the girl asked, a distinct whine creeping into her voice. "I'm just really tired."

"Sure," Faith said. "You know you have to call your grandmother before you fall asleep," she added.

"I know. I will. I promise. But I don't promise I won't fall asleep in the middle of talking to her."

In that moment Faith's own exhaustion caught up with her. She leaned on the check-in counter and watched the woman program their key cards.

"You know what's weird?" Faith asked after a second. The woman looked up as though Faith might be talking to her. "No. I meant that for my friend here." The woman returned to the task of writing the room number on the key card envelope, and drawing directional notes on the map of rooms.

"I give up," Sarah said, leaning on the counter with her eyes closed. "What's weird?"

"That whole thing with your father? Coming to my house with bagels, and you saw him there?"

"Yeah?"

"That was *today*. That was just this morning."

A long, long pause. Faith thought the girl might have fallen asleep on her feet, like a horse.

Then Sarah said, "Whoa. That *is* weird."

Faith woke in the night to a shout.

She sat up suddenly in bed and looked over at Sarah, but the girl seemed to be fast asleep. She clicked on the light between the beds, but it didn't wake the girl. Faith could see Sarah's eyes flicking back and forth under their lids, desperately. Tears ran down her face and onto her pillow. She had been crying in her sleep.

The girl shouted again.

"Mom!"

Faith jumped out of bed and covered the distance between them. Before she could get to Sarah, the girl shouted again.

"Mom!"

Faith shook her gently by the shoulder. She cried out one more time for her mom, then opened her eyes. She looked up at Faith.

"Oh," she said.

She sat up in the soft light, and Faith put one arm around her.

"That was weird," the girl said.

"Want to tell me about it?"

"I'm not sure," Sarah said. "I'm thinking."

They sat that way for a moment in silence. Faith glanced over once to see the girl's tears still flowing freely.

"Were you reliving something about when your mother died?" Faith asked after a time.

Yes, it was a personal question. Yes, Faith was pushing the girl. And maybe they didn't even know each other well enough for this kind of sharing. But it struck Faith that they were out in the world together, a hastily assembled team. They had no one but each other. If they weren't close enough to confide, she figured they had better learn to be, and in short order.

"No," Sarah said. "It was a weird dream. Not like anything that ever really happened. We were on the beach, my mom and me. The real beach, where we just were. And I was saying to my mom that I thought she died, that everybody told me she died. But there she was. She never said anything to me. She just kept looking in my eyes. And then this huge wave came and grabbed her up and pulled her out to sea. But not like a wave really would. It was a way that could only happen in a dream. Like she was standing up and facing me the whole time, and looking in my eyes. And I was yelling for her, but she just kept getting farther and farther away." An audible sob erupted out of her. It shook her body under Faith's arm. "I'm sorry I woke you up," Sarah added.

"Don't worry about it. Think you can get back to sleep?"

"Can you stay here a minute until I do?"

"Sure," Faith said.

She made herself comfortable with a pillow between herself and the headboard, half sitting up, one arm still around the girl's shoulder.

"We can still go back to the show tomorrow, right?" Sarah asked.

"I don't see why not. It's not like we have someplace better to go. Get some sleep now if you can."

Faith replayed vivid scenes from the horse show in her head as she waited.

In time she could hear the girl's sleep breathing—almost a light snore but not quite.

She tried, gently, but couldn't get her arm back without waking Sarah up.

So she stayed.

She got very little sleep after that.

Chapter Ten

Farm Sweet Farm

Faith was sitting in the barely cool shade of the tack stall, reading an e-book on her phone, when Sarah walked by leading the saddled and bridled mare.

She jumped up and followed the girl to the mare's stall, the oven-like heat hitting her in the face as she stepped outside. Nearly knocking her backward.

"How did it go?" she called.

Faith knew that John had just finished a ride on the mare, but she hadn't been able to bring herself to stand in the sun and watch.

While she waited in the shade of the barn row for the girl to answer, Faith leaned on the door of the mare's stall. Sarah had led the mare back in, slid the door most of the way closed, and was beginning to strip off her tack.

"Didn't look all that great to me," Sarah said, undoing the mare's girth. "But John said it was the best ride he's gotten out of her yet."

"Good. Maybe he'll keep her."

"Maybe," Sarah said. But her brow furrowed, as if she thought not.

"So . . . ," Faith began. And then stalled. Sarah

seemed to pick up the tension of what might come next. Faith could feel it crackle in the air between them. ". . . have you thought about where we might want to go after today?"

The girl slipped off the mare's bridle, and Faith could see lines of foamy sweat where the straps had been in contact with the horse's head.

Sarah held up one hand in a bold stop sign to keep Faith from saying more. But Faith had nothing more to say.

"Please," the girl said. "Please. Faith. I'm begging you. The day's not over. It's still today. Please, please just let me have today."

"Okay. Fair enough."

She wandered reluctantly out into the blast furnace of sun to find herself some lunch.

As Faith crossed back toward the barn with her bag of food, she noticed John and Sarah standing together at the board where scores were intermittently posted.

They seemed to be arguing.

Faith moved closer to hear what was going on. To see if everything was okay.

"It's not her fault," she heard the girl shout. "It's your fault. She's not Prix St. Georges. She's fourth level. If you want her to be Prix St. Georges, she can be. She will be. But you can't just wave a magic wand over her. She needs to school at that level for months. If you push her too fast, of course it's going to stress her out."

"If she's not Prix St. Georges material, then tell me how you manage to do a nearly perfect piaffe and passage on her."

"I didn't say she wasn't Prix St. Georges *material*. I said she wasn't Prix St. Georges. Yet. It's one thing to know a handful of the advanced movements. That doesn't mean she's ready to show at that level."

"Look, I know what I'm doing," John said, a bit more restrained but still agitated. "There's a method to my madness."

"I know what you're doing, too," Sarah shouted back. "Everybody here knows what you're doing. You want to say she's an FEI horse, so you can ask more money for her. But you're messing everything up by doing it, and now you're blaming the problems you're causing on her."

"Look. Kid. I asked you for your advice one time. It was not an open invitation."

The girl visibly fumed for a moment. Then she stomped off without offering a reply.

Faith moved closer to where John stood at the board, spent and dejected. He looked over and saw her there.

"Oh," he said. Then he didn't follow up with anything more.

For a moment they just stared at the scores together. Faith found the line for John Wintermeyer and Falkner's Midnight Sun. Their score was 58.357.

"So I take it a fifty-eight is not a good score?"

"The kid who was trying her out last night might have been happy enough with it. But for me it's pretty embarrassing. And that was the best ride I've had on her yet."

"What's an FEI horse?"

"A horse who rides in the FEI-level tests. Prix St. Georges, then Intermediare, then Grand Prix. The advanced classes. Those tests are prepared by the International Federation for Equestrian Sports."

"So horse people have problems with their acronyms?"

"Excuse me?"

"The letters of that don't form F-E-I. They form I-F-E-S."

"Oh. No, we're not stupid. We just do everything in French. Fédération Équestre Internationale. FEI."

"Got it," Faith said.

They began to walk back toward the barns together, John's shoulders slumped and his head hanging.

"Tell her to unbraid the mare and put her shipping boots on," he said. "If she's willing to. If not, I'll do it myself. Better I don't try to talk to her right now. I'm rolling out of here."

"I thought you had another ride on her this afternoon."

"I'm scratching her. If this is as good as it gets, I give up for now. I need to work this out in the schooling arena, not the show arena. I'm taking her home."

Faith looked up to see that they had reached the end of Barn B. They turned down the shady barn row together. Then Faith stopped and looked up at John, and he looked down at her.

She was thinking of the emotional devastation of the moment that was about to occur. But she had no idea how to prevent it, or even put it into words.

As if reading her mind, or at least her face, John spoke.

"Look, I have feelings," he said. "I have some empathy. Please don't think I don't. I know this is a terrible, terrible thing for Sarah. I swear if I could afford the loss, I'd hand the girl her horse back. But I paid a fortune for that mare. I'd be embarrassed to let you know how much. I'm already selling her at a price that represents all the loss I can afford. And it's not looking like I'll get it."

"Nobody expects you to give the horse back."

"Well, I wish I could. But I can't."

He turned to walk away. Faith stopped him by calling his name.

"John."

He turned back to her, but didn't speak. Just waited.

"You said you have nothing against free labor."

He smiled a crooked half smile. "I believe my exact words were 'What fool would?'"

"And you said you need to work out your issues with the mare in the schooling arena."

"Not sure where we're going with this," he said.

"Couldn't Sarah and I come back to your home barn with you? Just for a bit? She could groom and tack for you, and maybe ride the mare, and help you ride her in a way that'll get you higher scores. I mean, it costs you nothing. And it's worth a try. Right?"

For a moment, the strangely tall man just stood, not answering. Faith could feel the buzz of fear in her belly. Fear of the wrong answer, and the way it would cause the earth to fall away under the girl's feet. Faith had no idea where the girl would land, and no idea how to break a fall like that one.

He shrugged his shoulders. "Don't see any reason why not," he said. "Only . . . ask her to show me a little more respect in our conversations, okay?"

"She's really scared today. I think when I tell her you agreed to let her come back to your barn with the mare, she'll respect you till the day she dies."

"I have some slightly bad news and some really good news," Faith said to the girl. "And some lunch."

Sarah was sitting slumped in a corner of the

tack stall, a bridle hanging down on either side of her head, her eyes pressed shut.

"I'm not hungry," she said. "Just tell me the news. Good news first, please. I need some."

"We're going home with John and the mare to his barn."

Sarah leapt to her feet, eyes open wide. "That's great! That's . . . what's the bad news?"

"Well, just that they're leaving early. But I guess that's only bad news if we weren't invited to come along."

Sarah rushed at Faith as if she planned to tackle her and knock her down on the concrete of the tack stall floor. Instead she slowed at the moment of contact and threw her arms around Faith, holding her so tightly that Faith found it hard to breathe.

"I offered you as a free groom," Faith said.

"Not a problem."

"And you'll be helping him work out his problems with the mare."

"Definitely not a problem."

They stood silent and entwined for a moment, Faith still unable to draw a full, deep breath.

"I love you for this," Sarah said. Then she quickly let go and backed away, as if retreating from having gone a step too far. "I'll go unbraid her and put her shipping boots on," she said. "I'll even get his gelding ready to load, just to show how helpful I can be."

And with that, the girl was gone.

They drove together, Faith and the girl, south-bound on the 101 toward Los Alamos. Faith was following John's horse trailer. It was a massive thing—Faith thought it could probably hold six horses. It had six individual barred windows for horses to use to view their shifting world. But Faith knew the only horses inside it were Midnight and John's big Dutch gelding.

The girl was messing with her phone again, and it woke up a memory in Faith's brain.

"You didn't stop in and see your friends," she said.

"What friends?" Sarah seemed to break her obsession with the phone slowly, as if moving upward through thick mud.

"When we were driving to the horse park, you were talking on the phone with a man from your old barn, and you said you'd find him and say hello."

"I saw Dean," Sarah said. Simply. Almost bored.

"You did?"

"Yeah, I hung out with him and Cara and Lainie a couple of times. I did all kinds of stuff while you were sitting back at the barns in the shade."

"Oh," Faith said, feeling embarrassed. Maybe more than the situation required. "I don't do all that well with heat."

"You're from LA, too, though, right?"

"Santa Monica."

"Oh. Got it. In Moorpark it's hot. I'm used to it."

"I guess I was kind of hoping I could meet them," Faith said, even though it made her feel vulnerable to do so.

"Who?"

"Your friends from your old barn."

"Oh. Okay. You can. Next show."

"Which would be . . . ?"

Sarah was still staring at her phone as she spoke, so Faith initially thought she was reading a list off a website, or that someone had texted the information to the girl.

"Next weekend there's Somis. Then there's one in Rancho Murieta, but John might not want to go that far. It's all the way up near Sacramento. And one at the Earl Warren Showgrounds in Santa Barbara. He'll probably want to do that one."

The girl closed her eyes and continued, and Faith realized she was rattling off shows by heart.

"Then Burbank. San Juan Capistrano. And by mid-July we're back at the Paso Horse Park. But it's hard to say, you know, because those are just the ones *I* would go to. I have no idea what ones John thinks are important. There's something going on all the time in the summer, somewhere in California. But I don't know if he goes out every weekend."

As Sarah wrapped up her answer, Faith

210

followed John's trailer down an off-ramp, and they turned right and headed west on what looked like a shady, tree-lined country lane. But the speed limit was fifty-five, and Faith noticed that big trucks tore along it as if on a highway.

As they drove west, Faith watched her dashboard. The readout for the outside temperature dropped. From 101 down into the high nineties. That held steady for a time. Then it dropped one number every mile or so and held steady at eighty-six.

The trailer slowed in front of her and put on its right turn signal, and Faith slowed as well. She followed John down a dirt driveway with a closed gate halfway along it.

Behind the gate was a farm that looked beautiful enough to be captured by a landscape painter and hung in someone's living room: two long, deep-red barn buildings with gables and high windows; a life-size bronze statue of a racing horse, its jockey raising his crop for all of eternity; a covered arena as well as an outside dressage arena; an oval railed track for racehorses. Everywhere, trees shaded the dirt walks and barn rows, their leaves and smaller branches blowing in a strong wind.

"This place is beautiful," Faith said out loud.

"I'll say."

Faith leaned out her window and watched John do the same. He stretched his upper body out the window of his big white one-ton flatbed pickup and punched a button to open the gate.

"That seems strange," Faith said.

"What?"

"You just punch a button and the gate opens."

"What's strange about that?"

"Usually there's a code. If anybody can get in, why even have a gate?"

For a time, the girl didn't answer. Faith glanced over to see Sarah staring back at her skeptically, one eyebrow raised.

"It's so obvious," the girl said. "I'm just waiting for you to come up with it on your own."

Faith pulled through the gate behind John. The sign on the gate read "Moonshadow Farm."

"Sorry," she said after a time. "Not getting the obvious."

"The horses can't punch the button. It's not to keep people out, it's to keep horses in."

"Got it," Faith said. "I'm not a horse person. So they wander around free in there?"

"No, of course not. But stuff happens. You saw what happened to John when I first showed up. Horses get away sometimes."

John parked his truck and trailer in front of the nearest barn, and Faith pulled into the shade beyond the building so as not to block the back of his trailer during the unloading. Faith and the girl stepped out into the warm day. The wind was strong and cool, right off the ocean a mile or two on their west. Compared to where they had just been, eighty-six degrees felt like heaven.

Meanwhile, John was opening the back door of the trailer.

"Help me unload them," John called to Sarah. "And then you can be on your own for the rest of the day."

"No," Sarah called back. Just for a moment, Faith was shocked by the unexpected reaction. But a second later, the girl continued. "No, you go relax, John. I'll unload them. Just give me their stall numbers. I'll do it all. You had a show day, and not that good of one. I'll take care of the horses. That's what I'm here for."

The girl disappeared into the back of the trailer, and Faith stood out in the warm sun next to John. She looked up at him, sharing her reaction to Sarah's cooperative mood. He looked back.

"What did I tell you?" she said.

"I give up. What did you tell me?"

"About the respect."

"Oh. That. Right. Well, you did call that one. I have to say."

"This place is amazing, John. It's beautiful. You *own* this?"

He laughed out loud. It was a snorting, braying thing that came out sounding rude. But Faith was fairly sure he hadn't meant it to.

"Yeah, right," he said. "I should be so lucky. I board and train here. And give lessons. Believe me, if I owned this place, if I was rolling in this kind of property and dough, I'd give Sarah her horse back."

They both looked up to see Sarah standing at the open trailer door, leading Midnight. Her face said she had heard. She paused, based on what she had heard, and the horse paused because her girl did. But Sarah said nothing. Just tugged the lead rope gently and stepped down off the back of the trailer, Midnight following suit. The mare was wearing tall, padded shipping boots in a dramatic dark blue, covering all four of her lower legs. They looked stiff and obtrusive to Faith, as though it would be hard for a horse to walk in them.

As if reading that thought, Midnight picked up one hind leg, strangely high, and kicked out impatiently, as if that might shake off the boot. When it didn't, she walked on without further fuss.

Faith met John's eyes again.

"Well," he said. "It's not like she didn't know I wasn't giving her back. But anyway, I'm sorry."

"I don't think any of this is your fault, John. I think there's plenty of fault to go around, but you're just an innocent bystander. You're doing enough by letting her be here with the horse."

"That's no problem. I could use the help. I just worry how it's going to be for the girl when I find a buyer."

"Me too," Faith said.

She thought about Sarah practically begging her, earlier that day. *Please. Please, Faith. I'm begging you. The day's not over. It's still today. Please, please just let me have today.* Again, it seemed impossible that the words had been spoken earlier that same day. Or that Sarah's father had come over to her beach house with bagels the previous morning. The memories felt weeks old. Easily a month's worth of life changes had happened in the past two days.

"But anyway," she added, "that's not today. At least she's okay for now."

Faith walked beside the girl as she led John's huge bay gelding into the barn. It was shady and cool inside the barn aisle, with the wind blowing through like a tunnel. Faith found something beautiful in the sound of the horse's steel-shod hooves clopping on the concrete floor.

Sarah led the horse into an open stall filled deeply with blonde shavings, his hooves banging against the raised edge of the stall that held the shavings inside. The girl slid the door mostly closed, and began to pull apart the Velcro on the gelding's dark-red shipping boots. Faith watched her through the iron bars that made up the top half of the stall doors.

"He's a nice horse," Sarah said, pulling off a back boot.

"He seems nice, doesn't he? So mellow. I've never seen him react badly to anything."

"He's one of those bomb-proof horses," Sarah said, straightening up and arranging the boots with the smaller front ones inside the taller, larger back boots. "Which is nice in a way. But I think you pay the price for it in the show arena. Because he's not really very fiery. I think you need that fire to do upper-level dressage. Otherwise you spend most of your energy keeping the horse forward enough. But I guess John manages. He rides Grand Prix on him." She reached both hands out to the gelding's huge head, and he moved his muzzle close to her and took a bite of her T-shirt, mostly with his lips. "But nothing against you, buddy boy. No insult intended. You're a perfect example of exactly what you are."

Sarah kissed the horse on the flat part of his forehead and stepped out of the stall. She turned her eyes up to Faith.

"Well, this is pretty much heaven," she said.

"I was just thinking the same thing myself. And we can both use a little. So we should definitely enjoy this while we can."

Faith had been wandering the barn aisles for several minutes before the girl returned. She had identified a restroom between two stalls—clean and functional and including a shower that

216

looked like it hadn't been used in years. On the outside of the barn, under a shady overhang, stood several washing stations for the horses, with cross-ties and hoses, drains in their concrete floors.

Faith was examining one when she looked up to see that Sarah was back. The girl was carrying two large . . . well, Faith didn't know what they were. Only that they were big and flat and hidden inside green canvas carrying cases with vinyl handles.

"Not sure what you'll think of this," Sarah said, "but you were saying hotels were going to break us, so I'm hoping you might like it."

The girl turned and walked away, motioning for Faith to follow.

She followed Sarah along the deeply cool barn aisle and into what appeared to be an empty tack stall. No windows. Just a concrete floor and wooden walls, with a solid-wood sliding door. The girl flipped a switch, and a simple light fixture with a bare bulb came on in the middle of the ceiling. Faith saw hooks on the walls that she assumed had been intended for bridles, but they struck her as a decent place to hang a few clothes.

"But do we have permission to be here?" Faith asked.

"Yeah. John told everybody who works here, and nobody cares. They're happy he has some help with Midnight. They've been worried about that."

Meanwhile the girl was unzipping the cover on what Faith could now see was a camp cot. Not a mattress type of cot, but an aluminum frame with a plain canvas sling.

"Where'd you get those?"

"John loaned them to me. Where else? They come in handy at shows. If you want to stay close to the horses at night, or people use them for their grooms, or if they want to have a person nearby to check the horses all through the night. I'm more a fan of sleeping in a stall full of straw. But I figured you'd like this."

She set one up against a wall and motioned for Faith to try it. Faith sat on it carefully, then bounced slightly. It was more taut than she expected, but surprisingly comfortable.

"So . . . ," the girl began, "is this going to be okay?"

"It's fine with me," Faith said.

Faith saw all the breath flow out of the girl. Watched her exhale.

"Good," Sarah said. "Then we're good here. I'll go bring our stuff in from the car."

She was back less than a minute later, and Faith sat and watched as the girl hung their scant clothes on hooks on the wall.

"We don't have blankets," Sarah said. "But I know where there are some clean fly sheets. And some light cotton blankets for the horses. They'll do, I think."

"Not sure I can sleep without a pillow. I guess I can roll up some clothes for now."

"That's the spirit," Sarah said.

Faith wasn't sure if she was being derisive or genuinely supportive. Anything was possible now, with the girl so happy. Or, if not happy, at least temporarily buoyed. Any change in Sarah's personality was to be expected.

"Tomorrow I'm going to drive into Santa Barbara," Faith said. The girl stopped hanging clothes and turned to stare at her. "I'm going to trade in my car and get something different."

"Why? What's wrong with your car?"

"Nothing's wrong with it. Except that your father knows it. He's seen it a dozen times. He might even know the license number. I'll feel better if we're driving something he's never seen."

"Oh," Sarah said. She sat down hard on the end of Faith's cot. "I never thought of that."

"I give you permission to think about the horse and let me worry about stuff like that."

"Thank you."

"While I'm down there, I'll buy pillows."

"Get a couple towels," Sarah added.

"Right. Towels. Check."

Then the girl pulled to her feet and resumed arranging their new living quarters. It was

Spartan, to put it mildly. But, combined with the bathroom and shower down the aisle, it struck Faith as everything she and the girl needed.

At least for now.

A few minutes later the girl surprised her with a sudden statement. Or the beginning of one, anyway.

"Speaking of my father . . . ," she said.

But they hadn't been for a long time.

"What about him?"

"You don't think he'd look for me here, do you?"

"No. Of course not. If I thought he'd look for you here, we wouldn't be here."

"But he knows how much I want to see my horse."

"But why would anyone think John would let us hang around? I mean, that was a really odd set of circumstances that no one would imagine. Generally if a former horse owner went to see the horse in a new place . . . I mean, what new owner would let them stay longer than it took to say a quick hello?"

The girl said nothing for a time. Almost as though she never planned to.

"Yeah, that's true, I guess," she said at last.

They didn't talk about it again. But it left a bad taste in Faith's mouth.

She texted her friend Ava with the simple

message: I'm okay, by the way. Just so someone would know she was okay. And worry if they thought she wasn't. She had to walk out into the fading sunlight outside the barn to get the text to send.

It was dark out, but a little too early to go to sleep, when Faith suggested Sarah call her grandmother again. Sarah agreed quickly, but had to step out of the barn to get the reception she needed. Faith stayed behind, exhausted, her fully dressed body feeling as though it had sunk down and fused with the canvas cot.

Several minutes passed, and then the girl came back, extending the phone in Faith's direction.

"She wants to talk to you. But you have to take it outside, just right out into the air outside the barn doors, otherwise it cuts in and out too much." She extended the phone farther, as if nudging Faith to take it. "Here. Hurry, before it drops the call."

Faith sighed as quietly as possible, then forced her spent body to move again. Her limbs felt like concrete, but she pushed hard and they came halfway alive.

She didn't feel she had done that much at the horse show the past two days. Just walked around a lot in the heat. She wondered how Sarah must feel after her two days of grooming and riding. Then again, Sarah was used to grooming and riding. She was in shape for it. More importantly, she was fourteen. She was not in her late thirties like Faith. Not that late thirties is the least bit old, Faith thought. But on days like this she sure didn't feel fourteen.

She accepted the phone from the girl and carried it through the dim barn aisle. Past the horses, slumbering on their feet in their stalls. Their eyes popped open briefly as Faith came by, then drifted closed again.

Faith stepped out into the cool late-evening darkness. A nearly full moon shone its light on the neighboring hills. It glinted off the white railing of the racehorses' oval track. Soft lights glowed in three small cabin-like houses. People lived here on the farm, though she was not sure if John was one of them.

Faith could hear the soft nickering of a horse in the next barn over. Talking to a horse neighbor, or maybe to himself. Maybe just keeping himself company.

She was stalling and she knew it. She looked down at the lighted screen of the phone. The call had not dropped.

"Hi, Constance," she said, pressing the phone to her ear.

"Faith. Good. I just really wanted to thank you. I just had quite a talk with Sarah. She's so happy she's downright giddy."

"Yeah," Faith said. "It's nice. But it also

worries me a little. It's like her mood is way up because she's with her horse. I just don't want to know what happens when it drops. You know John has the mare up for sale, right?"

A long silence on the line. Long and freighted with just the sort of reservations Faith had been grappling with herself.

"No, she didn't tell me that," Constance said at last. "Only the good parts."

"He's not doing well selling her. She doesn't seem to want to work well for anyone except Sarah. Including John. If we play our cards right, and life cuts us a break, we might be able to stay with the mare all summer. Follow them from the farm to the shows and back to the farm."

"Good," Constance said. "Because this custody thing is complicated, and it's going to take time. It's going to take . . . well, I'm tempted to say a miracle. Nobody wants to hear why we're suspicious of him, or that he might be hiding something. They're pretty fact oriented. They want proof."

Faith wanted to know if the authorities were adamant to know the girl's whereabouts, but she couldn't bring herself to ask. Instead she asked, "Did you run into Sarah's father before you left the beach?"

"No. I got out fast. But he's watching my house. I think. I mean, somebody is."

A bank of floodlights came on suddenly in the

covered arena, and Faith watched at a distance as the silhouette of a rider led the silhouette of her horse up to a mounting block and mounted up. The pair rode inside, warming up at a brisk walk.

And Constance was still talking. "I think he was watching my house before I took her and ran to the beach," she said. "I think that's how he found us. He was following us around the whole time." A pause. "Mostly I just really wanted to thank you," Constance continued, as if she hadn't just dropped a bombshell about Harlan's watchful presence, "for being somebody I could trust. For proving I was right to put my trust in you. After you left I had this major panic attack because I sent Sarah off with a woman I hadn't known all that long. You know. That same old thing again. It was inevitable. But I knew you had her best interests at heart. I just knew it. I could feel it in my bones."

The horse and rider silhouette transitioned smoothly into a trot and began performing half passes. Or leg yields. Faith wasn't sure how to tell the difference.

"I definitely want her to be okay," Faith said. "Just keep your fingers crossed he doesn't suddenly find a buyer for that mare. I hate to think what happens after that. But for now, we're good here. For the moment I can honestly say we're okay right where we are."

. . .

By the time Faith had indulged Constance's need to talk and made her way back into the tack stall, the girl was asleep. The overhead light was blazing, but Sarah snored lightly with her head dropped back and her mouth open wide.

Maybe being only fourteen wasn't enough to buy your way out of utter exhaustion.

Faith picked up one of the clean horse blankets the girl had left folded in the corner—a white cotton blanket with blue crosshatched lines on its fabric—and draped it over the girl, careful not to hit her with any metal buckles.

Then she switched off the light and tried to get some sleep herself.

She woke in the middle of the night needing to use the bathroom. She rose carefully, quietly, so as not to wake the girl.

But as she eased back the rolling door, a soft light spread into the room. Some was from the nearly full moon outside the open barn doors. Part came from weak LED lights along the barn aisle that kept the horses from being cast into pitch-darkness.

By this light, Faith could see the girl's cot. It was empty.

Her first thought was that Sarah had gone to seek out the restroom herself. But as she stepped out into the cool concrete aisle, she heard the girl speaking quietly. Nearly in a whisper.

For a moment she followed the sound, wondering who Sarah could be talking to. But a few steps later, Faith saw the dark shape of the girl in Midnight's stall.

She was talking to her mare.

Faith turned and walked the opposite way, toward the restroom. It was none of her business what Sarah had to say to her horse. It was a conversation that Faith could stay out of, leaving the girl alone with what she loved most in the world. Letting her thoughts remain private.

No one needed to know except Midnight, and secrets are always safe with a horse.

Chapter Eleven

Like a Prodigy

When Faith got back to the Los Alamos farm in her "new" used car, no one was out riding on the property except Sarah and Midnight.

The sun was just about to disappear behind the western hills. The girl was practicing transitions in the outdoor dressage arena. Halt to canter, canter to halt. Also right-angle turns, working her mare in a ten-or-so-meter invisible box.

When she looked up and saw Faith she waved and let the mare's reins go long, allowing the horse's neck to stretch out and down.

Girl and horse walked to her, both looking relaxed.

"That looks like a pretty nice car," Sarah called when she was close enough to be heard. "Not that I had anything against your other car. How did you afford it?"

She rode the mare right up to the passenger side of the Volvo, then around the front fender in an approving half circle.

"Straight trade," Faith said. "No cash required. The back seat folds down. I thought that might come in handy at shows. Assuming there are going to be more shows."

"Oh, there are," the girl said. "Starting this weekend."

"And we're going?"

"Oh, yeah."

"Does he want you to ride her in the sales class thing?"

"There probably won't be one," Sarah said. "That was a new thing they were doing at the horse park. I think they might do it again in July. But most shows don't have that. But people still know which horses are for sale. And he'll still be looking for buyers."

"Oh," Faith said. The single word sounded down, because she was.

It struck her suddenly that she was tired from the day trip—and possibly other factors as well. They fell silent for a time, Midnight's soft-looking nose just inches from Faith's shoulder. For a moment she wanted to reach out and stroke the black velvet of the mare's coat. As though she had developed some affection for the animal, which came as a mild surprise. But Faith was afraid of the horse, too.

She raised one hand to shield her eyes from the setting sun and looked up at the girl.

"Why are *you* schooling her? Where's John?"

The girl shrugged. "I don't know. I think he went home. He got frustrated. You know. Everything always being a fight with the two of them. He told me I should school her all week, and then we'll see if it settles her down any for the show this weekend. I wasn't going to argue with him."

"No," Faith said. "I wouldn't imagine you would." Then she added, "John doesn't live here?"

"No. He lives in town."

"But you're sure it's okay that we do. For now."

"Yeah. I told you. I'm going to take her out on the trail. I heard there's a place you can ride off the property and up into the hills if you can open a gate from the back of your horse. Or at least remount from the ground after. John never takes them out on the trail. Never. I asked him. He just schools them all week and then goes to shows every weekend when there is one. Too much work and no relaxing, that's what I think. The trail once a week is good for their mind."

"It'll be dark soon."

"We'll be back in time," she said, and reined her mare around. With a barely perceptible press of Sarah's booted legs, the mare broke into a smooth trot. They headed west.

Faith watched until they were no bigger than a speck in the distance. Then she turned back toward the barn and was startled to see another woman standing nearby, watching the girl and mare go. She was maybe thirtysomething, slim and athletic-looking, in full riding gear. She even had her helmet on and a whip in her gloved hand. Faith had never seen her before.

"It's almost spooky," the woman said.

"What is?"

"It's just not something you expect a kid to be able to do by the time she's fourteen. She must be like the textbook definition of a natural. Reminds me of those five-year-olds who play perfect piano concertos and nobody can really explain how. She's like a prodigy."

"Oh," Faith said. "I guess I don't know enough about dressage to know how remarkable she is."

"Too bad," the woman said. "Because it's really something."

Then she dropped her head, shook it a few times, and wandered away.

Faith drove her new used Volvo south on the freeway, following John's massive trailer. Now and then she glanced over at the girl. Sarah sat slumped in the passenger seat, a gray file folder on her lap. She had the cover open and was staring at whatever was inside. But Faith couldn't see what it was.

"Day sheets?" she asked after a time.

"No," the girl said. Then she sighed. "I wouldn't have to stare at day sheets. I'm not riding. John's the one who has to keep track of his rides."

"Mind if I ask what's so fascinating?"

"It's not," Sarah said. "It's really, really dull."

She turned the open folder toward Faith, who

glanced away from the road quickly, then looked back. The last thing she wanted to do was take her eyes off the road when following the trailer and its precious cargo.

What she saw in that brief glance was a photo of John riding Midnight—the same photo she'd seen in the Sales Horse Presentation Class catalogue at the horse park—with text underneath.

"What does it say?"

"Same thing it said in the catalogue. It's just a flyer of that same catalogue stuff. Because there's no catalogue at this show. Told you it was dull."

The girl stared out the window for a moment. Faith thought she could feel Sarah wanting to say something. But, of course, she could be wrong.

Her brain suddenly filled with her friend Ava's advice.

What if you just tell your brain to shut up and go with the part of you that knows?

The girl spoke up suddenly.

"He wants me to put them up on the inside of the porta-potty doors. The women's ones."

"He doesn't want to sell her to a guy?"

"No, silly. He can put them in the men's ones himself."

"Oh. Right."

John exited onto a smaller freeway, headed east, in his huge truck and trailer. Faith followed.

"At the horse park, weren't the porta-potties all just unisex?"

"I think so. But at this farm they have three for the ladies and two for the guys. At least, that's how it was last year." She stared out the window for a few moments, then added, "I guess if I didn't do it, he'd never know."

"He might."

"He's not going in the ladies' ones."

"He might see somebody going in or coming out with the door wide open, though."

"And then maybe he'll just think somebody took it down and took it with them because they were interested." Sarah paused. Sighed deeply. All her energy seemed to drain out into the sigh. "I'm not going to do that, though. John's being nice to us. And even if he wasn't, I'm not going to lie to somebody's face like that. I'm not a liar."

"Good," Faith said. "I'm glad to know that."

"I'm not my father."

Faith pulled a long, deep breath at the mention of the man. As if shoring herself up.

"If I thought you were your father," she said, "I wouldn't be traveling with you."

They drove in silence for a time. The highway was a narrow two-lane rural road, passing farms and ranches. Horses grazed, cattle grazed. On one property, llamas or alpacas grazed. Faith had no idea how to tell the two animals apart.

"I kept meaning to thank you for that," Sarah said. Faith could feel effort behind the girl's words. They did not come easily. "Traveling with me, I mean. It's just . . . there was so much going on when we left the beach. I think we were all sort of in shock. But I wanted to say thank you for taking me like you did, so I didn't have to go back with my father. And especially for taking me to where Midnight was, not just where you wanted to go. I think most people would never have done that for me. And also I wanted to say I was sorry, for the trouble you had with him. Because if you hadn't gotten mixed up with me, you never would have gotten into that messed-up situation. But there was so much going on, and then none of that stuff got said even though I totally meant for it to."

Faith opened her mouth to answer, even though she wasn't sure what the answer was going to be.

The girl cut her off.

"Oh, we're here already," she said.

And that was the last they spoke of thank-yous and sorrys for the weekend and beyond.

Faith sat under a huge canopy on a folding chair at a concessions stand, watching a woman she didn't know ride a test. It was a fair distance from where she sat to the arena, but it felt important to Faith to stay in the shade.

It was the following late morning, just as the day eased into its overwhelming heat.

She looked up to see a man she'd never met standing over her, staring down at her. Something in her gut jumped, froze, then flipped over. At least, that was the way it felt.

"Sorry," he said. "Did I startle you?"

He was in his late thirties, prematurely bald, with soft-looking blond hair—what there was of it—and dressed in formal riding gear. The coat had tails, which Faith now knew signified the upper-level FEI classes.

"Not your fault," she said. "It seems to be my default mode."

"You're Sarah's new friend?"

"I am."

"Dean Burwell," he said, and stuck out his hand.

Faith shook it. But still she made no connection with who he was to Sarah, or to her.

"I'm Midnight's trainer and Sarah's riding instructor. Or at least I was, until a handful of weeks ago. From her old barn. Dressage Journeys in Moorpark."

"Dean," she said, and relaxed the rest of the way back to normal. At least, her new normal. "Right. I was there in the car with Sarah when she called you last weekend. I told her I wanted to meet you next time."

"I wanted to meet you, too," he said. "Buy you a soft drink?"

Faith looked at the bare table in front of her. It did seem odd, she supposed, to sit in this booth and eat and drink nothing. Truthfully, she was a little bit thirsty, but had fallen into the habit of saving money whenever possible.

"Sure," she said.

She stood.

They walked together to the table where drinks and sandwiches were being sold, one of his hands outstretched as if to guide her by the small of her back, but not touching her. It was an oddly formal gesture, she thought.

"We had no idea Midnight was being sold," he said, his voice dense with what sounded like genuine sorrow. "Not until the minute John Wintermeyer pulled his trailer onto our property and loaded her up. So far as we knew, Sarah and her grandmother were going to board the mare in Los Osos until they got all their trouble worked out. And then we figured they'd come back when they could. When John showed up with a bill of sale, we cried. Literally cried. All three of us. Cara and Lainie and me. And I'm not a crier. Last time I'd cried was twelve years ago when my mother died."

Faith chose a bottle of apple juice from a cooler filled with crushed ice. Its freezing wetness felt good in her hand. Dean grabbed a bottle of water and paid with a five, not bothering to wait for his change. Or maybe there was no change.

They found a seat at an empty table. The table Faith had been using was now taken.

"So you were close with Sarah?"

"Teach somebody to ride for ten years, yeah. You're going to feel close."

"Ten years? But Sarah's only . . ."

"Right. I know. She was *four* when her mother brought her in. Determined to ride. Nothing was going to stop her. We had a little pony at the time—well, we still have him but he's retired. He's old now. Hercules. Stands no higher than my waist. Her mother bought her a good helmet, and I tried to put the pony on a line for her. You know. Like a longe line. So I had some control. I mean, he was an angel of a pony, but still. The kid was four. But she was having none of it. She was going to ride that pony. By herself. And nobody was going to get in her way."

"Like a prodigy," Faith said.

Dean peered into her face for a moment. "Yes," he said. "I think that's more than fair to say. When her mother saw what a natural she was at riding, she relaxed some. Did you know she was only eight when her dad bought her that mare?"

Faith blinked a few times before answering. It just raised so many questions. In the end, she asked none of them.

She only said, "That's a lot of horse for an eight-year-old."

"She was, yeah. Especially since the mare was only a baby. Three years old. Heather was furious at him for doing it. Just furious. She thought he was going to get that girl killed. They almost divorced over it—she was that mad. Now, looking back, I guess we sort of all wish they had, but . . . well, anyway. Sarah and that horse were meant to be. They just bonded, right from the start. I'm not saying the mare didn't spook, or have her moments. But right from the start you could see her wanting to take care of that little girl. Also, that little girl was one hell of a rider. A prodigy, like you said. We used to joke that she had Velcro sticking her to the saddle. Nothing could peel her off. She never once came off that mare. But I guess it might have been partly because the mare didn't want her to come off. She was careful. She was very attached to the girl. I'm not the least bit surprised to hear she isn't working well for anybody else."

Faith took a long gulp of the cold juice. It shocked her going down, but in a good way. Again, her head was filled with questions. So many questions, jostling each other for a place in line.

Instead of any of them, she heard herself ask, "Are all horses so emotional?"

Dean sat back in his chair and smiled, but not really at or to Faith. It was as if he were sharing a good joke with himself in the privacy of his head.

"Here's the thing about horses," he said. "They're like people in one respect—that each one of them is a complete and total individual. People who are just looking at horses from a distance might not see that. But once you get in and work with them, you find out fast. They have their own likes and dislikes. They have people and horses they like and others they don't, and it might not be clear why. It's just a preference. They have their own opinions about things. Very distinct personalities. So, no, not every horse is quite as emotional as Midnight. But some are. And it's not unusual for a horse to want things a certain way and be pretty unhappy if he doesn't get it. Sorry. I guess I'm talking your ear off here."

"I don't mind about that. I've been trying to figure something out, but I can't, because I don't know enough about the situation. Sarah thinks one thing and John thinks another, and I don't know how to reconcile the two."

"And the thing is . . . ?"

"I guess just whether she's a horse somebody can really be safe riding. I mean, somebody who's not Sarah."

"There's a thing we call a 'safe' horse," he began. "It's really just an expression. No horse is guaranteed safe. They evolved to run away from danger, and any horse can spook and cause the rider problems. What we call a safe horse is one who's pretty quiet and unlikely to escalate a little spook into a big disaster. They're fairly few and far between. Most of the horses people call safe are really shut down or broken down, almost dead inside, and you wouldn't use them in dressage. Rental horses, mostly. I wouldn't call Midnight a safe horse in that context, no. But I rode her and never had an issue with her. I rode her every single lesson for fifteen minutes before putting Sarah on. It was part of the mare's training. Then again, I didn't take her to a new place where Sarah was out of the picture. It was all part of helping the girl ride her, and I think a horse can understand a thing like that."

They sat quietly for a moment, sipping their drinks. In the arena, an older woman was trotting a chunky, compact chestnut horse down the long side of the arena. Faith heard a bell ring.

"Argh," Dean said.

The woman slowed to a walk and turned, seeming to have lost the momentum, even the direction, of her ride.

"What was that all about?" she asked Dean.

"She went off course again. The judge rings the bell when the rider is off course. She can still finish her test, but that was her second off-course, so she loses four points. One more and she's disqualified."

They sat quietly for another minute or two. Watching. Wanting the woman not to go off course again, even though they didn't know her. Then Faith realized that Dean might know everybody here.

"You know that woman?" she asked.

"I don't."

"And yet here we are, hoping she doesn't make another mistake."

"Well, that's the better side of human nature," Dean said. "Let's not argue with that."

The woman rode her stocky horse down the centerline and executed her halt and salute at X.

Faith and Dean both let out a long sigh of relief.

"So, I know people think the mare is impossible," he said. "And, for that matter, I've talked to a few people who think Sarah is, too. But back at the barn, we just adored Sarah. I mean, yeah, she's a teenager. But we love her. She's a good kid. Things were really different for her before her mother died and her father sold the mare. That was a one-two punch that could bring down just about anybody. And it's just . . ."

He paused for a strange length of time, and Faith had another of those small knowings. Once again, she could feel that the person in front of her was trying to say something big. Important and big.

This time she simply believed what she knew.

"How do I say this?" he continued. "That girl and that mare, they belong together. They need to be together. That girl has put her whole life outside of school into riding dressage, and that horse is her partner. Her match. It's so wrong for them to be separated that we can hardly even sleep at night. It's like the world should have shifted off its axis because this is so wrong, what happened, and we can't figure out how life is just going on like it's all okay. The more time you spend around her, the more I hope you're getting that."

"I think I pretty well have it," Faith said. "I just don't know what anybody can do about it."

Dean looked up into her eyes, then quickly back down at the table. He ran his thumb along the wet label of his water bottle. Then he ran the same hand over his deeply receded hairline, leaving the light wisps of hair slightly wet.

This is it, Faith thought. *Here comes the thing he needs so badly to say.*

"I know you've done a lot for Sarah already," he said. "And I know I've got a lot of nerve even bringing this up. But I just have to take a shot here. I don't suppose there's any chance you could afford to buy Midnight back?"

Faith let out a choking sound, half laugh and half cough.

"He wants seventy-five thousand dollars for her!"

"Right. I know. I wish I could say that was inflated, but she's worth all that and more. Cara and Lainie and I tried to cobble some money together, but everything we had to spare added up to less than ten thousand dollars. We were just pathetically short."

"There's no way me going in with you gets the

pot to seventy-five. No way at all. I'm right in the middle of an uncomfortable divorce, and I just walked away from everything."

"Maybe . . . don't walk away from everything? I mean, assuming there's much there that you walked away from. Which of course I have no idea. Is there still time to change your mind and tell him you want half?" Dean dropped his face into his hands. He rubbed his eyes briskly and then popped up again, talking. "In case you're wondering, 'Does this guy know he's being unconscionably inappropriate here?' the answer is yes. He does. I have no right to ask you any of this, and I'm sorry. It's rude, and it's not like me to be rude. But it's so important. I just felt like I had to take a shot."

Faith sat back and watched him avoid her eyes. She realized she liked Dean more as a result of this impropriety. Not less. Because he was putting himself on the line for Sarah. Out of loyalty to the girl. And the horse.

"First of all," she began, "I'm not at all sure I'm safe with him at this point. So I don't really dare go back and tell him anything. But even if I hired an attorney to contact him . . . the money's just not there. He wasn't doing that well. *We* weren't doing that well, I guess I should say. I shouldn't put it all off on him. I could have worked, and then we would have had more saved up, but I didn't. The mortgage on the house is . . .

well, not literally underwater, but the equity in it adds up to nearly nothing. Plus he lives there, so I wouldn't want to force him to sell it. We do have some retirement savings, but my half of them falls a long way short of what I'd need to buy that mare. If John was selling her for fifty thousand dollars, I might possibly squeeze that out of the divorce if I had a ton of nerve to stand up to my angry ex. But John's selling her for a lot more, and he's made it clear that's as low as he can afford to go."

"I get it," Dean said, and took another long drink of water. "I get it completely. We're all in the same boat. I don't know too many people who have a spare seventy-five thousand dollars lying around. I'm sorry to put you on the spot. Don't feel bad, because what you're doing for Sarah right now is the next best thing. It's the best thing any of us can do for her. You're keeping her away from her father, and you're giving her the chance to stay with the mare for now. It's an amazing sacrifice, what you're doing. The last thing I want to do is make you feel you're not doing enough for Sarah. You are."

"It's okay," she said. And it was. "I get it."

Dean stood, as if to leave.

"Where *is* Sarah, anyway?" Faith added. "I haven't seen her all morning."

"Last I saw her she was putting the mare away. Some prospective buyer wanted to ride her, so

Sarah brought her out and tried to help it go well. It did *not* go well."

"Did she put somebody else off?"

"No. It wasn't that bad. But that was the only way it could have been worse. The lady tried to spur her forward and she bolted. First she wouldn't stop, then she stopped too fast. A lot of riders might have gone off at that point, but fortunately this one had a good seat. But suffice it to say the mare is not yet sold." He flipped his empty water bottle back and forth at the end of his fingers. "Well," he said. "It was a pleasure meeting you. But I have to go warm up. I ride in forty minutes."

"Good luck," she said, wondering if that was the right thing to say to a dressage rider on his way into a test. You sure as hell wouldn't want to say "Break a leg."

Dean walked away, the crisp figure of him—in his formal riding outfit—growing softer and more diffuse in the shimmering waves of summer heat.

Faith found Sarah in one of the warm-up arenas, warming up the mare for John's ride. The girl was dressed informally, in tan breeches and a gray T-shirt. The back and underarms of her shirt were soaked through with sweat as she rode Midnight in a sitting trot.

Not a minute later John showed up, fully

dressed for his class, and told her to jump down.

Sarah did.

Faith watched carefully, and saw the girl speaking softly to the mare, almost directly into her ear, as John mounted from the ground.

Then the girl walked out of the arena, joining Faith outside the rails. Together they leaned. And observed.

"You seem nervous," Faith said. Because somehow it felt better just to take the feeling head-on.

"I am," Sarah said.

"More so than usual?"

"Yeah."

For the next minute or two they watched John warm up in silence. The mare seemed fairly relaxed underneath him. She wasn't coming alive the way she did for Sarah. Neither was she misbehaving. And her neck was nicely round, showing acceptance of the bit and a good, relaxed submission.

Then it struck Faith as surprising that she knew all that. The world of dressage was rubbing off on her more quickly than she had realized.

"I begged her to be good for John," Sarah said, bumping Faith out of her thoughts. "I need her to do better on this test. Better than she did last weekend. Fifty-eight. That was pretty bad. She has to beat fifty-eight. Otherwise I'm afraid John's going to give up. If I worked with her all week and she's no better for him, I think he might just get frustrated and tell us to go away."

"So that's what you were saying in her ear."

"Oh. You saw that? Yeah." The girl turned her face away in embarrassment. "And I thought we could stay real close to the arena, where she can see me. Oh. He's going in! Come on. We need to stay close to her. Come on, Faith. Let's go."

She dragged Faith away by the sleeve, following John and the mare.

"Please be good, please be good, please be good," Sarah repeated under her breath. Over and over again.

John and the mare were riding their test in a covered arena. The low rails marking the twenty-by-sixty-meter dressage arena had been set up several feet inside a chest-high solid-wood barrier that formed the outside of the greater structure.

Faith and Sarah leaned on the solid fence and watched, hanging on every transition, every movement. So far Midnight and John seemed to be doing fairly well. At least, to Faith's untrained eye.

A moment later, the girl sucked in her breath audibly.

"Aw, man," she said. "That wasn't good. Two points off for that."

But Faith never learned what flaw the girl had witnessed. It had all looked fine to her.

Just for one breathtaking movement, the extended trot, the mare seemed to come out of her shell, offering the lift and reach she so naturally gave to Sarah.

Seconds later, in the tempi changes, she kicked out in back before settling and performing the flying lead change.

Sarah sucked in her breath again. Her hands flew up and covered her eyes.

"I can't look," she said. "I can't bring myself to look, Faith. Tell me how she's doing."

"Looks fine to me. But I don't know this work the way you do."

"Is she doing the changes?"

Faith watched for a few seconds before answering.

"Yeah. They look nice and even."

"No more kicking out?"

"No. Not yet. Okay, now they're doing the extended canter. Ooh. It looks good."

Sarah dropped her hands and opened her eyes.

"Nice," she said, drawing out the word into multiple syllables. "Oh, please be good, girl. Please, please, please be good."

Faith looked away from the performance entirely and watched the girl's face instead. It had gone ghostly white. Then, suddenly, it morphed into a spasm of pain.

Faith looked back into the arena to see John finishing his test on the halt and salute. But instead of rounding her neck nicely, the mare had thrown her head high, fighting against the reins. John worked for a second or two to get her back on the bit. Then he seemed to give up.

He saluted the judge, as if the halt had been properly executed, and rode Midnight out of the arena.

Sarah trotted to meet him at the gate, and Faith followed.

"There was a lot good about that ride," Sarah said as John rode out into the hot afternoon sun.

John smiled a wry, crooked smile. "If you mean some parts of it were better than others, I have to agree. Anyway, we'll see what the judge has to say."

They sat together in the concession booth, Faith and the girl, eating sandwiches in the blessed shade. Well, Faith was eating her sandwich. Sarah was ignoring hers.

"This is killing me," the girl said.

Her eyes remained glued to the board in the distance. It was on the inside of the wide-open door of the show office. From this vantage point, they could see the score sheets affixed to the board, waiting for more scores to be written. When someone finally came out to add scores, they would see.

John was standing in the blazing sun, just to the left of the board. Waiting.

"He's going to tell us to get lost," Sarah said. "I just know it."

"You don't know that," Faith said. "Your mind is just filling up with fears."

"What does he need me for? I'm just a big pain in his butt. The only reason he's keeping me around is in case I can help him with Midnight. But he's too impatient, you know? He wants everything to be perfect *right now*. He doesn't give things enough time to work themselves out. How somebody like him can be happy working with horses, I'll never know."

"He doesn't seem very happy," Faith said, "now that you mention it."

The girl launched out of her chair and sprinted at full speed toward the show office. Faith rose to follow at a brisk trot. Beyond the girl's head Faith could see a woman raising a pen or pencil to write on the sheets. A young man passed on his horse, and the horse spooked and reared at the sight of the sprinting girl, almost unseating its rider. Sarah ran on, seeming not to notice.

By the time Faith arrived at the open office door, the writer of scores had gone back inside, and Sarah and John were talking quietly.

Faith quickly scanned for John's name, followed by the horse Falkner's Midnight Sun.

His score was 62.897.

"Yeah, it's an *improvement,*" she heard John say. "Hardly anything to write home about, but it gives me hope. At least we're moving in the right direction. So here's what we'll do this week. We'll do things a little differently. Instead of you schooling her for me, you get on her for, say, twenty minutes a day. And then I'll get on after you. And you stay close by where she can see you the whole time I'm riding. And we'll see if we can't keep this streak of improvement going into next weekend's show."

Faith felt a heavy sliver of dread break away and leave her, like an iceberg calving. It was, in fact, more dread than she even knew she'd been holding.

It was a relief to feel it go.

MID-JULY, BACK TO THE MIDDLE
OF THE THING

Chapter Twelve

What She Should Have Told You

Faith sat in the driver's seat, her hands grasping the steering wheel until her knuckles blanched white. She braved a glance over at the girl. Sarah's face was turned away, but she did not seem to be looking out the window. Not that there was much to see. They were still parked in the trailer area of the horse park.

"I would drive away now," Faith said. "But I have no idea where we want to go."

No reply from the girl.

A movement caught Faith's eye through the windshield. She looked up to see Estelle LaMaster walking briskly toward her car. She hit the ignition button and powered down the window.

Estelle smiled, but it was a tight little thing with a great deal of sadness behind it. The older woman leaned down and stuck her face almost through the open window. Faith leaned back against the headrest to allow Estelle more room. Clearly it was the girl she had come to address.

"Darling," Estelle said. She waited for the girl to turn her face toward the new voice. Sarah never did. "I've come to apologize for John. Poor dear John. He means well—I believe that with every fiber of my being. But he doesn't always do well. In fact, often not. He's a bit shut down from his own emotions, so I guess he figures everyone will want to play a sad goodbye the way he would, which is to say, avoid it outright. But I thought you might want to see your mare before I take her home with me." She paused again, waiting for some reaction from the girl. None came. "It's up to you, of course."

A long, still silence.

Then Sarah popped the passenger door open and stepped out. She marched with a determination that surprised Faith, especially since the girl could not possibly know the specifics of where she was going.

Faith and Estelle followed, unable to catch up.

A moment later the girl stopped in her tracks and looked around.

"It's the horse box, darling," Estelle called.

Faith had no idea what a horse box was, but apparently Sarah knew. She headed straight to a silvery vehicle that looked like a small motorhome—a van cab up front with a tall box mounted on the chassis behind. Based on the number, size, and height of the windows, Faith assumed it was not designed as human living quarters. On its driver's side was a nearly life-size decal of a braided dressage horse silhouette, its rider in a classical top hat.

The girl trotted around the vehicle and disappeared.

Faith and Estelle followed.

On the van's right side, most of the wall of the box dropped down to form a ramp, rubber-covered to keep a horse's hooves from slipping as they walked up. The ramp was down, the whole side of the box open. Inside, Faith could see the mare, rear-facing, her halter clipped with a strap, munching hay from a hanging bag. Sarah trotted up the ramp. She ducked under a sturdy bar across the open doorway and stepped in, and Midnight turned her head to the girl and nickered in greeting.

"I've never seen anything like this for hauling a horse," Faith said. "And I've been hanging around at horse shows all summer."

"They're very popular in Europe," Estelle said. "In fact, some Americans call them Eurovans. They've been using them over there, France and Germany and the UK and the like, for decades now. They're only just starting to use them here, but I do think they'll catch on." She took hold of a bit of the fabric of Faith's sleeve. "Come," she said. "Let's let these two have their moment in privacy."

She led Faith several yards away, and they stopped and faced each other.

Estelle held out a business card.

"It's an open invitation," she said.

Faith took the card, not yet understanding what was an open invitation.

Fortunately, Estelle was still talking. "I live in the Santa Ynez Valley. Los Olivos. Not far at all from John's barn. Maybe fifteen or twenty miles south and east of there. Just a small horse property. Private. I don't board or train for others, so it's quiet. I have a guest room. Only one, though, so the two of you would have to be happy in two twin beds in the same room. But you're welcome to come for a visit if that's good enough for your comfort."

Faith laughed out loud. Partly because a huge chunk of tension and sadness had just rushed out of her. Partly at the idea that Faith would view two twin beds in a guest room as sparse accommodations.

"For the last six weeks we've been living on twin cots in the same tack stall. Covered by horse blankets. Unless we were at a show, in which case we didn't have all that luxury."

"I hope at least they were *clean* horse blankets."

"Yes. That much luxury we had."

"I think you'll find it comfortable, then," Estelle said. "And while the mare is new with us, as she's settling in and my granddaughter is getting to know her, well . . . that would be the ideal time, don't you think? In other words, soon."

"You have no idea how much you're helping her by offering."

"It's lovely for us as well. I know she'll be quite useful helping the mare with this transition. And I have grooms, so the girl won't be slave labor to me—no offense to John. You'll be my guests."

Faith looked up to see the girl standing behind Estelle, hands on her hips, looking more petulant than sad.

"Why didn't you wait and get a vet check first?" Sarah asked, her voice a hard bark. "Why would anybody pay this much for a horse without getting a vet check?"

Estelle turned to address the girl. "I *am* getting a pre-purchase exam for the mare," she said. "Of course I am. Where I come from, you don't even take a horse for free without a pre-purchase exam. It's not just the money you spend on the horse, but the money you'll spend on the vet care later."

"But you're taking her home," the girl said.

It struck Faith that Sarah was trying to invalidate the purchase—and thus the occasion of parting—somehow. As if finding a flaw in the logic of Estelle's business deal could turn the moment back around.

"But I haven't paid John for her or signed a bill of sale. That's contingent on a reasonably clean exam and good sets of X-rays. Why? Do you know something about the mare's condition that I should know?"

The girl allowed a pause, one Faith figured to be only two or three seconds long. But a lot rested on that pause, and Faith could feel a great deal packed into it. Sarah could throw a monkey wrench into everything with her answer. But only if she was willing to lie.

I'm not a liar. That's what the girl had said. *I'm not my father.*

"No, ma'am," Sarah said. "She's healthy and sound so far as I know."

"Good," Estelle said. "Hopefully the vet will agree."

Faith tried to move closer to the girl to tell her the good news. To break through Sarah's painful assessment that Midnight was driving away forever by sharing word of Estelle's invitation. But the girl stomped off before she could. And no matter how many times Faith called her name, Sarah never stopped or turned around.

"Thank you so much for your invitation," Faith said to Estelle. "We'll see you in a day or so. Two at most."

Then she turned and trotted after Sarah, who was headed for the car.

When Faith grew close to the Volvo, she unlocked it with her smart key. Sarah opened the door and dropped into the passenger seat without comment.

"I have good news," Faith said.

But the girl had slammed the car door already, and Faith was not sure Sarah could hear.

Faith got in on the driver's side and started the engine.

"Did you hear what I said?"

"No. But maybe because I don't want to hear anything, and I don't care."

"But it's good news."

"No such thing."

Faith popped the car into drive and pulled up the hill toward the gates.

"You're not catching my meaning here, Sarah. It's good news even by your standards. It's your kind of good news."

The girl looked over at Faith then, her face hopeful but afraid. As if hope were an indulgence she could scarcely afford.

Faith dropped Estelle's business card into Sarah's lap.

"She invited us to come to her place as guests. So you can help the mare settle in and help her granddaughter get to know her."

"Great! Let's go now! We'll follow her home. I want to go there right now."

"No," Faith said. She glanced over at the girl, who returned a scorched look but said nothing. "We'll go soon. But not now. There's something you need to do first. And if you stop to think a moment, I know you'll remember what it is."

An awkward silence.

Then Sarah said, "Oh. Right."

"Where is she now?"

"Home."

"Which is . . . ? I think she told me once, but I forgot."

"Thousand Oaks. Okay. I'll call her." She dug her phone out of her jeans pocket. "I shouldn't tell her on the phone, though, right?"

"Definitely not. We should meet somewhere random in between. It should be face to face."

Sarah pressed her thumb onto the screen a couple of times, then held the phone to her ear.

"Hey. Grandma. Hi. Yeah, it's me. We need to talk to you. Not just on the phone, though. Faith says we need to meet up somewhere. There's something I should have told you before. And I'm sorry because I didn't. And I need to tell it to you now."

"Tell her to make absolutely sure she's not followed."

Sarah held the phone to her chest and stared at Faith, a bit blankly. "Why would she be followed? How could she be followed?"

"Just tell her. Please."

The girl put the phone to her ear again. "Faith says make sure you're not followed." A pause. Then, "Okay. Bye." Sarah turned her gaze to Faith again. "She says she knows, and she's got a plan."

"Good."

"I don't get it. I mean, it's not like he's sitting outside her house watching her every move or anything."

Faith didn't answer. While she wasn't answering, she watched the girl's face change. It became more unsteady, figuratively a bit green, as if she were becoming seasick.

"Oh jeez," Sarah said. "Nobody told me that. That's sort of terrifying."

Faith sat on her hands on a smooth wooden bench with no back, watching through the pier railing as waves broke onto the sand.

Constance had chosen to meet at Stearns Wharf, the pier at the end of State Street in Santa Barbara. The sun had gone down, the last of the daylight fading fast. Faith could see the streetlights come on along Cabrillo Boulevard, lighting up a line of palm trees from behind. The moving car headlights grew brighter as she sat and watched, and the lights of the shops and restaurants stood out against the dimness. Meanwhile the mountains behind the city scene faded to nearly invisible, and the first stars came out above them.

Faith turned her head to sneak a glance at Sarah and her grandmother. They were standing at the railing several yards down, leaning and looking out into the harbor. They'd chosen the spot with the fewest tourists milling about. Faith could see only the outline of a lone fisherman a few yards farther down the pier.

It twisted deeply into Faith's belly to see them there, talking. Because she knew what was finally being said.

It was so ugly, what that poor girl had to say. And about her own father. She wondered how anyone could put a girl that age in such a position. But then, Faith figured, it's probably nothing anybody sets out to do. You act, and then you learn later what your actions have done to the people around you. Faith knew that from her own life, but only as a tiny microcosm of this level of disaster.

She watched Constance push off the railing and take hold of the girl by both shoulders. She shook Sarah. Slowly, like pulling and pushing. Toward her, then back again. Oddly, it didn't look or feel angry to Faith. It looked as though she were trying to get through to the girl, to get in. To help her words be absorbed.

A second or two later she pulled Sarah in for a long embrace.

Then they went back to leaning on the railing together. Sarah was looking off into the harbor. Constance had her face in her hands.

Faith looked away. Watched Santa Barbara bustle in the gathering dark of a summer Sunday evening.

A few minutes later Faith was startled by

someone plunking down onto the bench next to her. She looked over to see Sarah, who did not look in her direction. The girl just sat next to her and stared out at nothing, her face streaked with tears.

"You should go talk to her," Sarah said after a time. Her voice was smaller than Faith had ever heard it. She seemed to have lost her courage and most of her life force somewhere along her way through that impossible task.

"Why should *I* go talk to her?"

"Because I don't know what else to say."

They sat in silence for a moment.

Then Faith stood. "Stay close by," she said.

She walked slowly along the railing to where Constance stood leaning.

The older woman glanced over to see who had arrived, then turned her face out toward the sea again. Faith leaned on the railing, just a few inches from Constance's elbow. She said nothing for a long time. Neither woman said anything for a long time.

Constance was the one to break the silence.

"Part of me wants to say . . . Partly I feel like . . . Like . . . I knew it, I knew it, I knew it! I knew it was him all along. It was all his fault. It always is. And then another part of me wants to say, 'Oh my God, I had no idea!' I thought he *drove her to it*. I thought it was his fault, but I still thought she was the one who . . . And it doesn't make sense in my head, because now I'm having trouble figuring out how both those things can feel so real and so true at the same time."

"Every time I turn around life throws me a situation where two conflicting things are true at the same time. At least since I grew up and got married. Seems like the older I get, the less things want to agree to be only one way at a time."

Constance turned to her suddenly—Faith was almost tempted to feel that the older woman turned *on* her. There was an anger now in her movements, in her manner. In her very being.

"She told *you*," Constance said. "She told *you*, but she didn't tell me. She only told me now because you said she had to. Why did she tell you and not me? What does that say about my relationship with my only granddaughter?"

"That she loves you a lot."

Constance snorted a bitter laugh. In the brief silence that followed, Faith could hear the roar of a wave breaking on the beach.

"How do you figure?"

"She wanted to tell you, but she was afraid for you. She felt like you were right on the edge, emotionally. She didn't want to be the one to push you over."

A tourist family wandered up to the rail, a man and woman with a medium-sized girl, all three in shorts and flip-flops. The grown-ups looked at Constance and Faith and smiled. Then their smiles seemed to freeze and fade. They could see and feel the tension, the emotional undercurrent.

The man took hold of the sleeve of his daughter's T-shirt, and they hurried away.

"And this is a theory of yours?" Constance asked, her voice still hard.

"No. She told me."

"What did she tell you? What were her exact words? I need to know, Faith."

"She mentioned those old western movies where somebody goes off a cliff. And then the camera pans over the edge, and the person is holding on to this tiny little bush. Or weed, I think Sarah said. And its roots are pulling out, and the situation is getting more and more desperate. She said she didn't want to be the one to do that to you when you were trying to hold on."

Constance burst into tears. She pressed her face onto her folded forearms and sobbed into the safety of them.

Faith moved to put an arm around the older woman's shoulders, then froze and doubted herself. For a moment she just stood awkwardly, one arm raised but going nowhere. Her brain shifting back and forth regarding the right thing to do.

But it was so tiring, fighting with herself. So ever present and so utterly exhausting.

Faith placed one hand between Constance's

shoulder blades and left it there for several minutes, the silence only punctuated by breaking waves and the occasional audible sob.

In time, Constance picked up her head. Straightened.

Faith dug through her purse for the packet of fresh tissues, pulled one out and offered it up.

"Thank you," the older woman said. She wiped her eyes, then blew her nose lightly.

"How did you get away safely?" Faith asked, glancing over her shoulder at the girl, who was, blessedly, still sitting on the bench.

"I walked out my back door. Through my own yard and out the back gate. And then I walked all the way to my friend Janet's house and borrowed her car. Mine is still sitting in the driveway. I left the lights and the TV on."

"Good. That was smart."

"You know I have to take her back with me."

The words hit Faith like a raised ax, suddenly dropped. It had been up there for so long, poised. Faith had almost forgotten the threat of it.

I promised I'd take her to Estelle's. That was Faith's first thought. It probably wasn't the most important aspect of the moment, or the most compelling reason to keep the girl with her. But it was the most important aspect of Sarah's world. And the worse things got in Sarah's world, the more important it became to the girl to stay with her horse.

"Are you sure you need to do that?" Faith asked, simply.

"Of course. She has to tell the police what she just told me."

"I worry about that, though," Faith said. It felt as if her worries were forming in real time, coming together as she spoke them. "He still legally has custody. If you take her back now, I'm worried that they could give her back to him. Because he's only been *accused* of a crime. Isn't there some way you could set it up better than that? Tell them you have a witness? Have them set it up so that as soon as you bring her back to tell them what she saw, they can arrest him? And then I'm sure you can get temporary custody easily if he's been charged with a serious crime."

Constance said nothing for a time. Just waited for Faith to finish, then nodded a few times to herself. As though nudging her own thoughts along.

"That's actually good thinking," she said.

Faith breathed deeply for the first time that evening. If not longer.

"Where will you be in the meantime, though?" Constance asked. "She told me the mare was sold again. And if I need Sarah back, I'll need her back right away."

"That's no problem. We'll be in the Santa Ynez Valley. She's been invited to help the mare settle in with her new owner. We could be back in just a couple of hours if you need her."

"Okay, good. Then at least she'll be reasonably happy in the meantime."

Faith turned suddenly, to verify that Sarah was still on the bench where Faith had left her. It formed a twist in her stomach suddenly, imaging a scenario in which the girl was just gone. One in which they made the mistake of turning their backs on her, and her father grabbed her up and took her away.

It was the stuff of thriller movies. Then again, so was a father who shot his own wife.

But this was not a thriller movie.

Sarah was on the bench, right where Faith had left her.

"We'll keep in close touch," she said to Constance. Then she walked to where Sarah sat. "Come on," she said. "We're going to go."

"To see Midnight?"

"I think it's too late for that tonight. I think we should get a motel room for the night and go to Estelle's in the morning. But first we have to go back to Los Alamos and get all our stuff."

"Okay," Sarah said, seeming to brighten some.

She popped up from the bench and ran to her grandmother, throwing her arms around Constance and holding on for an extended time.

Then she trotted back to Faith, and they walked

together. Shoulder to shoulder on the wooden boards of the pier, headed for their parking lot.

"I thought I had to go back with her," Sarah said. "She said I had to when I first told her. You know. To give some kind of statement to the police."

"I talked her out of it," Faith said.

"Thank you."

"You're welcome. For now. But when she calls and says she needs you, we have to go. Right away. No delays."

"Okay. I understand."

They walked the rest of the way back to the car in silence.

Sarah rolled the door of the tack stall open, and they stepped inside. Faith reached for the light switch by feel and flipped it, flooding the concrete-and-wood room with light.

It struck Faith that she would miss this place—that over the last six weeks it had begun to feel something like a home. That was likely more true of the breathtaking farm setting overall than this cramped little windowless stall. And yet, somehow, even clearing out of this tack stall held a certain nostalgia. It may have been uncomfortable, but life certainly had a purpose during their time here—a sense that Faith was doing some tangible good for someone. Plus, she had felt safe here. Maybe it was foolish to have felt that way. But she had. It was definitely a place where Robert would never think to look. She had banked on the fact that Sarah's father wouldn't look here, either. As she had told Sarah, why would someone imagine that John would let the girl hang around? Faith had won that bet, at least so far.

Faith moved around the room, pulling her clothes down off the bridle hooks and stuffing them into her soft-side bag. In her peripheral vision, she saw the girl sink down onto her bare cot, her back up against the wooden-board wall.

Faith turned to face Sarah, her mouth open to speak. All ready to say, "Come on already. This is not the time. We need to get moving."

She took one good look at the girl's face and said nothing.

Sarah looked up and met her eyes briefly. She had her knees pulled up to her chest, arms wrapped around them and hugging tightly. Then she quickly looked away from Faith's eyes again.

"She's not coming back," Sarah said. "Is she?" The words floated into the world like sad little feathers. They had no weight. No true direction. They just drifted there, half an ounce of energy away from stalling altogether.

Then the girl pressed her face between her knees.

Faith moved across the small room and sat on the cot beside her.

"Who? The horse?"

A pause. Then the girl shook her head slightly, her face still pressed into that safe, dark space.

"You'll see your grandmother again. Probably soon."

But, even as she said it, Faith knew that wasn't it.

Another weak headshake from the girl.

"Oh," Faith said. And let the word sit a moment. Let it sink onto the concrete floor under its own onerous weight. "You're talking about your mom."

Sarah pulled her head up. Blinked into the light. She sniffled once, wiping her nose on the shoulder of her T-shirt sleeve. "Sounds incredibly stupid to say that, I know, because . . . duh."

"No, it doesn't sound stupid. I remember the feeling."

"You do?"

"Oh, yeah. All too well. You know it in your brain—of course you do. But then there's this other part of you, this other whole level, and down there it just doesn't make sense. It doesn't feel real. I kept having dreams like the one you had. Dreams where she wasn't dead at all—I would see her, and I'd say, 'Mom. They told me you were dead.' And it just made so much more sense that they would be wrong. That it was all just a big mistake somehow. It's not stupid. It has nothing to do with intelligence or stupidity.

That shock we feel at the beginning comes with its own denial, and it's not a bad thing. It's there for a reason. It cushions us until we're strong enough to take it all in. It's okay that a piece of it just came up for you now, but don't force it. It'll work itself out in time."

Faith stood, and moved over to her own cot. She sat facing the girl. It was dawning on her slowly that they were not going to a motel. That they were not going anywhere. Not tonight.

Sarah stretched out facedown on her cot, her forehead against her folded arms. After a minute or two she turned her head to face Faith.

"It's nice that you get it," she said. "That you've been there. Well—I don't mean it's good that you had to be there. Just that it's good to have somebody who gets it."

"I knew what you meant," Faith said.

She rose after a time and fetched one of the light cotton horse blankets folded and stacked in the corner. She spread one over the girl.

"I thought we had to go to a motel," Sarah said, sounding tired and weak.

"I changed my mind. I don't think we do. Nobody's going to come tell us we have to get out right now, tonight. The people who live and work here probably don't even know the mare was sold yet. We'll leave in the morning. Maybe that way we'll get a chance to say goodbye to John."

"And we'll go to Estelle's, right?"

"Right."

"Good."

Sarah turned toward the wall, as if entirely ready to drop off to sleep.

Faith took another horse blanket from the stack in the corner. She flipped off the overhead light and made herself comfortable on her own cot. It struck her that they were both fully dressed, but she had no energy to do anything about it.

Right around the time Faith was sure the girl must have fallen asleep, Sarah spoke up.

"Did you have somebody around who got it?"

"When my mom died, you mean?"

"Yeah. That."

"Not really. Well. Yes and no. Now I look back and see that my dad knew something about how I was feeling. At least, he was going through a huge loss at the same time. He got it. But I'm only able to see that looking back. At the time I was furious with him, and it created all this distance between us, so it didn't feel like having somebody there. Besides, I still don't know that he could really share what I was feeling, because losing your mother is different from losing a wife. I'm not trying to minimize what he lost. I'm sure it was terrible for him. But mothers are different. You have *one*. He went on, and years later he got married again. He was able to find another wife. But I never found another mother,

273

and I never will. But maybe this kind of talk is not helping you."

"No, it is."

"Good."

"But . . . if it's okay with you . . . I'm going to go back to that place where I don't really exactly believe it's a true thing at all."

"Not a bad idea," Faith said.

To Faith, it felt destined to be a night of hectic thoughts and emotional turmoil, enough to keep Faith tossing and turning. But she was wrong. They didn't. They couldn't. Faith was utterly exhausted, and she slept.

She woke in the night to the sound of someone whispering her name.

At first it was Robert. Or so she thought at the time. Because in her dream she was lying in her bed at home with Robert, wide awake and shaken after a particularly upsetting fight.

But the repetition of her name continued, and as it did the tone and tenor of the word seemed to change. First it seemed quieter, as if moving farther away. Then the register of the voice grew higher and less substantial, until it could not possibly be her husband speaking.

The dream let her go suddenly, and she sat up in bed with a start. Except it wasn't a bed, not really. It was the sling cot in the tack stall at Moonshadow Farm.

"I'm sorry I woke you up," Sarah said. "But I can't sleep and I was scared and I needed to ask you something."

"Okay, what?"

"Am I going to have to go to court and get up on that bench thing in front of everybody and look right in his face and say what I saw that night?"

"Um . . ."

Faith rubbed her eyes briskly. She felt three-quarters asleep, incapable of thinking. She didn't want to offer the wrong answer, and it seemed impossible to tell the girl what she was hoping to hear.

She moved the horse blanket off herself and swung her legs over the side of the cot, setting her bare feet on the cool concrete floor. She leaned on her knees for support before speaking again.

"I'm not somebody who knows a lot about legal stuff. But based on what little I know, probably one of two things will happen. Either he'll plead guilty, and they'll put him away for some time, and they won't need your help for that . . ."

"He won't plead guilty," Sarah said.

Faith could just barely make out the shape, the outline of the girl in the windowless dark. She was sitting up, hunched forward as if to protect her own soft underbelly.

"You don't know that."

"Trust me. He won't. I know him. He gets out of things. He talks his way out of them. He doesn't just go, 'Okay, here I am. You got me.'"

"Well, then, if he pleads not guilty, it'll go to a trial, I guess. And since what you saw that night is the only thing that's likely to change anybody's mind about it being a suicide . . . then, yeah. They'll probably need your testimony. But sometimes they make special arrangements for kids so they don't have to look a parent right in the eye and testify against them."

"I'm not a kid," Sarah said. "I'm fourteen. Nearly fifteen."

"I think the point still applies."

"Like what kind of arrangement?"

"Like . . . I've heard of kids being in another room with a trusted person, and maybe a therapist or something, and testifying into a camera. And the people in the courtroom can see it, but not the other way around. I don't know, Sarah. Don't take my word on any of this, please, because I don't know enough to make you any promises. But if you tell the police or the judge that it would be hard to do it looking right into your father's face . . . well, I think that's something they could understand."

They sat in the dark in silence for several minutes. Long enough that Faith wondered if they were done. If she could go back to sleep.

Then Sarah spoke, startling her.

"Maybe I'll just look him right in the face," she said.

"You don't have to decide tonight."

"But now I can't stop thinking about it. Now I have to go from staying awake because I thought I wouldn't have any choice to staying awake because I can't decide."

"What time is it?"

Sarah had a watch with a face that lit up when you pressed a button. She brought it up to her face and lit it up, and Faith could see the girl in the glow of the lighted dial. She could tell Sarah had been crying again.

"Four ten."

"Yes, it *is* too early to go to Estelle's. Before you even ask."

"Yeah, I figured. If I can't get back to sleep, can I wake you up at seven?"

"Sure, okay."

"And then we'll go to Estelle's?"

"Then we'll go out to breakfast, and when it gets to be a decent hour we'll go to Estelle's."

"Good. Thanks."

Faith lay back down and tried to find sleep exactly where she had left it. But it evaded her for at least an hour. Maybe more. Time was a slippery thing to judge that night.

"You're not sleeping," Sarah said, "are you?"

"No."

"I should have told her."

"Yes."

"I really screwed up by not telling everybody right away."

"Sarah. Listen. You're in a position no kid your age should ever have to be in. Nobody is watching you and judging how you're doing with this. You're not being graded. It's an impossible thing—a terrible thing. So just get through it any way you can, okay? Don't get too hung up on what it means to get through it just exactly right."

Chapter Thirteen

Knowing What You Don't Know

The gate to Estelle LaMaster's horse property was closed, and it didn't open with the simple press of a button. Instead it had a call button, which Faith pressed.

Then she and the girl sat for several minutes in the car in the gathering morning heat. It would have been wrong to say it was already hot at 8:00 a.m., but the threat of heat could not have been announced more clearly in that still valley air.

Sarah sat in the passenger seat, stony. Saying nothing. Looking at nothing.

Through the wrought-iron gate Faith could see a two-story white clapboard farmhouse, hundreds of years old from the look of it but nicely restored. A dark-red barn with white trim. An outdoor arena with dressage letter markers and a clean white rail. A covered arena. A small round pen with a roof.

A fit-looking man in his thirties came to the gate, and Faith stepped out.

"You would be Faith and Sarah," he said. He had a trace of an accent, possibly Australian, but Faith had a hard time placing it with confidence.

"I hope it's not too early to come visiting," she said.

The man laughed. He had closely cropped hair and wore jeans and heavy work boots. His plain white T-shirt was already soaked through with sweat.

"You haven't known Miss Estelle long, I take it."

"No. We just met her."

"She's up with the rooster every morning. Five o'clock she shows up in the barn. You just try to keep her down any longer than that. She works with the horses first thing. She says it's to beat the heat, but she does it all winter long, too, so you tell me."

He pressed a button mounted on a pole inside the gate. The wrought-iron bars slid open. Faith stepped back into her idling car and drove inside.

She leaned out her open driver's side window to ask him where to go, but he beat her to it.

He pointed.

To the right of the barn and slightly down the hill, Faith saw Estelle and a much younger woman leading Midnight into the covered round pen. The mare was in a high mood, head up and tossing, front hooves rising too high off the ground in a series of half rears.

"There she is!" Sarah said. "I see her!"

"You can park in the shade there by the barn," the man said, pointing again.

But Sarah had already jumped out and was trotting down the hill to her mare.

By the time Faith had parked and walked down to the round pen, the young woman—Faith assumed she was Estelle's granddaughter—was longeing the mare on a long line. She stood in the middle of the loose dirt of the pen and drove the horse around in a circle with no rider. The line was threaded through the ring of the horse's simple snaffle bit. Then it clipped to one of several rings on a wide belt around the mare's barrel, which Faith now knew enough to call a surcingle. The mare also wore a set of side reins, clipped to the bit ring and then back to the surcingle. Probably to keep her going with a rounded neck, Faith figured.

The young woman drove the mare from behind with a long whip to keep her trotting, but she never struck her with the whip. Never touched her, in fact. She just used the motion of it, which the horse could see going on behind her, to encourage forward movement.

The mare trotted well until she reached the spot where Sarah and Estelle leaned on the railing. Then she tried to stop. Every time around.

Faith could see that the young woman was growing frustrated.

Apparently the horse could sense the frustration as well, because she exploded. She jumped straight up into the air, kicking out violently, and thundered around the circle in a strong gallop, throwing bucks every few strides.

"Nana," the young woman called. "It would help if that girl wasn't standing there."

"Nonsense, love," Estelle called back. "She's a familiar person to the mare. That's why I have her here. To help."

"Well, she's not helping so far."

"Darling, it's fine what the mare's doing. It's normal. She's letting off steam. Which she can do safely in side reins and with no rider on her back—that's why you longe a horse. I wish I could have gotten you into a better habit with it right from the start. If you did this regularly, you wouldn't worry about what she's doing. You'd just let her work it out by moving forward."

As she listened to her grandmother, the young woman took her eyes off the horse and lowered the whip. Midnight took it as an invitation to trot to where Sarah stood and halt, her muzzle over the rail. Sarah petted the mare's face.

"Horses work out their anxiety through movement," Estelle said to her granddaughter.

"Like you haven't told me that a hundred times."

"And I'll continue to tell you until I see you incorporate it into your training program."

"She can move while I'm riding her, you know."

"I can't imagine you'd want to be on her back

while she was moving the way she did a moment ago." Estelle paused and looked over at Faith and Sarah. "I'm so sorry," she said. "I'm being terribly impolite. This is my granddaughter, Julia. Julia, these are the lovely people I was telling you about. Sarah and Faith. They're going to come in very handy helping the mare settle in."

"Pleased to meet you," Julia said. But she wasn't. Faith didn't feel that Julia bore any animosity toward them, but rather that she appeared not to have an ounce of attention to spare for the new people. "So how long do you want me to longe her before I get on?"

"Twenty-minute longe," Estelle said. "Ten minutes each side. And you don't get on her today. If you want to spend more time with her, you can walk her in hand as many times as you like for as long as you like. Show her every part of the place. That should help her settle."

Julia stood still in the center of the arena, whip drooping in one hand, line dragging the dirt in the other. She said nothing. But her mouth fell open, and it was abundantly clear that she was not happy with the answer.

"Now pick up the slack in that line, darling," Estelle said, "before the mare gets herself tangled."

Julia sighed and resumed longeing the mare. Or tried to, anyway. But the mare had her head close to her girl and did not care to move along. Julia got louder with the whip, still without actually touching the horse. She snapped it in the air in the mare's direction. Midnight surged forward, almost violently, then turned her haunches in toward the center of the arena and threw a powerful kick in Julia's general direction.

She settled briefly into a polite trot, then bolted forward, turning tightly into the rail, backing, and ending up with the line over her withers and caught up in the surcingle.

"No, darling," Estelle said, "no, no, no. You have to keep her moving forward no matter what."

"Well, that's what I was trying to do, Nana! Easy for you to say!"

Estelle clucked her tongue a couple of times. Then she ducked under the rope that sealed off the entrance to the arena. She moved smoothly to the mare, reassuring her with cooing sounds, and untangled the line.

"Give me," she said to her granddaughter, tugging on the line.

Julia dropped her end of it and offered the long whip to her grandmother, who positioned herself in the center of the pen.

"Wait," Julia said. "Don't start her until I duck out."

"You're not going anywhere, darling. Stand right behind me. When I get her going well, you're going to take over."

Julia sighed, once again loudly enough for Faith to hear her from outside the pen.

Estelle moved the horse into motion easily. Midnight trotted three circles around the pen, then Estelle asked her for more. The mare responded with a lovely trot, full of lift and energy, as though not bound by the rules of gravity like all other horses.

"Wow," Julia said. "She has beautiful gaits."

"I didn't buy her for no reason, love." Then, to the mare, "Can-ter." She separated out the syllables into two words with a singsongy voice. "Can-ter."

Midnight transitioned smoothly into a light, restrained canter. Then the mare took off again, hooves thundering, shaking the ground, causing Faith to instinctively step back from the rail.

"That's the good girl," Estelle cooed to the horse. "You just get it all out."

As if understanding English, the mare bucked wildly, over and over, throwing herself around the arena and an impossible distance into the air, coming down on her front hooves. Occasionally the mare would rear and fight with the line. Estelle seemed unconcerned. She just stayed a little behind the surcingle and used the visual cue of the whip to keep the horse from turning or backing up, or stopping for long.

After a few wild bucking spins around the circle, the mare settled into a strong gallop, neck foaming white with sweat. Five or six turns later, her gallop slowed to a canter.

"There," Estelle said. "See, you don't trouble yourself with her energy. You just let her get it out. But you keep her on the rail and moving forward no matter what."

"Nana," Julia said. "Please. There are people watching, and you're treating me like a beginner."

"Well, you are a beginner, darling, at longeing. I wanted you to practice far more over the years, and if you had, you'd be an expert by now. But you keep skipping that step. Now with a good older boy like Fergus you can get away with that, but you won't be getting away with it anymore. It's not my fault that you're an FEI rider with a hole in your training regimen."

She allowed Midnight to halt. The mare stood, neck rounded and head down, sides heaving, blowing through widely flared nostrils.

"Nana, you're embarrassing me in front of the company."

"Nonsense. Nobody knows how to do anything unless they practice it. Our guests didn't think you were born knowing everything." Estelle turned her attention to Sarah. "Sarah, darling. Did you longe her regularly when she was yours?"

"Yes, ma'am," Sarah called back. "Once a week no matter what. Plus anytime she seemed up, like after a day off or if the weather was stormy."

"Come work with her. I want to see how she goes for you."

"But Nana," Julia said, sounding scalded, "you said the mare was mine."

"She is yours, darling. Or she will be, after a clean vet check today. I should think you'd be as interested as I am in getting this transition right."

Julia shook her head and left the arena, walking quietly, if a bit petulantly, her head tilted down toward the dirt. Faith thought Julia would lean on the rail and watch, but she just kept walking, headed for the house.

"Pay her no mind, darling," Estelle said to Sarah when her granddaughter had walked out of earshot. "She's used to working with my old Grand Prix warmblood, Fergus. He makes it too easy, so I'm afraid she doesn't know how much she doesn't know. Now that Fergus is nineteen and needing more of a retirement schedule, she's in for a rude awakening. I think she would tell you she knows very well that horses don't come out of the box the way Fergus is now. She knows it with her brain. But I think she'll be quite surprised when she sees what goes into melding and pairing with a horse and making her your own. I'm pegging her as being up to the task, and we should all keep our fingers crossed that I'm not wrong. Now come work with this lovely girl, Sarah. It will do her good on her first day in an unfamiliar place. It should ease her fears."

Sarah ducked under the rope. She stopped briefly where Midnight stood, placing one reassuring hand on the mare's forehead. Then she moved to Estelle's side in the center of the arena.

"Vet check is today at ten thirty," Estelle said, handing Sarah the whip and the line. "I'd be most grateful if you'd come with us. I'm sure it would do a world of good keeping the mare calm."

Faith unpacked her bag, putting away the last of her clothes in the dresser and closet. Then she stood in the middle of the guest room alone, just taking it all in. It felt like an almost absurd, excessive degree of luxury compared to what she'd grown used to at Moonshadow Farm. Twin canopy beds with pillow shams and dust ruffles. Soft, clean carpeting. A bathroom with scented candles, guest soaps and towels, and a deep old-fashioned claw-foot tub.

She sat on the edge of one bed, bouncing slightly. She closed her eyes and sighed her contentment.

Just for a brief moment she pictured leaving this place. Wondered how long they would be allowed to stay here and where she would go when this odd segment of her life was over. She had just left a life when she met Sarah and her grandmother—a life that was now completely in the past—and had not yet built a new one on her own. So the idea of returning to her own life felt nebulous at best, meaningless at worst. How could she go back to a life that did not yet exist?

It disturbed her, that collection of thoughts and feelings. So she gathered herself up and trotted downstairs in search of company.

She found Estelle in the kitchen, filling an old-fashioned whistling teakettle.

"Ah, there you are," Estelle said. "I was just going to come ask you if you wanted a cup of tea before we head out for the vet's."

"That would be lovely," Faith said, and settled at the kitchen table.

"Will you be coming with us for that, or would you prefer to stay here?"

"I was thinking a nap in your lovely guest room would be just the thing."

"Fine, do that. It's quite boring, really. Standing around while a horse is X-rayed from every possible angle. You have to love the horse dearly or have a massive financial stake in her to take much interest in those proceedings."

Estelle set the kettle on the stove and lit the gas burner underneath it. Then she came to the table and sat with Faith.

"Where's Sarah?" Faith asked. But she had a pretty good idea.

"Can't say for a fact, but I could make an educated guess. Last I saw her she was in the barn with the mare, and that's still what I'd bet on. I hope I'm not overstepping my bounds here, but I'm going to ask you a personal question. Is your girl in some kind of trouble with the law? I hope you understand why it matters to me, what with her being a guest in my home and all that."

"No," Faith said, and then paused, feeling her shock. "No, Sarah isn't in any trouble. Why do you ask?"

"I overheard her talking on her cellular. I wasn't *purposely* eavesdropping, mind you, but we were in two different stalls in the barn, and voices carry. She made it sound as though the police wanted to talk to her. But she insisted on waiting until after the mare has finished with her pre-purchase exam. She had to fight quite hard for that, but I think she's still coming with us."

"Oh," Faith said. "Oh. Her grandmother must have called. She promised me we'd go right away when her grandmother called."

"I think she was worried about having made me a promise. And she's worried about the mare, of course. How everything must be so traumatic for her right now. It really is very hard for a horse to move to a new place, with all new horses and people. They're herd animals, of course, and they count on their herd for safety. And they rely on familiarity for safety. Even people are like that, but it's ten times harder for a horse, believe me. But back to the original question."

The kettle began to whistle. Estelle did not get up to make the tea.

"Sarah's not in any trouble with the police," Faith said.

"I'm glad to hear it," Estelle replied, loudly, to be heard over the sound of the screaming kettle.

"You go get that," Faith said. "And then we'll have our tea, and I'll explain."

"I'm going to go a little easy on the details," Faith said. Then she paused and blew on her tea. It was a strong black English breakfast, steeping in a ball diffuser with a chain. "But only because I'd like to assume that most of what Sarah says to me is in confidence. Anyway, here goes. She was the only witness to a crime. And at first she didn't tell anybody, because . . . well, that might be going down the road into a confidence. I'll just say it was a serious crime, and she's quite upset about it, as anybody would be." Faith paused. Sipped. Then she added, "It has to do with the death of her mother."

She looked up at Estelle. The older woman's eyes looked strangely wide open.

"You're not her mother?"

"I'm not."

"I always thought you were."

"I guess you see a girl her age and a woman my age, and it just makes sense."

"Oh, no. It's far more than just that, darling. You mother that girl. Do you not even know you're doing it? I don't mean that in a bad way

291

at all. But you guide her, and you advise her. And you comfort her. And she looks to you to get those needs met. It's a very mothering role you're playing."

"Oh," Faith said. And paused and sipped again. And wondered if she had known. Yes and no was the best answer she could muster. "Well. I guess it's as simple as . . . she needs somebody to. So I do."

"Yes," Estelle said, and nodded. She stirred a single teaspoonful of sugar into her tea. "I think very often in life we do something important for someone else for no better reason than that they need us to. And really, when you think about it . . . what more reason is needed?"

They sat and drank tea for a minute or two. Faith could feel Estelle wanting to ask more questions. Who wouldn't? But for the moment, both women were still.

"So . . . ," Estelle began, ". . . she lost her mother and she lost her horse. What a miserable era in the life of a girl. And losing her mother in some sort of terrible crime?"

It was a question, and it wasn't. It succeeded in being and not being at the same time.

"And in another way, she lost her father, too," Faith said, "because she doesn't want to be anywhere near him now."

Estelle nodded thoughtfully. Putting things together in her head, from the look of it.

Faith saw a movement at the corner of her eye and looked up to see Sarah standing in the open kitchen doorway. Faith had no idea how long the girl had been there or what she had heard.

"What are you two talking about?" Sarah asked. Guardedly, Faith thought.

For a split second, Faith opened her mouth to lie. But she caught herself just in time. She had done nothing wrong. And the truth was almost always better.

"You didn't tell me your grandmother called. Why didn't you tell me?"

"How did you know she called?"

"Because Estelle was in the barn and heard you talking to her."

"Oh."

The girl fell silent, as if going over in her head everything she might have revealed in that call.

"So why didn't you tell me? We had a deal, remember? That we'd drive down immediately as soon as your grandmother called."

"I would have told you. It was just a few minutes ago. I was in the barn. I'm just now coming in, and I was going to tell you."

"What about our deal that we would drive down right away?"

"It's okay. It's fine, Faith. She didn't want me to wait, but I promised Estelle I'd go with her to the vet. And then finally I just told her to ask the . . . you know. Guy. Who wants to talk to me.

And he said it was okay if we got there later in the day." Sarah turned her eyes to Estelle, as if desperate for a change of topic. "How long a drive is it to the vet?"

"Only fifteen or twenty minutes."

"Even so," Sarah said. "I should put her shipping boots on, right? And be ready to load in ten minutes or so?"

"Darling," Estelle said, "I have employees. Stan can load her up."

The girl looked crestfallen. Immediately, but also more and more deeply as the seconds ticked by. When she spoke, her voice came out weak and small.

"Don't you think she'd feel safer with me?"

"I only want you to know you're not my slave," Estelle said. "No offense to John, but he worked you too hard, and for no money. He took advantage of your eagerness to work around the mare. I don't want to exploit you. But if you're telling me it would truly, honestly make you happier to load the mare than to let Stan do it, then by all means make your-self happy. Just know that you don't have to constantly prove your usefulness to be welcome here. You and your . . . you and Faith are my guests."

"Thanks!" Sarah fairly shouted. She definitely sounded fully reinvigorated. "I'll go get her ready."

• • •

Faith was standing by her car with the keys in her hand when Estelle's horse box pulled back through the gate.

Sarah hopped out and moved to unlock the ramp side of the van, but Stan stepped in. As Faith had requested.

"I'll put the mare away," he said.

"No, I've got it," Sarah told him, almost pushing him out of the way.

"Sorry," he said, standing his ground. Then he indicated Faith with a flip of his chin. "Mother's orders."

"She's not my mother."

"Well, whoever she is," Stan said, "you're to report to her immediately."

"I'm just going to put the mare away," Sarah called to Faith.

"No. Let Stan do it. We're leaving now."

"I can just put her away first," Sarah whined.

"So can Stan. We made a promise. And we've already delayed it one time too many."

Sarah stood still a moment. Then she dropped her head and sighed, and Faith knew she had prevailed.

As the girl moved slowly toward her car, it struck Faith that Estelle was right. Faith had slipped into a mothering role without even realizing it.

"I'm hungry," Sarah whined. "Can't I even have something to eat first?"

"We'll stop and get something on the way down."

"What's the difference? That's not even any faster."

"You were at the vet for almost two and a half hours, Sarah. Your grandmother must be going crazy."

"It's not my fault. That's just how long it took!"

"Whatever. I plan to call Constance in the next minute or two and tell her we're on our way. And I need it to be the truth."

Several miles into the drive, when she had already turned south on the 101 freeway, Faith broke the silence.

"So how did the vet check go?"

"Good."

"No problems?"

"Nothing big. Nothing that was really a problem. Every horse has some little thing. But her naviculars are good. And her hocks. She just has this one bone spur, but the vet says it's inert and not facing any critical structures. So he says that's a blemish. You know. Not an unsoundness."

"Well, that might just as well have been in Greek for how much I understood it. But I get the general idea that she's in good shape."

"Yeah," the girl said.

Faith thought she heard a note of disappointment in the girl's voice. But she wrote it off as her imagination.

"So, was Julia a pain in the butt at the vet's?"

"She didn't go."

"Oh. That seems odd. I wonder why not."

"No idea," Sarah said.

They sank into an uncomfortable silence again.

A mile or two later, the girl spoke up again, surprising Faith.

"What did you tell Estelle?"

"As little as I could get away with. Just that you were the only witness to a crime."

"Why did you even tell her that much?"

"Because she thought you were the *perpetrator* of a crime. And we want to continue to be welcome at her house. Get it now?"

"Oh," Sarah said. "Yeah. I get it now. Hey. Can I tell you a secret?"

"Sure."

"I was hoping Midnight wasn't sound. And now I feel really guilty about that. But I felt like if she had a hidden fracture or something, or bad hocks . . . or the start of navicular disease . . . then she'd be worth hardly anything. Estelle wouldn't buy her, and John would have to practically give her away. These people like John and Estelle and Julia, they only want the mare for her talent. For whatever future she can have in dressage. But I love her even if she can't do the work. I'd love her even if I couldn't ride her. I'd still take care of her for the rest of her life, and I'd still want her. But then I started feeling bad for thinking that. Because I don't want her to be in any pain. And she loves the work. It's what she was bred to do. Born to do. And I shouldn't want to take that away from her. So now I think it was really bad to wish that. What do you think? Do you think that was bad?"

"I think it was very human," Faith said.

"Not exactly sure what you mean, but okay."

"It means I think anybody would feel that way."

"Oh. Okay. Faith. What if my grandmother wants me to stay? What if I say what I need to say, and they arrest him? And then we're safe from him. And he can't take me away. And then my grandmother wants me to stay down there with her. Then we can't go back to Estelle's."

"We'll cross that bridge when we come to it."

"That's not a good enough answer, Faith. This is important to me."

"I know it is, honey. I know. I'll try to help her understand how important it is. Maybe she would go stay at Estelle's with you for a few days."

"She won't want to do that. She hates new places."

"She took you to the beach house."

"Only because it was an emergency. And now that she's home, she's just really relieved to be home. She told me so. She won't want to go away again just so I can see my horse. Please, Faith. I need to go back to Estelle's. You need to help me get back there."

"I'll do my best," Faith said. "I can't do more than that."

She waited, but the girl never answered. Sarah was looking out the passenger window now. Refusing to connect.

"We'll look for a place to stop for lunch," Faith said after a time.

"I'm not hungry."

"You said you were."

"Yeah, well. Now that we're going down there and I have to talk to the police . . . I lost my appetite."

They rode in silence for a mile or two. Then Sarah added, "Also . . . I might have been trying to stall just a little bit."

"I sensed that," Faith said.

"Why do I have to do this? I hate this."

"I think you know why."

"Yeah. I guess I didn't really mean *why*. I guess I meant . . . I wish I didn't have to do it."

"I know. I get it."

"Why do people have to do things they hate so much? And that are so hard?"

"I wish I knew," Faith said. "Really, kiddo. You have no idea how much I wish I knew."

They drove the rest of the way down to Thousand Oaks in silence.

Chapter Fourteen

A Hell of a Thing

"Can Faith come in with me, too?" Sarah asked.

The girl's voice was strained thin with fear. Drenched in it.

They sat on a hard bench at the police station, Faith and Constance on either side, Sarah in between. Constance seemed to have a death grip on one of the girl's hands.

They all stared up at the officer, or detective, or whatever he was. He was a giant of a man in plain clothes, tall and broad shouldered and somewhat overweight. Not really a fat man, still Faith guessed he weighed close to three hundred pounds. His skin was pocked, his hair slicked back in a way that made it look oily.

The officer looked right into Faith's eyes. "Are you blood family?"

Faith shook her head. "No," she said. "No relation. Just a family friend."

"Let's stick with just your grandmother for now," he said to the girl.

Faith could hear Sarah draw her next breath, then push it out again. It sounded shaky.

The girl jumped to her feet, pulling Constance up by the hand. They followed the officer away, leaving Faith feeling distinctly alone on the bench.

Three other uniformed officers sat at desks in the outer room with Faith, one woman and two men, and as she glanced nervously around they occasionally caught her gaze and smiled.

After a few rounds of that, Faith stared out the window in silence.

A few minutes later, Constance came out and sat on the bench beside her.

"He asked you to leave?" Faith asked, taken aback. She thought she had read somewhere that a minor should always be allowed to have a parent or guardian present during any kind of questioning.

"No. Sarah did."

That simple statement hung in the air for a good minute or two before Faith dared address it.

"Did it make you feel . . . ?"

"No. It's okay. I thought about it. I thought a lot about what you said on the pier. And I get it. It fits with what I know about her. She's trying to protect me. The detective was getting into a lot of specifics about that night, and she kept looking over at me. Everything she said, she was trying to gauge how upset I was by it. It was constraining her. So I left her alone to do what she needed to do."

They sat in silence for a time. Maybe a minute. Maybe ten.

Then Constance said, "He told me something interesting. Not just now. Last time I was in here. He told me there was an anomaly on the medical examiner's report. I guess when I came in and told him what Sarah told me, he started looking back over the case. And there was an anomaly."

"What kind of anomaly?"

"He said there was no powder residue on Heather's hand."

"Powder?"

"Gunpowder."

"Oh. I'm still not sure . . ."

"There should have been gunpowder residue on her hand if she fired that gun. Everything else seemed to match up. The angle of the shot. And it was point blank against her head, but . . . there was just that one thing. No powder residue."

"Then why didn't they . . . ?" Again Faith couldn't seem to finish her thought. It seemed so obvious in her head and gut—all the things they should have done. But she couldn't seem to find the words.

"I asked," Constance said, sounding deeply exasperated. "I asked and I asked and I asked, and I never got a clear answer. The impression I got is that most cases aren't perfect and that they use more of a preponderance of the evidence. Like . . . they just have to decide. And in this case, I guess there was no one claiming it was any other way than what he said. There was one mistake in gathering the evidence, and that didn't help our situation. The police who secured the scene that night—they should have bagged her hands. And I guess one of the cops was new or something, or just moving too fast. And they skipped that step. So then if something that's supposed to be there is missing, it casts doubt. Maybe it wasn't really missing. Maybe it was more that the physical evidence wasn't preserved correctly. And all because they didn't . . ."

Constance trailed off. Faith had been looking out the window, watching birds flitting about in the leaves of a nearby tree. When Constance didn't go on, she glanced over at the older woman to see her dissolving into tears. Breaking down.

". . . bag my baby's hands!" she hissed, followed by a deep, racking sob. "My only little girl!"

Constance did not go on to explain why that mental image was such an offense. Then again, she didn't need to.

Faith wrapped herself around Constance and held her tightly, and the older woman fell the rest of the way apart in Faith's arms.

"This is good, though," Faith whispered. "I mean . . . I know it's hard. But there's more doubt now about his story. More than just Sarah's testimony. And that's good. Right?"

Before Constance could answer, they looked up to see Sarah and the detective standing over their bench. They both straightened quickly. Constance swiped tears away from her eyes, as if wanting to cover them over. As if they were a secret. As if anybody could fail to understand their presence in that moment.

The huge man looked down at Faith.

"Got a minute?" he asked.

"Okay," she said. But it sounded tentative. Because she had no idea what he could possibly want from her.

She stood, and followed him into his office.

It was a dank and dusty space. Small, with not enough light from the one narrow window. Several used disposable coffee cups sat on the windowsill, and on his desk. Faith could not imagine what resistance he could have to throwing them away.

She sat in a hard chair with no arms, in front of his desk. They looked at each other over a vast sea of paperwork.

"So, the girl told you this before she told anybody else," he said. It was not a question.

"Yes."

"Did she tell you why she waited so long?"

"She did. Yes. She was upset, and particularly wanting to protect her grandmother. She knew Constance should know, but she felt like her grandmother was just hanging on by a thread emotionally, and she didn't want to do anything to push her over the edge. And I'm sure you can appreciate . . . I mean, however she may feel about her father at this point, he's still her father. It's a very complicated position for a child to be in."

She paused, and waited. The detective was taking notes. Writing something down. By hand, with a pen. Faith wondered why he hadn't leapt into the information age. There was a desktop computer on one end of his desk, but it seemed to be turned off.

"Okay," he said. "Has Sarah ever said or done anything to make you think she's . . . less than fully truthful?"

Faith felt something uncomfortable rise in her. It took her a moment to realize it was anger. It tingled at the nape of her neck, making the little hairs stand on end.

"No! Why would you even ask that? She's very honest. Even when she could get something she wants by lying, she doesn't lie. She said to me, 'I'm not my father,' to explain why she tells the truth. Why would you doubt her?"

"Ma'am," he said, and his tone was intended to tamp her down. He was handling her, but not really in a dismissive or offensive way. "I assure you, this is nothing but standard procedure. I don't have any particular reason to doubt the girl. I'm just doing my job. If she goes into court and tells this story, well . . . you never really know what a judge or a jury will do, but there's a good chance this man will go away for a long time. I just want to know if you think she's telling the truth."

"Yes," Faith said. "I think she's telling the truth. It's something that just sort of . . . bubbled up out of her in the middle of the night. I could feel how much it had been weighing on her. And she had absolutely nothing to gain by saying it if it wasn't true."

"Unless she doesn't want to go back with her father."

"She doesn't. But this is *why* she doesn't. And yes, I believe she's being truthful. And from what I've seen of her father, I think everything he says is doubtful at best."

"Okay. That's fine. I'm not doubting either one of you. Just doing my job. Checking all the angles. That's all I needed from you. At least for the moment."

"So what happens now?"

"I think it's best if you keep the girl with you for a few more days. We'll go find her father and bring him in, but it might be wise to keep her in a safe place until we know we can find him. Until we know we've successfully charged him. We'll recommend no bail. We'll ask the judge for that, based on the safety of the girl. But, like I said before. Never know what a judge'll do."

"That's fine," Faith said. "We'll be in the Santa Ynez Valley if you need us."

As they drove up the 101 through the twisty, narrow pass at Gaviota—just a few minutes south of the San Marcos Pass turnoff they would take to get back to Estelle's—the girl spoke up for the first time.

"Um . . . ," she said, and then stared out the window for another half a minute or so. "Thanks. I was meaning to say that. You know. Just . . . thanks."

"For what?"

"Talking them into letting me go back to Estelle's with you."

"Oh. That. That kind of took care of itself. The guy . . . the . . . you know. Detective or whatever he was. He suggested you stay with me until they're sure they can charge your dad. And . . . before that, of course, they have to find him."

"Right," the girl said.

Then no more words were spoken for quite some time.

They drove out of the narrow pass and eventually into the small town of Buellton. There Sarah's phone rang.

The girl pulled the device from her pocket and stared at it as though it might be a poisonous variety of phone.

"It's my grandmother," she said. "Wonder what she wants."

"I know how you can find out."

Sarah rolled her eyes and picked up the call.

"Hi, Grandma."

Long pause while the girl listened.

"Oh. Okay," Sarah said after a couple of minutes. "I'll tell her."

Brief pause.

"Yeah. Okay. Bye."

The girl turned her eyes to Faith. Faith returned the look briefly, then had to put her eyes back on the road. She asked no questions. Just waited.

"They arrested my dad."

"That was fast."

"Yeah. He was home. They just went to his house. And there he was. And they arrested him."

"Well . . . good. That's good, right? Does she want you to come back right away?"

"No. She told me the same thing you just did. Stay put a little longer. Until they're sure they can charge him. And that he won't make bail."

"That might work out just right. A few more days at Estelle's. Then you can go home to your grandmother."

Faith knew that going home to her grandmother without the horse would be a major trauma for the girl. A crushing blow. But there was nothing Faith could do to stop it. There was nothing anybody could do to stop it as far as Faith could see. And she didn't try to inject that truth into the conversation, because she had no idea how to wrap it up in words. Also because she had made a silent, tacit agreement with the girl to push that reality as far down the road as possible.

"He won't make bail," Sarah said, knocking Faith out of her thoughts.

"How do you know?"

"Because he's got nobody left who'll give him that kind of money. Even his mother is done with him, especially when it comes to money."

They drove in silence for another few minutes. Faith took the turnoff for the 154. The San Marcos Pass. She watched her dashboard thermometer as the outdoor temperature rose one degree at a time, stopping on 104.

Just as they pulled onto the short road to Estelle's property, the girl spoke up again.

"They arrested my father. Because I told them to. That's a hell of a thing, don't you think?"

"Yeah," Faith said. "I would agree that that's a hell of a thing."

They lay in their individual canopy beds, side by side. The lights had been turned off, but a strong, full moon shone through the window overlooking the barn. Now and then Faith glanced over to see if the girl was asleep. Each time she could see Sarah's eyes blinking slowly.

"You awake?" the girl asked after a time.

"Yeah. Very much so."

Faith expected that Sarah would want to talk

about her father, or their visit to the police station earlier in the day. What the girl said next was a surprise.

"I'm so jealous of her."

"Who?"

"I would think you could guess."

"Not managing well so far."

"Julia."

"Oh. Julia."

"Why does she get so much? Why does she get everything she wants? She doesn't deserve it."

"Well . . . to be fair, Sarah, we hardly know her at all. There could be more to her than we've seen so far."

"I don't think she deserves my horse. Do you think she deserves my horse?"

Faith sighed. Tried for a positive answer. Fell short.

"Probably not. No."

"I can understand that she has a grandmother with plenty of money who gives her everything. And I can deal with that. I love my grandmother, and I wouldn't trade her for one with more money. I wish she could have afforded to buy me the horse back, but I still love her the way she is. So, fine, Julia's grandmother buys her pretty things. I just want to know why she had to buy her *my* pretty thing. Not calling Midnight a thing. Just . . . you know."

"Yeah. I know. But I thought it was good that

Estelle bought her. Because you knew she'd be okay at Estelle's."

"I thought so, yeah. Now I'm not so sure. I thought Estelle's granddaughter would be a really good person. Like her. And . . . Oh, it's kind of hard to say this, because it makes me feel like a terrible person, but . . . I hate it either way. If Midnight just loves it here, and totally gets used to it. And likes her new rider and doesn't miss me at all. That feels really bad. That's just horrible in its own way. But I don't want her to be unhappy here. I don't know what to want. I just don't even know what I'm supposed to want anymore, Faith."

She allowed a silence to fall. In case Faith wanted to fill it, maybe. But Faith had no idea what to say. She didn't know what Sarah should want anymore, either. After a few beats of silence, the girl went on.

"Why does stuff like this happen in the world, that just feels so unfair? And if you say 'Life is unfair,' I'm leaving."

"I wasn't going to say that."

"Good. My father used to say that. I hated it." A pause. Faith could see the girl turn her head to look off toward the barn in the moonlight. Toward the one "thing" she loved most in the world. "So what were you going to say?"

"Just that I don't know. I'm sorry. I realize I'm pathetic about things like that."

"No. You're not. I like that about you."

"That I don't know anything?" Faith asked with a wheezy little laugh.

"That when you don't know, you say you don't know. Most grown-ups try to bluff."

"Yeah. That's true. They don't know, either."

"Oh, I figured that out a long time ago," Sarah said.

Then the girl rolled one way, and Faith rolled the other, and they pretended they would sleep.

In the morning, Faith wandered around attempting to locate another living soul. First all through the house, then out onto the property.

She found everyone at the barn. Sarah, Estelle, Stan. They had three horses tied to a hitching post, one of them Midnight. Everyone was there except Julia.

"Ah! There you are," Estelle called to Faith. Almost too awake and cheerful to bear. "Good morning! We were just about to come in and fetch you. We're getting a horse ready for you. We're going on a little trail ride."

"Me?"

"Yes," Estelle said. "You."

Faith glanced at the girl, who was saddling her mare. Tried to catch her eye. But Sarah was lost in her head, in her own little world. Her face looked tight, her energy felt heavy and down. She seemed unwilling or unable to connect with anyone outside her own skin. Even the horse didn't seem to have her full attention.

"I don't ride," Faith said.

"No experience required for Reggie," Estelle replied. Simply, as though that closed the subject.

She pointed to the most enormous horse Faith could ever remember seeing, at least in person. He was a massively built chestnut with four high white stockings and a wide white blaze on his face. He turned to look at Faith, as if he knew he was the topic of conversation. His gaze looked soft and almost amused.

"He's enormous!"

"Gentle as a kitten, though," Stan said. "You won't have any trouble with this one."

As he spoke, he took the halter off Reggie's huge head and buckled it around the horse's neck. Then he raised the bridle and asked the horse to take the bit.

"How tall is this horse?" Faith asked the groom, stepping closer. She could feel her stomach buzz with fear at the idea of mounting the animal.

"Just a hair under eighteen hands."

"That's big," Faith said.

She knew Midnight was only sixteen-two— sixteen hands and two inches. And that had always seemed plenty big enough to Faith.

"Well, your eyes told you that much," Stan said. He followed the words with a wry smile.

"I was just thinking it's a long way to fall."

"Highly unlikely he would create a situation where you would. But, really, it's only six inches higher off the ground than Sarah's horse." He glanced over at Estelle, who didn't seem to have heard. "I meant Julia's horse. But here's the thing, anyway, Miss Faith. I wouldn't worry so much how far it is to the ground. I'd worry how much the horse wants to put you there. Mr. Reggie has no such plans."

He led the horse up to a three-step mounting block.

"Oh, wait," he said. "I need to get you a helmet. Here. Hold him, please."

He indicated to Faith that he wanted her to take the reins.

She did, hesitantly. Reggie sighed deeply, blowing through his huge nostrils. Then he dropped his head as though he had plenty of time for a nap before Stan returned. His eyes half-closed.

"This should do it," Stan said. He placed a helmet on her head and buckled the chin strap. "Now, come on. Your riding mates are mounted and ready to go. Let's get you up."

"I don't . . ." Faith trailed off, not even sure where to begin listing all the things she didn't.

"I'm holding him. So don't even worry about the reins for now. Just take hold of that strap."

"This strap?"

Faith pointed to a small, narrow rolled leather

314

strap that was clipped to either side of the pommel of Reggie's English saddle, spanning the short distance of his bony withers.

"The very one," Stan said. "Miss Estelle had me put that on to make you feel more secure. She said, 'I don't know that Miss Faith has ridden much, if at all, so fix her up with a Hail Mary strap.' "

Faith laughed out loud, but probably more as a result of nervousness than mirth.

"That's really what they call it?"

"Oh, not technically, I suppose. If you go to buy one, you'd ask for a grab strap or a handhold strap. But we call it that because . . . well, obvious reasons."

"Yes," Faith said. "Obvious."

"Go on up, ma'am."

Faith stepped up to the top of the mounting block and already felt too high off the ground. She grabbed the strap tightly in her right hand. Her knuckles brushed Reggie's withers, and he twitched as if shaking off a fly.

"Left foot in the stirrup. Swing up and over."

He raised his hands so they were braced behind her. Not touching her. Just back there should she lose her balance.

Next thing Faith knew she was sitting in the saddle, still holding tightly to the strap. She looked up to see Sarah and Estelle sitting their horses and patiently waiting. Stan handed her the reins, which she took with her left hand only because she did not care to let go. Stan turned the stirrups to face her, one side at a time, and she slipped her shoes into them.

"We'll put Faith in the middle," Estelle called to Sarah as the horses began to move.

Sarah rode around behind Faith, and they set off at a sedate walk. Reggie did indeed seem to be doing all the work, and needed no real direction from Faith. So Faith breathed deeply a few times and tried to let go of her fear.

They rode toward a gate in the white board fencing that surrounded Estelle's horse farm. The sun shone on them at a slant, only midmorning but already hot. It shone into Faith's eyes, and she had no free hand to shield them. She was unwilling to let go of either the reins or the Hail Mary strap. Nor did she care to close them. All that was left to her was squinting.

"Why are you riding Midnight?" Faith asked Sarah, turning her head back around to be heard. It also relieved the sun-in-her-eyes situation. "Why isn't Julia riding her?"

"Julia had a little accident."

"Oh. Oh, dear. That's too bad. Is she okay?"

"Sprained her wrist pretty bad," Sarah said. "But nothing's broken."

"How did she do that?"

"She came off a horse," the girl said. And seemed to want to leave it at that.

"Which horse?"

"Midnight."

They rode up to the gate, and Estelle moved her horse sideways and leaned down to unlatch the gate and swing it open. She rode through and then moved aside to let Faith and Sarah through. They grouped there mostly at a halt while Estelle closed the gate.

"Just this morning?" Faith asked. She was speaking to the girl, but she realized that now Estelle could hear as well. "She had an accident on the horse already this morning?"

"No," Estelle said. "It was yesterday afternoon. While you two were away in Southern California. Taking care of your business."

They rode off again, Estelle in the lead, Faith in the middle. The safest spot, she assumed. They headed up a steep hill, its grass golden brown from the summer sun.

"I thought she wasn't supposed to ride the mare yesterday," Faith said.

She had meant to say it only in the silence of her head, and regretted hearing the words come out loud and clear, filling the warm morning with something far better left unsaid.

"Yes," Estelle said. "Well, in any case, that was my recommendation to the girl. Woman, I guess I should say. She's really not a girl anymore, though she seems like it at times."

They rode in silence to the crest of the hill, and

Faith looked out over the valley in all directions. Rolling hills with fences following their dips and curves lay under a deep-blue, cloudless sky. Barns dotted the landscape, and horses grazed here and there, some wearing fly sheets or light summer blankets. In one fenced pasture, horses and cattle grazed together with what looked like ostriches or emus. They seemed not to bother to recognize that they were not all of a species.

"I hope I haven't made a mistake with her," Estelle added. "I thought she would step up to this. Well, I thought she needed to. But I guess I equated 'needed to' with 'would.' I hope I haven't misjudged her too badly. Hard to see clearly with your own kin."

They started down the other side, and Faith realized she had lost her fear of riding. Because the horse was so clearly going to keep doing exactly what he had been doing so far. Still, she held the Hail Mary strap.

They rode in a peaceful silence for ten minutes or more.

"My grandmother called this morning," Sarah said.

Faith saw Estelle turn her head slightly, and knew that the older woman could hear.

"Okay," Faith said. "What did she say?"

"He has an arraignment on Thursday. She wants us to come down for it."

"What day is this?"

"Tuesday," Estelle said when no answer seemed forthcoming from the girl.

"Okay," Faith said. "We'll drive down late tomorrow afternoon."

In the silence that followed, Faith thought she could hear a question in the air. Or maybe it was just the question in her own head.

This time, she wondered, would they be coming back? Or going anywhere together after their brief appearance in court?

They had always known this odd era of following the horse from place to place would end. It went without saying that it was finite. The only question was when. And it was a question they had both been doing their best to postpone.

"And then we'll come back after?" Sarah asked.

"I really don't know," Faith said. "So it's a good thing you don't mind it when I admit that. It depends on whether Estelle will host us any longer . . ."

"I'd be grateful for a few more days with you," Estelle said.

"Great!" Sarah nearly shouted. "It's settled!"

"It's not settled," Faith said. And felt like someone's mother again. "Not at all. It also depends on whether your grandmother will allow it. We've been away six weeks out of necessity. If there's an arraignment and the judge denies him bail, there's no more necessity. I'm assuming at that point your grandmother will want you back.

She didn't plan for us to stay away longer than necessary."

"Maybe the judge will give him bail," Sarah said, clearly grasping at options, "and then we'll have to wait and stay away while we see if he can get the money."

"Maybe," Faith said. "This is all we know for now."

Chapter Fifteen

Hail Mary

"Hold the strap, darling!" Estelle shouted to her granddaughter. "You have the one good hand at least."

The older woman stood in the center of the covered round pen, longeing Midnight with a long whip and a line. But Midnight wore a saddle. And a rider. Julia sat on her back, the reins tied into a knot and lying on the horse's neck, her right wrist immobilized in a splint with a stretchy tan cover. Her left hand simply poised in the air, looking deeply uncomfortable, as if knowing it had a job but seeming unable to find that job and do it.

"I don't need to hold the strap, Nana," she barked back. "I have a seat, you know."

Faith glanced over at Sarah, probably to see if she had any opinion on all this. The girl stood just inches from Faith's left elbow, leaning on the outside of the pen's railing, her eyes looking disconnected and far away. Faith wasn't even sure she was listening.

It was barely six o'clock on Wednesday morning. The day they had to leave for Southern California in order to be available bright and early

Thursday for the arraignment. Faith was doing her best to stay in the moment. Stay out of Southern California in her head. Not to mention court.

"I'm sure you have a decent rider's seat, darling," Estelle called back. "And I'm sure it was more than enough to keep you on Fergus. But this is not Fergus. And you don't want to aggravate that injury."

Estelle nudged the mare into a smooth trot with a wave of the whip and a cluck of her tongue. Julia sat it for a full circle around the pen, not posting, and holding her seat admirably well. Then she grabbed the strap.

"Why is it so hard to feel balanced without the reins?" she asked, her voice loud and a bit whiny.

"Because the reins are part of your structure, darling. They help with balance. Your body is all off-kilter without them. But it's a good chance to work on your seat independent of everything else. Now." Estelle stepped forward and almost invisibly asked the mare to halt. Midnight did. "Let's do a series of transitions. Trot to halt. Halt to trot."

Julia looked at her grandmother with narrowing eyes, as if translating each word from a foreign language in her head.

"You'll stop her?"

"No, darling. You will."

Julia picked up the knotted reins with her left.

"No reins," Estelle said. Quite firmly.

"Reins are helpful when you want to halt, Nana."

"But they shouldn't be necessary. Honestly, dear, if I had taught you to ride, I can't imagine you'd be showing in Intermediare without first having broken down some of these basics and working on their elements. Now tell me. Any fool can pull back on a set of reins. But you're an FEI rider. So what do you do when you want the horse to halt?"

Julia rolled her eyes, as if complaining that the test was too basic.

"Stretch up. Drop my seat. Close my knees."

"Of course. So why would you need me to stop the mare? I'm just here in case of emergency, darling. Because you're injured. Now you do this transition. Halt to trot."

Julia pressed her legs to the mare's sides. Midnight moved forward. She walked several steps, then broke into a bumpy trot.

"That was bad," Sarah said quietly. Almost into Faith's ear.

"She did get her trotting," Faith whispered back. "You know. Without a major incident or a world war."

Sarah laughed one bitter little bark. She stayed silent as Julia and the mare trotted by.

Then she leaned in and whispered, "It's supposed to be halt to trot. Not halt to walk to trot."

"Halt, darling," Estelle called.

The mare broke trot, walking a few uneven steps. She came almost to a halt, then surged forward again, violently, nearly unseating her rider.

Sarah called out into the arena, "If you close your knees, she'll halt. If you squeeze her with your thighs, she'll lose it. She hates that."

Julia guided the mare to a reasonably calm halt. Then she turned her face to Sarah and opened her mouth to speak.

Estelle raised one finger to her granddaughter in warning.

Julia closed her mouth again.

"This is exactly what Sarah is here for," Estelle said. "She knows the mare well. So just put your pride on the back burner for a moment and listen. I've had quite a few horses in my life who react badly to tension in the rider's thighs. She's a sensitive mare, and you're going to have to change how you ride for her. She's not going to change who she is as a horse for you."

"She's just so . . . ," Julia began. She squeezed her eyes closed, then opened them and glanced at Sarah briefly. "Difficult. Why do I have to have a horse who's so difficult?"

"Because she's brilliant, darling. And you said you wanted that. It's not that this mare is so very unusually hard to ride. She's just sensitive. Which is a blessing in the show arena because your aids will be absolutely invisible. Stop asking why you have to learn to ride a horse who requires more effort, and recognize that Fergus has been going way too easy on you for way too long. He absorbs your mistakes. He knows his job so well that he overrides any little errors in yours. Most horses won't do that for you, darling. It's time to step up."

"I'm done for today," Julia said, her face reddening.

"Why, you've barely begun!"

"My wrist hurts. I want to go inside."

Estelle sighed deeply. Then she reeled in the line as she walked to the mare's head. She held the horse's reins just behind the bit, and Julia jumped down and stomped away, ducking under the rope gate and heading toward the house.

Estelle raised her eyes to Sarah and indicated with a flip of her head that she wanted the girl to come in. Sarah perked up immediately. She bent at the waist and ducked through the rails, trotting through the groomed dirt to the spot where Estelle stood holding the mare.

The older woman said nothing. Just laced her fingers and reached out her joined hands, and Sarah placed a knee in them and swung up into the saddle.

As the girl undid the knot in the reins, Faith asked the question that had been weighing on her.

"You didn't teach Julia to ride?" she asked,

loudly enough for Estelle—who had moved into the center of the arena again—to hear.

"No, and I wish I had. I'm afraid her instructors indulged her. She just wanted to move up, move up. But it doesn't pay to jump levels too quickly. Not if you haven't absolutely nailed down the basics. Normally it'll show if there are holes in your schooling program, and I think it did to some degree with Julia. Her scores were nothing I would have been proud to show off. But Fergus made her look like a better rider than she was. It was my daughter's idea, to get a different riding teacher. She thought I was being too hard on the girl. I was as hard on her as I would be on any student. I wanted her to get it right. I wanted excellence for her. If you're not striving for excellence, why take on a task at all?"

As the older woman spoke, Sarah began to perform the transitions Estelle had wanted from her granddaughter. Trot to halt. Halt to trot. Faith could see none of the girl's aids. No trace of her instructions to the mare were visible to Faith's eye. And there was no walking in between the trot and the halt. Not even one step.

"My daughter reminded me of the time I tried to teach her to drive," Estelle continued. "To make her point about Julia and the riding lessons. That whole episode was . . . Well. Let's just say her second lesson was with a professional driving instructor and leave the story at that. Oh, and I'll add that we did put our relationship back together again, but it took a little time. There's wisdom, I think, in not complicating these blood family relationships. Trouble is, it has to be the right outside teacher."

Estelle was silent a moment, observing Sarah and the mare.

"That's brilliant, darling," she said. "She goes so beautifully for you. I think I'll have you take her out into the big arena and put a good forty-five minutes of disciplined schooling on her. I think I'll do the same myself with her tomorrow, while you're away. The mare's got herself in a bad pattern of being reactive with new riders. I'd like to see the habit go no further than this. Time for her to get back to doing what she knows so well."

They drove south together in silence, along the coast, north of Santa Barbara. Sarah seemed unusually fidgety. Although . . . Faith thought about it and decided *fidgety* wasn't a strong enough word. Something inside the girl seemed to jerk her body into new positions over and over, like a storm in her muscular system letting off sudden bolts of lightning.

It was hard for Faith to take her eyes off it, though she did watch the road more than anything else.

Sarah looked up and caught her watching.

"What?" the girl asked. Defensively, as though the only problem was that Faith had noticed.

"I didn't say a word," Faith said. Then, a few seconds later, she added, "I was just hoping you're okay."

That shattered the dam and it all came pouring out.

"Well, I'm not. Of course I'm not, Faith. How can I be? Why would you even ask that? I just wish I didn't have to do this. Why do I even have to do this? I don't want to go to court for any arraignment, and I don't want to see him, and I don't want him to see me. And I don't even get why I need to be there, because it's not like I have to testify against him or anything. Not tomorrow, anyway. Maybe later. But tomorrow he just stands up in court and either admits he did it or lies and says he didn't do it, except we all know he's going to lie, and I don't understand why he even needs me for that. Why anybody does. He can lie just fine on his own. He's been doing it all his life."

Faith took a breath or two and waited. Just to be sure the girl was done.

"Did you ask your grandmother why it's so important to her that you be there tomorrow?"

"Yes." The girl spoke that one word almost belligerently, her head turned away, looking out the window at the water.

Faith almost asked. Almost said something like

"What did she say?" But it was such an obvious question. It was so clear that she was asking for, waiting for, that information.

So she just waited. The girl could answer or not.

After a time, Sarah turned her head just slightly back from the window. Not enough to look at Faith. Just enough to telegraph that she was aware of Faith, and the conversation.

"She really wants to be there," Sarah said. Her voice was quieter now. Smaller and less angry. "I guess she sort of has to be there. I mean . . . the police didn't say she has to be or anything like that. But she has to be. She's sort of . . . obsessed with this whole thing now. You know. Making sure he gets caught for what happened. Well. He's caught already. But, you know. Punished, I guess. And now she can't let it go. So she has to be there so she can see and hear everything that happens the exact minute it happens. And she doesn't want to do it by herself. Which I guess I understand . . ."

Sarah seemed to trail off, leaving Faith unclear as to whether that had been the end of a sentence or not. She waited, but the girl did not appear to have more to say.

"Maybe you don't really have to see him, and he might not even see you. We could sit in a back corner and keep our heads down, and maybe he won't even know we were there."

As she spoke, Faith identified a ball of discomfort in her own gut. It had been growing there for a while, but she had been refusing to acknowledge it. But once she focused on it, its message felt clear. Faith didn't want to see Sarah's father, either.

Faith glanced over at the girl to see her looking vaguely squirmy, though she could not have put her finger on any one visual symptom that helped her arrive at that conclusion.

"What?" she asked the girl. "Is there something more?"

"There was another reason. You know. In what my grandma said. She said she wants him to see me there. She wants him to look right into my face. She thinks he has a conscience. Well, I guess almost everybody does. It's more a matter of whether they can remember where they put it. But she thinks if he looks into my face he'll find his. I'm not so sure she's right."

"Oh," Faith said. "Then I guess we can't hide in the corner."

Which meant Faith would likely come face to face with the man as well. But she pushed the thought away again, feeling that Sarah's problems were more grave. Also that Faith was a grown-up, and could be trusted to handle her own emotions.

"Did you know his father was a bank robber?" the girl asked suddenly.

"Your father's father?"

"Yeah."

"No. I had no idea. That's weird."

"It *is* weird. Isn't it?" The girl's voice had energized now. "I mean, most people think bank robbers are only in the movies."

"Well, I didn't exactly think that. You read about banks being robbed all the time."

"I guess," Sarah said. "But you don't really think about the robbers having kids and grand-kids."

"True."

They drove in silence for a minute or two, Faith looking out at the oil derricks off the coast. When she was a girl, a friend's mother had used to refer to them as pirate ships. To adjust her feelings about them, Faith supposed. Keep them from seeming like such a blight on the horizon.

"Is he in jail, your grandfather?"

"No. He's dead."

"Oh. I'm sorry."

"He was in jail. But he escaped. With five other guys. The other four got caught again and put back. My grandfather stayed outside, on the run, for like seven months. I think it was seven months. Then he robbed another bank and got shot by a guard he didn't know was there. This was all before I was born. But, you know. You hear about it."

"That's quite a family history, kiddo."

"I know, right?"

"How old was your dad during all this?"

"I think he was thirteen when his dad first went to jail. And around seventeen when he died."

"I'm curious as to why you brought this up."

Sarah shrugged and looked out toward the pirate ships. Then again, maybe they were only oil derricks to her.

"Just talking," she said.

"Were you thinking maybe this kind of stuff runs in his family?"

Then Faith desperately wished she could pull the words back inside again. It wasn't until they were out in the world that she realized she might have accidentally suggested such behavior could run all the way down through the family genes to Sarah. Which she hadn't meant, and didn't believe.

But the girl didn't seem to read anything troubling into the question.

"I wasn't thinking that, no. I was just thinking it must have been a really hard way to grow up."

"Oh," Faith said.

She said nothing more for several miles. Neither one of them said more all the way through Santa Barbara.

Then Carpinteria.

Almost into Ventura.

Faith chewed on the inside of her lip and mulled over the fact that Sarah was reaching for a reason why her father was the way he was. Rehumanizing him in her mind. Because he was still her father, in spite of everything. After everything.

What's more, Faith had to think about the fact that the girl was probably right. People generally are the way they are for reasons.

"She's not going to work out for Julia, you know," Sarah said, bumping her out of her thoughts. "You know that, right?"

"I guess I'd say it's not looking good."

"It's hopeless."

"I don't know that anything is hopeless. Maybe Estelle will keep the mare for herself."

"Be nice if she would. Now *that* could work out. But I doubt it. She's seventy-eight, you know."

"I didn't know that. I had no idea she was that old. Are you sure? Who told you she was seventy-eight?"

"Stan. She doesn't really show anymore. Every now and then she'll do a sort of exhibition ride at a big show, usually a championship one. But the training schedule you have to keep to ride a horse in Grand Prix . . . you know, to keep yourself and the horse sharp for that level, well . . . it's a lot of work. And she's retired from that."

"She may still be able to help Julia step up to ride the mare."

"No," Sarah said. And it was a definitive

answer. It left no room for doubt, and no thought of error. "No, she can teach Julia to ride. But she can't teach her what kind of person to be. Julia's already what she is, and Estelle can't do anything about it."

When Constance opened the door of her home, Faith was shocked by the older woman's appearance. Her skin looked sallow and pale, more creased than Faith remembered. She seemed not to have slept in days. Her hair was unkempt.

She grabbed Sarah up into her arms, and they embraced for a long time on her welcome mat.

"Come in," she said. "Come in. I made spaghetti and garlic bread. I hope that's okay. And a salad, of course. Something on our plates has to be green."

"That sounds great," Faith said.

"I'm not hungry," Sarah said. "I'm just tired. I'm just going to go to my room and lie down."

Sarah trotted up the stairs and disappeared.

Faith looked at Constance, who looked back briefly. The older woman cut her eyes away.

"She's upset about tomorrow," Faith said.

"Of course she is. We all are. I mean, we both are."

"No," Faith said. "We all are."

Constance's weary eyes came up to hers again, searching. It took her a moment. The count of three, maybe. Then she got it.

"Oh my goodness, yes," she said. "I'm sorry. I forgot about that whole thing with you and Sarah's father. You thought you were dating a nice man."

"For a minute there. It's not like much happened."

"Oh, plenty happened," Constance said. "He earned your trust under false pretenses. It was a betrayal. Like everything else he does. Like everything else he's ever done."

They stood aimlessly for a moment, not sure what to do with their bodies. Not sure if there was more to say.

Then Constance said, "Come into the kitchen with me. I have to stir the sauce."

And they walked together, Faith following.

"I made you a bed on the couch," Constance continued, on their way into the kitchen. "I hope that will be good enough."

"It's fine. Thank you. I'm sorry we're so late getting down here. There was traffic, and some construction going through the pass."

Faith had just glanced at the clock on the microwave and noted, to her surprise, that it was nearly eight in the evening.

"I'm not worried about that," Constance said, measuring out dry spaghetti in her hand one serving at a time and dropping it into the pot of boiling water. "I'm just so relieved to have Sarah home again. It's going to help me a lot to have her back. I mean, assuming the judge doesn't do something crazy like let him out on bail until the trial."

Faith breathed deeply against a ball of anxiety that had risen up into her chest. It seemed to be lodged in the space between her lungs. It hurt to try to draw a full breath around it.

"About that . . . ," Faith began.

Immediately she could feel Constance's anxiety rise up to guard against her words. She could see it on the older woman's face, but she could literally feel it as well. It had an electrical charge. It crackled in the air between them.

"She can't stay with the horse forever," Constance said.

"I know. She knows. But she's been invited to stay for a little while. Just to help with the transition. Just for the first few days. It's barely even been two days, and it's not going well so far. Her new rider already came off the horse and sprained her wrist. If Sarah stays down here now, doesn't even go back for a few days to help . . . well, I worry that it won't work out and she'll always blame herself for the fact that it didn't."

Constance dropped a small handful of salt into the boiling pot, and it fizzed up white as she stirred it in.

"There's really no good ending to this," Constance said. Her voice sounded hard. Unfriendly to the point of raising a knot of fear in Faith's gut. "Once she went back to see the horse, it's nothing but trauma for her, no matter how it ends. I think if it had been me, I wouldn't have taken her to visit the horse in the first place. I don't know that it was wise."

She stopped stirring and raised her eyes to Faith. Faith had opened her mouth to speak, but no words were coming out. The older woman's eyes softened suddenly, and the anger fell away.

She rushed in and threw her arms around Faith, who was too shocked to hold her in return.

"Oh, Faith, I'm sorry. I've been so upset. But the last thing I want to do is take it out on you. You've done so much for Sarah. And for me. You've been wonderful."

She let go of Faith. Stepped back. Both women trained their gazes more or less on the kitchen linoleum.

Faith breathed deeply for the first time in a long time.

"It was great for her to go see the horse," Constance said, her words all in a rush. Tumbling against one another. "I think it helped her make it through the summer. It got her through this hardest time after her mother . . . I just worry about what happens when those two come apart again. I'm scared about that. And I don't know what the answer is. I don't know if it was right or wrong for her to be spending this time with the

337

horse. I don't know the answer. But I do know you were trying to act in her best interest."

They stood awkwardly for a moment, still not looking at each other.

Then Faith said, "A few more days, Constance. Just give her a few more days to feel she's done everything she can to help this new home work out for the mare. No matter how hard it is for her to say goodbye again, I really think it will be better than if we tear her away now."

"I suppose," Constance said. "Maybe I'm being selfish. If a few days will help her, then you should try that. I've been without her this long. I'll survive a few more days. I'll go get her and tell her to come down for dinner."

"She said she wasn't hungry," Faith said as Constance hurried out of the kitchen.

"In my house, you come to dinner," Constance said over her shoulder and without stopping. "She doesn't have to eat, but she should come to the table."

Then she was out of earshot and gone.

Faith sat down hard on a thinly padded chair at the kitchen table. Watched steam rise from the pot of boiling spaghetti, and the smaller pot of sauce. Looked out the window at a squirrel running along the high branches of a tree in Constance's side yard. But the windows grew opaque with steam, and it became harder and harder to see him. As though life outside this house, this set of troubles, was growing dimmer and fading away.

"You have to come see this with me," Constance said, startling her. "I need help deciding something."

Faith rose and followed the woman through the dining room, down a hallway, and up the stairs to the second floor.

They stuck their heads into Sarah's bedroom.

The girl was lying on the bed with her eyes closed, as if sleeping. But she was crying. Sobbing audibly, her body shaking with the sobs, and with tears running freely down her face.

"Is she asleep?" Faith asked quietly.

"Sound asleep. At first I thought she was awake but she just didn't want to see me there. But I spoke to her. And she's sleeping. And now I don't know what to do. I don't know if I should wake her."

"I wouldn't worry much about her coming to dinner," Faith said. "What does it matter in the great scheme of things?"

"I didn't mean that. I meant . . . should I wake her? You know how when a child is having a nightmare and they're acting afraid in their sleep? You wake them. You kiss them awake to save them from it. So they'll see there's nothing to be afraid of. But what do you do when a child is heartbroken in her sleep but the world you're waking her up into is no better?"

"Wow," Faith said. "That's a hard one."

She paused, in case it was a rhetorical question. But she could feel Constance waiting for an answer. Desperate for any advice.

"I guess . . . I would say . . . let her cry it out. I've seen her cry a few times, but you just know there must be more in there. It needs to get out. So badly that it's coming out in her sleep. I think we should just let her clear some more of this away. It's not like we can really stop it anyway. All she can do is bottle it up. Or not."

"Good," Constance said, sounding more settled now. "That's good thinking. Come on downstairs, and we'll have some dinner."

Faith did.

They ate their spaghetti and garlic bread and salad in absolute silence. If there was anything more in the world for the two women to say to each other, neither seemed able to find it.

Chapter Sixteen

Better Than Never

Faith sat nervously on the edge of a hard bench in the courtroom, Sarah to her right, Constance on the other side of the girl.

They had been waiting this way for close to half an hour. Her father had not been brought in, and they had no clue when he would be.

The room was clean and upscale. Big windows, with drawn dark-tan blinds that blocked out the world beyond. Men in dark uniform slacks and tan short-sleeved shirts stood. Some mingled. One uniformed officer in blue leaned his back against a wall. A woman in a neat-looking pantsuit sat at a table facing the empty judge's bench and a smaller bench-style desk for a court reporter, but Faith had no idea if she was Harlan Deaver's attorney.

Faith closed her eyes and tried to calm her lower belly by sheer force of will. Failing that, she attempted to mentally project herself somewhere else. Anywhere else.

Oddly enough, at least in her mind, she landed in the cool tack stall at Moonshadow Farm. Because they had been safe there. And not right on the edge of losing everything. Well . . . losing the mare. And, at the moment, Midnight seemed to be everything. The loss of the horse and the loss of everything felt indistinguishable in Faith's head.

She opened her eyes again. Leaned over the girl and whispered to Constance.

"It's been three days since they arrested him."

Constance blinked a few times, quickly. As though Faith had wakened her.

"Has it? No, I don't think so. It's been two."

"They arrested him on Monday."

"No," Constance whispered back. "They brought him in for questioning on Monday evening. They arrested him and charged him with a crime on Tuesday."

"Oh," Faith said. "Oh. Okay. That explains a lot."

The girl must have gotten those logistics wrong as she passed information from her grandmother to Faith. It made more sense this way, because Faith had heard or read somewhere that a defendant has to be arraigned within forty-eight hours of his arrest, assuming no weekdays or holidays.

Faith closed her eyes and tried to go away again in her head.

She didn't get far.

"I feel like I'm about to be sick," Sarah said under her breath. Whether she meant the words for Faith or her grandmother remained unclear.

Faith opened her eyes and glanced over at the girl, and at Constance beyond. The girl did look a little green. And Constance was in a world very far away. Farther than just Moonshadow Farm in Los Alamos. She seemed not to have heard.

"Literally?" Faith asked quietly. "Like you're going to throw up?"

"Maybe. I'm not sure. Might have been something I ate."

"You didn't eat anything."

"Oh. Right. Must've been that, then."

It struck Faith suddenly that she had forgotten to tell the girl about the conversation she'd had with Constance the previous evening. About the hard-won few days Faith had negotiated so they could go back to Estelle's. It was important, but Faith had wakened up nervous and preoccupied, and somehow it had remained lodged in a segment of her mind she had not been able to access.

She opened her mouth to say something about it. This was not the time, but at least she could get out a short version of it.

Before she could speak, Sarah spit out three elongated, shocked words under her breath.

"Oh. My. God."

Faith turned her head to see . . . him. She wanted to say Greg, but he wasn't Greg. He was Harlan Deaver, a stranger to her. He had already passed them, being led up the aisle by two uniformed officers. He appeared not to have noticed them sitting there, but maybe he simply chose not to react. His gaze was trained straight ahead, and he did not look back. He wore a two-piece orange prison outfit. He seemed to have his hands together in front of him, but Faith couldn't tell from behind if he was handcuffed or not.

She glanced over at her two friends. Sarah was biting her lower lip, and her eyes looked almost entirely vacant. Constance had her gaze trained on the man like a laser. She reminded Faith of a cat watching a moving object with intense fascination.

A judge stepped into the room from her chambers beyond and everyone rose, because a strong male voice asked them to.

It said, "All rise."

She was an older woman, the judge. Close to eighty from the look of it, with black hair going to pure white at the temples and hairline. She sat at the bench, and everyone else sat again.

Well. Almost everyone else. Harlan Deaver did not sit.

He stood, and his attorney stood. Someone was reciting something to him, but Faith couldn't hear what it was. The judge had a microphone, but no one else in the court did.

Faith watched carefully, and saw that Harlan was raising his right hand. So she assumed he was being sworn in. And it was difficult and awkward to raise his right hand, because he was indeed handcuffed. So his left hand had to hover a few inches below his right until the moment he said, "Yes, sir. I do." Meanwhile he was creating a clear view of his handcuffs for everyone in the courtroom. As if he intended to show them off.

"I'm gonna throw up," Sarah hissed into her ear.

She pushed by Faith and ran toward the courtroom doors.

Faith glanced over at Constance, but the older woman didn't seem to know the girl was gone. So Faith ran after Sarah.

Just as she reached the doors that the girl had pushed through, she heard the tapping of a gavel, and a woman who must have been the judge saying, "Can we have silence in the courtroom?" into a microphone.

Faith didn't know if she and the girl were the disturbance in question, but she assumed they were.

She pushed the door open quietly and stepped out into the hall.

No Sarah.

There was a ladies' room off to the right, clearly marked with a Plexiglas sign that stuck out at a right angle from the wall. Faith trotted down the empty hallway, pushed the swinging door open, and stepped inside.

One stall door was closed, and from behind

it Faith heard the terrible sound of retching. Painful-sounding, desperate heaves, the kind that try to turn a person inside out.

On a brief break in between them, Faith said, quietly, "I'm here. Just so you know."

No reply.

A long silence fell, free of the horrible sounds of regurgitation.

After a time the girl said, "I heard you come in." Her voice sounded weak. Spent.

"How did you know it wasn't your grandmother coming through the door?"

"Because she's frozen like a statue. I couldn't get in to wherever she was. Believe me. I tried."

Another long, blessedly silent pause.

Then the stall door swung in and the girl stepped out, her face frighteningly white. She crossed the ladies' room linoleum to the sink, swaying once as if she might faint dead away. Faith rushed in to help, but Sarah had already caught herself with both hands against the sink.

She turned on the water and filled both her hands with it, rinsing her mouth. Then she spit, dried her face with a paper towel, and stared at her own eyes in the mirror.

"Was it the handcuffs?" Faith asked.

"Was what the handcuffs?"

"Seeing your dad in handcuffs?"

"I told you I felt sick before he even came in."

"Oh. That's right. You did, didn't you?"

"I thought it was just something I didn't eat."

And on that sentence, surprisingly, the girl smiled. Just the tiniest bit. It was only an ironic little twist of her mouth. But Faith was happy to see Sarah's sense of humor peek out, and grateful that it had not utterly abandoned her.

"But I guess it could have been all this," Sarah added. She frowned into her own face in the mirror. "You know. Tension and stuff. It *is* weird to see your own father in handcuffs. Especially when you sort of put them on him yourself. Not literally, but . . . you know what I mean."

"You did exactly what needed to be done, Sarah."

"I know. I know I did. It's just weird."

"Yeah. I know. Well, no, I don't know. Not really. But I can imagine."

A strange, queasy look came over the girl's face.

"Uh-oh," she said.

She turned suddenly and darted into the stall again, falling forward onto her knees.

Faith stepped in behind her and crouched over her, gathering up the girl's long hair to keep it out of the way. Then she reached around and pressed one hand to Sarah's forehead and held it there. Because Faith's mother had used to do that for her when she was sick. She had completely and utterly forgotten the gesture. It only came back to her at the moment she performed the act herself.

She kept her eyes averted and her mind as blank as possible until the girl was done with what sounded like dry heaving. Or until she appeared to be done, anyway.

"Is that it?" she asked gently.

"I think so," Sarah said. And spit.

Faith took her hand off the girl's forehead and flushed the toilet for her without looking.

"We should go back in as soon as you think you can. Your grandmother's all alone in there. And she was very specific about not wanting that."

"Right," Sarah said, and struggled to get to her feet.

Faith helped.

She walked the girl over to the sink, where Sarah rinsed her mouth again and splashed water on her own face.

"Okay," Sarah said, connecting with Faith's eyes in the mirror. "I'm not sure what's going to happen with my stomach. But I'll try."

They stepped out into the hall together. Faith still had one arm around the girl's shoulders to steady her. When they reached the swinging doors into the courtroom, Faith reached a hand out and pushed one of the doors open, guiding the girl through.

There they almost literally ran into Sarah's father.

He was being walked out of the courtroom by the two uniformed officers. One on each side, holding the handcuffed man's arms at the elbow. The three of them formed a wide parade, not easy to get around in the aisle between benches. So they all stalled there, just looking each other in the face.

Faith watched the world grow a faint white at the edges of her vision, as though her grip on consciousness was not assured. She could only imagine how the girl must feel.

Harlan Deaver was not looking at Faith. He was looking into the eyes of his daughter. And his daughter was looking back.

They stood that way for a long—bizarrely long—three or four seconds.

Then Sarah pushed by one of the officers and hurried up the aisle to her grandmother. Faith followed.

"We missed the whole thing," Faith whispered to Constance as she sat back down, still a little shaky. She leaned over the girl to speak, so as not to cause another gaveled warning with her words. "What happened?"

Thankfully, Constance seemed to have broken free of her trance.

"They read him the charges," she said. "Second-degree murder, and making a false statement to a police officer. And how much time he could be sentenced to for each count. He pled not guilty, just like we knew he would. Oh, and the judge denied him bail. Something about a whiff of trying to intimidate a witness. She didn't say much about the details of that, but I think we know what she meant. I guess the police who arrested him asked for no bail. For Sarah's sake. From what I understand, she doesn't have to do what they ask, but in this case she did."

Sarah was staring over her shoulder at the back of the courtroom, so Faith turned to see what was so interesting.

He was still there.

Harlan Deaver stood huddled by the door with the two officers and his attorney. For a strangely long time they massed there, talking. Too loudly for the judge's tastes, most likely, but not loud enough for Faith to make out their individual words.

"What are they doing?" Faith said out loud, quietly, to no one. Facing no one. She just asked.

As she did, the attorney split off from the group and walked back up to the front of the courtroom.

"Your Honor—" she began.

The judge gaveled her into silence.

"We're done with your client, counselor," the judge said closely—too closely—into the microphone. It howled with feedback, causing Faith to jump. "We're ready to call the next defendant."

"If I may, Your Honor," the attorney said, "I realize this is irregular. But my client wants to change his plea."

"He can do that at the next hearing. In three weeks."

"He can, Your Honor. But I just thought . . . in the interest of saving the court's time and the taxpayers' money . . ."

She paused.

The whole world paused. Or so it seemed to Faith.

The judge sighed deeply.

"All right. I'll allow it. But let's make this quick."

She raised her eyes to the back of the room and nodded.

Harlan Deaver was led back up the aisle. Faith watched over her shoulder. Constance and Sarah did not. This time he looked right into Faith's eyes. Hooked her with the compelling cool gray of his own.

Faith knew exactly what she expected to see.

Every time she had locked gazes with the man, she had experienced a combination of attraction and fear, and a confusion over whether her attachment to those eyes, and their draw, could be trusted.

This time she waited for the positive parts of the feeling to be utterly absent, and to see only evil and justification for her fear in his eyes. She waited for everything to fall away except the danger of him.

It didn't happen.

Instead he looked helpless and demoralized, which should not have come as a surprise. After all, he was handcuffed, and in police custody. And there was something else, but Faith struggled to place it.

She connected with a sudden memory in her head. Sarah, in a clean stall full of straw at the horse park in the middle of the night. Saying, "He was . . . ashamed. Like . . . really, really ashamed."

But that wasn't quite it.

It was something more akin to regret. Like he had never intended his life or anything in it to lead him into a position like this one. And yet here he was.

Then he drew level with Faith, and passed her.

He did not look back.

"All right," the judge said, sounding put-upon and irritated. "Harlan Jeffrey Deaver, you've been read the charges against you. Tell the court . . . how do you plead?"

"Guilty, Your Honor."

"I see," the judge said.

She drew a long, slow breath.

Then she began to ask a series of questions that Faith only half followed because her head was swimming with surprise and random thoughts. But each question seemed geared toward asking Sarah's father to affirm that he knew he was giving up various rights by entering this plea, and assuring that he understood each point, and that he was sure it was what he wanted to do.

After each question he answered, "Yes, Your Honor," in a small and humbled voice.

"Well, then, Mr. Deaver. Please tell the court in your own words what happened on the night in question." She lifted a legal-length paper from her desk, brought it closer to her face, and scanned it quickly, holding a pair of reading glasses between her eyes and the sheet. "The night of May nineteenth."

"Yes, Your Honor," he said again.

Then he just stood and breathed for a few seconds, as if filling himself with whatever courage he was about to need. Faith could see his back and shoulders rise and fall with the force of the breaths.

"Um . . . it was just after midnight, so actually it was the morning of the twentieth . . . but I guess that doesn't matter. Anyway, my wife and I had been fighting, which we did pretty regularly, but this time was different. I'm not sure different how. Well, I know how, I'm just not sure if I can say it right. Getting it into words might be hard, but I'll try. It's like she was . . . not . . . affected by me at all—like she'd pulled away somehow, and I was trying to draw her out with my words, but I couldn't even find her. It scared me. Nothing like that had ever happened before. And then she started yelling these really bad things about me. I mean . . . I can't even repeat them. It's nothing I'd even say out loud, but it felt like she had a knife and she kept stabbing me with it, except it wasn't a knife, it was just words. She was looking out the window and yelling these things. She wouldn't even look at me.

"There was a gun in the drawer of the bedside table. For home defense only, you know—in case of robbery. I just wanted her to stop talking. I thought I could scare her into not talking. So I went over to where she was standing at the window, and I held it right up against the side of her head and I told her, 'No more.' Like, just stop talking. And she looked over at me with this total look of . . ."

He paused for a long time. Long enough that Faith expected the judge to force the issue. Before she could, as if sensing the end of his slack, he restarted himself.

". . . like I repulsed her. Like she had no respect for me at all. Like I was a worm or something, something she'd be disgusted to scrape off her shoe. She laughed at me. I couldn't believe it. I was holding a gun to her head, and she laughed at me. I was just . . . powerless. There was nothing I could do to get through to her.

"I know this is going to sound hard to believe, but I swear to God I didn't know I pulled the trigger until I heard the gun go off. I never thought, *I'll pull the trigger now.* There was no thought about that at all. I'm not saying I did it by accident exactly—I know now that I did it, but I was so outside myself . . . it's like I was outside my body. I did it without ever knowing I was going to. I don't even know if that makes sense or not, but I swear I'm explaining it the best way I know how."

The judge nodded. Waited. In case there might be more.

Then she said, her lips close to the microphone, "And then you put the gun in your wife's hand to make it look like a suicide?"

"Well, yes and no, Your Honor."

"Has to be one or the other, Mr. Deaver. Did you or didn't you?"

"I did. But not then. Not right away. I ran out of the room and out into the hallway. I was just going to call 9-1-1. I don't know what I would have said, I was just trying to get an ambulance even though I mostly knew it was too late for one. But I guess I was in shock and not seeing things clearly. I couldn't think. And then once I got out into the hall I ran into my daughter. Not literally, but . . . she was there. I guess she'd heard everything. Or enough, anyway. And I looked at her and she looked at me, and I thought, *She probably doesn't have a mother anymore, and if I tell the truth about what happened, she won't have a father, either.* It just broke my heart. So that's when I . . . changed . . . some things. About the scene."

"More detail, please, Mr. Deaver," the judge said. "The law thrives on specificity."

"Okay. I . . . went back in. To the bedroom. Which I really didn't want to do, of course. I'd dropped the gun on the bed before I ran out of the room. I picked it up and I wiped my prints off it with a tissue and held it with my shirttail, and then I wrapped her hand around it. And I went back downstairs and called 9-1-1, and when the police came I told them we'd been fighting, but that I'd gone downstairs to have a drink when I heard the shot. Oh, and I scrubbed my hands with sink cleanser because I thought the police might be able to find gunpowder residue on my hands. I think I saw that on a TV show, but I don't remember exactly."

"And you didn't think your daughter would tell the police her version of the events?"

"I . . ." With that, Harlan Deaver appeared to step off another verbal cliff. The question seemed to have short-circuited him. It took him an awkward length of time to pull himself together and continue. "I don't know, Your Honor. I don't know how to answer that question. I wasn't thinking clearly, to put it mildly. I didn't know what she would do."

"I see," the judge said. "So you not only falsified evidence at the scene and made a false statement to those officers, but you made a knowingly false statement to the court a few minutes ago, under oath. You said you were not guilty of the crimes you've been charged with, but now you say you consciously knew that you *were* guilty."

Harlan Deaver's head dropped forward. He must have grown tired of holding it up and wanted to rest his chin on his chest. He mumbled something, but Faith couldn't make out the words.

Apparently neither could the judge.

"Excuse me?" she asked, her voice booming into the microphone.

"I said, 'Yes, Your Honor.' "

"All right. I think we're nearly done here. Bail is denied, same as it was when you said you were innocent. A sentencing hearing will be scheduled for three weeks from today if possible. I only have one other question, Mr. Deaver, before they take you away and we move on to our next defendant like we thought we were about to do five or ten minutes ago. Would you please tell the court what brought on this sudden change of heart?"

Again, Harlan Deaver mumbled something too quiet to hear.

"With sufficient volume, Mr. Deaver. Please."

"My daughter, Your Honor."

"What about your daughter?"

"I saw her. Just now as I was leaving the courtroom. And I thought about how there would be a trial, and she'd have to get up on the stand and say what she saw that night. No, that's not quite right. I didn't even think of it, exactly. It just kind of slammed into me. It was just there all of a sudden. We'd be testifying against each other, and if I was still maintaining that I'd done nothing wrong . . . then I'd have to . . . I'd have to say she was lying. I'd have to call my own daughter a liar. And she's not. I've told a lot of stories in my life, I guess because I thought I had to—because I'd gotten myself into some mess that I thought was too big to face, so I lied to save my skin and get out of it. But I guess everybody has a line. I think you know what I mean by a line. I didn't know where mine was, but I found out just now. I wasn't going to call my own daughter a liar when I know she's not. I love my daughter. Whatever you think of me and whatever I've done, I'm telling you right now I love that little girl. She doesn't deserve that. That would have been over the line even for me. Why do you think I was following her and trying to get her back? I wasn't going to hurt her. I wanted her back. She was all I had left."

The judge looked down at him from the bench with an expression that struck Faith as pity. Or at least something closely related.

Harlan Deaver looked down at the carpet in shame. Faith couldn't even see his face. But she could feel his shame. It was in his body language. It was there in the room. It all but filled up the breathable air, leaving no room for anything else to exist.

"You wanted to brainwash her," Constance hissed under her breath.

But Sarah shushed her grandmother.

"I suppose the court thanks you for your honesty, Mr. Deaver," the judge said. "It goes without saying that it arrived far too late, but better that than never, I suppose. Now this arraignment is complete, and it's time to bring in the next defendant. Well past time, in fact."

And then, just like that, it was all over.

Harlan Deaver was led out of the courtroom by the two armed officers.

Nobody met anybody else's eyes.

"I need to go back to Estelle's," Sarah said to her grandmother. She was leaning on Faith's car, looking down at the tarmac of the municipal parking lot. "I'm sorry, but I really need to. I know you want me home, Grandma, but it's so important. Maybe you could come to Estelle's with me." She raised her eyes hopefully on the last sentence.

"No, honey," Constance said. "I can't. You know how I need to be in my own home, especially when I'm upset. But you can go with Faith."

Sarah's eyes came up to Constance's face, filled with something close to disbelief.

"Just like that? Just that easy?"

"We talked about it last night," Faith said. "Your grandmother and I talked while you were sleeping. She was kind enough to agree to let you go to Estelle's for a few more days."

"I thought we said a couple more," Constance interjected.

"Pretty sure we said a few."

"Well. Whatever, I guess. Once you're up there I can't force you back anyway. I'm just trusting you to come back as soon as you know everything's okay with the horse."

Faith watched the girl and her grandmother hug goodbye and knew that elusive "everything's okay" moment would never arrive. Nothing was ever likely to be fully okay between Julia and the mare. "Everything" was cleanly out of reach.

But they would come back.

It would break Sarah's heart all over again, but they would come back. Because they had to. There really was no other way for this to end as far as Faith could see.

"So, I have a question," Faith said when they were almost back to Estelle's.

She had taken the 154 out of Santa Barbara, the San Marcos Pass from the southeastern end, to see if it would be faster. It was more direct but with a lower speed limit. They were looking out and down over Cachuma Lake as Faith spoke up.

Sarah seemed to gather herself to listen—to bring her whole self back into the car with Faith. Maybe she had been half-asleep. Maybe just very far away.

"Okay," she said.

"Do you believe everything he said in that courtroom today?"

"Not really. Not everything. But he was being pretty honest. I mean, that was more honesty than I've heard out of his mouth at one time . . . well, I guess ever. I already knew it wasn't premeditated or anything. He loved her. I knew he didn't mean for it to turn out like that. Anyway, I know when he's lying. Always. He has a tell. Good thing he doesn't know he has it, or he'd fix it somehow. He has a really good poker face, which makes sense, since he learned it during actual poker. But when he lies, he starts talking faster and his voice gets higher. It's not super obvious. If you don't know him, you might not even notice. I'll bet the judge never noticed. But when you really know him like I do . . ."

She trailed off, and Faith waited to see if there was more.

It surprised her that the girl felt so talkative. But maybe it shouldn't have. That was Faith's next thought. Of course Sarah needed to talk this

361

over with someone. Faith was mostly relieved and honored to be the trusted someone.

"So what did he say today that was a lie?"

"The part about how he only tampered with the crime scene for me. So I wouldn't lose both parents. He might have thought about that later. But that whole 'I did it for my daughter and not for me' thing was a story for the judge. He was just scared, and he didn't want to go to jail."

"And now there he is," Faith said. "In jail."

"Yeah. I was just thinking that. All this trouble to try to avoid going to jail. To get out of paying for what he did. And now there he is. If it was me, I would have just called 9-1-1 and said what happened. Not added all those extra false statements and perjury charges."

"If it had been you, it never would have happened."

"Oh," Sarah said. "That's a good point, too."

Chapter Seventeen

Absolution, Maybe

They sat at the breakfast table with Estelle. Faith was drinking a second cup of coffee. She had finished her eggs. Sarah was mostly pushing hers around with her fork, and staring down at the plate.

"I have a request of you this morning," Estelle said.

Faith could tell those words had been directed to the girl, but Sarah was still staring at her uneaten eggs and didn't seem to notice. After a moment of silence during which no one else answered, the girl lifted her head and looked at Estelle.

"Who? Me?"

"Yes, darling. You. I'd like to do another of those lessons with Julia on a longe line. I think it has to be that way right now, because she can't properly hold both reins. I think it's the only safe way to do it. I was hoping this morning you could take the line and give her a lesson on the mare. Keep her safe. You can control the mare on a longe line, correct?"

"Yes, ma'am," Sarah said.

"Good. And give her the pointers she needs,

please. But here comes the important part of the request. I need you to make a bit of an adjustment in your attitude toward Julia. Wait. Let me rephrase that. 'Attitude' is such a loaded word. I'd like you to try a different approach. Julia thinks you look down on her. That you feel you're the better rider. That's why she gets so defensive. And I'm not blaming you, darling. Truth is—and you must never repeat this to anyone—you *are* the better rider, despite being eight years younger and two levels behind in the show arena. You have a better grasp of the basics, you're more effective, and you look prettier in the saddle. But I'd like you to put that behind you today and try to advise Julia as an equal. Does that make sense? And, more importantly, does it feel like something you can do?"

"I can *do it,*" Sarah said. "I'm not sure she's willing to *let me* do it."

"She'll let you. I had a long talk with her while you were away. She knows she needs help if she's ever to have a future with that beautiful mare. She just can't tolerate feeling you're looking down on her. And I'm not even going to be there, because I think on an emotional level I'll only get in the way. She can tell me later how it went. And so can you."

The girl sighed deeply. And, surprisingly, popped a big bite of eggs into her mouth. She chewed slowly, then swallowed.

"I'm willing to give it a try if she is," Sarah said.

Julia was waiting for them out by the barn. Horseless. Just standing in the sun, wearing expensive tall boots and tan breeches. A white short-sleeved riding shirt with red bars on the sleeves. And, of course, her wrist brace.

"I asked Stan to go get Sol and tack her up," she said as Faith and Sarah came within earshot.

For a moment, Sarah seemed not to focus on the obvious.

She only said, "I could've tacked her and brought her up."

"Let Stan do it. He *works* here."

A brief pause, during which Faith wondered if she was the only one wondering.

Then Sarah seemed to backtrack in her head and trip over the information that had originally passed her by.

"Wait. You asked him to go get *who?*"

"Sol. It's her new barn name."

"Why does she need a new barn name?"

"I don't know. Didn't you ever get a new horse and want to name her yourself?"

"Not really," Sarah said. Faith could tell the girl was doing her best to contain herself. "I only ever got one horse. And her registered name is Falkner's Midnight Sun, so why would I want to change that? I mean, Midnight is part of her name. It's just a short version of her name."

"But Sol means sun. As in, Falkner's Midnight Sun. I thought that was clever."

Sarah shifted back and forth in her boots a little, as if standing still were out of the question.

"I just don't see what's wrong with Midnight," she said after a time.

"Oh, it's just so . . ." Julia paused to gather her words. She either didn't have any handy or didn't like the ones she had. "Midnight for a black animal. I don't know. It's like the name a little kid would give to a black cat if you let him decide on his own."

"Well, I was only eight when I got her," Sarah said, her voice rising now. Leaning in slightly. "But I didn't just make it up. It's on her papers."

"I didn't mean to offend you," Julia said. But it might have been just shy of sincere. "I'm only saying that she's mine now, and I want her to have a barn name that I *like*."

Sarah rose up onto her toes and leaned in. She opened her mouth, but no words came out. Faith thought the girl's face looked a little too red.

Stan walked out of the barn leading the fully tacked mare and led the horse between the two girls, effectively ending the standoff.

"Here's Midnight," he said.

Faith thought Stan might not have heard about the name change yet. But as Julia led the mare to the mounting block with her one good hand, Stan turned to Sarah and gave the girl a conspiratorial wink.

Then he disappeared back into the barn.

"Okay, here's an exercise," Sarah called to Julia.

She stood in the middle of the round pen, holding the longe whip and line. Julia sat the mare on the rail, in a halt position, reins knotted and sitting idle on the horse's neck.

"Remember when your grandmother wanted you to practice halting the mare with no reins? It helps you focus on the other aids involved with the halt. I'd like to see her neck rounder right now. She can go a lot rounder than this. Normally I know you'd work the bit to ask her to round. But she can do it just from your leg and your structure. So try engaging your core and giving her a tiny little aid with your legs. She might think you want her to move forward, but I'll be your reins. I'll ask her to stand in place. Okay?"

"Okay," Julia said. "Let's try it."

She sat up very straight in the saddle. Probably gave a small aid with her legs, but Faith never saw it.

The mare moved forward.

Sarah stopped her after only one step.

"Try again," Sarah said.

She stood a little forward in the mare's line of sight and held one hand out in a signal to the horse to stand.

There was no movement on the part of the rider as far as Faith could see. But the mare dropped her head and rounded her neck beautifully.

"Good one!" Sarah called out. "See? That was just the right amount of aid."

Faith's phone rang.

She pulled it out of her pocket and stared at it to see who was calling.

The caller ID line read "Ventura County Department of Corrections."

Faith picked up the call, thinking it was Constance. Somehow Constance was at the jail today, she thought. Maybe she had some kind of news. Maybe she'd tried to call Sarah, but what if the girl had left her phone in the house? It could be urgent.

"Hello?" she said.

Nothing happened. There seemed to be no one on the line.

Then she heard a click, followed by a recorded message. A robotic woman's voice informed her that she had a collect call from an inmate at the Ventura County Jail, and told her what numbers to press to accept or reject the call and its charges.

She paused a moment, unsure of what to do.

She still thought it must be Constance, somehow forced to use the automated collect call system at the jail. Or maybe some jail administrator needing to speak to Sarah.

Faith pressed one.

"Hello?" a tentative male voice asked.

Faith could feel a tingling begin at the nape of her neck and cascade down her spine like ice water. It was Harlan Deaver on the other end of the line. Unmistakably Harlan Deaver. Her first impulse was to hang up. And she almost did. But she was curious about one thing. So curious that she had considered a letter or even a hard-to-imagine prison visit to get an answer. Maybe she could get one now. And then never come near him again as long as she lived, not even on the phone. Even if she had to change her number for safety.

"How did you get this number?" she asked, probably too loudly.

She turned her back to the rail and walked away from the round pen and the lesson as briskly as possible.

"You don't want to know," he said. "You really don't want to know."

Faith stopped walking at the big outdoor arena.

Estelle was schooling Reggie, the huge chestnut gelding with the high white socks who had carried Faith so ably on the trail. Faith knew that ride had been only a couple of days earlier, but any part of Faith's life prior to the arraignment felt like ancient history now.

"What do you want?" she asked him, allowing all her anger to rise up into her throat. Into her voice. To protect her. "And before you even

369

answer, I want to say one thing in no uncertain terms. I picked up this call because I didn't understand it was you. You're probably right that I don't want to know how you got the number. But I'll give you this one chance to tell me what you want, and I want one piece of information from you, and then you're going to lose this number and never try to contact me again. Is that something you can commit to?"

"Yes," he said. "I get it."

"Good. Talk fast. I'm paying for this call."

"I just wanted to say I was sorry."

"For what specifically?"

"For . . . what happened with us. You know. My not being entirely honest about who I was and what I wanted."

"Not *entirely* honest? Is that some kind of joke? You told me your name was Greg."

"Okay. Okay. You win. Not honest at all."

A pause fell on both ends of the line. Estelle and her gelding were performing a half pass, diagonally across the arena, the horse's legs neatly crossing over one another in a perfectly choreographed lateral movement. It struck Faith as almost painfully beautiful. But maybe it was only beautiful, and the pain was a separate entity. Or maybe it just hurt to witness beauty at a moment like this.

"I can usually do that pretty well with strangers," Harlan said. "I can get away with it

370

in my own head. But then you weren't a stranger anymore, and I liked you. I didn't want to fool you when I liked you, but I couldn't think of any way out of it by then. But I just wanted to say that if I had that to do over again, I wouldn't have lied to you, because you're too good to lie to."

Faith felt another surge of anger rise up from a place just below her stomach.

"If you're saying . . ."

"What? What did I say wrong this time?"

"If you're saying you wanted to get to know me better a couple or three weeks after your wife died . . . because *you* shot her . . ."

"No," he said, frustrated and desperate. "No, I wasn't saying that. Of course I wasn't looking for romance right after what happened. I'm not a monster. I just meant . . . I watched you with Sarah, and I saw how good you were with her and what good care you took of her. And the way you stepped in and tried to give her what she was missing from her mother at that point. And it just made me sorry I took advantage of you."

"Oh," Faith said. She paused to watch Reggie perform a canter pirouette, simply because it was beautiful. "That apology I guess I can accept."

"Good," he said. "Then my work here is done. And, as you say, you're paying for this call."

"Wait," Faith said. "Wait, before you hang up. There's one thing I really want to know."

"Okay . . ." But he sounded guarded.

"Why did you sell her horse?"

"Oh," he said. "That."

"You must have known that it would just about kill her. Especially right after losing her mother."

"Right. Well. Here's the thing about that. Here was my conundrum. It would figuratively kill Sarah if I did and literally kill me if I didn't. I owed some money. To a guy you don't want to owe money to."

"I don't believe he would literally have killed you."

"You don't know this guy. He's a few good deeds short of a model citizen."

"I'm sure that's true, but if he killed you, then he'd never get his money."

"Let me tell you how this goes, Faith, since you're lucky enough not to know. There are two categories of debtor. One who doesn't have it now and one who never will. If you just don't have it now, you might lose a finger. Or the ability to ever use a knee again. But if he thinks you'll never have it, then you might have to serve as an example for others."

"And how would he know whether you'd *ever* have it?"

"Just a judgment call. But I'll tell you, when your own mother gives up on you, don't expect much credit-related confidence from a loan shark."

In the pause that followed, it occurred to Faith

that there had been no one in the courtroom to support Harlan. No mother. No family on his side at all.

"Look," he said, "you want me to say I felt bad about the horse? Of course I felt bad. But I thought it over, and I figured Sarah would be better off with one dead parent and a sold horse than two dead parents."

Harlan stopped talking and waited. Gave her time to respond.

Reggie flew along the rail in a flashy extended trot, legs thrusting out to chew up the groomed dirt. Faith watched him and realized she felt better. That Harlan's explanation about the horse had helped her. Because a moment earlier, when he had offered her a genuine apology, she'd almost had to accept that he was a marginally decent guy. And that definitely did not compute in Faith's brain. That would have forced her to question how a basically decent man could put a gun to his wife's head and pull the trigger. But now Harlan had come back around to being who and what he was. Unfortunately the crumb of decency she had witnessed could not be utterly dismissed. It had reared its head, and it was real. There was decency in there somewhere. A thin thread of it, anyway. But it was still mostly covered in gambling debts and rash acts and lies.

"This will sound like a terrible thing to say,"

Faith told him. "But I think Sarah would have been better off *with* Midnight and *without* you."

"Wow," he said, his voice breathy. "You're right." Just for a moment, Faith thought she was having to deal with another visit from his scant store of decency. "That *is* a terrible thing to say."

"Don't ever call here again," she said.

"Got it," he said.

And she hung up on him.

Estelle cantered her horse to where Faith stood at the rail and transitioned directly to a halt. She looked down at Faith from her high perch.

"Are you all right, darling?"

"Oh. You heard that?"

"No, not a word. All I could hear was the wind in my ears. But you looked dreadfully upset the whole time."

"That was Sarah's father," she said. "Calling me from jail."

"Oh, dear. I can see how that might be upsetting. What did he want from you?"

"Hard to say. Absolution, maybe. Not for his crime. He knows better than to ask for that, and I'm not the one he'd ask, anyway. For something different. Something that was between us. Yes, it was strange, but I'll be okay. I didn't give him anything he didn't deserve, and I made it very clear that we'll never be talking again."

To Faith's surprise, Estelle reached a gloved hand out and down to her, palm facing Faith.

And just held it there. It took Faith a moment to realize that it was the offer of a high five.

She slapped the gloved palm firmly.

"Well done, then," the older woman said.

She and Reggie cantered away.

Faith fell in step with Sarah as she led the mare back toward the barn.

"What was that all about?" the girl asked when she saw Faith. "Who was that who called you?"

"You don't usually ask personal questions like that," Faith said, because she was hoping to avoid saying. What good could it bring into Sarah's world? And didn't the girl have enough on her plate as it stood?

"Sorry. I didn't mean to be too personal. I just heard you say, 'How did you get this number?' And you sounded super upset. I thought maybe your ex found you or something."

"No, it wasn't Robert."

They walked together into the cool shade of the barn.

Faith made a decision by checking with her gut. That place Ava had told her to trust.

"It was your father."

"My father?" Sarah said. She stopped walking and just froze there in the concrete barn aisle, holding the mare's reins and looking directly into Faith's face. "Can he even call from where he is?"

"If he calls collect, yeah."

"What did he want?"

"To apologize," Faith said simply.

"For . . . how do you just apologize for *killing* someone? And why would he call *you?*"

"No, not that. I think he knows there's no apologizing for that. Just for that weird thing that happened between us at the beach."

"Oh. Right."

Sarah seemed to unstick herself. She led the mare into her open stall, slid the door mostly closed, and began to strip off the horse's tack, her forehead furrowed down into a frown.

Faith leaned on the bars and watched.

"I used your little trick," she said.

"What little trick?"

"To know when he's lying and when he's telling the truth. I listened closely. And it really worked."

"What was the lie?"

Faith didn't answer for a time. Just weighed whether it had been a mistake to bring this up.

"I'm just not sure . . . ," she began. "I'd have to tell you what we were talking about, and I don't know if it would make you feel better or worse."

Sarah frowned again. She reached through the partly open stall door and hung the bridle up on the halter hook by feel.

"It'd be kind of weird if you knew something

about this whole thing that I didn't. Don't you think?"

"Oh," Faith said. "Yeah. I guess it would. Well. I asked him why he sold Midnight."

"I could've told you that," the girl said. "He owed money to a loan shark."

"You knew that? How did you know?"

"Because he always owes money to a loan shark. But anyway, what was the lie?"

"He said he was faced with this choice, and he made it for *you*. Because he thought you'd be better off with no horse, but him alive. It reminded me of what he said to the judge. But that's not how I knew. I listened to his voice. I remembered what you said about his tell. And I could hear it. He was lying. He was thinking of himself, not you."

"Yup," Sarah said. "Could've told you that, too. What did you say?"

"It might sound terrible."

"I still want to know."

She stepped out of the stall holding the saddle and slid the door fully closed.

"I told him I thought you would have been better off with the horse."

"Hmm," Sarah said. "Bet he didn't liked hearing *that*."

"I guess I wasn't too interested in telling him what he wanted to hear."

She carried the saddle to Estelle's tack room,

Faith following behind. The girl did not go on to say if she agreed with Faith's assessment. Then again, Faith thought, she shouldn't have to. A girl her age should never be forced to make such a choice.

"So how did the lesson go?" Faith asked.

"Kind of . . . weirdly okay. Not great. But not bad at all. And I'm really having trouble figuring out if I should be happy about that or not."

Faith stopped in the shade of a huge old gnarled scrub oak tree on her way back to the house. She leaned on its trunk and slid her phone out of her pocket. Opened the message app.

Ava was still the last person she had texted.

Hey, she typed, and pressed send. Just to make sure Ava was even around.

While she waited, she watched heat waves distort the air between herself and the horizon. A hot breeze came through from the west and rattled the leaves over her head, and she closed her eyes and sighed contentedly. Because she knew the day would get cooler from here on.

Hey, Ava typed back.

I owe you an apology.

No you don't.

Well I say I do. So there.

For what?

For ignoring our friendship.

No, Ava typed. With her signature brevity.

No what? No I'm not sorry? Or no I don't
need to be sorry?

More like you'd better not be. I mean,
you texted me nearly every day to let me
know you were okay. As far as longer
instances of chatting, we have one of those
friendships that can be set down. When
we need to set it down, we do. Don't even
treat me like one of those people who need
reassurance.

Faith smiled to herself.

She almost typed out the whole reason she had
thought about Ava in the first place. To tell her
that the advice about trusting herself—the part of
her that knows—had been coming in handy. But
Ava didn't need or even want that reassurance.
Oh, Faith would tell her. Anyway. Sometime.
Whether Ava wanted to hear it or not. But that
would be better later and in person.

Got it, she typed, and hit send.

How are things with you and that girl?

Complex question.

Life's like that. Whenever you're ready. 10-4 good buddy.

Faith slid the phone back in her pocket and braved the heat, uphill, to the house.

"Faith," Sarah whispered. "Are you asleep?"

Faith was not asleep.

She sat up in bed and gave her eyes a minute to adjust. Sarah sat up, too, swinging her legs off the edge of the bed and resting her feet on the braided rug between the twin beds of Estelle's guest room.

"I think I want to just . . . ," Sarah began.

Then the girl stalled and did not finish the thought.

"What?" Faith asked after a time.

"I think we should just . . ."

Still no end to the sentence. No indication of what the girl thought they should just do.

"Sorry," Faith said. "If I could finish the thought for you, I would. But I have no idea where you're headed with this."

"Go home," the girl said.

"Oh. I'm surprised to hear you say that."

"I know."

"To your grandmother's house?"

"Yeah."

"Any special reason?"

For a minute or more they just sat there in the dark. If Faith could have turned on a light, she might have been able to know more. See it in the girl's face, maybe. As it was, Sarah was just a silhouette, one with no clues and nothing it cared to reveal.

"I just can't stand it," Sarah said, finally.

Faith could have asked what it was the girl couldn't stand. But instead she waited, trusting the information to come.

"Ever since I saw Midnight again, she hasn't been getting along with anybody. Not John, not anybody who tried to buy her. Well . . . Estelle. But that's different. Who could not like Estelle? Especially if you're a horse. But then today it sort of seemed like she was ready to get along with Julia. And I hate it so much, Faith. I don't want to watch it. It's like watching somebody you love holding hands with somebody new. It's torture. All this time I kept thinking how bad it would be if she never got along with Julia. Or if she got sold again. Or just thinking of the awfulness of having to say goodbye to her and go home. And I never once thought there would be something worse. But then this morning she was pretty okay with Julia, and I honestly think that was worse than saying goodbye and going where I don't have to watch. So now I just want to go home."

"Okay," Faith said. "It was always up to you. We can leave in the morning if you like."

"Yeah," Sarah said.

Faith thought from the girl's voice that she might be crying. Or right on the edge of it. Just at that place where emotions twist your mouth around and cause a word to come out sounding shaky and strange. But in the dark it was hard to tell.

"Before you even give Julia one more lesson?"

"Doesn't have to be. I could do one more. Not for her, though. For Estelle. Because she's been nice to us."

"Okay," Faith said. "If that's really what you want. We'll leave right after that."

Sarah lay down again in the dark.

Just as Faith was sure the girl had no more to say and was ready to drop off to sleep, Sarah spoke up again. It was sudden, and strangely loud.

"And that 'Sol' thing. 'She's mine now so I want her to have a barn name *I* like.' I mean, what was up with that, Faith?"

"Yeah," Faith said. "I know. That was a bit much."

Chapter Eighteen

Stars Askew

Faith puttered around Estelle's guest room packing their things—both hers and Sarah's. She had promised the girl she would be ready to drive away when the lesson was over.

She slung both bags over her shoulder and carried them downstairs.

Estelle was in the kitchen, standing by the window. Looking out at something with apparent fascination.

Faith dropped the bags outside the kitchen doorway and walked up behind the older woman to see what she found so interesting. Turned out there was a decent view of the round pen from here. Distant, but workable.

"How's it going?" Faith asked.

"I hate to get my hopes up, but . . . surprisingly well. Seems almost like a breakthrough. But I hope I didn't just jinx it. Oh. And a message from Sarah. She asked you, when you get all of your things in the car, to please park by the front doors of the barn and wait for her. She wants to be alone when she says goodbye to her mare, and then afterward she wants not to speak to anyone. Not so much as a word. She was quite clear on that point. Vehement, in fact. She just wants to drive away as quickly as possible. Can I make you a tea for the road?"

"That would be lovely," Faith said.

She sat briefly at Estelle's table for what she assumed would be the last time. Again Faith felt a pang of regret over leaving a place that should not have felt like home. Not after so short a time. Perhaps a home of her own would solve that issue, she thought.

"You've been very kind to us," she said to Estelle.

"Nonsense, darling, I've enjoyed having both of you here. Terrible to have to say it, but I enjoy your company more than that of my own granddaughter. You won't repeat that, of course."

"I won't," Faith said.

Estelle came and sat across the table from her as the kettle heated.

"Sarah's a remarkable girl. Very strong."

"I hope so," Faith said. "She's about to need it."

"She can come visit the mare sometime if she likes. We could arrange it for a time when Julia's not around."

"It's a generous offer," Faith said. "But I don't think she will. I don't think she'll be able to bear to."

"Very well," Estelle said. "But if she changes her mind, you know where we are."

• • •

Faith sat in the Volvo with the engine running, because it would have been too hot in the car without air-conditioning. Now and then she looked through the passenger window and into the barn aisle, but saw nothing.

A minute or two later she heard and felt her car door opening. But when she turned her head, no one was stepping in on the passenger side. She craned her neck around farther and saw Sarah slam the back door and stretch out—as much as the width of the seat would allow—facedown in the back.

"What are you doing back there?" she asked.

"Please just drive. I'm begging you."

"I'm not comfortable with driving on the highway with you not in a seat belt. I'm sorry. I know I'm breaking your request, but I just have to say it."

Sarah sighed. Sat up. Faith could see the girl had been crying. Sarah pulled the shoulder belt out as far as it would go, adjusted the slack into the lap part of the belt, clicked it into place, and flopped onto her face again. It looked uncomfortable to Faith, but the girl seemed to want to stay with the system.

She drove through Estelle's gate.

Down the short, quiet country road to the 154.

Northwest to the 101.

South toward Southern California.

She glanced at the girl in the rearview mirror. Sarah hadn't moved a muscle.

"You okay back there?"

For a moment, silence.

Then Sarah said, "I really meant it about the talking."

"Sorry."

"I don't mean to sound cold. If I wanted to talk to anybody, I'd talk to you. But I don't."

"Got it," Faith said.

When they arrived at Constance's house, Sarah jumped out of the back seat without a word. She trotted up the porch steps, where her grandmother stood in the open doorway, waiting to greet her.

She did not greet her grandmother. She pushed by her and disappeared inside.

Faith hauled their bags out of the back of the car and carried them up the steps to the porch, where Constance stood, smiling sadly.

"I wouldn't take it personally," Faith said.

"I don't. It would be lovely if I were a horse. I could probably help her a lot more if I were. But I'm not and I never will be."

"Right," Faith said. "I can't be much help to her on that score, either." She stepped into Constance's house. The air-conditioning was running, and it felt blissfully cool. "Where did she go?"

"Three guesses."

"She ran up to her room and slammed the door."

"Exactly. I'm not sure if I should go up there."

"I'd give her some time," Faith said.

The two women stood facing each other in the foyer, saying nothing. Neither seeming to know what would come next. Or even what should.

"Glass of wine?" Constance asked.

"Isn't it only a little after noon?"

"I just thought it was one of those days."

"I see your point," Faith said. "We'll issue ourselves an exemption from the usual life rules."

They sat in a glass nursery of a room on the back of Constance's house, shaded by trees that Faith thought looked like some type of willow. It was cool, and the wine was good.

For several minutes, no one had spoken. As if Sarah's feelings about words had proven contagious.

"I'm having trouble," Constance said, "trying not to hate him."

"That's understandable."

"I don't want it, though. It feels like poison."

Faith sipped her wine and absorbed that thought. Wondered if there was anything she could do to help with it. Who was she, after all, to advise two women who had lost so much? It's not like she had her own life all in order.

"Does your Buddhism have anything to offer you for that?"

"Oh, yes," Constance said. "Quite a bit. But you have to be willing to utilize it. I'm not there yet. I'm not even close. I feel like I haven't made any progress at all."

"It hasn't been very long."

"That's true."

"I had a friend once . . . ," Faith began, ". . . well, an acquaintance, really, who was a Western Buddhist. He used to pray for the people he had the most trouble with. He would say a prayer for them to be filled with loving-kindness."

"I can't imagine doing that with Harlan. How can I possibly? Why would I? He deserves no happiness. Not even a speck. Why should I wish for him to have something he doesn't deserve?"

"Well," Faith said, and paused on the thought. Going over it in her head, the only place it had ever lived. To be sure it was worth saying. To be sure it even made sense and felt true. "Here's what I thought was interesting about the idea. Let's say you pray for Harlan to be filled with loving-kindness. I'm not saying he immediately will be, of course. But just to speak in the abstract for a moment. If he were, he wouldn't be any threat to the world. If he had been happy all along, your daughter would be alive. None of this would ever have happened."

"That's an interesting take on things," Constance said. "I'll have to give it some thought.

Because I can't keep living like this. He's in my head all the time. It's killing me."

"He doesn't deserve that space in your head."

"No. He doesn't."

Faith almost told her about the phone call from Harlan. His genuine apology to her. But she didn't. Because Constance had no space in her heart to hear it. Even the tiniest suggestion of a thread of decency in the man would slide off Constance unheard.

Instead they drank the rest of their wine in silence.

It was about seven in the evening—after Constance had fed her a good dinner, and while the older woman was washing up the dishes— that Faith announced it was time for her to go.

"If she was wanting to talk to me, I'd stay," Faith said. "If I was any use to her right now at all. But she's just up in her room with the door closed. And I feel like I need to go back to the beach house. I've forgotten what it feels like to be me—just me without all of this. I'd like to sleep for days and just be alone and figure out where I go from here."

"I think you've done more than enough," Constance said. "And I can't tell you how much we appreciate it."

"I'll go tell her goodbye."

Faith walked down the cool hallway and up

the stairs. She rapped gently on the girl's closed bedroom door.

"Go away," Sarah called through the door.

"That's exactly what I'm about to do. I just wanted to say goodbye."

The door opened abruptly, though only a crack, and Faith found herself looking into Sarah's red and swollen eyes.

"You're going?"

"I thought I would, yes."

"Don't go."

"I just figured . . . you don't want to talk. You want to be alone. Which is fine. I understand. But it doesn't require me. You don't even know if I'm out here or not."

"But I thought you were. And I thought you still would be. And that was good. I liked that. Just knowing you were out here. Please stay."

"For how long?"

"I don't know. As long as you can."

Faith sighed. Reset her internal clock, pushing the beach house, the sleep, the solitude, and the introspection further down the road.

"I'll stay tonight," Faith said. "And then in the morning we'll see where things stand."

Faith woke in the morning with the sun in her eyes. And, just like that first morning at the beach house, she was jolted by the fear of not understanding where she was.

She sat up and looked around, but—still in the grip of a dream—she could see only that she was on a foldout couch in a room that felt unfamiliar.

Then her eyes landed on a picture of Sarah and Midnight and Dean. It was on the mantelpiece in a silver frame. Sarah sat astride the mare in show attire, Dean stood in the dirt beside them. Both smiled broadly for the camera. Midnight wore a two-tone blue ribbon attached to her bridle.

Faith plopped back down on her pillow and breathed deeply.

She was at Constance's house.

And, at the exact moment she realized she was there, she understood how badly she needed not to be.

Faith needed to go home. Until she had a new home she could call her own, she needed to go back to the beach. At least there she had a home that belonged to her family, that she had been given permission to use. Her patience regarding being a guest with no set address had reached the end of its tether and snapped. Just that quickly.

She rose and dressed. Brushed her teeth and her hair. Packed the few bits of her belongings that she had even bothered to unpack in the first place.

Constance was nowhere around, so Faith trotted up the stairs to Sarah's room and tapped quietly on the door.

"You can come in, Faith," the girl said.

Faith opened the door.

The photos she had first seen on the walls in Sarah's room at the beach bungalow were here now. Constance must have moved everything out of that beach rental while they were gone.

"How did you know it was me and not your grandmother?"

"She's meditating."

"Oh. Meditating. Right. I forgot."

Faith crossed the room and sat on the edge of the girl's bed. Sarah was under the covers, at least to her waist, leaning her upper body back against the wall. She was wearing white pajamas two or three sizes too big, with red hearts. Faith draped an arm around the girl's shoulders. Much to Faith's surprise, Sarah snuggled closer and rested her head against the side of Faith's neck.

"I hope you'll understand what I'm about to tell you," Faith said.

"You need to go home."

"How did you know?"

"Because . . . who wouldn't need to? We've been away for almost two months. I still can't believe you were willing to do all that for me, but you did, so how can I sit here and not understand that you want to go home? I'm sorry about yesterday. I was feeling super emotional."

"It's fine," Faith said. "I'm better off driving after a good night's sleep."

"I didn't think it would end like this," Sarah said.

"It's not ending. We'll see plenty of each other. Just give me two or three days to sort myself out. You and your grandmother can come up to the beach for a visit anytime after that."

"That would be nice," the girl said. "But that actually wasn't what I meant. I meant me and Midnight. *That* story. I thought it would end with her coming back to me. Even though there was no possible way she could. But I just didn't get that somehow. It's like it was just too wrong to be possible. Like something in the universe would see that it was just too wrong for us to be apart, and make sure it didn't end that way. But it didn't work with my mother, so I don't know why I thought it would work with my horse."

They sat quietly for a minute, Sarah still leaning into that contact.

"Will you be okay until the next time we see each other?" Faith asked.

"Not really. But . . . don't take this the wrong way . . . it's not like I'd be fine if you were here. I hope you know what I mean by that."

"I do. I wish we could be there in some meaningful way for somebody when they're in pain. In a way that would actually solve something. But I feel like we're pretty powerless to help each other a lot of the time." Another silent moment. Then Faith added, "You'll tell your grandmother I said goodbye?"

Sarah nodded silently against Faith's neck. Then she sat up to allow Faith to go, which Faith did.

She looked back briefly from the doorway.

"Thank you," Sarah said.

"You're welcome. It was good for me, too."

"Good how?"

"I learned some things about myself. I'll call in a day or two and see how you're doing."

Then Faith let herself out of the house.

Faith was halfway to the freeway when her phone rang. She pulled over to see who was calling. But the number was unfamiliar. It was in the 805 area code, same as Cayucos. Then again, that was a massive and strangely shaped area code, miles and miles long, probably because it covered a lot of sparsely populated territory.

She picked up the call.

"Oh good, you're there, darling," a familiar voice said.

"Estelle. I'm surprised."

"I hope I'm not bothering you. What are you right in the middle of? Anything?"

"Driving. But I pulled over."

"Where are you? Is Sarah still with you?"

"Thousand Oaks. And no. She's back with her grandmother. We parted ways just a few minutes ago. It was hard."

"I can imagine. Don't tell me you're about to drive right by here."

"Pretty much, yeah. Why?"

"I was going to offer to come to you. But if you're coming right by my neck of the woods . . . I don't suppose I could talk you into coming by here for a tea? I have something I'd like to discuss with you."

Faith pulled up to the familiar gate, powered down her window, and reached out to push the call button. She was surprised to see Estelle waiting for her on the other side of the gate. Standing in the shade, leaning on the pole that held the electric gate controller. Waiting, as far as Faith could figure.

The gate slid open and Faith drove in, parking in her familiar spot in the shade of the barn.

Estelle waited for her to step out, and they walked uphill toward the house together, side by side. Slowly, as if killing time.

"Where's Julia?" Faith asked. "I expected to see her riding the mare."

"Home with her mother," Estelle said.

There was a subtext there. Faith could both hear it and feel it. Something lay brewing under the older woman's words.

"She didn't ride today?" Faith asked, poking gently at whatever was hiding.

"Depends on what you call riding. She rode the

mare for maybe two minutes. Maybe three. Then she performed quite a lovely halt, considering she had no reins, and jumped off. And do you know what she said to me? 'It's too hard, Nana.' Turns out she had already spoken to her mother about buying her a different horse. Which of course my daughter is going to do. She knew better than to ask *me* to buy her another one. I've had it."

They reached the wooden steps to Estelle's porch. Faith paused for a moment at the base of them.

"Oh no," she said. "The mare is for sale again? No wonder you asked me if Sarah was with me. She'll be brokenhearted when she finds out."

Faith looked up into the older woman's face and realized Estelle was deeply upset by her granddaughter's behavior. That she was nearly beside herself. But—Estelle being Estelle—she was handling those emotions with remarkable grace.

"Come inside and have some tea" was all the older woman said.

Faith followed her into the house and sat at the familiar kitchen table.

"I thought things were going well between Julia and the mare."

"So did I, my friend," Estelle said, puttering near the stove. "So did I."

"They were having something of a break-through."

Estelle lit the gas burner under the kettle and then settled at the table across from Faith. She sighed out a deep breath.

"It may sound strange to say, but I think the breakthrough was our problem. Before yesterday, you might have noticed that relations between Julia and the mare were more in the category of a disaster. And my granddaughter is good with disasters. They bring out her stubbornness, which is actually a quality I admire in her. I used to admire many things about Julia, but those qualities are dwindling, I'm afraid. When the mare didn't want her, she had something to fight back against. She was determined to prevail. Then the horse decided to accept her. When all that drama dropped away, I think she simply found herself looking down the road at a lot of hard work. Just work, day after day. Which is what it means to ride dressage. I'm not sure my granddaughter ever fully made her peace with that reality. Dressage is a journey, and Julia is only interested in destinations."

They sat in silence until the kettle began to whistle.

"So you'll sell her again?" Faith asked as Estelle moved to the stove and turned off the flame.

"I don't see that I have any other good choices. If I were a younger woman, even ten years younger, I'd keep the mare for myself. She's a once-in-a-lifetime horse. I haven't known her long, but I think I have the experience to make that judgment. She has a future in dressage. I'd be tempted even to call it a destiny. I would only be wasting her. I can't bear to see a horse like that go to waste."

She poured two mugs of tea and set them on either side of the table to steep. Then she sat across from Faith, and leaned her chin on her hands.

"I know you're not a horsewoman," she said. "Not by nature and not by experience, though I expect you got quite the crash course in dressage this summer. Do you know enough about the situation to know what a magical pairing it was, that girl and that horse?"

"I think I know," Faith said. "But I think I know because I kept seeing it through the eyes of other people, who really knew."

"That might do." Estelle's fingers wandered across the table to a small, flat leather case. She picked it up and began to fidget with it as she spoke. "I had a brother," she said. "He's deceased now. He played classical guitar. From the time he was so small he could barely *hold* a guitar, he played. Before he ever took a lesson, he played like an angel. People could barely breathe as they listened. Then when he was sixteen he lost a hand in an industrial accident. And that was that. I never got over the sense that the world was wrong without his music. As though the stars would forever be lined up incorrectly. I wanted him to compose or some such thing, but he soured on music and turned away. I never lost that sense that the stars were all in disarray. And I don't want to see that happen again. I just can't go through it a second time.

"Now before I get your hopes up too high, Faith, I have to qualify. I'm fairly comfortable financially, but horses are an expensive avocation. I'm not a rich enough woman to gift the horse back. But here's what I was thinking."

She looked down at the thin leather case in her hand. Pulled a blank note card out of it, stiff stock the size of an index card. She reached into her skirt pocket and produced a silver pen.

"If someone were to want to buy the mare, the price would be just what I paid for her. It's a fair price. In a few years, people will look back on that price and laugh. She could be worth hundreds of thousands. But that requires a steady training regimen. And besides, I don't need to profit. Just to recover what I lost while amusing my spoilt granddaughter for what amounted to a whole week."

Estelle looked down at the blank card and wrote something on it. Something brief. A handful of pen strokes. Then she turned the card upside down, hiding whatever she had written against the table.

"Now let's say you knew someone who wanted to buy the mare not for themselves, but for Sarah. And to line up the stars again. Or let's even say you *were* such a person. Then my asking price would go down considerably."

Estelle slid the card across the table to Faith.

Her hands trembling, Faith picked it up and turned it over. It was engraved on the top with the name Estelle LaMaster in maroon letters. With astonishing neatness, Estelle had written a sum.

$35,000.

Faith stared at the card, her brain running in half a dozen directions at once. It kept tripping over itself by trying to do too much too fast. Plus, whichever way her thoughts ran, they hit the same tether. She didn't have $35,000.

"This is a very generous offer," she said. "It's less than half what you paid."

"No, it's exactly half what I paid. I didn't give John his full asking price."

"It's still very generous."

Faith could feel herself avoiding the word "but." Talking around the fact that she didn't have the money.

"I'm not a perfect person by any means, Faith, but I do genuinely love horses. I love what I do because I care about them so. There's a thing that happens to horses who are sold to too many owners—a sort of spiraling slide down into misery. The more times they're sold, the more

400

sour they get, and the more sour they get, the more times they're sold. I care too much for that beautiful animal to see that happen. And in addition to caring for horses, I care for the vulnerable young girls who love them. Especially the ones who are humble enough and grateful enough to appreciate a fine horse when they have one. So please, Faith. For me if not for the girl. Tell me you can make this happen."

Faith stared at the card for a moment longer. Then she opened her mouth to break Estelle's heart. Hell, everybody's heart. Even the stars would be wounded by her answer. Because she could not make it happen.

A memory caught her suddenly, and she closed her mouth. Or the memory closed it for her. Dean Burwell had told her that he and those two women from the barn had raised nearly $10,000. Maybe they still could. So, then, only $25,000 that she didn't have. Maybe Constance had something to give. Maybe Faith's father and his wife would lend her some money.

Or . . . what had Dean said? When she'd told him she had walked out of her marriage with the clothes on her back. "Maybe . . . don't walk away from everything?" She had dismissed the idea because it wasn't $75,000, no matter how brave she could be in the face of an angry Robert.

"How much time do I have?" she asked Estelle.

"You tell me how much time you need, and

401

that's how much time you'll have. All I ask is that if you know you won't succeed, you'll tell me the truth about it. If it really could happen this way, I'm happy enough to wait."

Faith pulled off Estelle's road onto its dirt shoulder just before turning back onto the 154. She opened the message app, then closed it again. She touched the phone symbol and called Ava at work.

"What's up?" her friend asked in place of hello. "You don't usually call. You okay?"

"Yeah. I am. But I need your help making sure I'll continue to be."

"Not following."

"I'm going to go see Robert. Shut up. Don't open your mouth yet. It's for a noble reason. I'm changing my mind about letting him keep everything. I want half."

"Then you need to get a nice team of attorneys to do this for you."

"No. I can't. He'll play games with the attorneys and tie this up for months. You know how he is." Through the windshield she watched cars and trucks flash by on the 154. Then a truck towing a four-horse trailer. For a flash of a moment she allowed herself to imagine it was delivering a wrongly sold horse to his or her rightful owner, so the stars could line up again. "I have to do this," she said. "But I'll be safe. I promise. I'll meet him in a public place. Like a restaurant. I'll tell you where we'll be and when I'm going in. And I'll leave my phone on the table or in my lap like I'm expecting an important call, and every five or ten minutes I'll text you a thumbs-up so you know I'm okay. And then I'll call you when I get out of there."

"And park where he can't see your new car?"

"Yes, that, too."

Though, frankly, Faith had not thought of that. She might have later.

A long silence on the line. A long line of cars headed into Santa Barbara for the morning. Everybody living a life that seemed so much simpler than Faith's. But maybe that was only on the outside of them.

"I did always think it was wrong to give him everything," Ava said. "All right. Keep me posted."

They said their goodbyes, clicked off the call, and Faith stared at her phone. Unblocked her ex. She tried to tap his work number, to call, but couldn't bring herself to do it. Fear jangled in her stomach, throwing the whole world off-kilter.

She opened the message app again.

She typed, Would like to meet very soon to discuss settlement.

Then she sat back and waited. But, as it turned out, only for half a minute.

I see, his text said. *I could look at my schedule.*

Sooner is better. I was thinking maybe after you get off work tonight.

Faith waited. The tension grew in the waiting. Robert was typing, she could see that. But she had no idea what he was typing. And it was taking a long time. The tone made her jump when his message landed.

So let me get this straight. You walk out more than two months ago. I hear nothing. I know nothing. I have no address for you. You don't answer calls or texts. You block my number. Keep me waiting for months. Now you want something and it has to be right now.

Faith breathed around the tingling fear in her belly and lungs, and tried to think of an answer. She knew it should include an apology. Because she could see his point. But it needed to be followed by a strong bid to stick to her schedule. And she wasn't sure how to do that skillfully. And successfully.

Before she could even raise the phone to answer, another text landed.

Okay fine. Whatever. Where do you want to meet?

I was thinking that restaurant we used to like so much.

Which one?

The one with the view of the water.

Eduardo's?

Yeah that's the one.

I can be there by seven.

Faith breathed deeply. Saw another horse trailer go by, a small two-horse on a bumper-pull hitch. It felt like a sign of encouragement.

Thank you, she typed. See you at seven.

Chapter Nineteen

The Scary Guy

"Where are you?" Ava asked.

Faith held the phone against her ear with her shoulder and pulled her makeup kit out of her bag. Carried it into the bathroom.

"I'm at that hotel where I stayed when I first left home. You know. While my dad was canceling rentals at the beach house. I'm going to meet Robert at seven at Eduardo's. Wait a minute."

Faith looked down at the makeup kit in her hand. Why was she putting on makeup for Robert? She hadn't worn makeup since leaving home. Her goal was not to attract him. She cocked her arm back and sailed the zippered bag onto the hotel bed, in the general area of her suitcase.

"Wait for what? What are we doing, Faith?"

"Nothing. I was just thinking. So I had to get a room because it was barely the middle of the morning and I made an appointment in Santa Monica for seven o'clock tonight. I wasn't going to drive all the way up to the beach house in Cayucos and then back down. I had to have someplace to be in the meantime. Plus, it's probably going to be too late for that long drive after dinner. So, look. Gotta go. I'll text you just as I walk in."

"Wait."

"Wait what, Ava?"

"Are you scared?"

It was unfortunate that her friend had asked. Because Faith had to stop rushing around, both in her hotel room and in her head. And the minute she stopped, it caught up with her.

"Of course I'm scared."

"Good. Shows you understand what you're up against."

He was already there when Faith walked in. Sitting at a table by the window. Looking out over the water.

He looked terrible. That was Faith's first thought. He had grown a beard, but it was not neatly trimmed. It was shot through with gray, despite the fact that his hair was still brown. He had lost weight, and his face seemed more creased, his eyes more sunken. He had aged ten years since she left him.

She stepped up to the table, her heart hammering.

He looked up and met her eyes. He pushed up to his feet, as if to be gentlemanly. But it only reminded Faith that he was huge. That he towered over her. It was impossible to gauge which intention Robert had in mind. Both, maybe.

They sat.

"You look like hell," he said.

Oddly, Faith felt a wave of gratitude and relief rise out of her. Because she was done with him. She had gotten away. How many times had he done that? How many times had Faith politely withheld any thoughts that might have hurt his feelings while he threw insults into her face like hurled stones?

"I'm not wearing makeup anymore," she said.

"I can't imagine why not."

"Can't you? *You* walk in here without makeup. You just show the world the face you've got, and the world accepts it. But this is a dumb thing to be arguing about."

"I agree," he said.

He picked up his menu and opened its cover, staring inside. Faith did the same. A young waiter came by and asked if they wanted wine or cocktails. Robert ordered a bourbon. Faith ordered hot tea.

"I want half of what we both worked so hard for," Faith said when the waiter had gone again.

"I figured as much when you said you wanted to talk settlement. I'm not going to sell the house. I'll fight you on that. I need it to live in, and there's barely enough equity to make it worthwhile. That only leaves the retirement savings."

"Which are about a hundred and five thousand?"

"No. Not that much. I had to hit it right after you left."

"So what's left? You didn't spend it all, did you?"

"Of course not. It's a little over ninety-five, I think."

"Good. Because I need at least thirty-five."

Faith stopped talking, and wished she had said less. She shouldn't have let on how much she needed, or even that it was a pressing need. She should simply have stayed with the nonspecific request that half their savings were hers.

Robert sat back in his chair and eyed her with a look that made her feel he had caught her at something.

"Yeah," he said. "I figured it was something like that. Suddenly you need money. I want to know what's going on here. I have a right to know why you need so much money all of a sudden. If I'm going to tear up our savings, I have a right to know why."

Faith felt rage rise up through her chest. She opened her mouth and set it free. "No, you don't, Robert. No you . . ." She realized her voice was rising and that the couple at the next table had tensed up, unable not to listen. She lowered her voice and softened an expletive. "No you effing don't. You're not my father, and I'm not a child. This is a community property state and that money's half mine no matter what I want it for."

The waiter came and brought Robert his drink and Faith her tea. They fell silent until he left again. Then Faith waited to see if Robert had any answer. But he was only staring into his glass with a sullen look on his face.

"You want to know why I left you, Robert?" she said quietly. "You really want to know? This. This is why."

He snorted laughter. Derisive laughter that tried to pin Faith as being foolish and wrong. "*This* . . . hadn't happened yet."

"Are you kidding me? Are you seriously kidding me? This happened every day. Every freaking day, Robert. You wouldn't let me buy my own car. You said we didn't have enough money and there wasn't enough need for one. You could drive me to work and pick me up and we could save money. So then you knew exactly where I was the minute I got off work. And every time I wanted to go anywhere—to the library, to visit Ava, you 'had a right to know where your car was.' That's what you said. *Your* car. Not *our* car. You had a right to know where I was taking *your* car. You're a very controlling man, Robert, and I get that you don't see it. You're never just straight-out controlling. You always have a better excuse for why you need to monitor my every move. You believe whatever you want. I don't care anymore, and it's none of my business. But let me tell you one thing. I lived under that control. I know how it feels. You call it anything you want, but I've been on the receiving end of it. Now you sit here and tell me I can't have my half of what we saved unless you know what it's for and you approve its use. Do you really not get how wrong that is?"

Faith braced herself for an explosion. But Robert only stared into his glass again. Or maybe still. She hadn't been watching him the whole time she spoke.

Having reminded herself of Ava by mentioning her, she reached for her phone, which was sitting on her cloth napkin, and sent her a thumbs-up icon as a text message.

She looked up to see Robert watching her with narrowed eyes.

"What was that? What you just did?"

"You're doing it again, Robert."

"You're sending someone messages like an SOS. Or lack of same. You set up some kind of safety thing with someone for this meeting."

"So what if I did?"

"I don't understand that, Faith. What did I ever do to make you treat me like I'm so dangerous? Did I beat you? Did you ever have to call the police or go to the hospital? How am I so horrible that you need an emergency contact just to have dinner with me?"

Faith looked out the window at the water, not knowing whether or not she should answer. She looked back at Robert. He was working his jaw in that way of his. Grinding his molars. Nothing would make him madder than no answer at all.

"Okay. Let me see. There was that time you held me by the hair while you told me how furious you were with me for getting home twenty minutes late with *your* car. Or that time you grabbed me by the upper arms and shook me back and forth, and you were holding so tightly i left bruises. I had to wear long sleeves to the gym for two weeks. And when I told you my upper arms bruised easily, you did that more often, not less. Or that time when I tried to leave the house to get away from one of your rages, and you threatened to put my dog out on the street if I left And then when I scooped up the dog to take him with me, you threatened to lock me out with the chain and never let me back in. Then there was the time I was reading that book that my father gave me, and you pulled it out of my hands and tore it in half. Or the time I'd been working on that special dinner for over an hour and you took the pot away and dumped it upside down into the sink. Should I go on, Robert? Because I could go on. And all this happened when we were together and in love and honoring and cleaving and all that good stuff we told the minister. Now that I've left you, you'll have to excuse me for thinking that your reactions might be bigger than anything I've seen before."

Robert stared down into his bourbon and said nothing for a time. His jaw was no longer working. An aura of shame hung around his head, like Harlan in the courtroom, but smaller. Not enough to use up every ounce of oxygen in the room.

"I asked why you wanted the money out of concern for you," he said. "I thought you might be in some kind of trouble."

"No you didn't. But I'll tell you anyway. Not because I need to, but because I have nothing to hide."

The waiter arrived at their table, got a whiff of their energy, and bounced back a step.

"We need another minute," Robert said.

The waiter hurried away.

"I need to buy a dressage horse."

His eyes came up to hers. Gauging her sincerity. He seemed to hear the sentence as a joke, and was checking to see if she'd meant it that way.

"A dressage horse."

"Yes."

"Those prissy little horses who do ballet?"

"They're mostly big horses and not prissy at all. It's a very demanding sport."

"So you've decided you're going to learn a new demanding sport at your age."

"No. The horse is not for me."

Robert sat back in his chair with a thump. "I knew it. You're seeing a guy, and he's working you for money."

"I'm not seeing a guy. It's for a young woman.'

"Please tell me you're not seeing a young woman."

"I'm not *seeing* anyone, Robert," she said. Too loudly. The couple at the next table tensed again. Faith lowered her voice. "Can you get past that in your head? I made friends with a teenage girl and her grandmother. This girl is a dressage rider. She lost her horse, and I'm trying to get the horse back for her."

Robert looked into her face for a long time, and clearly never found what he was looking for.

"I don't get it."

"I know you don't. And, you know what? You don't need to. I told you the truth. Why I'm asking for half our savings. Now you just need to tell me if we can work it out amicably, over this table. Or, if not, what I'll have to go through to get what's mine."

He picked up his menu again. Faith texted another thumbs-up to Ava, then quickly decided on the fresh mahi-mahi. She caught the waiter's eye and gave him silent permission to approach their table again.

"The prime rib," Robert said when he looked up to see the waiter there. "Clam chowder. Garlic bread instead of potato. And my wife will have—"

Faith flashed back to a time in their relationship when he had taken the liberty of ordering for her.

Surely he knew better by now. Just to be on the safe side, she interrupted him.

"Mahi-mahi," she said. "Salad with house dressing."

The waiter took their menus from them and peeled away from the table.

"And I'm not your wife," she added quietly.

"So you're not coming back."

"No."

"I'm surprised. I thought you were coming back."

"I'm not," she said.

They sat looking over the water for a minute or two. Seeming more at peace with each other. Maybe just understanding each other at long last. Faith didn't know if enough time had gone by to text another thumbs-up to Ava. She did anyway, just to be safe.

"I'm going to want you to sign something," he said. "I'll have our attorney draw up an agreement that says if I give you half the savings, that's the end of it. That you won't be coming back later because you found another unrelated random child who wants another prissy horse that dances."

"That's not a problem," she said, ignoring the rest of the affront.

"It won't be thirty-five thousand dollars."

"Why won't it be? You said we had over ninety-five."

"Are you familiar with the phrase 'substantial interest penalty for early withdrawal'? Plus it's tax-deferred retirement savings. Once you cash it out, you'll have to pay taxes on it. Federal and state. Both."

"What do you think it'll come to?"

Robert sighed, a little too theatrically. Slid his phone out of an inside breast pocket of his blazer.

"Okay, let me go out to the broker's website. I have to remember the password for that account. Unless I have it in my password app. Wait. Let me look. Oh. Good. There it is."

Faith sipped her tea and waited, nursing a tightness around her lungs. She thought of the horse trailers going by on the 154. Maybe they signified nothing. Maybe she had come all this way just to fall short again.

"Okay," he mumbled to himself. "Now divide by two. Do I know there will be a substantial interest penalty for early withdrawal? Yes I do." He touched the screen a few times. Then he looked up at Faith. "Any idea what your income will be this year?"

"Well, the year's more than half over," she said. "And I haven't worked so far. My dad's helping me out. This might be it for the year."

"Okay," he mumbled. "So figuring the tax bracket on . . . Twenty-five percent to the feds, most likely. Eight or nine to the state. Wait, I have to go to the calculator app here." He punched in a few numbers. "This is an estimate. I can't say for a fact what the IRS will do. I don't know what you might have in the way of deductions. But if you take the money and pay the taxes right away as an estimate so it doesn't hit you all at once next April . . . you should be left with about twenty-nine grand."

"How long before I actually have that in hand?"

"Three business days, most likely."

"Okay," Faith said. Disappointed and excited at the same time. "I'll take it."

Maybe Estelle would accept a little less. Or maybe Constance or Dean could help bring up the total. If not, maybe she would ignore the taxes. For now, anyway. Just buy the horse. Come April she could set up a payment plan with the IRS. It might cost a bundle in penalties and interest, but maybe it would be worth it.

The waiter arrived with their dinners, knocking Faith out of her tangle of thoughts. She stared at her plate and realized that she only wanted to go now. She didn't want to stay and have dinner with Robert. But she had committed to it. So she texted another thumbs-up to Ava and stayed.

They spoke very little over dinner. Barely more than the occasional small talk one might expect from a stranger.

After he paid the check and just before they parted ways at the door, he made it clear that the earlier parts of their conversation—subjects he had seemed to absorb without much issue at the time—were still bothering him.

"When you love someone, you overlook things like that," he said.

"What, you mean like the bruises and the hair?"

"Yeah."

"I should think that when you love someone, you override the temptation to hurt them like that."

"But it wasn't that much hurt."

"I'll be the judge of that."

"I'm just saying . . . people've had worse. It's not the worst thing ever. You're a strong lady. You could have dealt with it."

"Yeah," Faith said. She leaned her back against the restaurant door. Looked straight into Robert's eyes. He looked away. "Yeah, I'm strong enough to deal with it. But then I started wondering . . . why would I want to? And why should I have to?"

She turned her back on him and pushed the door open, prepared to step out into the night. In that almost dreamlike—or nightmarish—moment, she felt the sickening sensation of his hand closing on her upper arm, turning her. Holding her. Hurting her.

"Now wait just a minute," he said.

And then she had broken his hold on her. Just like that. It was immediate. Decisive. It surprised him. She could see that now by the look on his face.

She had learned it in her self-defense class.

It was a smooth, simple movement involving bringing her arms up and out and turning her body so that her raised arms knocked his away. But she hadn't even done it fully consciously. More like an instinctive reaction.

She stood with her hands raised protectively, watching him watch her.

She almost said something to him. Something like "You really don't want to go there, now do you?" But it would have been unnecessary. Almost anticlimactic. She didn't need to say anything, because he had gone there. Of course he had. He was Robert. But it hadn't worked. It didn't work anymore.

She saw a movement beyond his shoulder. A young and very tall waiter had moved up behind Robert, and was waiting to catch her eye. But he wasn't really a big young man. He seemed thin and insubstantial. But he was apparently willing to help.

"You all right, ma'am?" the young man asked. "You need any help here?"

"I'm not sure," she said. "I'll know more in a minute."

Robert turned and took the measure of the young waiter with his gaze. She watched his face break into a forced and somewhat artificial sneer when he saw he outweighed the boy.

"*You're* going to help her?" he asked, ignoring the fact that she had just proven she didn't need much help. "You and who else?"

A large, heavy young busboy stepped up behind the waiter and stood with his arms crossed, his face serious. Then a diner, a man in his forties, stepped away from his wife and his dinner and stood behind the busboy.

Faith breathed in relief, knowing it was over.

Robert turned to her, seething. "You're not worth this," he said, his words hard edged, like knives. But they didn't cut her. Because it didn't matter what he said anymore.

Then he slammed the restaurant door open with his shoulder and walked away into the night.

Faith watched him go for a second, then turned her attention to the three men.

"Thank you," she said. "I think I had that, but I still appreciate the backup."

"I'd like to walk you to your car," the large busboy volunteered.

"I really don't think that'll be necessary. I know some self-defense."

"Do it for me, then," he said. "I'd really like a break."

Faith felt herself smile. It felt vaguely foreign, yet entirely welcome.

"Fair enough," she said. "Just to get you outside."

On the way to the car with him, she sent Ava a text. It said, I'm out.

Ava texted her back immediately. Is he going to give you the money?

Probably not. He was going to, but then the evening took a bad turn. You know. The way things do with him. But I'll get an attorney and get it out of him anyway.

Think the lady with the horse will wait?

No idea, Faith texted back.

Faith sat on the edge of her hotel bed and glanced at the clock. It was after nine in the evening. Possibly late to call Constance, who got up at five to meditate. Or was it four?

Faith took the chance, and Constance picked up on the second ring.

"Faith," she said. "I'm sorry I wasn't able to say goodbye this morning."

"That was just *this morning?* Whoa. A lot has happened since then. Listen. Constance. Is Sarah where she can hear you?"

"No, she's upstairs in her room. Why?"

"I just don't want her to hear your end of this."

"Okay, I'll take the phone outside just to be safe. Give me a minute."

Faith walked to the window with her phone.

Drew back the curtain and looked out, and was filled with revulsion by the city landscape. After the beach at Cayucos and the horse farms in the Santa Ynez Valley, Faith could not imagine how anyone could enjoy such a view. She dropped the curtain and it swung closed again.

"Okay," Constance said. "What's wrong?"

"Nothing. It's not a problem. Well, it could be. Or it could be a very wonderful thing, but I don't want Sarah to know, because if she got her hopes up and it didn't work out, she'd be crushed. There's a chance I might be able to afford to buy Midnight back. But it's very much in doubt whether my ex will send the money or withhold it to be a jerk. Also, even if he sends it, I'm a little short. But I'm hoping I can raise a little right away to put a deposit on the horse with Estelle. You know. So she doesn't sell her to someone else."

A long silence on the line. Faith could not imagine why Constance's reaction was so delayed.

"For *Sarah?*"

"Yes, of course for Sarah. I don't ride."

"You would spend all that money for Sarah?"

"It's less money at this point than you probably think. But yes, of course I would. I would have all along if I'd had it. But I didn't have it."

"How much do you need?"

"About six thousand."

"Oh," Constance said. And Faith knew the answer just by the sag in her voice. "I don't have that much. No."

"I have another possibility. The people at Sarah's old barn might help. But if we still fall short, is there any part of that amount you could manage?"

"I *could,*" Constance said. "I could drain my savings and put in a piece of what you need. But then the horse would be home and I'd have no savings. And it's not cheap to keep a horse."

Faith said nothing, stunned by the fact that she hadn't thought of that. Constance kept talking.

"Board and feed is the main thing, but that was never a problem because Sarah worked it off. Anything that goes directly to Dressage Journeys they'll let her work off. They just love her there, and she's very useful. But that still leaves shots, worming, shoeing. Medical insurance for the horse, because that's the only way we'd be able to afford the vet bills if she got injured or had colic."

"Can you afford all that if we can get the horse home?"

"I think I'll manage it, yes. I just don't think I can do both. Hey. I have a thought. Sarah's dressage saddle was very expensive—over six thousand dollars new. It's eight years old, but they maintain their value quite well. We might be able to get half that for it."

"Kind of a 'Gift of the Magi' situation, though,

don't you think? Then she has a horse but no saddle."

"Oh. Right. But if it comes right down to that . . . Dean would let her use one of his, I would think."

"Okay. It's a thought. I'm just going to try to get some sleep tonight. You do the same. In the morning I'll talk to Dean. I doubt there's anybody at the barn this late at night. And not a word to Sarah."

"No, of course not. I understand completely."

"Good," Faith said. "Talk to you in the morning."

Then, before she could click off the call, Constance said, "Faith. Wait."

"Yes?"

"No matter how this works out, thank you. *Now* go get some sleep."

As it turned out, Faith got precious little sleep.

At a little after five in the morning Faith found a listing for Dressage Journeys in Moorpark and called, but got only a recorded message.

She stepped out of the hotel, ate a light breakfast at a coffee shop across the street.

Then she went back to her room. Called again. Same result.

Faith gathered up her belongings quickly, checked out of her room, and loaded her bag into the car.

She opened the web browser on her phone, found the website for Dressage Journeys, and peered at the little map on the directions page while her car warmed up. Then she opened the address in her maps app and began to drive, braving the morning traffic north out of the city.

She had learned enough about horse barns that summer to understand one thing clearly: dressage riders don't sit in front of their business phones. The fact that they weren't answering didn't mean they weren't there. Especially in hot weather like this, when schooling mostly takes place early in the morning.

She turned on her air conditioner and sat miserably in traffic, wondering how she had managed to live with traffic jams for so much of her life. *Funny how you get used to things,* she thought. *You don't even notice how much they're grinding on you.* Like the time Faith quit smoking and got well over the course of a couple of weeks, as if recovering from a cold or the flu. But she hadn't even known she'd been sick.

But once you step out of all that. Into a healthier life. Well, then there's just no going back again.

Dressage Journeys reminded Faith of Moon-shadow Farm. The same basic equestrian amenities—cross-ties, wash racks, longe arena, dressage arena. But it was more compact, every-thing wedged into a smaller parcel of land. The area around it was much more built up and populated. There was no racetrack. And the one barn was more utilitarian and less rustic. A big-city version of the heavenly—if hot—place Faith had spent her summer.

Two female riders were schooling their horses in the dressage arena, carefully working around one another. Passing left to left with surprising accuracy and not much room to spare.

Faith parked her car under a tree and stepped out, nearly running into Dean.

He was leading a sweaty, fully tacked bay toward the barn, his helmet under his arm, his sparse hair shining with sweat. He stopped short when he saw her, and so did his horse.

"Faith?" he asked, leaning in to peer at her face. "What are you doing here? Wait—I didn't mean that the way it sounded. You're welcome here anytime. I guess I meant . . . to what do I owe the pleasure?"

"I needed to talk to you about something. Remember that conversation we had at the show over the summer?"

"In excruciating detail. If you've come to punch me out because you're still mad about that, have at it."

He offered one shoulder in her direction.

"No. I . . . might be able to afford to buy Midnight back. Maybe soon, or maybe there'll be some more hoops to jump through to get the money. That's all really in doubt right now. But whenever I get it . . . assuming I get it . . . I'm still a little short."

Faith watched Dean's eyes change as he absorbed her words. As he adapted his view of the world to include this news.

"For Sarah," he said. Not a question. A confirmation.

"Of course for Sarah. Why does everybody keep asking me that? I'm not a rider, and if I thought I wanted to be, I'd get a beginner's horse. I remembered how you said you and the two women—I'm sorry but I don't remember their names now—tried to get some money together to buy her. I was wondering if you still could."

"How did you— No, never mind that. Let's get right down to business. How much are you short?"

"Six thousand."

He furrowed his brow, which Faith knew was a bad sign.

"Oh," he said. "Oh. Wow. Worked better back then, I'm afraid. Lainie bought a new horse since then, and I just had the transmission replaced in my truck."

"Even if you could get us closer . . ."

"Here," Dean said. "Hold this."

He handed her the reins of the big bay and trotted away.

Faith stood awkwardly in the sun, intimidated

by the sheer bulk of the horse. He turned his deep-brown liquid eye on her, and she stared back.

"Hey, boy," she said, despite not knowing if the horse was a boy or a girl.

She looked over to see Dean trotting into the dressage arena, and calling the two mounted riders to him. But they were much too far away for Faith to hear what they were saying.

She looked back to see that the bay had moved a step closer to her and was extending his soft muzzle, touching her shirt pocket. Then he bumped her front jeans pockets, first one side, then the other. Finally he peeled his lips back and gently took a piece of the fabric of her jeans between his teeth.

"Good boy," Faith said. "Go away now."

She took a step back, gently pulling her jeans out of his grasp. He took a step in, and they repeated the dance a second time, almost identical to the first.

"Don't let him do that to you," Dean said.

Faith looked up to see him trotting in her direction. He took the reins from her and bumped the bay under the nose with his palm. The horse popped his head up into the air and withdrew his muzzle immediately.

"He's looking for carrots," Dean said. "But it's rude. And he knows better." He leveled a stern gaze on the horse, who turned his head away in what looked for all the world like shame.

"Oh," Faith said. "I didn't know I had that option."

"We can still put together five," he said.

"That's good!"

"It's not all you need."

"No, but it's a deposit I can give Estelle. And if my ex decides not to be a jerk, it brings me up to thirty-four. That's so close!"

Dean said nothing for a moment. Just examined her face for clues.

"How can you . . . thirty-five? How can that be all you need?"

Faith reached up to her shirt pocket for Estelle's note card. She had been carrying it with her since the older woman pushed it across the table to her. Close to her heart, like some kind of talisman. She slipped it out of her pocket and handed it to Dean.

"Special price. For anybody who's buying the mare to return her to Sarah."

She watched Dean's eyes soften as he stared at the card. For a moment she thought she even saw them glisten, as if tearing up.

"That Estelle LaMaster is a class act," he said. "Always has been, from what I've heard. Will be till the day she dies, I'll put money on it. You think she'll take thirty-four?"

"I think she would if it came right down to that. But there has to be a way to raise a thousand. It's going to be a while before I know what's happening with my part of the money. I have time to think of something."

Dean looked up. Handed her back the card.

"Not to be too personal," he said. "Not really any of my business. But you had nothing when I first talked to you."

"I took your advice."

"Really? You went back to your ex and demanded your due?"

"I actually did."

"Whoa," Dean said. "No wonder Sarah likes you so much. You're awesome."

Faith drove north on the 101, through Buellton, fully intending to stop at Estelle's. She would tell the older woman how much she'd been able to raise as a deposit. She would ask her to please nail down the sale right there and then—maybe for a thousand less, maybe with a thousand owing. She would have to sound more positive about her part of the money—which was most of it—than the situation likely warranted. But she had to try to make it work.

Instead she drove right by the exit for the 154.

It was a sudden idea. Possibly crazy. But it had entered her mind with such force and conviction that she believed it somehow. Right or wrong, she had to try it now. At least she had to see it through.

She drove a few minutes farther north to

Los Alamos, and took the familiar exit to Moonshadow Farm.

He won't even be there, she thought as she drove down the long tree-lined road. She glanced at her watch. It was after nine o'clock. He might be done with his horses and at home by now. But someone at the barn would have his number, or his home address.

Faith turned into the driveway and pulled up to the gate, leaning out her open window and punching the button. As soon as she drove through the open gate, she saw him. He was in the outside arena, schooling a horse in the hot sun. It was a slim gray, a horse Faith had never seen before.

She parked in her usual spot in the shade of the barn and walked to the rail of the arena.

He saw her then, and rode to where she stood.

"Forget something?" he asked. A bit guarded, Faith thought.

"Not exactly. Who's this?" She indicated his mount.

"This is my new horse. He's a wonderful horse." His tone sounded mildly sarcastic. "He doesn't hate me even a little bit. He's never bucked me off. He doesn't seem to have somebody else just over the horizon who he likes much better." The horse shifted his weight underneath John, who patted him on the neck. "And he's nice and tall. So only my ankles hang down under the bottom of the girth. He's only third level right now. So I have to bring him up. But because I have to bring him up, I didn't pay an arm and a leg for him. Unlike some horses I know."

Faith shielded her eyes against the sun and looked up at his face. "Ah. So you're a little more flush for cash now. That's good."

He frowned down at her. "You didn't come here soliciting for something. Did you?"

"Well . . . kind of."

"You seriously came back here to ask me for money?"

"Not for me. For a good cause. I'm almost able to buy that mare back for Sarah. I'm just a little short."

"Oh," John said. For the first time since Faith had arrived, he dropped all trace of artifice and emotional distance. She watched it fall away. "That would be great." He sat his horse in stillness a moment. Maybe putting it all together in his head. "How much are you short?"

"About . . ." Faith felt her face tighten. Her forehead scrunch down. She had to try to speak as if her part of the money were a reality. But it wasn't. And even if it had been, it was hard to say the amount. ". . . a thousand?" Then she talked quickly to cover the tension. "I'm not saying you owe it. She did do a lot of work for you, but it was never with the understanding that she would be paid. And I'm not trying to guilt you into it. I'm just . . . asking."

Silence.

Then, to her surprise, John put his calves to his new horse and rode away. He began to canter the gray in a series of figure eights from one end of the arena to another, changing the horse's bend and lead as they crossed the centerline. Simple changes, meaning he changed leads through a step or two at the walk.

Faith waited, but time stretched out. And she had no indication that he intended to ride back.

She could only take it as a no.

She almost walked away. But it felt cowardly just to leave. He could say no. He could resent her for asking. But he could at least answer.

She gathered up all her voice and energy and shouted across the arena to him. "John Wintermeyer, are you ignoring me?"

"No," he shouted back. "I'm thinking."

So Faith waited in the hot sun while he thought.

It was maybe three minutes later when he trotted down the centerline toward her and halted at the rail.

"All right," he said. "I'm in for a grand."

"Really? John, that's great!"

"Well, I did say I would do it for her if I could afford it. And I can't really pretend that a grand is more than I can afford. Besides, it's mostly selfish. I'm tired of feeling guilty. I was guilty that I'd bought the mare and guilty that I sold her. I'm going to jump down and write you a check right now, and when I tear it off the pad and hand it to you, I plan to never feel guilty about any of it ever again."

"Sounds like a deal to me," Faith said.

It was only two days later when Faith got the call from her stepmother. But they had been two long, gut-wrenching days. She had unblocked Robert, assuming he would email, text, or call. But he had done none of the three.

"Marilyn," she said, thinking something must have happened to her father. She was not close with her stepmother, and they didn't call just to chat or check in.

"You got a registered letter from Robert," she said. "I guess he figured he could use this as a last known address sort of thing."

"Open it," Faith said without thought or hesitation. She felt her heart begin to hammer, growing in resonance. "Read it to me."

Her stomach jangled while she waited.

"Oh," Marilyn said quietly. Almost as if to herself. "Hmm."

"What does it say?"

"I'm not sure you want me to read this to you. Word for word. Also, I'm not sure I want to. It's long and kind of . . . ugly."

"I have to know, though. Can you give me the gist of it?"

"Okay." Another unbearable pause. "He's

sending you a legal form," Marilyn began. "And . . . yes, it's here behind the letter. He says you need to sign it and have it notarized. Basically, I guess it says you'll never ask him for any more money again after this. And then he says he'll send you a certified check within three business days. And he says he'll sign your divorce papers, but then he never wants to see you or hear from you again."

Silence on both ends of the line as Faith absorbed this news.

"That sounds like Robert," she said after a time. "You can't fire me, I quit."

"He also says quite a bit more about *why* he never wants to see you or hear from you again . . ."

"I don't care about that. That doesn't matter."

"It's not very happy stuff," Marilyn said. Then, after a pause, she added, "But really . . . when you think about it . . . that's not bad, how he wants to end it."

Faith heard herself laugh openly, probably tension rushing out of her mixed with relief.

"Oh, yeah, I'll take that deal every day of the week," she said.

Chapter Twenty

Belated Birthdays and Blank Journals

Not a minute before Faith walked out the door, Constance called to announce that they had a problem.

"She doesn't want to go," Constance said. "You know how she's been so down and discouraged, and she knows there'll be lots of people there and she'll be the center of attention. *You* know she'll feel better when she sees her present. And *I* know it. But I can't figure out how to convince Sarah without ruining the surprise. So she's refusing to go. And I can't break through that logjam."

Faith carried the phone out to the car with her. It was time to get on the road. It was a long drive to Moorpark, and she still believed the gathering would come off on time. She refused to question whether it would come off at all.

"If we have to spoil the surprise, then we do," Faith said, dropping into the driver's seat. "But let me take a shot at it anyway. Can you get her on the line?"

"I can try."

While she was waiting, Faith put the call

on speaker and drove out of the beach house driveway. Toward Highway 1 southbound.

"Hi," Sarah said. She sounded like a parody of a depressed teen. Her voice was barely audible. Deep. Without energy or conviction.

"Quick question, kid. Do you trust me?"

"I can't do this today, Faith. I just can't. All these people are going to be trying to cheer me up . . ."

"Kiddo, something is going to happen at the party that *will* cheer you up. And nobody's going to have to try. It's supposed to be a surprise, but—"

"Nothing could cheer me up," Sarah interjected.

"You're not letting me talk. It's a surprise, but I'll ruin it if I have to. If I have to tell you about it to get you there, then I will, because you *have* to be there. You just have to be. And when you're there, and you see your present, then you'll turn to me and say, 'Okay, Faith. I get it now. Why I had to be here. And I'm so glad I didn't blow it.' So back to my original question. Do you trust me?"

"My birthday is over already. We just missed it, okay? It was less important than everything else that was going on, and it's just gone. Let it be gone. We don't need to dredge it up again."

"You're not answering my question."

Faith pulled onto the highway. It was still foggy in fingers along the coast. Morro Rock wore a piece of that fog like a cap.

"Yeah," Sarah said, her voice still limp. "I do."

"Then be there. For me if for no other reason."

A long silence on the line. Then a huge sigh.

"Okay. When are you coming down?"

"I'm driving right now."

"It'll be good to see you, at least."

"Oh, it'll be good for more reasons than that," Faith said.

Estelle was already there when Faith arrived at Dressage Journeys with her small, flat gift-wrapped package. Cara and Lainie were there, setting up a picnic table of refreshments, including a decorated cake covered with a picnic-style dome of screening to protect it from hungry flies. There were half a dozen other people there, seeming part of the festivities, but Faith had never met them. Other boarders and riders, maybe. They were too old to be friends from Sarah's school.

Sarah and Constance had not arrived yet, as far as Faith could see.

She waved to Estelle and then quickly found Dean in the barn, tacking up Midnight.

"Oh, we're bringing her out all ready to ride?"

"Well . . . yeah," Dean said. "I mean . . . I can't imagine her not wanting to jump on first thing. Can you?"

"What about the ribbon? Did we decide against the ribbon?"

"More like it decided against us. I have a nice big bow, but I was just a tiny bit short of enough ribbon to put it around her neck. I taped it on her, but every time she moved her neck it pulled the tape off. I could tape it onto her bridle when I get that on."

"Good. Do that. I gift wrapped the mare's papers and the bill of sale."

"I'm too excited," he said. "And it's unlike me. I'm such a coolheaded guy usually. Too much so, I'm told. And I've been like a kid at Christmas all day. And it's not even Christmas for *me*."

Faith had opened her mouth to answer, when she heard her name called. She turned to see Constance standing in the open doorway of the barn.

"We have another problem, Faith. I can't get her out of the car. You managed to get her into it, at least. Do your magic again, please. If you can."

Faith walked out into the hot sun and stood next to Constance, who pointed to her car. Sarah sat in the passenger seat, eyes closed, face cast downward. It occurred to Faith that maybe they had waited too long to spring this on the girl. Even an extra day or two in a mood like this must have felt like torment to Sarah. Faith would have to apologize for that, when it was over.

She walked to the unlocked car and sat in the driver's seat. The engine was not running.

Without air-conditioning it was downright oppressive inside. The air felt almost too hot to breathe.

"So, it's like this," Faith said. "I know you think we can't possibly have a present that can change how much you're hurting. But we think we do. And . . . spoiler alert: we're right and you're wrong. And since *we* know what it is, and *you* don't, you should consider the possibility that we're right. So jump out of the car. And let us give you your present. And if we're wrong, and it doesn't change your mood completely, you have my permission to go home. Deal?"

"I can go home the minute I see what it is?"

"If you still want to. But you won't."

Sarah glanced over at the wrapped gift in Faith's hand.

"There's more to it than this," Faith said.

Sarah sighed and popped open the passenger door. Stepped out into the heat. Faith did the same.

"Attention, attention, attention," Faith called out as they reached the barn. Individual conversations broke off. "I hope you'll forgive the rush, but Sarah's not feeling much into this, so we're not going to put off giving her the present a moment longer. She thinks she's not going to stay after she sees it. But we think she will. So let's go ahead and see who's right. Dean?"

Dean stepped out of the barn, leading the mare.

He had washed her. Faith could see that, now that she was out in the sun. Her black coat gleamed where the light hit it. She wore her dressage saddle with a whip tucked under the leather of the left stirrup. She wore the big red bow on the far left of the browband of her bridle, just under her ear.

Sarah looked at the mare, and everyone looked at Sarah.

"Oh, she's here," Sarah said. "That's nice."

She spoke without much emotion. Just a flat statement. Then a silence fell that could just about have swallowed the world.

The only person who could bring herself to speak after that surprise was Sarah herself.

"No, really," she said, turning her face toward Estelle. "It was nice of you to bring her. So I can ride her while she's here. That was nice."

"She doesn't understand," Estelle said. And everyone seemed to breathe again. "Darling, the mare is not a birthday guest. She's your present."

"She's—" Sarah said.

Then she just stood there, statue-like, looking like she might be about to cry.

Faith stepped up to her and handed her the gift-wrapped package. "These are her papers. And the bill of sale. I had her put in my name. Just so there can't be any funny business with your father, and anybody he might have doing business for him while he's in jail. The day you turn eighteen, I'll sell her to you for a dollar. You trust me until then, right?"

"You—" Sarah said, and got no further.

Dean led the mare up to where she stood, since movement on Sarah's part appeared to be out of the question. He held his interlaced hands together to give her a leg up, but she only stared at him. Then she dropped to her knees and began to cry. No sobs. No sound. Just tears flowing down her face at an alarming rate.

Dean tried to help her to her feet, but her bones seemed to have turned to jelly. She sank back down again, her face turned up to her mare.

"Honey, are you okay?" Constance asked, rushing to her side.

Sarah nodded. Silently. Tears still flowing.

"Are you crying because you're happy?"

She nodded again, though she looked pitiful, eyes huge and red, face twisted with emotion. Then a series of sounds erupted from the girl. Faith could only describe it in her mind as a cross between sobs and hiccups.

Dean got her to her feet, and tried and failed again to help her into the saddle.

"Oh, you're trembling all over," he said.

Cara and Lainie rushed up behind the girl to hold her up, but her collapse into almost hysterical sobbing only grew more complete. Dean passed off the mare's reins to Faith, and tried to help. He stood looking right into the girl's face, asking over and over if she was okay.

Finally he began to pat both her cheeks firmly, with increasing vigor. A gentle version of the slap in the face used—maybe only in movies—to break someone out of her hysteria.

Still Sarah sobbed and hiccupped, her body so limp that her two barn friends were the only thing keeping her from hitting the ground.

Faith looked away from the scene to see the mare staring at her with soft, dark eyes. Amicably, Faith thought. As if Faith were a trusted friend. The horse reached out with her velvety muzzle, and Faith stroked it.

"Welcome back where you belong, friend," she said.

Then they all stood by helplessly as Sarah cried it out. There didn't seem to be anything else they could do.

"She loves it when we turn her out here," Dean said.

He and Sarah had stripped off the mare's tack, and were leading her to a small fenced pasture, ostensibly to have time to run.

"No kidding," Sarah said. "Remember when she was three and ran herself into the fence and almost killed herself and that other horse?"

Everybody laughed about that, which seemed

odd to Faith. Maybe they only laughed because it was over. And everybody had survived.

Dean unclipped the lead rope and quickly slammed the gate, and the mare ran. And ran. And ran.

The guests ate cake while they watched her run. They sat on cheap folding lawn chairs in any available shade, and smiled. And patted the girl on the back anytime they walked by her. And thought of reasons to walk by her, it seemed to Faith, just so they could pat her back again.

"You know it wasn't supposed to be this way," Dean said. "We had it all worked out. The best-laid plans, as they say. You were going to get on and do an amazing exhibition ride for everyone present. Everyone was going to ooh and aah. Lainie was going to videotape it for posterity."

Lainie waved a small video camera in the air.

"We didn't factor in that all your seams would dissolve and you'd be like a limp rag doll with your insides all over the ground. Unable to sit in a saddle. I've known you for almost nine years, and I've never seen you unable to sit in a saddle before today. Not even when you had the flu that time."

"I'm sorry," Sarah said. But she clearly wasn't. Nor did she need to be. "I just . . . I didn't see that coming. I thought you guys had a horse for me, but it would be a different horse, and I wouldn't want to hurt your feelings, but I wouldn't want him. Oh! Lainie! She's rolling! Get video of her rolling."

But Lainie was talking to someone and didn't hear.

"Great," Dean said. "Less than twenty minutes after her bath. That's got to be a new record for shortest period of horse cleanliness."

Faith rose, pulled her phone out of her pocket. She walked to the gate of the turnout pasture and began to videotape the mare rolling.

A minute later Sarah appeared at her side, and they leaned on the fence together. Faith wondered how many fences they had leaned on together since the summer began. As traditions go, she figured it wasn't a bad one.

"I can't help noticing you're not leaving," Faith said.

Sarah laughed. "Okay. Fine. You want me to say it? I'll say it. You were right and I was wrong."

"A record-breaking statement coming from a fifteen-year-old. So what day was your actual birthday? And why didn't you tell me?"

"The day we had to go to court for the arraignment. And I was throwing up."

"Oh," Faith said. "That kind of answers both questions at once."

The mare was still rolling. It was a delightfully undignified series of movements, wiggly, with her hooves punching up into the air in no particular order. And Faith was still taping. Which meant she was recording the conversation as well.

"I still don't really get it," Sarah said. "Who bought her for me?"

"Kind of . . . everybody. Estelle actually put in more than anybody, by selling her back for half what she paid. A special price for anybody who wanted to return her to you. Then I was the second-highest contributor. Dean and Cara and Lainie come next. And . . . you might have trouble believing this, but John kicked in some."

"John Wintermeyer?"

"Yeah. That John."

"He didn't come, though."

"No. If he'd come, he'd have had to admit he's a nice guy. And you know how he is. Oh, and your grandmother helped, because she's the one signing on for the ongoing expenses."

They watched in silence as the mare pulled to her feet and shook herself. She stood spraddle-legged, a surprisingly immature gesture. She looked right at Faith and Sarah. Then she flew straight up into the air and exploded into galloping again, like a dog overwhelmed by the urge to play.

"I don't get it, though," Sarah said. "I mean . . . it's so incredibly wonderful that part of me doesn't even want to say a word . . ."

"But . . ."

"But I was with you all summer. And you didn't have almost half what John paid for her. You didn't have anything."

"Right. I didn't. Uh . . . remember when I told you I was willing to walk out of my marriage with more or less the clothes on my back? And you were a bit critical of that plan? To put it mildly? Well, I thought better of the idea. I changed my mind."

The mare finally stopped running. She stuck her head through the boards of the fence and tried to graze on the dry, scrubby grass outside.

Faith looked over to see the girl staring at her, eyes wide.

"You went to see the scary guy for *me?*"

"I did. That and . . . so the stars would line up right."

"I don't know what that means."

"Never mind. I'll tell you the whole thing sometime."

"But it was . . . it was like . . . *thousands of dollars*. And you got it. And then you spent it all on something for *me?*"

"I wasn't going to have it either way. If I hadn't needed to spend it on something for you, I never would have gone and gotten it. So what's the difference? I'm a big girl. My hands aren't broken. I can work a job. I'll be okay."

They watched the mare again for a moment, though she wasn't providing much amusement.

Faith was still recording. For some reason she felt compelled to have this exchange between them saved.

"I still can't believe you did that," Sarah said. And Faith could hear that she was crying again. Calmly and quietly this time. "You're not going to go away and forget me now, are you?"

"You would be a hard person to forget."

"You'll still visit, and we can still come up to the beach?"

"You'd better."

"And when we start showing again, you'll come and watch us ride?"

"Try to keep me away."

They fell silent, and Faith pressed the screen icon to stop recording.

"I'll send you a copy of this," she said. "Now let's get back to the party. Everybody wants a piece of you today."

On the drive home, only a couple dozen miles south of the beach house, Faith heard a text pop up onto her phone. She pulled off the highway at the next exit to read it.

It was from Sarah.

I'm sorry. I'm really really sorry Faith. I never really said thank you the way I wanted to. I wanted to say it like a thousand times. But I was sort of in shock. Is it okay if I text you every single morning for the rest of our lives to tell you how grateful I am?

Faith typed her reply.

You don't have to. I believe you. I never doubted that you appreciated it. But you can say it every day if you want.

Faith pressed send, and waited. But apparently Sarah had already turned off her phone and gone to bed. It had been a long and emotional day, after all.

Faith arrived home after ten o'clock, utterly exhausted. She fell asleep on top of the covers with all of her clothes on. Even her shoes.

Sometime in the middle of the night she woke, sat up, and—as had been so common lately—could not make an immediate connection to where she was. Her eyes were open, and she thought she was looking out the window onto the dark beach. And she could see the shape of a small, slight human being there, in the sand outside her window. In a lotus position, as if meditating.

But slowly her mind cleared, and the person in the sand faded away. That part had only been a dream. In fact, as her eyes focused and the dream let go of her, she could see only the window from her bed on the second floor. Not beyond it, because the curtains were drawn. And not down to the sand in front of her porch unless she got up and crossed to the window to look.

She didn't.

She sat nursing the parts of the emptiness that had not gone away. It was not an unpleasant emptiness. Not at all. It put Faith in mind of a blank journal, waiting for a hand to come and fill it in. Except a journal tends to be filled with the life that's just taken place. This blankness was waiting to see what Faith would do next.

It could be anything. She could write the next phase of her life to be anything she wanted it to be. If she could find enough courage, she might even choose to let this new life write her.

In time she lay back down and slept long and well until morning.

When Faith woke and turned on her phone, a text was waiting for her. The first outpouring of bubbly, effusive, nearly breathless gratitude from the same young girl who could barely hold her head up all summer.

As it would turn out, the first of many.

Book Club Questions

1. In *Just After Midnight*, the author brings readers into the fascinating world of dressage, a highly skilled manner of riding horses that is performed in exhibition and competition. How does this use of setting and showmanship enhance the reader's experience of the story?

2. In what ways does Sarah's horse, Midnight, play a pivotal part in both women's journey, and touch the life of everyone she comes in contact with?

3. Both Sarah and Faith are on the run, trying to avoid facing conflicts from their past. Do you agree with their choice to run rather than stay and confront both Faith's husband, Robert, and Sarah's father, Harlan, head-on?

4. What do you think is the primary motivating factor for Faith to step up and help an almost-stranger, Sarah? How might the outcome of the story change if they had not found each other?

5. Why do you think Faith takes a self-defense course? Is this something you've ever considered,

and how does it ultimately benefit her in the story?

6. A sense of foreboding follows Faith throughout the story as she seeks to find herself and create a new direction for her life. Why is her final confrontation with Robert necessary to help open the door for her new life? Do you believe that we sometimes have to deal with the past to move ahead into the future?

7. The reader learns early on in the novel that Harlan is probably responsible for killing his wife. On top of that, he broke his daughter's heart by selling Midnight. Knowing his circumstances, do you feel he redeemed himself in the courtroom scene? Why or why not?

8. Learning to listen to your intuition is a prevalent theme in the book, particularly when a sense of danger is involved on any level. Why do you think Faith had such a difficult time responding to her own gut knowledge?

9. The kindness of strangers plays a large part in the final restaurant scene with Robert and Faith. Are there times in your life when the kindness of strangers has been there when you needed it most?

10. We often see the best of humanity come out in the worst of times. How does Sarah's love for Midnight act as a catalyst to unite the characters in this book under a common cause?

About the Author

Catherine Ryan Hyde is the author of more than thirty published and forthcoming books. An avid hiker, traveler, equestrian, and amateur photographer, she has released her first book of photos, *365 Days of Gratitude: Photos from a Beautiful World.*

Her novel *Pay It Forward* was adapted into a major motion picture, chosen by the American Library Association for its Best Books for Young Adults list, and translated into more than twenty-three languages for distribution in over thirty countries. Both *Becoming Chloe* and *Jumpstart the World* were included on the ALA's Rainbow List, and *Jumpstart the World* was a finalist for two Lambda Literary Awards. *Where We Belong* won two Rainbow Awards in 2013, and *The Language of Hoofbeats* won a Rainbow Award in 2015.

More than fifty of her short stories have been published in the *Antioch Review*, *Michigan Quarterly Review*, the *Virginia Quarterly Review*, *Ploughshares*, *Glimmer Train*, and many other journals and in the anthologies *Santa Barbara Stories* and *California Shorts* and the bestselling anthology *Dog Is My Co-Pilot*. Her stories have been honored by the Raymond Carver Short

Story Contest and the Tobias Wolff Award and nominated for *Best American Short Stories*, the O'Henry Award, and the Pushcart Prize. Three have been cited in *Best American Short Stories*.

She is founder and former president (2000–2009) of the Pay It Forward Foundation and still serves on its board of directors. As a professional public speaker, she has addressed the National Conference on Education, twice spoken at Cornell University, met with AmeriCorps members at the White House, and shared a dais with Bill Clinton.

For more information and book club questions, please visit the author at www.catherineryan hyde.com.

Center Point Large Print
600 Brooks Road / PO Box 1
Thorndike, ME 04986-0001 USA

(207) 568-3717

US & Canada:
1 800 929-9108
www.centerpointlargeprint.com